# DUNE
## MESSIAH

A holy war has made Paul Atreides the religious and political leader of a thousand planets. The malign sisterhood of the Bene Gesserit, unable to dominate the man they have made a god, set out to destroy him.

Paul, who is able to foresee the plans of his enemies, resolves to adapt and shape them to a goal that is as shocking as it is unexpected.

*Dune Messiah* — long-awaited successor to double award-winner *Dune* — is an epic of imperial intrigue that spans the universe, rich and strange in its evocation of the history, institutions and people of a far future age.

*Also by Frank Herbert and available from
New English Library*

THE HEAVEN MAKERS
DUNE
CHILDREN OF DUNE
THE WORLDS OF FRANK HERBERT
DRAGON IN THE SEA
WHIPPING STAR
THE GREEN BRAIN
SANTAROGA BARRIER
THE GODMAKERS
THE EYES OF HEISENBERG

# DUNE
## MESSIAH

## FRANK
## HERBERT

**NEW ENGLISH LIBRARY**
TIMES MIRROR

A shorter version of this book appeared in Galaxy Magazine for July – September, 1969, copyright © 1969 by Galaxy Publishing Corporation

First published in Great Britain by Victor Gollancz Ltd, in 1971
© by Frank Herbert 1969

\*

FIRST NEL PAPERBACK EDITION SEPTEMBER 1972
Reprinted September 1972
New edition December 1974
Reprinted August 1975
New edition February 1977
Reprinted September 1977
Reprinted February 1978
This new edition August 1978
Reprinted May 1979

\*

*NEL Books are published by*
*New English Library Limited from Barnard's Inn, Holborn, London EC1N 2JR.*
*Made and printed in Great Britain by Hunt Barnard Printing Ltd., Aylesbury, Bucks.*

45004156 5

# Prologue

## THE WEIRD OF DUNE

Dune is the planet Arrakis, an arid world of great deserts where life survives against terrifying odds. The semi-nomadic Fremen of Dune base all their customs on water scarcity and face the deserts in stillsuits which recover all moisture. Gigantic sand worms and savage storms are a constant menace to them. Dune's only resource is the melange, an addictive drug produced by the worms. This 'spice' aids longevity and gives an adept some ability to foresee the future.

PAUL ATREIDES was the son of Dune's ruler. When his father was killed in a war with the rival Harkonnen nobility, Paul fled into the desert with his pregnant mother, the LADY JESSICA. She was an adept, trained by the Bene Gesserit – a female order devoted to the mental arts and the control of genetic lines. According to them, Paul was of a line that was to produce a kwisatz haderach, the messiah of the future.

Duncan Idaho was killed in saving them. Paul fought his way to acceptance by the Fremen, and even learned to control and ride the sand worms. In one of their rituals, he took a massive dose of drugs which produced a permanent change in him, giving him full vision of the future – or futures. His mother also took the drug, trying to control it by Bene Gesserit methods. As a result, Paul's sister ALIA was made aware of all her mother's knowledge while still in the womb, and was fully cognitive at birth.

In time, Paul became the accepted leader of the Fremen. He mated with a Fremen girl, CHANI, and adopted most of their customs. But his Atreides mind had been trained to disciplines unknown to Fremen, and he gave them an organisation and mission they had not known before. He also planned to change the climate of Dune to bring water to the planet.

Before his plans were fully developed, the Harkonnens again struck at Dune and its capital, Arrakeen. In spite of the supposedly invincible Sardaukar soldiers, Paul's Fremen forces overcame the enemy in a great battle.

In the treaty Paul imposed, he gained a power base that would enable him to begin carving out a star empire. He also took the Imperial heir, PRINCESS IRULAN, as his consort, though he refused to consummate the marriage, remaining true to Chani.

In the ensuing twelve years, he created his empire. But now all the ancient power groups are beginning to unite and conspire against him and against the legend of Muad'dib, as he is called.

*Such a rich store of myths enfolds Paul Muad'dib, the Mentat Emperor, and his sister, Alia, it is difficult to see the real persons behind these veils. But there were, after all, a man born Paul Atreides and a woman born Alia. Their flesh was subject to space and time. And even though their oracular powers placed them beyond the usual limits of time and space, they came from human stock. They experienced real events which left real traces upon a real universe. To understand them, it must be seen that their catastrophe was the catastrophe of all mankind. This work is dedicated, then, not to Muad'dib or his sister, but to their heirs – to all of us.*

– Dedication in the Muad'dib Concordance as copied
from The Tabla Memorium of the Mahdi Spirit Cult

Muad'dib's Imperial reign generated more historians than any other era in human history. Most of them argued a particular viewpoint, jealous and sectarian, but it says something about the peculiar impact of this man that he aroused such passions on so many diverse worlds.

Of course, he contained the ingredients of history, ideal and idealised. This man, born Paul Atreides in an ancient Great Family, received the deep *prana-bindu* training from the Lady Jessica, his Bene Gesserit mother, and had through this a superb control over muscles and nerves. But more than that, he was a *mentat*, an intellect whose capacities surpassed those of the religiously proscribed mechanical computers used by the ancients.

Above all else, Muad'dib was the *kwisatz haderach* which the Sisterhood's breeding program had sought across thousands of generations.

The kwisatz haderach, then, the one who could be 'many places at once,' this prophet, this man through whom the Bene Gesserit hoped to control human destiny – this man became Emperor Muad'dib and executed a marriage of convenience with a daughter of the Padishah Emperor he had defeated.

Think on the paradox, the failure implicit in this moment, for you surely have read other histories and know the surface facts. Muad'dib's wild Fremen did, indeed, overwhelm the Padishah Shaddam IV. They toppled the Sardaukar legions, the allied forces of the Great Houses, the Harkonnen armies and the mercenaries bought with money voted in the Landsraad. He brought the Spacing Guild to its knees and placed his own sister, Alia, on the religious throne the Bene Gesserit had thought their own.

He did all these things and more.

Muad'dib's Qizarate missionaries carried their religious war across space in a Jihad whose major impetus endured only twelve standard years, but in that time, religious colonialism brought all but a fraction of the human universe under one rule.

He did this because capture of Arrakis, that planet known more often as Dune, gave him a monopoly over the ultimate coin of the realm – the geriatric spice, melange, the poison that gave life.

Here was another ingredient of ideal history: a material whose psychic chemistry unraveled Time. Without melange, the Sisterhood's Reverend Mothers could not perform their feats of observation and human control. Without melange, the Guild's Steersmen could not navigate across space. Without melange, billions upon billions of Imperial citizens would die of addictive withdrawal.

Without melange, Paul-Muad'dib could not prophesy.

We know this moment of supreme power contained failure. There can be only one answer, that completely accurate and total prediction is lethal.

Other histories say Muad'dib was defeated by obvious plotters – the Guild, the Sisterhood and the scientific amoralists of the Bene Tleilax with their Face-Dancer disguises. Other histories point out the spies in Muad'dib's household. They make much of the Dune Tarot which clouded Muad'dib's powers of prophecy. Some show how Muad'dib was made to accept the services

8

of a *ghola*, the flesh brought back from the dead and trained to destroy him. But certainly they must know this ghola was Duncan Idaho, the Atreides lieutenant who perished saving the life of the young Paul.

Yet, they delineate the Qizarate cabal guided by Korba the Panegyrist. They take us step by step through Korba's plan to make a martyr of Muad'dib and place the blame on Chani, the Fremen concubine.

How can any of this explain the facts as history has revealed them? They cannot. Only through the lethal nature of prophecy can we understand the failure of such enormous and far-seeing power.

Hopefully, other historians will learn something from this revelation.

> — Analysis of History: Muad'dib
> by Bronso of Ix

*There exists no separation between gods and men; one blends softly casual into the other.*

– Proverbs of Muad'dib

Despite the murderous nature of the plot he hoped to devise, the thoughts of Scytale, the Tleilaxu Face Dancer, returned again and again to rueful compassion.

*I shall regret causing death and misery to Muad'dib,* he told himself.

He kept this benignity carefully hidden from his fellow conspirators. Such feelings told him, though, that he found it easier to identify with the victim than with the attackers – a thing characteristic of the Tleilaxu.

Scytale stood in bemused silence somewhat apart from the others. The argument about psychic poison had been going on for some time now. It was energetic and vehement, but polite in that blindly compulsive way adepts of the Great Schools always adopted for matters close to their dogma.

'When you think you have him skewered, right then you'll find him unwounded!'

That was the old Reverend Mother of the Bene Gesserit, Gaius Helen Mohiam, their hostess here on Wallach IX. She was a black-robed stick figure, a witch crone seated in a floater chair at Scytale's left. Her aba hood had been thrown back to expose a leathery face beneath silver hair. Deeply pocketed eyes stared out of skull-mask features.

They were using a *mirabhasa* language, honed phalange consonants and jointed vowels. It was an instrument for conveying fine emotional subtleties. Edric, the Guild Steersman, replied to the Reverend Mother now with a vocal curtsy contained in a sneer – a lovely touch of disdainful politeness.

Scytale looked at the Guild envoy. Edric swam in a container of orange gas only a few paces away. His container sat in the center of the transparent dome which the Bene Gesserit had built for this meeting. The Guildsman was an elongated figure, vaguely humanoid with finned feet and hugely fanned membraneous hands – a fish in a strange sea. His tank's vents emitted a pale orange cloud rich with the smell of the geriatric spice, melange.

'If we go on this way, we'll die of stupidity!'

That was the fourth person present – the *potential* member of the conspiracy – Princess Irulan, wife (*but not mate*, Scytale reminded himself) of their mutual foe. She stood at a corner of Edric's tank, a tall blond beauty, splendid in a robe of blue whale fur and matching hat. Gold buttons glittered at her ears. She carried herself with an aristocrat's hauteur, but something in the absorbed smoothness of her features betrayed the controls of her Bene Gesserit background.

Scytale's mind turned from nuances of language and faces to nuances of location. All around the dome lay hills mangy with melting snow which reflected mottled wet blueness from the small blue-white sun hanging at the meridian.

*Why this particular place?* Scytale wondered. The Bene Gesserit seldom did anything casually. Take the dome's open plan: a more conventional and confining space might've inflicted the Guildsman with claustrophobic nervousness. Inhibitions in his psyche were those of birth and life off-planet in open space.

To have built this place especially for Edric, though – what a sharp finger that pointed at his weakness.

What here, Scytale wondered, was aimed at me?

'Have you nothing to say for yourself, Scytale?' the Reverend Mother demanded.

'You wish to draw me into this fools' fight?' Scytale asked. 'Very well. We're dealing with a potential messiah. You don't launch a frontal attack upon such a one. Martyrdom would defeat us.'

They all stared at him.

'You think that's the only danger?' the Reverend Mother

demanded, voice wheezing.

Scytale shrugged. He had chosen a bland, round-faced appearance for this meeting, jolly features and vapid full lips, the body of a bloated dumpling. It occurred to him now, as he studied his fellow conspirators, that he had made an ideal choice – out of instinct perhaps. He alone in this group could manipulate fleshly appearances across a wide spectrum of bodily shapes and features. He was the human chameleon, a Face Dancer, and the shape he wore now invited others to judge him too lightly.

'Well ?' the Reverend Mother pressed.

'I was enjoying the silence,' Scytale said. 'Our hostilities are better left unvoiced.'

The Reverend Mother drew back, and Scytale saw her reassessing him. They were all products of profound prana-bindu training, capable of muscle and nerve control that few humans ever achieved. But Scytale, a Face Dancer, had muscles and nerve linkages the others didn't even possess plus a special quality of *sympatico*, a mimic's insight with which he could put on the psyche of another as well as the other's appearance.

Scytale gave her enough time to complete the reassessment, said: 'Poison !' He uttered the word with the atonals which said he alone understood its secret meaning.

The Guildsman stirred and his voice rolled from the glittering speaker globe which orbited a corner of his tank above Irulan. 'We're discussing *psychic* poison, not a physical one.'

Scytale laughed. Mirabhasa laughter could flay an opponent and he held nothing back now.

Irulan smiled in appreciation, but the corners of the Reverend Mother's eyes revealed a faint hint of anger.

'Stop that !' Mohiam rasped.

Scytale stopped, but he had their attention now, Edric in a silent rage, the Reverend Mother alert in her anger, Irulan amused but puzzled.

'Our friend Edric suggests,' Scytale said, 'that a pair of Bene Gesserit witches trained in all their subtle ways have not learned the true uses of deception.'

Mohiam turned to stare out at the cold hills of her Bene Gesserit homeworld. She was beginning to see the vital thing here, Scytale realised. That was good. Irulan, though, was another matter.

'Are you one of us or not, Scytale ?' Edric asked. He stared out of tiny rodent eyes.

'My allegiance is not the issue,' Scytale said. He kept his attention on Irulan. 'You are wondering, Princess, if this was why you came all those parsecs, risked so much?'

She nodded agreement.

'Was it to bandy platitudes with a humanoid fish or dispute with a fat Tleilaxu Face Dancer?' Scytale asked.

She stepped away from Edric's tank, shaking her head in annoyance at the thick odor of melange.

Edric took this moment to pop a melange pill into his mouth. He ate the spice and breathed it and, no doubt, drank it, Scytale noted. Understandable, because the spice heightened a Steersman's prescience, gave him the power to guide a Guild heighliner across space at translight speeds. With spice awareness he found that line of the ship's future which avoided peril. Edric smelled another kind of peril now, but his crutch of prescience might not find it.

'I think it was a mistake for me to come here,' Irulan said.

The Reverend Mother turned, opened her eyes, closed them, a curiously reptilian gesture.

Scytale shifted his gaze from Irulan to the tank, inviting the Princess to share his viewpoint. She would, Scytale knew, see Edric as a repellent figure: the bold stare, those monstrous feet and hands moving softly in the gas, the smoky swirling of orange eddies around him. She would wonder about his sex habits, thinking how odd it would be to mate with such a one. Even the field-force generator which recreated for Edric the weightlessness of space would set him apart from her now.

'Princess,' Scytale said, 'because of Edric here, your husband's oracular sight cannot stumble upon certain incidents, including this one ... presumably.'

'Presumably,' Irulan said.

Eyes closed, the Reverend Mother nodded. 'The phenomenon of prescience is poorly understood even by its initiates,' she said.

'I am a full Guild Navigator and have the Power,' Edric said.

Again, the Reverend Mother opened her eyes. This time, she stared at the Face Dancer, eyes probing with that peculiar Bene Gesserit intensity. She was weighing minutiae.

'No, Reverend Mother,' Scytale murmured, 'I am not as simple as I appeared.'

'We don't understand this Power of second sight,' Irulan said. 'There's a point. Edric says my husband cannot see, know or predict what happens within the sphere of a Navigator's influence. But how far does that influence extend?'

'There are people and things in our universe which I know only by their effects,' Edric said, his fish mouth held in a thin line. 'I know they have been here . . . there . . . somewhere. As water creatures stir up the currents in their passage, so the prescient stir up Time. I have seen where your husband has been; never have I see him nor the people who truly share his aims and loyalties. This is the concealment which an adept gives to those who are his.'

'Irulan is not yours,' Scytale said. And he looked sideways at the Princess.

'We all know why the conspiracy must be conducted only in my presence,' Edric said.

Using the voice mode for describing a machine, Irulan said: 'You have your uses, apparently.'

*She sees him now for what he is,* Scytale thought. *Good!*

'The future is a thing to be shaped,' Scytale said. 'Hold that thought, Princess.'

Irulan glanced at the Face Dancer.

'People who share Paul's aims and loyalties,' she said. 'Certain of his Freman legionaries, then, wear his cloak. I have seen him prophesy for them, heard their cries of adulation for their Mahdi, their Muad'dib.'

*It has occurred to her,* Scytale thought, *that she is on trial here, that a judgement remains to be made which could preserve her or destroy her. She sees the trap we set for her.*

Momentarily, Scytale's gaze locked with that of the Reverend Mother and he experienced the odd realisation that they had shared this thought about Irulan. The Bene Gesserit, of course, had briefed their Princess, primed her with the *lie adroit.* But the moment always came when a Bene Gesserit must trust her own training and instincts.

'Princess, I know what it is you most desire from the Emperor,' Edric said.

'Who does not know it?' Irulan asked.

'You wish to be the founding mother of the royal dynasty,' Edric said, as though he had not heard her. 'Unless you join us, that will never happen. Take my oracular word on it. The Emperor married you for political reasons, but you'll never share his bed.'

'So the oracle is also a voyeur,' Irulan sneered.

'The Emperor is more firmly wedded to his Fremen concubine

than he is to you!' Edric snapped.

'And she gives him no heir,' Irulan said.

'Reason is the first victim of strong emotion,' Scytale murmured. He sensed the outpouring of Irulan's anger, saw his admonition take effect.

'She gives him no heir,' Irulan said, her voice measuring out controlled calmness, 'because I am secretly administering a contraceptive. Is that the sort of admission you wanted from me?'

'It'd not be a thing for the Emperor to discover,' Edric said, smiling.

'I have lies ready for him,' Irulan said. 'He may have truthsense, but some lies are easier to believe than the truth.'

'You must make the choice, Princess,' Scytale said, 'but understand what it is protects you.'

'Paul is fair with me,' she said. 'I sit in his Council.'

'In the twelve years you've been his Princess Consort,' Edric asked, 'has he shown you the slightest warmth?'

Irulan shook her head.

'He deposed your father with his infamous Fremen horde, married you to fix his claim to the throne, yet he has never crowned you Empress,' Edric said.

'Edric tries to sway you with emotion, Princess,' Scytale said. 'Is that not interesting?'

She glanced at the Face Dancer, saw the bold smile on his features, answered it with raised eyebrows. She was fully aware now, Scytale saw, that if she left this conference under Edric's sway, part of their plot, these moments might be concealed from Paul's oracular vision. If she withheld commitment, though . . .

'Does it seem to you, Princess,' Scytale asked, 'that Edric holds undue sway in our conspiracy?'

'I've already agreed,' Edric said, 'that I'll defer to the best judgement offered in our councils.'

'And who chooses the best judgement?' Scytale asked.

'Do you wish the Princess to leave here without joining us?' Edric asked.

'He wishes her commitment to be a real one,' the Reverend Mother growled. 'There should be no trickery between us.'

Irulan, Scytale saw, had relaxed into a thinking posture, hands concealed in the sleeves of her robe. She would be thinking now of the bait Edric had offered: *to found a royal dynasty!* She would be wondering what scheme the conspirators had provided to protect themselves from her. She would be weighing many things.

'Scytale,' Irulan said presently, 'it is said that you Tleilaxu have an odd system of honour: your victims must always have a means of escape.'

'If they can but find it,' Scytale agreed.

'Am I a victim?' Irulan asked.

A burst of laughter escaped Scytale.

The Reverend Mother snorted.

'Princess,' Edric said, his voice softly persuasive, 'you already are one of us, have no fear of that. Do you not spy upon the Imperial Household for your Bene Gesserit superiors?'

'Paul knows I report to my teachers,' she said.

'But don't you give them the material for strong propaganda against your Emperor?' Edric asked.

*Not 'our' Emperor*, Scytale noted. *'Your' Emperor. Irulan is too much the Bene Gesserit to miss that slip.*

'The question is one of powers and how they may be used,' Scytale said, moving closer to the Guildsman's tank. 'We of the Tleilaxu believe that in all the universe there is only the insatiable appetite of matter, that energy is the only true *solid*. And energy learns. Hear me well, Princess: energy learns. This, we call power.'

'You haven't convinced me we can defeat the Emperor,' Irulan said.

'We haven't even convinced ourselves,' Scytale said.

'Everywhere we turn,' Irulan said, 'his power confronts us. He's the kwisatz haderach, the one who can be many places at once. He's the Mahdi whose merest whim is absolute command to his Qizarate missionaries. He's the mentat whose computational mind surpasses the greatest ancient computers. He is Muad'dib whose orders to the Fremen legions depopulate planets. He possesses oracular vision which sees into the future. He has that gene pattern which we Bene Gesserits covet for – '

'We know his attributes,' the Reverend Mother interrupted. 'And we know the abomination, his sister Alia, possesses this pattern. But they're also humans, both of them. Thus, they have weaknesses.'

'And where are those human weaknesses?' the Face Dancer asked. 'Shall we search for them in the religious arm of his Jihad? Can the Emperor's Qizara be turned against him? What about the civil authority of the Great Houses? Can the Landsraad Congress do more than raise a verbal clamor?'

'I suggest the Combine Honnete Ober Advancer Mercantiles,' Edric said, turning in his tank. 'CHOAM is business and business follows profits.'

'Or perhaps the Emperor's mother,' Scytale said. 'The Lady Jessica, I understand, remains on Caladan, but is in frequent communication with her son.'

'That traitorous bitch,' Mohiam said, voice level. 'Would I might disown my own hands which trained her.'

'Our conspiracy requires a level,' Scytale said.

'We are more than conspirators,' the Reverend Mother countered.

'Ah, yes,' Scytale agreed. 'We are energetic and we learn quickly. This makes us the one true hope, the certain salvation of humankind.' He spoke in the speech mode for absolute conviction, which was perhaps the ultimate sneer coming, as it did, from a Tleilaxu.

Only the Reverend Mother appeared to understand the subtlety. 'Why?' she asked, directing the question at Scytale.

Before the Face Dancer could answer, Edric cleared his throat, said: 'Let us not bandy philosophical nonsense. Every question can be boiled down to the one: "Why is there anything?" Every religious, business and governmental question has the single derivative: 'Who will exercise the power?' Alliances, combines, complexes, they all chase mirages unless they go for the power. All else is nonsense, as most thinking beings come to realise.'

Scytale shrugged, a gesture designed solely for the Reverend Mother. Edric had answered her question for him. The pontificating fool was their major weakness. To make sure the Reverend Mother understood, Scytale said: 'Listening carefully to the teacher, one acquires an education.'

The Reverend Mother nodded slowly.

'Princess,' Edric said, 'make your choice. You have been chosen as an instrument of destiny, the very finest . . . '

'Save your praise for those who can be swayed by it,' Irulan said. 'Earlier, you mentioned a ghost, a revenant with which we may contaminate the Emperor. Explain this.'

'The Atreides will defeat himself!' Edric crowed.

'Stop talking riddles!' Irulan snapped. 'What is this ghost?'

'A very unusual ghost,' Edric said. 'It has a body and a name. The body – that's the flesh of a renowned sword-master known as Duncan Idaho. The name . . . '

'Idaho's dead,' Irulan said. 'Paul has mourned the loss often in my presence. He saw Idaho killed by my father's Sardaukar.'

'Even in defeat,' Edric said, 'your father's Sardaukar did not abandon wisdom. Let us suppose a wise Sardaukar commander recognised the swordmaster in a corpse his men had slain. What then? There exist uses for such flesh and training . . . if one acts swiftly.'

'A Tleilaxu ghola,' Irulan whispered, looking sideways at Scytale.

Scytale, observing her attention, exercised his Face-Dancer powers – shape flowing into shape, flesh moving and readjusting. Presently, a slender man stood before her. The face remained somewhat round, but darker and with slightly flattened features. High cheekbones formed shelves for eyes with definite epicanthic folds. The hair was black and unruly.

'A ghola of this appearance,' Edric said, pointing to Scytale.

'Or merely another Face Dancer?' Irulan asked.

'No Face Dancer,' Edric said. 'A Face Dancer risks exposure under prolonged surveillance. No; let us assume that our wise Sardaukar commander had Idaho's corpse preserved for the axolotl tanks. Why not? This corpse held the flesh and nerves of one of the finest swordsmen in history, an adviser to the Atreides, a military genius. What a waste to lose all that training and ability when it might be revived as an instructor for the Sardaukar.'

'I heard not a whisper of this and I was one of my father's confidantes,' Irulan said.

'Ahh, but your father was a defeated man and within a few hours you had been sold to the new Emperor,' Edric said.

'Was it done?' she demanded.

With a maddening air of complacency, Edric said: 'Let us presume that our wise Sardaukar commander, knowing the need for speed, immediately sent the preserved flesh of Idaho to the Bene Tleilax. Let us suppose further that the commander and his men died before conveying this information to your father – who couldn't have made much use of it anyway. There would remain then a physical fact, a bit of flesh which had been sent off to the Tleilaxu. There was only one way for it to be sent, of course, on a heighliner. We of the Guild naturally know every cargo we transport. Learning of this one, would we not think it additional wisdom to purchase the ghola as a gift befitting an Emperor?'

'You've done it then,' Irulan said.

Scytale, who had resumed his roly-poly first appearance, said: 'As our long-winded friend indicates, we've done it.'

'How has Idaho been conditioned?' Irulan asked.

'Idaho?' Edric asked, looking at the Tleilaxu. 'Do you know of an Idaho, Scytale?'

'We sold you a creature called Hayt,' Scytale said.

'Ah, yes – Hayt,' Edric said. 'Why did you sell him to us?'

'Because we once bred a kwisatz haderach of our own,' Scytale said.

With a quick movement of her old head, the Reverend Mother looked up at him. 'You didn't tell us that!' she accused.

'You didn't ask,' Scytale said.

'How did you overcome your kwisatz haderach?' Irulan asked.

'A creature who has spent his life creating one particular representation of his selfdom will die rather than become the antithesis of that representation,' Scytale said.

'I do not understand,' Edric ventured.

'He killed himself,' the Reverend Mother growled.

'Follow me well, Reverend Mother,' Scytale warned, using a voice mode which said: You are not a sex object, have never been a sex object, cannot be a sex object.

The Tleilaxu waited for the blatant emphasis to sink in. She must not mistake his intent. Realisation must pass through anger into awareness that the Tleilaxu certainly could not make such an accusation, knowing as he must the breeding requirements of the Sisterhood. His words, though, contained a gutter insult, completely out of character for a Tleilaxu.

Swiftly, using the mirabhasa placative mode, Edric tried to smooth over the moment. 'Scytale, you told us you sold Hayt because you shared our desire on how to use him.'

'Edric, you will remain silent until I give you permission to speak,' Scytale said. And as the Guildsman started to protest, the Reverend Mother snapped: 'Shut up, Edric!'

The Guildsman drew back into his tank in flailing agitation.

'Our own transient emotions aren't pertinent to a solution of the mutual problem,' Scytale said. 'They cloud reasoning because the only relevant emotion is the basis fear which brought us to this meeting.'

'We understand,' Irulan said, glancing at the Reverend Mother.

'You must see the dangerous limitations of our shield,' Scytale said. 'The oracle cannot chance upon what it cannot understand.'

'You are devious, Scytale,' Irulan said.

*How devious she must not guess,* Scytale thought. *When this is done, we will possess a kwisatz haderach we can control. These others will possess nothing.*

'What was the origin of your kwisatz haderach?' the Reverend Mother asked.

'We've dabbled in various pure essences,' Scytale said. 'Pure good and pure evil. A pure villain who delights only in creating pain and terror can be quite educational.'

'The old Baron Harkonnen, our Emperor's grandfather, was he a Tleilaxu creation?' Irulan asked.

'Not one of ours,' Scytale said. 'But then nature often produces creations as deadly as ours. We merely produce them under conditions where we can study them.'

'I will not be passed by and treated this way!' Edric protested. 'Who is it hides this meeting from –'

'You see?' Scytale asked. 'Whose best judgement conceals us? What judgement?'

'I wish to discuss our mode of giving Hayt to the Emperor,' Edric insisted. 'It's my understanding that Hayt reflects the old morality that the Atreides learned on his birthworld. Hayt is supposed to make it easy for the Emperor to enlarge his moral nature, to delineate the positive-negative elements of life and religion.'

Scytale smiled, passing a benign gaze over his companions. They were as he'd been led to expect. The old Reverend Mother wielded her emotions like a scythe. Irulan had been well trained for a task at which she had failed, a flawed Bene Gesserit creation. Edric was no more (and no less) than the magician's hand: he might conceal and distract. For now, Edric relapsed into sullen silence as the others ignored him.

'Do I understand that this Hayt is intended to poison Paul's psyche?' Irulan asked.

'More or less,' Scytale said.

'And what of the Qizarate?' Irulan asked.

'It requires only the slightest shift in emphasis, a glissade of the emotions, to transform envy into enmity,' Scytale said.

'And CHOAM?' Irulan asked.

'They will rally round profit,' Scytale said.

'What of the other power groups?'

'One invokes the name of government,' Scytale said. 'We will annex the less powerful in the name of morality and progress.

Our opposition will die of its own entanglements.'

'Alia, too ?'

'Hayt is a multi-purpose ghola,' Scytale said. 'The Emperor's sister is of an age when she can be distracted by a charming male designed for that purpose. She will be attracted by his maleness and by his abilities as a mentat.'

Mohiam allowed her old eyes to go wide in surprise. 'The ghola's a mentat ? That's a dangerous move.'

'To be accurate,' Irulan said, 'a mentat must have accurate data. What if Paul asks him to define the purpose behind our gift ?'

'Hayt will tell the truth,' Scytale said. 'It makes no difference.'

'So you leave an escape door open for Paul,' Irulan said.

'A mentat!' Mohiam muttered.

Scytale glanced at the old Reverend Mother, seeing the ancient hates which colored her responses. From the days of the Butlerian Jihad when 'thinking machines' had been wiped from most of the universe, computers had inspired distrust. Old emotions colored the human computer as well.

'I do not like the way you smile,' Mohiam said abruptly, speaking in the truth mode as she glared up at Scytale.

In the same mode, Scytale said: 'And I think less of what pleases you. But we must work together. We all see that.' He glanced at the Guildsman. 'Don't we, Edric ?'

'You teach painful lessons,' Edric said. 'I presume you wished to make it plain that I must not assert myself against the combined judgements of my fellow conspirators.'

'You see, he can be taught,' Scytale said.

'I see other things as well,' Edric growled. 'The Atreides holds a monopoly on the spice. Without it I cannot probe the future. The Bene Gesserit lose their truthsense. We have stockpiles, but these are finite. Melange is a powerful coin.'

'Our civilisation has more than one coin,' Scytale said. 'Thus, the law of supply and demand fails.'

'You think to steal the secret of it,' Mohiam wheezed. 'And him with a planet guarded by his mad Fremen!'

'The Freman are civil, educated and ignorant,' Scytale said. 'They're not mad. They're trained to believe, not to know. Belief can be manipulated. Only knowledge is dangerous.'

'But will I be left with something to father a royal dynasty ?' Irulan asked.

They all heard the commitment in her voice, but only Edric smiled at it.

'Something,' Scytale said. 'Something.'

'It means the end of this Atreides as a ruling force,' Edric said.

'I should imagine that others less gifted as oracles have made that prediction,' Scytale said. 'For them, *mektub al mellah*, as the Freman say.'

'The thing was written with salt,' Irulan translated.

As she spoke, Scytale recognised what the Bene Gesserit had arrayed here for him – a beautiful and intelligent female who could never be his. *Ah, well*, he thought, *perhaps I'll copy her for another.*

*Every civilisation must contend with an unconscious force which can block, betray or countermand almost any conscious intention of the collectivity.*

— Tleilaxu Theorem (unproven)

Paul sat on the edge of his bed and began stripping off his desert boots. They smelled rancid from the lubricant which eased the action of the heel-powered pumps that drove his stillsuit. It was late. He had prolonged his nighttime walk and caused worry for those who loved him. Admittedly, the walks were dangerous, but it was a kind of danger he could recognise and meet immediately. Something compelling and attractive surrounded walking anonymously at night in the streets of Arrakeen.

He tossed the boots into the corner beneath the room's lone glowglobe, attacked the seal strips of his stillsuit. Gods below, how tired he was! The tiredness stopped at his muscles, though, and left his mind seething. Watching the mundane activities of everyday life filled him with profound envy. Most of that nameless flowing life outside the walls of his Keep couldn't be shared by an Emperor – but . . . to walk down a public street without attracting attention: what a privilege! To pass by the clamoring of mendicant pilgrims, to hear a Fremen curse a shopkeeper: 'You have damp hands!' . . .

Paul smiled at the memory, slipped out of his stillsuit.

He stood naked and oddly attuned to his world. Dune was a world of paradox now – a world under siege, yet the center of power. To come under siege, he decided, was the inevitable fate of power. He stared down at the green carpeting, feeling its rough texture against his soles.

The streets had been ankle deep in sand blown over the Shield Wall on the stratus wind. Foot traffic had churned it into choking dust which clogged stillsuit filters. He could smell the dust even now despite a blower cleaning at the portals of his Keep. It was an odor full of desert memories.

*Other days . . . other dangers.*

Compared to those other days, the peril in his lonely walks remained minor. But, putting on a stillsuit, he put on the desert. The suit with all its apparatus for reclaiming his body's moisture guided his thoughts in subtle ways, fixed his movements in a desert pattern. He became wild Fremen. More than a disguise, the suit made of him a stranger to his city self. In the stillsuit, he abandoned security and put on the old skills of violence. Pilgrims and townfolk passed him then with eyes downcast. They left the wild ones strictly alone out of prudence. If the desert had a face for city folk, it was a Fremen face concealed by a stillsuit's mouth-nose filters.

In truth, there existed now only the small danger that someone from the old *sietch* days might mark him by his walk, by his odor or by his eye. Even then, the chances of meeting an enemy remained small.

A swish of door hangings and a wash of light broke his reverie. Chani entered bearing his coffee service on a platinum tray. Two slaved glowglobes followed her, darting to their positions: one at the head of their bed, one hovering beside her to light her work.

Chani moved with an ageless air of fragile power – so self-contained, so vulnerable. Something about the way she bent over the coffee service reminded him then of their first days. Her features remained darkly elfin, seemingly unmarked by their years – unless one examined the outer corners of her whiteless eyes, noting the lines there: 'sandtracks,' the Fremen of the desert called them.

Steam wafted from the pot as she lifted the lid by its Hagar emerald knob. He could tell the coffee wasn't yet ready by the way she replaced the lid. The pot – fluting silver female shape, pregnant – had come to him as a *ghanima*, a spoil of battle won when he'd slain the former owner in single combat. Jamis, that'd been the man's name . . . Jamis. What an odd immortality death had earned for Jamis. Knowing death to be inevitable, had Jamis carried that particular one in his mind?

Chani put out cups: blue pottery squatting like attendants beneath the immense pot. There were three cups: one for each drinker and one for all the former owners.

'It'll only be a moment,' she said.

She looked at him then, and Paul wondered how he appeared in her eyes. Was he yet the exotic offworlder, slim and wiry but water-fat when compared to Fremen? Had he remained the Usul of his tribal name who'd taken her in 'Fremen *tau*' while they'd been fugitives in the desert?

Paul stared down at his own body: hard muscles, slender . . . a few more scars, but essentially the same despite twelve years as Emperor. Looking up, he glimpsed his face in a shelf mirror – blue-blue Fremen eyes, mark of spice addiction; a sharp Atreides nose. He looked the proper grandson for an Atreides who'd died in the bull ring creating a spectacle for his people.

Something the old man had said slipped then into Paul's mind: *'One who rules assumes irrevocable responsibility for the ruled. You are a husbandman. This demands, at times, a selfless act of love which may only be amusing to those you rule.'*

People still remembered that old man with affection.

*And what have I done for the Atreides name?* Paul asked himself. *I've loosed the wolf among the sheep.*

For a moment, he contemplated all the death and violence going on in his name.

'Into bed now!' Chani said in a sharp tone of command that Paul knew would've shocked his Imperial subjects.

He obeyed, lay back with his hands behind his head, letting himself be lulled by the pleasant familiarity of Chani's movements.

The room around them struck him suddenly with amusement. It was not at all what the populace must imagine as the Emperor's bedchamber. The yellow light of restless glowglobes moved the shadows in an array of colored glass jars on a shelf behind Chani. Paul named their contents silently – the dry ingredients of the desert pharmacopoeia, unguents, incense, mementos . . . pinch of sand from Sietch Tabr, a lock of hair from their firstborn . . . long dead . . . twelve years dead . . . an innocent bystander killed in the battle that had made Paul Emperor.

The rich odor of spice-coffee filled the room. Paul inhaled, his glance falling on a yellow bowl beside the tray where Chani was preparing the coffee. The bowl held ground nuts. The inevitable poison-snooper mounted beneath the table waved its insect arms over the food. The snooper angered him. They'd never needed snoopers in the desert days!

'Coffee's ready,' Chani said. 'Are you hungry?'

His angry denial was drowned in the whistling scream of a spice lighter hurling itself spaceward from the field outside Arrakeen.

Chani saw his anger, though, poured their coffee, put a cup near his hand. She sat down on the foot of the bed, exposed his legs, began rubbing them where the muscles were knotted from walking in the stillsuit. Softly, with a casual air which did not deceive him, she said: 'Let us discuss Irulan's desire for a child.'

Paul's eyes snapped wide open. He studied Chani carefully. 'Irulan's been back from Wallach less than two days,' he said. 'Has she been at you already?'

'We've not discussed her frustrations,' Chani said.

Paul forced his mind to mental alertness, examined Chani in the harsh light of observational minutiae, the Bene Gesserit Way his mother had taught him in violation of her vows. It was a thing he didn't like doing with Chani. Part of her hold on him lay in the fact he so seldom needed his tension-building powers with her. Chani mostly avoided indiscreet questions. She maintained a Fremen sense of good manners. Hers were more often practical questions. What interested Chani were facts which bore on the position of her man – his strength in Council, the loyalty of his legions, the abilities and talents of his allies. Her memory held catalogs of names and cross-indexed details. She could rattle off the major weakness of every known enemy, the potential dispositions of opposing forces, battle plans of their military leaders, the tooling and production capacities of basic industries.

Why now, Paul wondered, did she ask about Irulan?

'I've troubled your mind,' Chani said. 'That wasn't my intention.'

'What was your intention?'

She smiled shyly, meeting his gaze. 'If you're angered love, please don't hide it.'

Paul sank back against the headboard. 'Shall I put her away?' he asked. 'Her use is limited now and I don't like the things I sense about her trip to the Sisterhood.'

'You'll not put her away,' Chani said. She went on massaging his legs, spoke matter-of-factly: 'You've said many times she's

26

your contact with our enemies, that you can read their plans through her actions.'

'Then why ask about her desire for a child ?'

'I think it'd disconcert our enemies and put Irulan in a vulnerable position should you make her pregnant.'

He read by the movement of her hands on his legs what that statement had cost her. A lump rose in his throat. Softly, he said: 'Chani, beloved, I swore an oath never to take her into my bed. A child would give her too much power. Would you have her displace you ?'

'I have no place.'

'Not so, Sihaya, my desert springtime. What is this sudden concern for Irulan ?'

'It's concern for you, not for her! If she carried an Atreides child, her friends would question her loyalties. The less trust our enemies place in her, the less use she is to them.'

'A child for her cou'd mean your death,' Paul said. 'You know the plotting in this place.' A movement of his arm encompassed the Keep.

'You must have an heir !' she husked.

'Ahhh,' he said.

So that was it: Chani had not produced a child for him. Someone else, then, must do it. Why not Irulan ? That was the way Chani's mind worked. And it must be done in an act of love because all the Empire avowed strong taboos against artificial ways. Chani had come to a Fremen decision.

Paul studied her face in this new light. It was a face he knew better in some ways than his own. He had seen this face soft with passion, in the sweetness of sleep, awash in fears and angers and griefs.

He closed his eyes, and Chani came into his memories as a girl once more – veiled in springtime, singing, waking from sleep beside him – so perfect that the very vision of her consumed him. In his memory, she smiled . . . shyly at first, then strained against the vision as though she longed to escape.

Paul's mouth went dry. For a moment, his nostrils tasted the smoke of a devastated future and the voice of another kind of vision commanding him to disengage . . . disengage . . . disengage. His prophetic visions had been eavesdropping on eternity for such a long while, catching snatches of foreign tongues, listening to stones and to flesh not his own. Since the day of his first encounter with terrible purpose, he had peered at the future,

27

hoping to find peace.

There existed a way, of course, He knew it by heart without knowing the heart of it – a rote future, strict in its instructions to him: disengage, disengage, disengage . . .

Paul opened his eyes, looked at the decision in Chani's face. She had stopped massaging his legs, sat still now – purest Freman. Her features remained familiar beneath the blue *nezhoni* scarf she often wore about her hair in the privacy of their chambers. But the mask of decision sat on her, an ancient and alien-to-him way of thinking. Fremen women had shared their men for thousands of years – not always in peace, but with a way of making the fact nondestructive. Something mysteriously Fremen in this fashion had happened in Chani.

'You'll give me the only heir I want,' he said.

'You've *seen* this?' she asked, making it obvious by her emphasis that she referred to prescience.

As he had done many times, Paul wondered how he could explain the delicacy of the oracle. the Timelines without number which vision waved before him on an undulating fabric. He sighed, remembered water lifted from a river in the hollow of his hands – trembling, draining. Memory drenched his face in it. How could he drench himself in futures growing increasingly obscure from the pressures of too many oracles?

'You've not *seen* it, then,' Chani said.

That vision-future scarce any longer accessible to him except at the expenditure of life-draining effort, what could it show them except grief? Paul asked himself. He felt that he occupied an inhospitable middle zone, a wasted place where his emotions drifted, swayed, swept outward in unchecked restlessness.

Chani covered his legs, said: 'An heir to House Atreides, this is not something you leave to chance or one woman.'

That was a thing his mother might've said, Paul thought. He wondered if the Lady Jessica had been in secret communication with Chani. His mother would think in terms of House Atreides. It was a pattern bred and conditioned into her by the Bene Gesserit, and would hold true even now when her powers were turned against the Sisterhood.

'You listened when Irulan came to me today,' he accused.

'I listened.' She spoke without looking at him.

Paul focused his memory on the encounter with Irulan. He'd let himself into the family salon, noted an unfinished robe on Chani's loom. There'd been an acrid wormsmell to the place, an evil odor which almost hid the underlying cinnamon bite of melange. Someone had spilled unchanged spice essence and left it to combine there with a spice-based rug. It had not been a felicitous combination. Spice essence had dissolved the rug. Oily marks lay congealed on the plastone floor where the rug had been. He'd thought to send for someone to clean away the mess, but Harah, Stilgar's wife and Chani's closest feminine friend, had slipped in to announce Irulan.

He'd been forced to conduct the interview in the presence of that evil smell, unable to escape a Fremen superstition that evil smells foretold disaster.

Harah withdrew as Irulan entered.

'Welcome,' Paul said.

Irulan wore a robe of gray whale fur. She pulled it close, touched a hand to her hair. He could see her wondering at his mild tone. The angry words she'd obviously prepared for this meeting could be sensed leaving her mind in a welter of second thoughts.

'You came to report that the Sisterhood has lost its last vestige of morality,' he said.

'Isn't it dangerous to be that ridiculous ?' she asked.

'To be ridiculous and dangerous, a questionable alliance,' he said. His renegade Bene Gesserit training detected her putting down an impulse to withdraw. The effort exposed a brief glimpse of underlying fear, and he saw she'd been assigned a task not to her liking.

'They expect a bit too much from a princess of the blood royal,' he said.

Irulan grew very still and Paul became aware that she had locked herself into a viselike control. A heavy burden, indeed, he thought. And he wondered why prescient visions had given him no glimpse of this possible future.

Slowly, Irulan relaxed. There was no point in surrendering to fear, no point in retreat, she had decided.

'You've allowed the weather to fall into a very primitive pattern,' she said, rubbing her arms through the robe. 'It was dry and there was a sandstorm today. Are you never going to let it rain here ?'

'You didn't come here to talk about the weather,' Paul said. He felt that he had been submerged in double meanings. Was Irulan trying to tell him something which her training would not permit her to say openly ? It seemed that way. He felt that he had been cast adrift suddenly and now must thrash his way back to some steady place.

'I must have a child,' she said.

He shook his head from side to side.

'I must have my way!' she snapped. 'If need be, I'll find another father for my child. I'll cuckold you and dare you to expose me.'

'Cuckold me all you wish,' he said, 'but no child.'

'How can you stop me?'

With a smile of utmost kindness, he said: 'I'd have you garroted, if it came to that.'

Shocked silence held her for a moment and Paul sensed Chani listening behind the heavy draperies into their private apartments.

'I am your wife,' Irulan whispered.

'Let us not play these silly games,' he said. 'You play a part, no more. We both know who my wife is.'

'And I am a convenience, nothing more,' she said, voice heavy with bitterness.

'I have no wish to be cruel to you,' he said.

'You chose me for this position.'

'Not I,' he said. 'Fate chose you. Your father chose you. The Bene Gesserit chose you. The Guild chose you. And they have chosen you once more. For what have they chosen you, Irulan?'

'Why can't I have your child?'

'Because that's a role for which you weren't chosen.'

'It's my right to bear the royal heir! My father was —'

'Your father was and is a beast. We both know he'd lost almost all touch with the humanity he was supposed to rule and protect.'

'Was he hated less than you're hated?' she flared.

'A good question,' he agreed, a sardonic smile touching the edges of his mouth.

'You say you've no wish to be cruel to me, yet . . .'

'And that's why I agreed that you can take any lover you choose. But understand me well: take a lover, but bring no sour-fathered child into my household. I would deny such a child. I don't begrudge you any male alliance as long as you are discreet . . . and childless. I'd be silly to feel otherwise under the circumstances. But don't presume upon this license which I freely bestow. Where the throne is concerned, I control what blood is heir to it. The Bene Gesserit doesn't control this, nor does the Guild. This is one of the privileges I won when I smashed your father's Sardaukar legions out there on the Plain of Arrakeen.'

'It's on your head, then,' Irulan said. She whirled and swept out of the chamber.

Remembering the encounter now, Paul brought his awareness out of it and focused on Chani seated beside him on their bed. He could understand his ambivalent feelings about Irulan, understand Chani's Fremen decision. Under other circumstances Chani and Irulan might have been friends.

'What have you decided?' Chani asked.

'No child,' he said.

Chani made the Fremen crysknife sign with the index finger and thumb of her right hand.

'It could come to that,' he agreed.

'You don't think a child would solve anything with Irulan?' she asked.

'Only a fool would think that.'

'I am not a fool, my love.'

Anger possessed him. 'I've never said you were! But this isn't some damned romantic novel we're discussing. That's a real princess down the hall. She was raised in all the nasty intrigues of an Imperial Court. Plotting is as natural to her as writing her stupid histories!'

'They are not stupid, love.'

'Probably not.' He brought his anger under control, took her hand in his. Sorry. But that woman has many plots – plots within plots. Give in to one of her ambitions and you could advance another of them.'

Her voice mild, Chani, said: 'Haven't I always said as much?'

'Yes, of course you have.' He stared at her. 'Then what are you really trying to say to me?'

She lay down beside him, placed her head against his neck. 'They have come to a decision on how to fight you,' she said. 'Irulan reeks of secret decisions.'

Paul stroked her hair.

Chani had peeled away the dross.

Terrible purpose brushed him. It was a *coriolis* wind in his soul. It whistled through the framework of his being. His body knew things then never learned in consciousness.

'Chani, beloved,' he whispered, 'do you know what I'd spend to end the Jihad – to separate myself from the damnable godhead the Qizarate forces onto me?'

She trembled. 'You have but to command it,' she said.

'Oh, no. Even if I died now, my name would still lead them. When I think of the Atreides name tied to this religious butchery . . . '

'But you're the Emperor! You've –'

'I'm a figurehead. When godhead's given, that's the one thing the so-called god no longer controls.' A bitter laugh shook him. He sensed the future looking back at him out of dynasties not even dreamed. He felt his being cast out, crying, unchained from the rings of fate – only his name continued. 'I was chosen,' he said. 'Perhaps at birth . . . certainly before I had much say in it. I was chosen.'

'Then un-choose,' she said.

His arm tightened around her shoulder. 'In time, beloved. Give me yet a little time.'

Unshed tears burned his eyes.

'We should return to Sietch Tabr,' Chani said. 'There's too much to contend with in this tent of stone.'

He nodded, his chin moving against the smooth fabric of the scarf which covered her hair. The soothing spice smell of her filled his nostrils.

Sietch. The ancient Chakobsa word absorbed him: a place of retreat and safety in a time of peril. Chani's suggestion made him long for vistas of open sand, for clean distances where one could see an enemy coming from a long way off.

'The tribes expect Muad'dib to return to them,' she said. She lifted her head to look at him. 'You belong to us.'

'I belong to a vision,' he whispered.

He thought then of the Jihad, of the gene mingling across parsecs and the vision which told him how he might end it. Should he pay the price? All the hatefulness would evaporate. dying as fires die – ember by ember. But . . . oh! The terrifying price!

*I never wanted to be a god*, he thought. *I wanted only to disappear like a jewel of trace dew caught by the morning. I wanted to escape the angels and the damned – alone . . . as though by an oversight.*

'Will we go back to the Sietch?' Chani pressed.

'Yes,' he whispered. And he thought: *I must pay the price.*

Chani heaved a deep sigh, settled back against him.

*I've loitered*, he thought. And he saw how he'd been hemmed in by boundaries of love and the Jihad. And what was one life, no matter how beloved, against all the lives the Jihad was certain to take? Could single misery be weighed against the agony of multitudes?

'Love?' Chani said, questioning.

He put a hand against her lips.

*I'll yield up myself*, he thought. *I'll rush out while I yet have the strength, fly through a space a bird might not find.* It was a useless thought, and he knew it. The Jihad would follow his ghost.

What could he answer? he wondered. How explain when people taxed him with brutal foolishness? Who might understand?

*I wanted only to look back and say: 'There! There's an existence which couldn't hold me. See! I vanish! No restraint or net of human devising can trap me ever again. I renounce my religion! This glorious instant is mine! I'm free!'*

*What empty words!*

'A big worm was seen below the Shield Wall yesterday,' Chani said. 'More than a hundred meters long, they say. Such big ones come rarely into this region any more. The water repels them, I suppose. They say this one came to summon Muad'dib home to his desert.' She pinched his chest. 'Don't laugh at me!'

'I'm not laughing.'

Paul, caught by wonder at the persistent Fremen mythos, felt a heart constriction, a thing inflicted upon his lifeline: *adab*, the demanding memory. He recalled his childhood room on Caladan then . . . dark night in the stone chamber . . . a vision! It'd been one of his earliest prescient moments. He felt his mind dive into the vision, saw through a veiled cloud-memory (vision-within-vision) a line of Fremen, their robes trimmed with dust. They paraded past a gap in tall rocks. They carried a long, cloth-wrapped burden.

And Paul heard himself say in the vision: 'It was mostly sweet . . . but you were the sweetest of all . . .'

Adab released him.

'You're so quiet,' Chani whispered. 'What is it?'

Paul shuddered, sat up, face averted.

'You're angry because I've been to the desert's edge,' Chani said.

He shook his head without speaking.

'I only went because I want a child,' Chani said.

Paul was unable to speak. He felt himself consumed by the raw power of that early vision. Terrible purpose! In that moment, his whole life was a limb shaken by the departure of a bird . . .

and the bird was *chance*. Free will.

*I succumbed to the lure of the oracle*, he thought.

And he sensed that succumbing to this lure might be to fix himself upon a single-track life. Could it be, he wondered, that the oracle didn't *tell* the future ? Could it be that the oracle *made* the future ? Had he exposed his life to some web of underlying threads, trapped himself there in that long-ago awakening, victim of a spider-future which even now advanced upon him with terrifying jaws.

A Bene Gesserit axiom slipped into his mind: *To use raw power is to make yourself infinitely vulnerable to greater powers.*

'I know it angers you,' Chani said, touching his arm. 'It's true that the tribes have revived the old rites and the blood sacrifices, but I took no part in those.'

Paul inhaled a deep, trembling breath. The torrent of his vision dissipated, became a deep, still place whose currents moved with absorbing power beyond his reach.

'Please,' Chani begged. 'I want a child, our child. Is that a terrible thing ?'

Paul caressed her arm where she touched him, pulled away. He climbed from the bed, extinguished the glowglobes, crossed to the balcony window, opened the draperies. The deep desert could not intrude here except by its odors. A windowless wall climbed to the night sky across from him. Moonlight slanted down into an enclosed garden, sentinel trees and broad leaves, wet foliage. He could see a fish pond reflecting stars among the leaves, pockets of white floral brilliance in the shadows. Momentarily, he saw the garden through Fremen eyes: alien, menacing, dangerous in its waste of water.

He thought of the Water Sellers, their way destroyed by the lavish dispensing from his hands. They hated him. He'd slain the past. And there were others, even those who'd fought for the sols to buy precious water, who hated him for changing the old ways. As the ecological pattern dictated by Muad'dib remade the planet's landscape, human resistance increased. Was it not presumptuous, he wondered, to think he could make over an entire planet – everything growing where and how he told it to grow ? Even if he succeeded, what of the universe waiting out there ? Did it fear similar treatment ?

Abruptly, he closed the draperies, sealed the ventilators. He turned toward Chani in the darkness, felt her waiting there. Her

water rings tinkled like the almsbells of pilgrims. He groped his
way to the sound, encountered her outstretched arms.

'Beloved,' she whispered. 'Have I troubled you?'

Her arms enclosed his future as they enclosed him.

'Not you,' he said. 'Oh . . . not you.'

*The advent of the Field Process shield and the lasgun with their explosive interaction, deadly to attacker and attacked, placed current determinatives on weapons technology. We need not go into the special role of atomics. The fact that any Family in my Empire could so deploy its atomics as to destroy the planetary bases of fifty or more other Families causes some nervousness, true. But all of us possess precautionary plans for devastating retaliation. Guild and Landsraad contain the keys which hold this force in check. No, my concern goes to the development of humans as special weapons. Here is a virtually unlimited field which a few powers are developing.*

— Muad'dib: Lecture of the War College
from The Stilgar Chronicle

The old man stood in his doorway peering out with blue-in-blue eyes. The eyes were veiled by that native suspicion all desert folk held for strangers. Bitter lines tortured the edges of his mouth where it could be seen through a fringe of white beard. He wore no stillsuit and it said much that he ignored this fact in the full knowledge of the moisture pouring from his house through the open door.

Scytale bowed, gave the greeting signal of the conspiracy.

From somewhere behind the old man came the sound of a rebec wailing through the atonal dissonance of *semuta* music. The old man's manner carried no drug dullness, an indication that semuta was the weakness of another. It seemed strange to

Scytale, though, to find that sophisticated vice in this place.

'Greetings from afar,' Scytale said, smiling through the flat-featured face he had chosen for this encounter. It occurred to him, then, that this old man might recognise the chosen face. Some of the older Fremen here on Dune had known Duncan Idaho.

The choice of features, which he had thought amusing, might have been a mistake, Scytale decided. But he dared not change the face out here. He cast nervous glances up and down the street. Would the old man never invite him inside?

'Did you know my son?' the old man asked.

That, at least, was one of the countersigns. Scytale made the proper response, all the time keeping his eyes alert for any suspicious circumstances in his surroundings. He did not like his position here. The street was a cul-de-sac ending in this house. The houses all around had been built for veterans of the Jihad. They formed a suburb of Arrakeen which stretched into the Imperial Basin past Tiemag. The walls which hemmed in this street presented blank faces of dun plasmeld broken by dark shadows of sealed doorways and, here and there, scrawled obscenities. Beside this very door someone had chalked a pronouncement that one Beris had brought back to Arrakis a loathsome disease which deprived him of his manhood.

'Do you come in partnership,' the old man asked.

'Alone,' Scytale said.

The old man cleared his throat, still hesitating in that maddening way.

Scytale cautioned himself to patience. Contact in this fashion carried its own dangers. Perhaps the old man knew some reason for carrying on this way. It was the proper hour, though. The pale sun stood almost directly overhead. People of this quarter remained sealed in their houses to sleep through the hot part of the day.

Was it the new neighbor who bothered the old man? Scytale wondered. The adjoining house, he knew, had been assigned to Otheym, once a member of Muad'dib's dreaded Fedaykin death commandos. And Bijaz, the catalyst-dwarf, waited with Otheym.

Scytale returned his gaze to the old man, noted the empty sleeve dangling from the left shoulder and the lack of a stillsuit. An air of command hung about this old man. He'd been no foot slogger in the Jihad.

'May I know the visitor's name?' the old man asked.

Scytale suppressed a sigh of relief. He was to be accepted, after all. 'I am Zaal,' he said, giving the name assigned him for this mission.

'I am Farok,' the old man said, 'once Bashar of the Ninth Legion in the Jihad. Does this mean anything to you?'

Scytale read menace in the words, said: 'You were born in Sietch Tabr with allegiance to Stilgar.'

Farok relaxed, stepped aside. 'You are welcome in my house.'

Scytale slipped past him into a shadowy atrium – blue tile floor, glittering designs worked in crystal on the walls. Beyond the atrium was a covered courtyard. Light admitted by translucent filters spread an opalescence as silvery as the white-night of First Moon. The street door grated into its moisture seals behind him.

'We were a noble people,' Farok said, leading the way toward the courtyard. 'We were not of the cast-out. We lived in no *graben* village . . . such as this! We had a proper sietch in the Shield Wall above Habbanya Ridge. One worm could carry us into Kedem, the inner desert.'

'Not like this,' Scytale agreed, realising now what had brought Farok into the conspiracy. The Fremen longed for the old days and the old ways.

They entered the courtyard.

Farok struggled with an intense dislike for his visitor, Scytale realised Fremen distrusted eyes that were not the total blue of the Ibad. Offworlders, Fremen said, had unfocused eyes which saw things they were not supposed to see.

The semuta music had stopped at their entrance. It was replaced now by the strum of a baliset, first a nine-scale chord, then the clear notes of a song which was popular on the Naraj worlds.

As his eyes adjusted to the light, Scytale saw a youth sitting cross-legged on a low divan beneath arches to his right. The youth's eyes were empty sockets. With that uncanny facility of the blind, he began singing the moment Scytale focused on him. The voice was high and sweet:

> 'A wind has blown the land away
> And blown the sky away
> And all the men!
> Who is this wind?
> The trees stand unbent,

38

Drinking where men drank.
I've known too many worlds,
Too many men,
Too many trees,
Too many winds.'

Those were not the original words of the song, Scytale noted.
Farok led him away from the youth and under the arches on the
opposite side, indicated cushions scattered over the tile floor. The
tile was worked into designs of sea creatures.

'There is a cushion once occupied in sietch by Muad'dib,'
Farok said, indicating a round, black mound. 'It is yours now.'

'I am in your debt,' Scytale said, sinking to the black mound.
He smiled. Farok displayed wisdom. A sage spoke of loyalty even
while listening to songs of hidden meaning and words with
secret messages. Who could deny the terrifying powers of the
tyrant Emperor?

Inserting his words across the song without breaking the
meter, Farok said: 'Does my son's music disturb you?'

Scytale gestured to a cushion facing him, put his back against
a cool pillar. 'I enjoy music.'

'My son lost his eyes in the conquest of Naraj,' Farok said. 'He
was nursed there and should have stayed. No woman of the People
will have him thus. I find it curious, though, to know I have
grandchildren on Naraj that I may never see. Do you know the
Naraj worlds, Zaal?'

'In my youth, I toured there with a troupe of my fellow Face
Dancers,' Scytale said.

'You are a Face Dancer, then,' Farok said. 'I had wondered at
your features. They reminded me of a man I knew here once.'

'Duncan Idaho?'

'That one, yes. A swordmaster in the Emperor's pay.'

'He was killed, so it is said.'

'So it is said,' Farok agreed. 'Are you truly a man, then? I've
heard stories about Face Dancers that . . . ' He shrugged.

'We are Jadacha hermaphrodites,' Scytale said, 'either sex at
will. For the present, I am a man.'

Farok pursed his lips in thought, then: 'May I call for refresh-
ments? Do you desire water? Iced fruit?'

'Talk will suffice,' Scytale said.

'The guest's wish is a command,' Farok said, settling to the
cushion which faced Scytale.

'Blessed is Abu d' Dhur, Father of the Indefinite Roads of Time,' Scytale said. And he thought: *There! I've told him straight out that I come from a Guild Steersman and wear the Steersman's concealment.*

'Thrice blessed,' Farok said, folding his hands into his lap in the ritual clasp. They were old, heavily veined hands.

'An object seen from a distance betrays only its principle,' Scytale said, revealing that he wished to discuss the Emperor's fortress Keep.

'That which is dark and evil may be seen for evil at any distance,' Farok said, advising delay.

*Why?* Scytale wondered. But he said: 'How did your son lose his eyes?'

'The Naraj defenders used a stone burner,' Farok said. 'My son was too close. Cursed atomics! Even the stone burner should be outlawed.'

'It skirts the intent of the law,' Scytale agreed. And he thought: *A stone burner on Naraj! We weren't told of that. Why does this old man speak of stone burners here?*

'I offered to buy Tleilaxu eyes for him from your masters,' Farok said. 'But there's a story in the legions that Tleilaxu eyes enslave their users. My son told me that such eyes are metal and he is flesh, that such a union must be sinful.'

'The principle of an object must fit its original intent,' Scytale said, trying to turn the conversation back to the information he sought.

Farok's lips went thin, but he nodded. 'Speak openly of what you wish,' he said. 'We must put our trust in your Steersman.'

'Have you ever entered the Imperial Keep?' Scytale asked.

'I was there for the feast celebrating the Molitor victory. It was cold in all that stone despite the best Ixian space heaters. We slept on the terrace of Alia's Fane the night before. He has trees in there, you know – trees from many worlds. We Bashars were dressed in our finest green robes and had our tables set apart. We ate and drank too much. I was disgusted with some of the things I saw. The walking wounded came, dragging themselves along on their crutches. I do not think our Muad'dib knows how many men he had maimed.'

'You objected to the feast?' Scytale asked, speaking from a knowledge of the Fremen orgies which were ignited by spice-beer.

'It was not like the mingling of our souls in the sietch,' Farok

40

said. 'There was no tau. For entertainment, the troops had slave girls, and the men shared the stories of their battles and their wounds.'

'So you were inside that great pile of stone,' Scytale said.

'Muad'dib came out to us on the terrace,' Farok said. ' "Good fortune to us all," he said. The greeting drill of the desert in that place!'

'Do you know the location of his private apartments?' Scytale asked.

'Deep inside,' Farok said. 'Somewhere deep inside. I am told he and Chani live a nomadic life and that all within the walls of their Keep. Out to the Great Hall he comes for the public audiences. He has reception halls and formal meeting places, a whole wing for his personal guard, places for the ceremonies and an inner section for communications. There is a room far beneath his fortress, I am told, where he keeps a stunted worm surrounded by a water moat with which to poison it. Here is where he reads the future.'

*Myth all tangled up with facts*, Scytale thought.

'The apparatus of government accompanies him everywhere,' Farok grumbled. 'Clerks and attendants and attendants for the attendants. He trusts only the ones such as Stilgar who were very close to him in the old days.'

'Not you,' Scytale said.

'I think he has forgotten my existence,' Farok said.

'How does he come and go when he leaves that building?' Scytale asked.

'He has a tiny 'thopter landing which juts from an inner wall,' Farok said. 'I am told Muad'dib will not permit another to handle the controls for a landing there. It requires an approach, so it is said, where the slightest miscalculation would plunge him down a sheer cliff of wall into one of his accursed gardens.'

Scytale nodded. This, most likely, was true. Such an aerial entry to the Emperor's quarters would carry a certain measure of security. The Atreides were superb pilots all.

'He uses men to carry his *distrans* messages,' Farok said. 'It demeans men to implant wave translators in them. A man's voice should be his own to command. It should not carry another man's message hidden within its sounds.'

Scytale shrugged. All great powers used the distrans in this age. One could never tell what obstacle might be placed between sender and addressee. The distrans defied political cryptology because it relied on subtle distortions of natural sound patterns which could be scrambled with enormous intricacy.

'Even his tax officials use this method,' Farok complained. 'In my day, the distrans was implanted only in the lower animals.'

*But revenue information must be kept secret,* Scytale thought. *More than one government has fallen because people discovered the real extent of official wealth.*

'How do the Fremen cohorts feel now about Muad-dib's Jihad?' Scytale asked. 'Do they object to making a god out of their Emperor?'

'Most of them don't even consider this,' Farok said. 'They think of the Jihad the way I thought of it – most of them. It is a source of strange experiences, adventure, wealth. This graben hovel in which I live' – Farok gestured at the courtyard – 'it cost sixty lidas of spice. Ninety kontars! There was a time when I could not even imagine such riches.' He shook his head.

Across the courtyard, the blind youth took up the notes of a love ballad on his baliset.

*Ninety kontars,* Scytale thought. *How strange. Great riches, certainly. Farok's hovel would be a palace on many another world, but all things were relative – even the kontar. Did Farok, for example, know whence came his measure for this weight of spice? Did he ever think to himself that one and a half kontar once limited a camel load? Not likely. Farok might never even have heard of a camel or of the Golden Age of Earth.*

His words oddly in rhythm to the melody of his son's baliset, Farok said: 'I owned a crysknife, water rings to ten liters, my own lance which had been my father's, a coffee service, a bottle made of red glass older than any memory in my sietch. I had my own share of our spice, but no money. I was rich and did not know it. Two wives I had: one plain and dear to me, the other stupid and obstinate, but with form and face of an angel. I was a Fremen Naib, a rider of worms, master of the leviathan and of the sand.'

The youth across the courtyard picked up the beat of his melody.

'I knew many things without the need to think about them,' Farok said. 'I knew there was water far beneath our sand, held there in bondage by the Little Makers. I knew that my ancestors sacrificed virgins to Shai-hulud . . . before Liet-Kynes made us stop. It was wrong of us to stop. I had seen the jewels in the mouth of a worm. My soul had four gates and I knew them all.'

He fell silent, musing.

'Then the Atreides came with his witch mother,' Scytale said.

'The Atreides came,' Farok agreed. 'The one we named Usul in our sietch, his private name among us. Our Muad'dib, our Mahdi! And when he called for the Jihad, I was one of those who asked: 'Why should I go to fight there? I have no relatives there.' But other men went – young men, friends, companions of my childhood. When they returned, they spoke of wizardry, of the power in this Atreides *savior*. He fought our enemy, the Harkonnen. Liet-Kynes, who had promised us a paradise upon our planet, blessed him. It was said this Atreides came to change our world and our universe, that he was the man to make the golden flower blossom in the night.'

Farok held up his hands, examined the palms. 'Men pointed to First Moon and said: "His soul is there." Thus, he was called Muad'dib. I did not understand all this.'

He lowered his hands, stared across the courtyard at his son. 'I had no thoughts in my head. There were thoughts only in my heart and my belly and my loins.'

Again, the tempo of the background music increased.

'Do you know why I enlisted in the Jihad?' The old eyes stared hard at Scytale. 'I heard there was a thing called a sea. It is very hard to believe in a sea when you have lived only here among our dunes. We had no seas. Men of Dune had never known a sea. We had our windtraps. We collected water for the great change Liet-Kynes promised us . . . this great change Muad'dib is bringing with a wave of his hand. I could imagine a *qanat*, water flowing across the land in a canal. From this, my mind could picture a river. But a sea?'

Farok gazed at the translucent cover of his courtyard as though trying to probe into the universe beyond. 'A sea,' he said, voice low. 'It was too much for my mind to picture. Yet, men I knew said they had seen this marvel. I thought they lied, but I had to know for myself. It was for this reason that I enlisted.'

The youth struck a loud final chord on the baliset, took up a new song with an oddly undulating rhythm.

'Did you find your sea?' Scytale asked.

Farok remained silent and Scytale thought the old man had not heard. The baliset music rose around them and fell like a tidal movement. Farok breathed to its rhythm.

'There was a sunset,' Farok said presently. 'One of the elder artists might have painted such a sunset. It had red in it the color

43

of the glass in my bottle. There was gold . . . blue. It was on the world they call Enfeil, the one where I led my legion to victory. We came out of a mountain pass where the air was sick with water. I could scarcely breathe it. And there below me was the thing my friends had told me about: water as far as I could see and farther. We marched down to it. I waded out into it and drank. It was bitter and made me ill. But the wonder of it has never left me.'

Scytale found himself sharing the old Fremen's awe.

'I immersed myself in that sea,' Farok said, looking down at the water creatures worked into the tiles of his floor. 'One man sank beneath that water . . . another man arose from it. I felt that I could remember a past which had never been. I stared around me with eyes which could accept anything . . . anything at all. I saw a body in the water – one of the defenders we had slain. There was a log nearby supported on that water, a piece of a great tree. I can close my eyes now and see that log. It was black on one end from a fire. And there was a piece of cloth in that water – no more than a yellow rag . . . torn, dirty. I looked at all these things and I understood why they had come to this place. It was for me to see them.'

Farok turned slowly, stared into Scytale's eyes. 'The universe is unfinished, you know,' he said.

*This one is garrulous, but deep*, Scytale thought. And he said: 'I can see it made a profound impression on you.'

'You are a Tleilaxu,' Farok said. 'You have seen many seas. I have seen only this one, yet I know a thing about seas which you do not.'

Scytale found himself in the grip of an odd feeling of disquiet.

'The Mother of Chaos was born in a sea,' Farok said. 'A Qizara Tafwid stood nearby when I came dripping from that water. He had not entered the sea. He stood on the sand . . . it was wet sand . . . with some of my men who shared his fear. He watched me with eyes that knew I had learned something which was denied to him. I had become a sea creature and I frightened him. The sea healed me of the Jihad and I think he saw this.'

Scytale realised that somewhere in this recital the music had stopped. He found it disturbing that he could not place the instant when the baliset had fallen silent.

As though it were relevant to what he'd been recounting, Farok said: 'Every gate is guarded. There's no way into the Emperor's fortress.'

'That's its weakness,' Scytale said.

Farok stretched his neck upwards, peering.

'There's a way in,' Scytale explained. 'The fact that most men – including, we may hope, the Emperor – believe otherwise ... that's to our advantage.' He rubbed his lips, feeling the strangeness of the visage he'd chosen. The musician's silence bothered him. Did it mean Farok's son was through transmitting? That had been the way of it, naturally: the message condensed and transmitted within the music. It had been impressed upon Scytale's own neural system, there to be triggered at the proper moment by the distrans embedded in his adrenal cortex. If it was ended, he had become a container of unknown words. He was a vessel sloshing with data: every cell of the conspiracy here on Arrakis, every name, every contact phrase – all the vital information.

With this information, they could brave Arrakis, capture a sandworm, begin the culture of melange somewhere beyond Muad'dib's writ. They could break the monopoly as they broke Muad'dib. They could do many things with this information.

'We have the woman here,' Farok said. 'Do you wish to see her now?'

'I've seen her,' Scytale said. 'I've studied her with care. Where is she?'

Farok snapped his fingers.

The youth took up his rebec, drew the bow across it. Semuta music wailed from the strings. As though drawn by the sound, a young woman in a blue robe emerged from a doorway behind the musician. Narcotic dullness filled her eyes which were the total blue of the Ibad. She was a Fremen, addicted to the spice, and now caught by an offworld vice. Her awareness lay deep within the semuta, lost somewhere and riding the ecstacy of the music.

'Otheym's daughter,' Farok said. 'My son gave her the narcotic in the hope of winning a woman of the People for himself despite his blindness. As you can see, his victory is empty. Semuta has taken what he hoped to gain.'

'Her father doesn't know?' Scytale asked.

'She doesn't even know,' Farok said. 'My son supplies false memories with which she accounts to herself for her visits. She thinks herself in love with him. This is what her family believes. They are outraged because he is not a complete man, but they won't interfere, of course.'

The music trailed away in silence.

. At a gesture from the musician, the young woman seated herself beside him, bent close to listen as he murmured to her.

'What will you do with her?' Farok asked.

Once more, Scytale studied the courtyard. 'Who else is in this house?' he asked.

'We are all here now,' Farok said. 'You've not told me what you'll do with the woman. It is my son who wishes to know.'

As though about to answer, Scytale extended his right arm. from the sleeve of his robe, a glistening needle darted, embedded itself in Farok's neck. There was no outcry, no change of posture. Farok would be dead in a minute, but he sat unmoving, frozen by the dart's poison.

Slowly, Scytale climbed to his feet, crossed to the blind musician. The youth was still murmuring to the young woman when the dart whipped into him.

Scytale took the young woman's arm, urged her gently to her feet, shifted his own appearance before she looked at him. She came erect, focused on him.

'What is it, Farok?' she asked.

'My son is tired and must rest,' Scytale said. 'Come. We'll go out the back way.'

'We had such a nice talk,' she said. 'I think I've convinced him to get Tleilaxu eyes. It'd make a man of him again.'

'Haven't I said it many times?' Scytale asked, urging her into a rear chamber.

His voice, he noted with pride, matched his features precisely. It unmistakably was the voice of the old Fremen, who certainly was dead by this time.

Scytale sighed. It had been done with sympathy, he told himself, and the victims certainly had known their peril. Now, the young woman would have to be given her chance.

*Empires do not suffer emptiness of purpose at the time of their creation. It is when they have become established that aims are lost and replaced by vague ritual.*

– Words of Muad'dib
by Princess Irulan

It was going to be a bad session, this meeting of the Imperial Council, Alia realised. She sensed contention gathering force, storing up energy – the way Irulan refused to look at Chani, Stilgar's nervous shuffling of papers, the scowls Paul directed at Korba the Qizara.

She seated herself at the end of the golden council table so she could look out the balcony windows at the dusty light of the afternoon.

Korba, interrupted by her entrance, went on with something he'd been saying to Paul. 'What I mean, m'Lord, is that there aren't as many gods as once there were.'

Alia laughed, throwing her head back. The movement dropped the black hood of her aba robe. Her features lay exposed – blue-in-blue 'spice eyes,' her mother's oval face beneath a cap of bronze hair, small nose, mouth wide and generous.

Korba's cheeks went almost the color of his orange robe. He glared at Alia, an angry gnome, bald and fuming.

'Do you know what's being said about your brother?' he demanded.

'I know what's being said about your Qizarate,' Alia countered.

47

'You're not divines, you're god's spies.'

Korba glanced at Paul for support, said: 'We are sent by the writ of Muad'dib, that He shall know the truth of His people and they shall know the truth of Him.'

'Spies,' Alia said.

Korba pursed his lips in injured silence.

Paul looked at his sister, wondering why she provoked Korba. Abruptly, he saw that Alia had passed into womanhood, beautiful with the first blazing innocence of youth. He found himself surprised that he hadn't noticed it until this moment. She was fifteen – almost sixteen, a Reverend Mother without mother-hood, virgin priestess, object of fearful veneration for the super-stitious masses – Alia of the Knife.

'This is not the time or place for your sister's levity,' Irulan said.

Paul ignored her, nodded to Korba. 'The square's full of pilgrims. Go out and lead their prayer.'

'But they expect *you*, m'Lord,' Korba said.

'Put on your turban,' Paul said, 'They'll never know at this distance.'

Irulan smothered irritation at being ignored, watched Korba arise to obey. She'd had the sudden disquieting thought that Edric might not hide her actions from Alia. *What do we really know of the sister ?* she wondered.

Chani, hands tightly clasped in her lap, glanced across the table at Stilgar, her uncle, Paul's Minister of State. Did the old Fremen Naib ever long for the simpler life of his desert sietch ? she wondered. Stilgar's black hair, she noted, had begun to gray at the edges, but his eyes beneath heavy brows remained far-seeing. It was the eagle stare of the wild, and his beard still carried the catchtube indentation of life in a stillsuit.

Made nervous by Chani's attention, Stilgar looked around the Council Chamber. His gaze fell on the balcony window and Korba standing outside. Korba raised outstretched arms for the bene-diction and a trick of the afternoon sun cast a red halo onto the window behind him. For a moment, Stilgar saw the Court Qizara as a figure crucified on a fiery wheel. Korba lowered his arms, destroyed the illusion, but Stilgar remained shaken by it. His thoughts went in angry frustration to the fawning supplicants waiting in the Audience Hall, and to the hateful pomp which surrounded Muad'dib's throne.

Convening with the Emperor, one hoped for a fault in him, to find mistakes, Stilgar thought. He felt this might be sacrilege, but wanted it anyway.

Distant crowd murmuring entered the chamber as Korba returned. The balcony door thumped into its seals behind him, shutting off the sound.

Paul's gaze followed the Qizara. Korba took his seat at Paul's left, dark features composed, eyes glazed by fanaticism. He'd enjoyed that moment of religious power.

'The spirit presence has been invoked,' he said.

'Thank the lord for that,' Alia said.

Korba's lips went white.

Again, Paul studied his sister, wondered at her motives. Her innocence masked deception, he told himself. She'd come out of the same Bene Gesserit breeding program as he had. What had the kwisatz haderach genetics produced in her? There was always that mysterious difference: she'd been an embryo in the womb when her mother had survived the raw melange poison. Mother and unborn daughter had become Reverend Mothers simultaneously. But simultaneity didn't carry identity.

Of the experience, Alia said that in one terrifying instant she had awakened to consciousness, her memory absorbing the uncounted other-lives which her mother was assimilating.

'I became my mother and all the others,' she said. 'I was unformed, unborn, but I became an old woman then and there.'

Sensing his thoughts on her, Alia smiled at Paul. His expression softened. *How could anyone react to Korba with other than cynical humor?* he asked himself. *What is more ridiculous than a Death Commando transformed into a priest?*

Stilgar tapped his papers. 'If my liege permits,' he said. 'These are matters urgent and dire.'

'The Tupile Treaty?' Paul asked.

'The Guild maintains that we must sign this treaty without knowing the precise location of the Tupile Entente,' Stilgar said. 'They've some support from Landsraad delegates.'

'What pressures have you brought to bear?' Irulan asked.

'Those pressures which my Emperor has designated for this enterprise,' Stilgar said. The stiff formality of his reply contained all his disapproval of the Princess Consort.

'My Lord and husband,' Irulan said, turning to Paul, forcing him to acknowledge her.

*Emphasising the titular difference in front of Chani,* Paul thought, *is a weakness.* In such moments, he shared Stilgar's dislike for

Irulan, but sympathy tempered his emotions. What was Irulan but a Bene Gesserit pawn?

'Yes?' Paul said.

Irulan stared at him. 'If you withheld their melange...'

Chani shook her head in dissent.

'We tread with caution,' Paul said. 'Tupile remains the place of sanctuary for defeated Great Houses. It symbolises a last resort, a final place of safety for all our subjects. Exposing the sanctuary makes it vulnerable.'

'If they can hide people they can hide other things, Stilgar rumbled. 'An army, perhaps, or the beginnings of melange culture which –'

'You don't back people into a corner,' Alia said. 'Not if you want them to remain peaceful.' Ruefully, she saw that she'd been drawn into the contention which she'd foreseen.

'So we've spent ten years of negotiation for nothing,' Irulan said.

'None of my brother's actions is for nothing,' Alia said.

Irulan picked up a scribe, gripped it with white-knuckled intensity. Paul saw her marshal emotional control in the Bene Gesserit way: the penetrating inward stare, deep breathing. He could almost hear her repeating the litany. Presently, she said: 'What have we gained?'

'We've kept the Guild off balance,' Chani said.

'We want to avoid a showdown confrontation with our enemies,' Alia said. 'We have no special desire to kill them. There's enough butchery going on under the Atreides banner.'

*She feels it, too*, Paul thought. Strange, what a sense of compelling responsibility they both felt for that brawling, idolatrous universe with its ecstasies of tranquility and wild motion. *Must we protect them from themselves?* he wondered. *They play with nothingness every moment – empty lives, empty words. They ask too much of me.* His throat felt tight and full. How many moments would he lose? What sons? What dreams? Was it worth the price his vision had revealed? Who would ask the living of some far distant future, who would say to them: 'But for Muad'dib, you would not be here.'

'Denying them their melange would solve nothing,' Chani said. 'So the Guild's navigators would lose their ability to see into timespace. Your Sisters of the Bene Gesserit would lose their truthsense. Some people might die before their time. Communication would break down. Who could be blamed?'

'They wouldn't let it come to that,' Irulan said.

'Wouldn't they?' Chani asked. 'Why not? Who could blame the Guild? They'd be helpless, demonstrably so.'

'We'll sign the treaty as it stands,' Paul said.

'M'Lord,' Stilgar said, concentrating on his hands, 'there is a question in our minds.'

'Yes?' Paul gave the old Fremen his full attention.

'You have certain . . . powers,' Stilgar said. 'Can you not locate the Entente despite the Guild?'

*Powers!* Paul thought. Stilgar couldn't just say: '*You're prescient. Can't you trace a path in the future that leads to Tupile?*'

Paul looked at the golden surface of the table. Always the same problem: How could he express the limits of the inexpressible? Should he speak of fragmentation, the natural destiny of all power? How could someone who'd never experienced the spice change of prescience conceive an awareness containing no localised sensory captives?

He looked at Alia, found her attention on Irulan. Alia sensed his movement, glanced at him, nodded toward Irulan. Ahhh, yes: any answer they gave would find its way into one of Irulan's special reports to the Bene Gesserit. They never gave up seeking an answer to their kwisatz haderach.

Stilgar, though, deserved an answer of some kind. For that matter, so did Irulan.

'The uninitiated try to conceive of prescience as obeying a *Natural Law*,' Paul said. He steepled his hands in front of him. 'But it'd be just as correct to say it's heaven speaking to us, that being able to read the future is a harmonious act of man's being. In other words, prediction is a natural consequence in the wave of the present. It wears the guise of nature, you see. But such powers cannot be used from an attitude that prestates aims and purposes. Does a chip caught in the wave say where it's going? There's no cause and effect in the oracle. Causes become occasions or convections and confluences, places where the currents meet. Accepting prescience, you fill your being with concepts repugnant to the intellect. Your intellectual consciousness, therefore, rejects them. In rejecting, intellect becomes a part of the process, and is subjugated.'

'You cannot do it?' Stilgar asked.

'Were I to seek Tupile with prescience,' Paul said, speaking directly to Irulan, 'this might hide Tupile.'

'Chaos!' Irulan protested. 'It has no . . . no . . . consistency.'

'I did say it obeys no Natural Law,' Paul said.

'Then there are limits to what you can see or do with your powers ?' Irulan asked.

Before Paul could answer, Alia said: 'Dear Irulan, prescience has no limits. Not consistent ? Consistency isn't a necessary aspect of the universe.'

'But he said . . . '

'How can my brother give you explicit information about the limits of something which has no limits ? The boundaries escape the intellect.'

*That was a nasty thing for Alia to do.* Paul thought. It would alarm Irulan, who had such a careful consciousness, so dependent upon values derived from precise limits. His gaze went to Korba, who sat in a pose of religious reverie – *listening with the soul.* How could the Qizarate use this exchange ? More religious mystery ? Something to evoke awe ? No doubt.

'Then you'll sign the treaty in its present form ?' Stilgar asked.

Paul smiled. The issue of the oracle, by Stilgar's judgement, had been closed. Stilgar aimed only at victory, not at discovering truth. Peace, justice and a sound coinage – these anchored Stilgar's universe. He wanted something visible and real – a signature on a treaty.

'I'll sign it,' Paul said.

Stilgar took up a fresh folder. 'The latest communication from our field commanders in Sector Ixian speaks of agitation for a constitution.' The old Fremen glanced at Chani, who shrugged.

Irulan, who had closed her eyes and put both hands to her forehead in mnemonic impressment, opened her eyes, studied Paul intently.

'The Ixian Confederacy offers submission,' Stilgar said, 'but their negotiators question the amount of the Imperial Tax which they –'

'They want a legal limit to my Imperial will,' Paul said. 'Who would govern me, the Landsraad or CHOAM ?'

Stilgar removed from the folder a note on *instroy* paper. 'One of our agents sent this memorandum from a caucus of the CHOAM minority.' He read the cipher in a flat voice: 'The Throne must be stopped in its attempt at a power monopoly. We must tell the truth about the Atreides, how he maneuvers behind the triple sham of Landsraad legislation, religious sanction and bureaucratic efficiency.' He pushed the note back into the folder.

'A constitution,' Chani murmured.

Paul glanced at her, back to Stilgar. *Thus the Jihad falters*, Paul thought, *but not soon enough to save me.* The thought produced emotional tensions. He remembered his earliest visions of the Jihad-to-be, the terror and revulsion he'd experienced. Now, of course, he knew visions of greater terrors. He had lived with the real violence. He had seen his Fremen, charged with mystical strength, sweep all before them in the religious war. The Jihad gained a new perspective. It was finite, of course, a brief spasm when measured against eternity, but beyond lay horrors to overshadow anything in the past.

*All in my name*, Paul thought.

'Perhaps they could be given the *form* of a constitution,' Chani suggested. 'It needn't be actual.'

'Deceit *is* a tool of statecraft,' Irulan agreed.

'There are limits to power, as those who put their hopes in a constitution always discover,' Paul said.

Korba straightened from his reverent pose. 'M'Lord?'

'Yes?' And Paul thought, *Here now! Here's one who may harbor secret sympathies for an imagined rule of Law.*

'We could begin with a religious constitution,' Korba said, 'something for the faithful who –'

'No!' Paul snapped. 'We will make this an Order in Council. Are you recording this, Irulan?'

'Yes, m'Lord,' Irulan said, voice frigid with dislike for the menial role he forced upon her.

'Constitutions become the ultimate tyranny,' Paul said. 'They're organised power on such a scale as to be overwhelming. The constitution is social power mobilised and it has no conscience. It can crush the highest and the lowest, removing all dignity and individuality. It has an unstable balance point and no limitations. I, however, have limitations. In my desire to provide an ultimate protection for my people, I forbid a constitution. Order in Council, this date, etcetera, etcetera.'

'What of the Ixian concern about the tax, m'Lord?' Stilgar asked.

Paul forced his attention away from the brooding, angry look on Korba's face, said: 'You've a proposal, Stil?'

'We must have control of taxes, Sire.'

'Our price to the Guild for my signature on the Tupile Treaty,' Paul said, 'is the submission of the Ixian Confederacy of our tax. The Confederacy cannot trade without Guild transport. They'll pay.'

'Very good, m'Lord.' Stilgar produced another folder, cleared his throat. 'The Qizarate's report on Salusa Secundus. Irulan's father has been putting his legions through landing maneuvers.'

Irulan found something of interest in the palm of her left hand. A pulse throbbed at her neck.

'Irulan,' Paul asked, 'do you persist in arguing that your father's one legion is nothing more than a toy?'

'What could he do with only one legion?' she asked. She stared at him out of slitted eyes.

'He could get himself killed,' Chani said.

Paul nodded. 'And I'd be blamed.'

'I know a few commanders in the Jihad,' Alia said, 'who'd pounce if they learned of this.'

'But it's only his police force!' Irulan protested.

'Then they have no need for landing maneuvers,' Paul said. 'I suggest that your next little note to your father contain a frank and direct discussion of my views about his delicate position.'

She lowered her gaze. 'Yes, m'Lord. I hope that will be the end of it. My father would make a good martyr.'

'Mmmmmm,' Paul said. 'My sister wouldn't send a message to those commanders she mentioned unless I ordered it.'

'An attack on my father carries dangers other than the obvious military ones,' Irulan said. 'People are beginning to look back on his reign with a certain nostalgia.'

'You'll go too far one day,' Chani said in her deadly serious Fremen voice.

'Enough!' Paul ordered.

He weighed Irulan's revelation about public nostalgia – ah, now! that'd carried a note of truth. Once more, Irulan had proved her worth.

'The Bene Gesserit send a formal supplication,' Stilgar said, presenting another folder. 'They wish to consult you about the preservation of your bloodline.'

Chani glanced sideways at the folder as though it contained a deadly device.

'Send the Sisterhood the usual excuses,' Paul said.

'Must we?' Irulan demanded.

'Perhaps . . . this is the time to discuss it,' Chani said.

Paul shook his head sharply. They couldn't know that this was part of the price he had not yet decided to pay.

But Chani wasn't to be stopped. 'I have been to the prayer wall of Sietch Tabr where I was born,' she said. 'I have submitted to

54

doctors. I have knelt in the desert and sent my thoughts into the depths where dwells Shaihulud. Yet' – she shrugged – 'nothing avails.'

*Science and superstition, all have failed her*, Paul thought. *Do I fail her, too, by not telling her what bearing an heir to House Atreides will precipitate?* He looked up to find an expression of pity in Alia's eyes. The idea of pity from his sister repelled him. *Had she, too, seen that terrifying future?*'

'My Lord must know the dangers to his realm when he has no heir,' Irulan said, using her Bene Gesserit powers of voice with an oily persuasiveness. 'These things are naturally difficult to discuss, but they must be brought into the open. An Emperor is more than a man. His figure leads the realm. Should he die without an heir, civil strife must follow. As you love your people, you cannot leave them thus?'

Paul pushed himself away from the table, strode to the balcony windows. A wind was flattening the smoke of the city's fires out there. The sky presented a darkening silver-blue softened by the evening fall of dust from the Shield Wall. He stared southward at the escarpment which protected his northern lands from the coriolis wind, and he wondered why his own peace of mind could find no such shield.

The Council sat silently waiting behind him, aware of how close to rage he was.

Paul sensed time rushing upon him. He tried to force himself into a tranquility of many balances where he might shape a new future.

*Disengage . . . disengage . . . disengage,* he thought. What would happen if he took Chani, just picked up and left with her, sought sanctuary on Tupile? His name would remain behind. The Jihad would find new and more terrible centers upon which to turn. He'd be blamed for that, too. He felt suddenly fearful that in reaching for any new thing he might let fall what was most precious, that even the slightest noise from him might send the universe crashing back, receding until he never could recapture any piece of it.

Below him, the square had become the setting for a band of pilgrims in the green and white of the hajj. They wended their way like a disjointed snake behind a striding Arrakeen guide. They reminded Paul that his reception hall would be packed with supplicants by now. Pilgrims! Their exercise in homelessness had become a disgusting source of wealth for his Imperium. The hajj filled the spaceways with religious tramps. They came and they came and they came.

*How did I set this in motion ?* he asked himself.

It had, of course, set itself in motion. It was in the genes which might labor for centuries to achieve this brief spasm.

Driven by that deepest religious instinct, the people came, seeking their resurrection. The pilgrimage ended here – 'Arrakis, the place of rebirth, the place to die.'

Snide old Fremen said he wanted the pilgrims for their water. What was it the pilgrims really sought ? Paul wondered. They said they came to a holy place. But they must know the universe contained no Eden-source, no Tupile for the soul. They called Arrakis the place of the unknown where all mysteries were explained. This was a link between their universe and the next. And the frightening thing was that they appeared to go away satisfied.

*What do they find here ?* Paul asked himself.

Often in their religious ecstasy, they filled the streets with screeching like some odd aviary. In fact, the Fremen called them 'passage birds.' And the few who died here were 'winged souls.'

With a sigh, Paul thought how each new planet his legions subjugated opened new sources of pilgrims. They came out of gratitude for 'the peace of Muad'dib.'

*Everywhere there is peace*, Paul thought, *Everywhere . . . except in the heart of Muad'dib.*

He felt that some element of himself lay immersed in frosty hoar-darkness without end. His prescient power had tampered with the image of the universe held by all mankind. He had shaken the safe cosmos and replaced security with his Jihad. He had out-fought and out-thought and out-predicted the universe of men, but a certainty filled him that this universe still eluded him.

This planet beneath him which he had commanded be remade from desert into a water-rich paradise, it was alive. It had a pulse as dynamic as that of any human. It fought him, resisted, slipped away from his commands . . .

A hand crept into Paul's. He looked down to see Chani peering up at him, concern in her eyes. Those eyes drank him, and she whispered: 'Please, love, do not battle with your ruh-self.' An outpouring of emotion swept upward from her hand, buoyed him.

'Sihaya,' he whispered.

'We must go to the desert soon,' she said in a low voice.

He squeezed her hand, released it, returned to the table where he remained standing.

Chani took her seat.

Irulan stared at the papers in front of Stilgar, her mouth a tight line.

'Irulan proposes herself as mother of the Imperial heir,' Paul said. He glanced at Chani, back to Irulan, who refused to meet his gaze. 'We all know she holds no love for me.'

Irulan went very still.

'I know the political arguments,' Paul said. 'It's the human arguments which concern me. I think if the Princess Consort were not bound by the commands of the Bene Gesserit, if she did not seek this out of desires for personal power, my reaction might be very different. As matters stand, though, I reject this proposal.'

Irulan took a deep, shaky breath.

Paul, resuming his seat, thought he had never seen her under such poor control. Leaning toward her, he said: 'Irulan, I am truly sorry.'

She lifted her chin, a look of pure fury in her eyes. 'I don't want your pity!' she hissed. And turning to Stilgar: 'Is there more that's urgent and dire?'

Holding his gaze firmly on Paul, Stilgar said: 'One more matter, m'Lord. The Guild again proposes a formal embassy here on Arrakis.'

'One of the deep-space kind?' Korba asked, his voice full of fanatic loathing.

'Presumably,' Stilgar said.

'A matter to be considered with the utmost care, m'Lord,' Korba warned. 'The Council of Naibs would not like it, an actual Guildsman here on Arrakis. They contaminate the very ground they touch.'

'They live in tanks and don't touch the ground,' Paul said, letting his voice reveal irritation.

'The Naibs might take matters into their own hands, m'Lord,' Korba said.

Paul glared at him.

'They are Fremen, after all, m'Lord,' Korba insisted. 'We well remember how the Guild brought those who oppressed us. We have not forgotten the way they blackmailed a spice ransom from us to keep our secrets from our enemies. They drained us of every –'

'Enough!' Paul snapped. 'Do you think *I* have forgotten?'

As though he had just awakened to the import of his own words, Korba stuttered unintelligibly, then: 'M'lord, forgive me. I did not mean to imply you are not Fremen. I did not...'

'They'll send a Steersman,' Paul said. 'It isn't likely a Steersman would come here if he could see danger in it.'

Her mouth dry with sudden fear, Irulan said: 'You've... *seen* a Steersman come here?'

'Of course I haven't *seen* a Steersman,' Paul said, mimicking her tone. 'But I can see where one's been and where one's going. Let them send us a Steersman. Perhaps I have a use for such a one.'

'So ordered,' Stilgar said.

And Irulan, hiding a smile behind her hand, thought: *It's true then. Our Emperor cannot see a Steersman. They are mutually blind. The conspiracy is hidden.*

*'Once more the drama begins.'*
– The Emperor Paul Muad'dib
on his ascension to the Lion Throne

Alia peered down from her spy window into the great reception hall to watch the advance of the Guild entourage.

The sharply silver light of noon poured through clerestory windows onto a floor worked in green, blue and eggshell tiles to simulate a bayou with water plants and, here and there, a splash of exotic color to indicate bird or animal.

Guildsmen moved across the tile pattern like hunters stalking their prey in a strange jungle. They formed a moving design of gray robes, black robes, orange robes – all arrayed in a deceptively random way around the transparent tank where the Steersman-Ambassador swam in his orange gas. The tank slid on its supporting field, towed by two gray-robed attendants, like a rectangular ship being warped into its dock.

Directly beneath her, Paul sat on the Lion Throne on its raised dais. He wore the new formal crown with its fish and fist emblems. The jeweled golden robes of state covered his body. The shimmering of a personal shield surrounded him. Two wings of bodyguards fanned out on both sides along the dais and down the steps. Stilgar stood two steps below Paul's right hand in a white robe with a yellow rope for a belt.

Sibling empathy told her that Paul seethed with the same agitation she was experiencing, although she doubted another could detect it. His attention remained on an orange-robed attendant whose blindly staring metal eyes looked neither to right nor to left. This attendant walked at the right front corner of the Ambassador's troupe like a military outrider. A rather flat face beneath curly black hair, such of his figure as could be seen beneath the orange robe, every gesture shouted a familiar identity.

It was Duncan Idaho.

It could not be Duncan Idaho, yet it was.

Captive memories absorbed in the womb during the moment of her mother's spice change identified this man for Alia by a rihani decipherment which cut through all camouflage. Paul was seeing him, she knew, out of countless personal experiences, out of gratitude and youthful sharing.

It was Duncan.

Alia shuddered. There could be only one answer: this was a Tleilaxu ghola, a being reconstructed from the dead flesh of the original. That original had perished saving Paul. This could only be a product of the axolotl tanks.

The ghola walked with the cock-footed alertness of a master swordsman. He came to a halt as the Ambassador's tank glided to a stop ten paces from the steps of the dais.

In the Bene Gesserit way she could not escape, Alia read Paul's disquiet. He no longer looked at the figure out of his past. Not looking, his whole being stared. Muscles strained against restrictions as he nodded to the Guild Ambassador, said: 'I am told your name is Edric. We welcome you to our Court in the hope this will bring new understanding between us.'

The Steersman assumed a sybaritic reclining pose in his orange gas, popped a melange capsule into his mouth before meeting Paul's gaze. The tiny transducer orbiting a corner of the Guildsman's tank reproduced a coughing sound, then the rasping, uninvolved voice: 'I abase myself before my Emperor and beg leave to present my credentials and offer a small gift.'

An aide passed a scroll up to Stilgar, who studied it, scowling, then nodded to Paul. Both Stilgar and Paul turned then toward the ghola standing patiently below the dais.

'Indeed my Emperor has discerned the gift,' Edric said.

'We are pleased to accept your credentials,' Paul said. 'Explain the gift.'

Edric rolled in the tank, bringing his attention to bear on the ghola. 'This is a man called Hayt,' he said, spelling the name. 'According to our investigators, he has a most curious history.

He was killed here on Arrakis . . . a grievous head-wound which required many months of regrowth. The body was sold to the Bene Tleilax as that of a master swordsman, an adept of the Ginaz School. It came to our attention that this must be Duncan Idaho, the trusted retainer of your household. We bought him as a gift befitting an Emperor.' Edric peered up at Paul. 'Is it not Idaho, Sire?'

Restraint and caution gripped Paul's voice. 'He has the aspect of Idaho.'

*Does Paul see something I don't?* Alia wondered. *No! It's Duncan!*

The man called Hayt stood impassively, metal eyes fixed straight ahead, body relaxed. No sign escaped him to indicate he knew himself to be the object of discussion.

'According to our best knowledge, it's Idaho,' Edric said.

'He's called Hayt now,' Paul said. 'A curious name.'

'Sire, there's no divining how or why the Tleilaxu bestow names,' Edric said. 'But names can be changed. The Tleilaxu name is of little importance.'

*This is a Tleilaxu thing*, Paul thought. *There's the problem.* The Bene Tleilax held little attachment to phenomenal nature. Good and evil carried strange meanings in their philosophy. What might they have incorporated in Idaho's flesh – out of design or whim?

Paul glanced at Stilgar, noted the Fremen's superstitious awe. It was an emotion echoed all through his Fremen guard. Stilgar's mind would be speculating about the loathsome habits of Guildsmen, of Tleilaxu and of gholas.

Turning towards the ghola, Paul said: 'Hayt, is that your only name?'

A serene smile spread over the ghola's dark features. The metal eyes lifted, centered on Paul, but maintained their mechanical stare. 'That is how I am called, my Lord: Hayt.'

In her dark spy hole, Alia trembled. It was Idaho's voice, a quality of sound so precise she sensed its imprint upon her cells.

'May it please my Lord,' the ghola added, 'if I say his voice gives me pleasure. This is a sign, say the Bene Tleilax, that I have heard the voice . . . before.'

'But you don't know this for sure,' Paul said.

'I know nothing of my past for sure, my Lord. It was explained that I can have no memory of my former life. All that remains from before is the pattern set by the genes. There are, however, niches into which once-familiar things may fit. There are voices, places, foods, faces, sounds, actions – a sword in my hand, the controls of a 'thopter . . . '

Noting how intently the Guildsmen watched this exchange, Paul asked: 'Do you understand that you're a gift?'

'It was explained to me, my Lord.'

Paul sat back, hands resting on the arms of the throne.

*What debt do I owe Duncan's flesh?* he wondered. *The man died saving my life. But this is not Idaho, this is a ghola.* Yet, here were body and mind which had taught Paul to fly a 'thopter as though the wings grew from his own shoulders. Paul knew he could not pick up a sword without leaning on the harsh education Idaho had given him. A ghola. This was flesh full of false impressions, easily misread. Old associations would persist. *Duncan Idaho.* It wasn't so much a mask the ghola wore as it was a loose, concealing garment of personality which moved in a way different from whatever the Tleilaxu had hidden here.

'How might you serve us?' Paul asked.

'In any way my Lord's wishes and my capabilities agree.'

Alia, watching from her vantage point, was touched by the ghola's air of diffidence. She detected nothing feigned. Something ultimately innocent shone from the new Duncan Idaho. The original had been worldly, devil-may-care. But this flesh had been cleansed of all that. It was a pure surface upon which the Tleilaxu had written . . . what?

She sensed the hidden perils in this gift then. This was a Tleilaxu thing. The Tleilaxu displayed a disturbing lack of inhibitions in what they created. Unbridled curiosity might guide their actions. They boasted they could make *anything* from the proper human raw material – devils or saints. They sold killer-mentats. They'd produced a killer medic, overcoming the Suk inhibitions against the taking of human life to do it. Their wares included willing menials, pliant sex toys for any whim, soldiers, generals, philosophers, even an occasional moralist.

Paul stirred, looked at Edric. 'How has this *gift* been trained?' he asked.

'If it please my Lord,' Edric said, 'it amused the Tleilaxu to train this ghola as a mentat and philosopher of the Zensunni. Thus, they sought to increase his abilities with the sword.'

'Did they succeed?'

'I do not know, my Lord.'

Paul weighed the answer. Truthsense told him Edric sincerely believed the ghola to be Idaho. But there was more. The waters of Time through which this oracular Steersman moved suggested dangers without revealing them. *Hayt*. The Tleilaxu name spoke of peril. Paul felt himself tempted to reject the gift. Even as he felt the temptation, he knew he couldn't choose that way. This flesh made demands on House Atreides – a fact the enemy well knew.

'Zensunni philosopher,' Paul mused, once more looking at the ghola. 'You've examined your own role and motives ?'

'I approach my service in an attitude of humility, Sire. I am a cleansed mind washed free of the imperatives from my human past.'

'Would you prefer we called you Hayt or Duncan Idaho ?'

'My Lord may call me what he wishes, for I am not a name.'

'But do you *enjoy* the name Duncan Idaho ?'

'I think that was my name, Sire. It fits within me. Yet . . . it stirs up curious responses. One's name, I think, must carry much that's unpleasant along with the pleasant.'

'What gives you the most pleasure ?' Paul asked.

Unexpectedly, the ghola laughed, said: 'Looking for signs in others which reveal my former self.'

'Do you see such signs here ?'

'Oh, yes, my Lord. Your man Stilgar there is caught between suspicion and admiration. He was friend to my former self, but this ghola flesh repels him. You, my Lord, admired the man I was . . . and you trusted him.'

'Cleansed mind,' Paul said. 'How can a cleansed mind put itself in bondage to us ?'

'Bondage, my Lord ? The cleansed mind makes decisions in the presence of unknowns and without cause and effect. Is this bondage ?'

Paul scowled. It was a Zensunni saying, cryptic, apt – immersed in a creed which denied objective function in all mental activity. *Without cause and effect !* Such thoughts shocked the mind. *Unknowns ?* Unknowns lay in every decision, even in the oracular vision.

'You'd prefer we called you Duncan Idaho ?' Paul asked.

'We live by differences, my lord. Choose a name for me.'

'Let your Tleilaxu name stand,' Paul said. 'Hayt – there's a name inspires caution.'

Hayt bowed, moved back one step.

And Alia wondered: *How did he know the interview was over ?*

63

*I knew it because I know my brother. But there was no sign a stranger could read. Did the Duncan Idaho in him know?*

Paul turned toward the Ambassador, said: 'Quarters have been set aside for your embassy. It is our desire to have a private consultation with you at the earliest opportunity. We will send for you. Let us inform you further, before you hear it from an inaccurate source, that a Reverend Mother of the Sisterhood, Gaius Helen Mohiam, has been removed from the heighliner which brought you. It was done at our command. Her presence on your ship will be an item in our talks.'

A wave of Paul's left hand dismissed the envoy. 'Hayt,' Paul said, 'stay here.'

The Ambassador's attendants backed away, towing the tank. Edric became orange motion in orange gas – eyes, a mouth, gently waving limbs.

Paul watched until the last Guildsman was gone, the great doors swinging closed behind them.

*I've done it now,* Paul thought. *I've accepted the ghola.* The Tleilaxu creation was bait, no doubt of it. Very likely the old hag of a Reverend Mother played the same role. But it was the time of the tarot which he'd forecast in an early vision. The damnable tarot! It muddied the waters of Time until the prescient strained to detect moments but an hour off. Many a fish took the bait and escaped, he reminded himself. And the tarot worked for him as well as against him. What he could not see, others might not detect as well.

The ghola stood, head cocked to one side, waiting.

Stilgar moved across the steps, hid the ghola from Paul's view. In Chakobsa, the hunting language of their sietch days, Stilgar said: 'That creature in the tank gives me the shudders, Sire, but this *gift!* Send it away!'

In the same tongue, Paul said: 'I cannot.'

'Idaho's dead,' Stilgar argued. 'This isn't Idaho. Let me take its water for the tribe.'

'The ghola is my problem, Stil. Your problem is our prisoner. I want the Reverend Mother guarded most carefully by the men I trained to resist the wiles of Voice.'

'I like this not, Sire.'

'I'll be cautious, Stil. See that you are, too.'

'Very well, Sire.' Stilgar stepped down to the floor of the hall, passed close to Hayt, sniffed him and strode out.

*Evil can be detected by its smell,* Paul thought. Stilgar had

64

planted the green and white Atreides banner on a dozen worlds, but remained superstitious Fremen, proof against any sophistication.

Paul studied the gift.

'Duncan, Duncan,' he whispered. 'What have they done to you?'

'They gave me life, m'Lord,' Hayt said.

'But why were you trained and given to us?' Paul asked.

Hayt pursed his lips, then: 'They intend me to destroy you.'

The statement's candor shook Paul. But then, how else could a Zensunni-mentat respond? Even in a ghola, a mentat could speak no less than the truth, especially out of Zensunni inner calm. This was a human computer, mind and nervous system fitted to the tasks relegated long ago to hated mechanical devices. To condition him also as a Zensunni meant a double ration of honesty . . . unless the Tleilaxu had built something even more odd into this flesh.

Why, for example, the mechanical eyes? Tleilaxu boasted their metal eyes improved on the original. Strange, then, that more Tleilaxu didn't wear them out of choice.

Paul glanced up at Alia's spy hole, longed for her presence and advice, for counsel not clouded by feelings of responsibility and debt.

Once more, he looked at the ghola. This was no frivolous gift. It gave honest answers to dangerous questions.

*It makes no difference that I know this is a weapon to be used against me,* Paul thought.

'What should I do to protect myself from you?' Paul asked. It was direct speech, no royal 'we,' but a question as he might have put it to the old Duncan Idaho.

'Send me away, m'Lord.'

Paul shook his head from side to side. 'How are you to destroy me?'

Hayt looked at the guards, who'd moved closer to Paul after Stilgar's departure. He turned, cast his gaze around the hall, brought his metal eyes back to bear on Paul, nodded.

'This is a place where a man draws away from people,' Hayt said. 'It speaks of such power that one can contemplate it comfortably only in the remembrance that all things are finite. Did my Lord's oracular powers plot his course into this place?'

Paul drummed his fingers against the throne's arms. The mentat sought data, but the question disturbed him. 'I came to this position by strong decisions . . . not always out of my other . . . abilities.'

'Strong decisions,' Hayt said. 'These temper a man's life. One can take the temper from fine metal by heating it and allowing it to cool without quenching.'

'Do you divert me with Zensunni prattle ?' Paul asked.

'Zensunni has other avenues to explore, Sire, than diversion and display.'

Paul wet his lips with his tongue, drew in a deep breath, set his own thoughts into the counterbalance poise of the mentat. Negative answers arose around him. It wasn't expected that he'd go haring after the ghola to the exclusion of other duties. No, that wasn't it. Why a *Zensunni*-mentat ? Philosophy . . . words . . . contemplation . . . inward searching . . . He felt the weakness of his data.

'We need more data,' he muttered.

'The facts needed by a mentat do not brush off onto one as you might gather pollen on your robe while passing through a field of flowers,' Hayt said. 'One chooses his pollen carefully, examines it under powerful amplification.'

'You must teach me this Zensunni way with rhetoric,' Paul said.

The metallic eyes glittered at him for a moment, then 'M'Lord, perhaps that's what was intended.'

*To blunt my will with words and ideas ?* Paul wondered.

'Ideas are most to be feared when they become actions,' Paul said.

'Send me away, Sire,' Hayt said, and it was Duncan Idaho's voice full of concern for 'the young master'.

Paul felt trapped by that voice. He couldn't send that voice away, even when it came from a ghola. 'You will stay,' he said, 'and we'll both exercise caution.'

Hayt bowed in submission.

Paul glanced up at the spy hole, eyes pleading for Alia to take this *gift* off his hands and ferret out its secrets. Gholas were ghosts to frighten children. He'd never thought to know one. To know this one, he had to set himself above all compassion . . . and he wasn't certain he could do it. *Duncan . . . Duncan . . .* Where was Idaho in this shaped-to-measure flesh ? It wasn't flesh . . . it was a shroud in fleshy shape ! Idaho lay dead forever on the floor of an Arrakeen cavern. His ghost stared out of metal eyes. Two beings stood side by side in this revenant flesh. One was a threat with its force and nature hidden behind unique veils.

Closing his eyes, Paul allowed old visions to sift through his awareness. He sensed the spirits of love and hate spouting there in a rolling sea from which no rock lifted above the chaos. No place at all from which to survey turmoil.

*Why has no vision shown me this new Duncan Idaho?* he asked himself. *What concealed Time from an oracle? Other oracles, obviously.*

Paul opened his eyes, asked: 'Hayt, do you have the power of prescience?'

'No, m'Lord.'

Sincerity spoke in that voice. It was possible the ghola didn't know he possessed this ability, of course. But that'd hamper his working as a mentat. What was the hidden design?

Old visions surged around Paul. Would he have to choose the terrible way? Distorted Time hinted at this ghola in that hideous future. Would that way close in upon him no matter what he did?

*Disengage . . . disengage . . . disengage . . .*

The thought tolled in his mind.

In her position above Paul, Alia sat with chin cupped in left hand, stared down at the ghola. A magnetic attraction about this Hayt reached up to her. Tleilaxu restoration had given him youth, an innocent intensity which called out to her. She'd understood Paul's unspoken plea. When oracles failed, one turned to real spies and physical powers. She wondered, though, at her own eagerness to accept this challenge. She felt a positive desire to be near this *new* man, perhaps to touch him

*He's a danger to both of us,* she thought.

*Truth suffers from too much analysis.*
                              —Ancient Fremen Saying

'Reverend Mother, I shudder to see you in such circumstances,'
Irulan said.

She stood just inside the cell door, measuring the various
capacities of the room in her Bene Gesserit way. It was a three-
meter cube carved with cutterays from the veined brown rock
beneath Paul's Keep. For furnishings, it contained one flimsy
basket chair occupied now by the Reverend Mother Gaius Helen
Mohiam, a pallet with a brown cover upon which had been
spread a deck of the new Dune Tarot cards, a metered water tap
above a reclamation basin, a Fremen privy with moisture seals.
It was all sparse, primitive. Yellow light came from anchored
and caged glowglobes at the four corners of the ceiling.

'You've sent word to the Lady Jessica?' the Reverend Mother
asked.

'Yes, but I don't expect her to lift one finger against her firstborn,' Irulan said. She glanced at the cards. They spoke of the
powerful turning their backs on supplicants. The card of the
Great Worm lay beneath Desolate Sand. Patience was counseled.
*Did one require the tarot to see this?* she asked herself.

A guard stood outside watching them through a metaglass
window in the door. Irulan knew there'd be other monitors on
this encounter. She had put in much thought and planning before
daring to come here. To have stayed away carried its own perils,
though.

The Reverend Mother had been engaged in *prajna* meditation
interspersed with examinations of the tarot. Despite a feeling that

68

she would never leave Arrakis alive, she had achieved a measure of calm through this. One's oracular powers might be small, but muddy water was muddy water. And there was always the Litany Against Fear.

She had yet to assimilate the import of the actions which had precipitated her into this cell. Dark suspicions brooded in her mind (and the tarot hinted at confirmations). Was it possible the Guild had planned this?

A yellow-robed Qizara, head shaved for a turban, beady eyes of total blue in a bland round face, skin leathered by the wind and sun of Arrakis, had awaited her on the heighliner's reception bridge. He had looked up from a bulb of spice-coffee being served by an obsequious steward, studied her a moment, put down the coffee bulb.

'You are the Reverend Mother Gaius Helen Mohiam?'

To replay those words in her mind was to bring that moment alive in the memory. Her throat had constricted with an unmanageable spasm of fear. How had one of the Emperor's minions learned of her presence on the heighliner?

'It came to our attention that you were aboard,' the Qizara said. 'Have you forgotten that you are denied permission to set foot on the holy planet?'

'I am not on Arrakis,' she said. 'I'm a passenger on a Guild heighliner in free space.'

'There is no such thing as free space, Madame.'

She read hate mingled with profound suspicion in his tone.

'Muad'dib rules everywhere,' he said.

'Arrakis is not my destination,' she insisted.

'Arrakis is the destination of everyone,' he said. And she feared for a moment that he would launch into a recital of the mystical itinerary which pilgrims followed. (This very ship had carried thousands of them.)

But the Qizara had pulled a golden amulet from beneath his robe, kissed it, touched it to his forehead and placed it to his right ear, listened. Presently, he restored the amulet to its hidden place.

'You are ordered to gather your luggage and accompany me to Arrakis.'

'But I have business elsewhere!'

In that moment, she suspected Guild perfidy . . . or exposure through some transcendant power of the Emperor or his sister. Perhaps the Steersman did not conceal the conspiracy, after all.

The abomination, Alia, certainly possessed the abilities of a Bene Gesserit Reverend Mother. What happened when those powers were coupled with the forces which worked in her brother?

'At once!' the Qizara snapped.

Everything in her cried out against setting foot once more on that accursed desert planet. Here was where the Lady Jessica had turned against the Sisterhood. Here was where they'd lost Paul Atreides, the kwisatz haderach they'd sought through long generations of careful breeding.

'At once,' she agreed.

'There's little time,' the Qizara said. 'When the Emperor commands, all his subjects obey.'

*So the order had come from Paul!*

She thought of protesting to the heighliner's Navigator-Commander, but the futility of such a gesture stopped her. What could the Guild do?

'The Emperor has said I must die if I set foot on Dune,' she said, making a last desperate effort. 'You spoke of this yourself. You are condemning me if you take me down there.'

'Say no more,' the Qizara ordered. 'The thing is ordained.'

That was how they always spoke of Imperial commands, she knew. *Ordained!* The holy ruler whose eyes could pierce the future had spoken. What must be must be. He had seen it, had He not?

With the sick feeling that she was caught in a web of her own spinning, she had turned to obey.

And the web had become a cell which Irulan could visit. She saw that Irulan had aged somewhat since their meeting on Wallach IX. New lines of worry spread from the corners of her eyes. Well . . . time to see if this Sister of the Bene Gesserit could obey her vows.

'I've had worse quarters,' the Reverend Mother said. 'Do you come from the Emperor?' And she allowed her fingers to move as though in agitation.

Irulan read the moving fingers and her own fingers flashed an answer as she spoke, saying: 'No – I came as soon as I heard you were here.'

'Won't the Emperor be angry?' the Reverend Mother asked. again, her fingers moved: imperative, pressing, demanding.

'Let him be angry. You were my teacher in the Sisterhood, just as you were the teacher of his own mother. Does he think I will turn my back on you as she has done?' And Irulan's finger-talk made excuses, begged.

The Reverend Mother sighed. On the surface, it was the sigh of a prisoner bemoaning her fate, but inwardly she felt the response as a comment on Irulan. It was futile to hope the Atreides Emperor's precious gene pattern could be preserved through this instrument. No matter her beauty, this Princess was flawed. Under the veneer of sexual attraction lived a whining shrew more interested in words than in actions. Irulan was still a Bene Gesserit, though, and the Sisterhood reserved certain techniques to use on some of its weaker vessels as insurance that vital instructions would be carried out.

Beneath small talk about a softer pallet, better food, the Reverend Mother brought up her arsenal of persuasion and gave her orders: the brother-sister crossbreeding must be explored. (Irulan almost broke at receiving this command.)

'I must have my chance!' Irulan's fingers pleaded.

'You've had your chance,' the Reverend Mother countered. And she was explicit in her instructions: Was the Emperor ever angry with his concubine? His unique powers must make him lonely. To whom could he speak in any hope of being understood. To the sister, obviously. She shared this loneliness. The depth of their communion must be exploited. Opportunities must be created to throw them together in privacy. Intimate encounters must be arranged. The possibility of eliminating the concubine must be explored. Grief dissolved traditional barriers.

Irulan protested. If Chani were killed, suspicion would fasten immediately upon the Princess-Consort. Besides, there were other problems. Chani had fastened upon an ancient Fremen diet supposed to promote fertility and the diet eliminated all opportunity for administering the contraceptive drugs. Lifting the suppressives would make Chani even more fertile.

The Reverend Mother was outraged and concealed it with difficulty while her fingers flashed their demands. Why had this information not been conveyed at the beginning of their conversation? How could Irulan be that stupid? If Chani conceived and bore a son, the Emperor would declare the child his heir!

Irulan protested that she understood the dangers, but the genes might not be totally lost.

*Damn such stupidity!* the Reverend Mother raged. Who knew what suppressions and genetic entanglements Chani might introduce from her wild Fremen strain? The Sisterhood must have

71

only the pure line! And an heir would renew Paul's ambitions, spur him to new efforts in consolidating his Empire. The conspiracy could not afford such a setback.

Defensively, Irulan wanted to know how she could have prevented Chani from trying this diet?

But the Reverend Mother was in no mood for excuses. Irulan received explicit instructions how to meet this new threat. If Chani conceived, an abortifact must be introduced into her food or drink. Either that, or she must be killed. An heir to the throne from that source must be prevented at all costs.

An abortifact would be as dangerous as an open attack on the concubine, Irulan objected. She trembled at the thought of trying to kill Chani.

Was Irulan deterred by danger? the Reverend Mother wanted to know, her finger-talk conveying deep scorn.

Angered, Irulan signaled that she knew her value as an agent in the royal household. Did the conspiracy wish to waste such a valuable agent? Was she to be thrown away? In what other way could they keep this close a watch on the Emperor? Or had they introduced another agent into the household? Was that it? Was she to be used now, desperately, and for the last time?

In a war, all values acquired new relationships, the Reverend Mother countered. Their greatest peril was that House Atreides should secure itself with an Imperial line. The Sisterhood could not take such a risk. This went far beyond the danger to the Atreides genetic pattern. Let Paul anchor his family to the throne and the Sisterhood could look forward to centuries of disruption for its programs.

Irulan understood the argument, but she couldn't escape the thought that a decision had been made to spend the Princess-Consort for something of great value. Was there something she should know about the ghola? Irulan ventured.

The Reverend Mother wanted to know if Irulan thought the Sisterhood composed of fools. When had they ever failed to tell Irulan all she *should* know?

It was no answer, but an admission of concealment, Irulan saw. It said she would be told no more than she needed to know.

How could they be certain the ghola was capable of destroying the Emperor? Irulan asked.

She could just as well have asked if melange were capable of destruction, the Reverend Mother countered.

It was a rebuke with a subtle message, Irulan realised. The

Bene Gesserit 'whip that instructs' informed her that she should have understood long ago this similarity between the spice and the ghola. Melange was valuable, but it exacted a price – addiction. It added years to a life – decades for some – but it was still just another way to die.

The ghola was something of deadly value.

The obvious way to prevent an unwanted birth was to kill the prospective mother before conception, the Reverend Mother signaled, returning to the attack.

*Of course*, Irulan thought. *If you decide to spend a certain sum, get as much for it as you can.*

The Reverend Mother's eyes, dark with the blue brilliance of her melange addiction, stared up at Irulan, measuring, waiting, observing minutiae.

*She reads me clearly*, Irulan thought with dismay. *She trained me and observed me in that training. She knows I realise what decision has been taken here. She only observes now to see how I will take this knowledge. Well, I will take it as a Bene Gesserit and a princess.*

Irulan managed a smile, pulled herself erect, thought of the evocative opening passage of the Litany Against Fear:

'*I must not fear. Fear is the mind-killer. Fear is the little-death that brings total obliteration. I will face my fear . . .*'

When calmness had returned, she thought: *Let them spend me. I will show them what a princess is worth. Perhaps I'll buy them more than they expected.*

After a few more empty vocalisations to bind off the interview, Irulan departed.

When she had gone, the Reverend Mother returned to her tarot carts, laying them out in the fire-eddy pattern. Immediately, she got the Kwisatz Haderach of the Major Arcana and the card lay coupled with the Eight of Ships: the sibyl hoodwinked and betrayed. These were not cards of good omen: they spoke of concealed resources for her enemies.

She turned away from the cards, sat in agitation, wondering if Irulan might yet destroy them.

*The Fremen see her as the Earth Figure, a demi-goddess whose special charge is to protect the tribes through her powers of violence. She is Reverend Mother to their Reverend Mothers. To pilgrims who seek her out with demands that she restore virility or make the barren fruitful, she is a form of anti-mentat. She feeds on that strong human desire for the mysterious. She is living proof that the 'analytic' has limits. She represents ultimate tension. She is the virgin-harlot – witty, vulgar, cruel, as destructive in her whims as a coriolis storm.*

> – St Alia of the Knife
> as taken from The Irulan Report

Alia stood like a black-robed sentinel figure on the south platform of her temple, the Fane of the Oracle which Paul's Fremen cohorts had built for her against a wall of his stronghold.

She hated this part of her life, but knew no way to evade the temple without bringing down destruction upon them all. The pilgrims (damn them!) grew more numerous every day. The temple's lower porch was crowded with them. Vendors moved among the pilgrims, and there were minor sorcerers, haruspices, diviners, all working their trade in pitiful imitation of Paul Muad'dib and his sister.

Red and green packages containing the new Dune Tarot were prominent among the vendors' wares, Alia saw. She wondered about the tarot. Who was feeding this device into the Arrakeen market? Why had the tarot sprung to prominence at this particular time and place? Was it to muddy Time? Spice addiction always conveyed some sensitivity to prediction. Fremen were notoriously fey. Was it an accident that so many of them dabbled in portents and omens here and now? She decided to seek an answer at the first opportunity.

There was a wind from the southeast, a small leftover wind blunted by the scarp of the Shield Wall which loomed high in these northern reaches. The rim glowed orange through a thin dust haze underlighted by the late afternoon sun. It was a hot wind against her cheeks and it made her homesick for the sand, for the security of open spaces.

The last of the day's mob began descending the broad greenstone steps of the lower porch, singly and in groups, a few pausing to stare at the keepsakes and holy amulets on the street vendors' racks, some consulting one last minor sorcerer. Pilgrims, supplicants, townfolk, Fremen, vendors closing up for the day – they formed a straggling line that trailed off into the palm-lined avenue which led to the heart of the city.

Alia's eyes picked out the Fremen, marking the frozen looks of superstitious awe on their faces, the half-wild way they kept their distance from the others. They were her strength and her peril. They still captured giant worms for transport, for sport and for sacrifice. They resented the offworld pilgrims, barely tolerated the townfolk of graben and *pan*, hated the cynicism they saw in the street vendors. One did not jostle a wild Fremen, even in a mob such as the ones which swarmed to Alia's Fane. There were no knifings in the Sacred Precincts, but bodies had been found ... later.

The departing swarm had stirred up dust. The flinty odor came to Alia's nostrils, ignited another pang of longing for the open *bled*. Her sense of the past, she realised, had been sharpened by the coming of the ghola. There'd been much pleasure in those untrammeled days before her brother had mounted the throne – time for joking, time for small things, time to enjoy a cool morning or a sunset, time ... time ... time ... Even danger had been good in those days – clean danger from known sources. No need then to strain the limits of prescience, to peer through murky veils for frustrating glimpses of the future.

Wild Fremen said it well: 'Four things cannot be hidden – love, smoke, a pillar of fire and a man striding across the open bled.'

With an abrupt feeling of revulsion, Alia retreated from the platform into the shadows of the Fane, strode along the balcony which looked down into the glistening opalescence of her Hall of Oracles. Sand on the tiles rasped beneath her feet. *Supplicants always tracked sand into the Sacred Chambers!* She ignored attendants, guards, postulants, the Qizarate's omnipresent priest-sycophants, plunged into the spiral passage which twisted upward to her private quarters. There, amidst divans, deep rugs, tent hangings and mementos of the desert, she dismissed the Fremen amazons Stilgar had assigned as her personal guardians. *Watchdogs, more likely!* When they had gone, muttering and objecting, but more fearful of her than they were of Stilgar, she stripped off her robe, leaving only the sheathed crysknife on its thong around her neck, strewed garments behind as she made for the bath.

He was near, she knew – that shadow-figure of a man she could sense in her future, but could not see. It angered her that no power of prescience could put flesh on that figure. He could be sensed only at unexpected moments while she scanned the lives of others. Or she came upon a smoky outline in solitary darkness when innocence lay coupled with desire. He stood just beyond an unfixed horizon, and she felt that if she strained her talents to an unexpected intensity she might see him. He was *there* – a constant assault on her awareness: fierce, dangerous, immoral.

Moist warm air surrounded her in the bath. Here was a habit she had learned from the memory-entities of the uncounted Reverend Mothers who were strung out in her awareness like pearls on a glowing necklace. Water, warm water in a sunken tub, accepted her skin as she slid into it. Green tiles with figures of red fish worked into a sea pattern surrounded the water. Such an abundance of water occupied this space that a Fremen of old would have been outraged to see it used merely for washing human flesh.

*He* was near.

It was lust in tension with chastity, she thought. Her flesh desired a mate. Sex held no casual mystery for a Reverend Mother who had presided at the sietch orgies. The *tau* awareness of her *other-selves* could supply any detail her curiosity required. This feeling of nearness could be nothing other than flesh reaching for flesh.

Need for action fought lethargy in the warm water.

Abruptly, Alia climbed dripping from the bath, strode wet

and naked into the training chamber which adjoined her bedroom. The chamber, oblong and skylighted, contained the gross
and subtle instruments which toned a Bene Gesserit adept into
ultimate physical and mental awareness/preparedness. There
were mnemonic amplifiers, digit mills from Ix to strengthen and
sensitise fingers and toes, odor synthesisers, tactility sensitisers,
temperature gradient fields, pattern betrayers to prevent her
falling into detectable habits, alpha-wave-response trainers,
blink-synchronisers to tone abilities in light/dark/spectrum
analysis ...

In ten-centimeter letters along one wall, written by her own
hand in mnemonic paint, stood the key reminder from the Bene
Gesserit Creed:

'Before us, all methods of learning were tainted by instinct.
We learned how to learn. Before us, instinct-ridden researchers
possessed a limited attention span – often no longer than a single
lifetime. Projects stretching across fifty or more lifetimes never
occurred to them. The concept of total muscle/nerve training
had not entered awareness.'

As she moved into the training room, Alia caught her own
reflection multiplied thousands of times in the crystal prisms of a
fencing mirror swinging in the heart of a target dummy. She saw
the long sword waiting on its brackets against the target, and she
thought: *Yes! I'll work myself to exhaustion – drain the flesh and
clear the mind.*

The sword felt right in her hand. She slipped the crysknife
from its sheath at her neck, held it sinister, tapped the activating
stud with the sword tip. Resistance came alive as the aura of the
target shield built up, pushing her weapon slowly and firmly
away.

Prisms glittered. The target slipped to her left.

Alia followed with the tip of the long blade, thinking as she
often did that the thing could almost be alive. But it was only
servomotors and complex reflector circuits designed to lure the
eyes away from danger, to confuse and teach. It was an instrument geared to react as she reacted, an anti-self which moved as
she moved, balancing light on its prisms, shifting its target,
offering its counter-blade.

Many blades appeared to lunge at her from the prisms, but
only one was real, She countered the real one, slipped the sword
past shield resistence to tap the target. A marker light came alive:
red and glistening among the prisms ... more distraction.

77

Again the thing attacked, moving at one-marker speed now, just a bit faster than it had at the beginning.

She parried and, against all caution, moved into the danger zone, scored with the crysknife.

Two lights glowed from the prisms.

Again, the thing increased speed, moving out on its rollers, drawn like a magnet to the motions of her body and the tip of her sword.

Attack – parry – counter.

Attack – parry – counter . . .

She had four lights alive in there now, and the thing was becoming more dangerous, moving faster with each light, offering more areas of confusion.

Five lights.

Sweat glistened on her naked skin. She existed now in a universe whose dimensions were outlined by the threatening blade, the target, bare feet against the practice floor, sense/nerves/ muscles – motion against motion.

Attack – parry – counter.

Six lights . . . seven . . .

Eight!

She had never before risked eight.

In a recess of her mind there grew a sense of urgency, a crying out against such wildness as this. The instrument of prisms and target could not think, feel caution or remorse. And it carried a real blade. To go against less defeated the purpose of such training. That attacking blade could maim and it could kill. But the finest swordsmen in the Imperium never went against more than seven lights.

Nine!

Alia experienced a sense of supreme exaltation. Attacking blade and target became blurs among blurs. She felt that the sword in her hand had come alive. She was an anti-target. She did not move the blade; it moved her. .

Ten!

Eleven!

Something flashed past her shoulder, slowed at the shield aura around the target, slid through and tripped the deactivating stud. The lights darkened. Prisms and target twisted their way to stillness.

Alia whirled, angered by the intrusion, but her reaction was thrown into tension by awareness of the supreme ability which had hurled that knife. It had been a throw timed to exquisite nicety – just fast enough to get through the shield zone and not too fast to be deflected.

And it had touched a one-millimeter spot within an eleven-light target.

Alia found her own emotions and tensions running down in a manner not unlike that of the target dummy. She was not at all surprised to see who had thrown the knife.

Paul stood just inside the training room doorway, Stilgar three steps behind him. Her brother's eyes were squinted in anger.

Alia, growing conscious of her nudity, thought to cover herself, found the idea amusing. What the eyes had seen could not be erased. Slowly, she replaced the crysknife in its sheath at her neck.

'I might've known,' she said.

'I presume you know how dangerous that was,' Paul said. He took his time reading the reactions on her face and body: the flush of her exertions coloring her skin, the wet fullness of her lips. There was a disquieting femaleness about her that he had never considered in his sister. He found it odd that he could look at a person who was this close to him and no longer recognise her in the identity framework which had seemed so fixed and familiar.

'That was madness,' Stilgar rasped, coming up to stand beside Paul.

The words were angry, but Alia heard awe in his voice, saw it in his eyes.

'Eleven lights,' Paul said, shaking his head.

'I'd have made it twelve if you hadn't interfered,' she said. She began to pale under his close regard, added: 'And why do the damned things have that many lights if we're not supposed to try for them?'

'A Bene Gesserit should ask the reasoning behind an open-ended system?' Paul asked.

'I suppose you never tried for more than seven!' she said, anger returning. His attentive posture began to annoy her.

'Just once,' Paul said. 'Gurney Halleck caught me on ten. My punishment was sufficiently embarrassing that I won't tell you what he did. And speaking of embarrassment . . . '

'Next time, perhaps you'll have yourselves announced,' she said. She brushed past Paul into the bedroom, found a loose gray robe, slipped into it, began brushing her hair before a wall mirror. She felt sweaty, sad, a post coitum kind of sadness that left her with a desire to bathe once more . . . and to sleep. 'Why're you here?' she asked.

'My Lord,' Stilgar said. There was an odd inflection in his voice that brought Alia around to stare at him.

'We're here at Irulan's suggestion,' Paul said, 'as strange as that may seem. She believes, and information in Stil's possession appears to confirm it, that our enemies are about to make a major try for –'

'My Lord!' Stilgar said, his voice sharper.

As her brother turned, questioning, Alia continued to look at the old Fremen Naib. Something about him now made her intensely aware that he was one of the primitives. Stilgar believed in a supernatural world very near him. It spoke to him in a simple pagan tongue dispelling all doubts. The natural universe in which he stood was fierce, unstoppable, and it lacked the common morality of the Imperium.

'Yes, Stil,' Paul said. 'Do you want to tell her why we came?'

'This isn't the time to talk of why we came,' Stilgar said.

'What's wrong, Stil?'

Stilgar continued to stare at Alia. 'Sire, are you blind?'

Paul turned back to his sister, a feeling of unease beginning to fill him. Of all his aides, only Stilgar dared speak to him in that tone, but even Stilgar measured the occasion by its need.

'This one must have a mate!' Stilgar blurted. 'There'll be trouble if she's not wed, and that soon.'

Alia whirled away, her face suddenly hot. *How did he touch me?* she wondered. Bene Gesserit self-control had been powerless to prevent her reaction. How had Stilgar done that? He hadn't the power of the Voice. She felt dismayed and angry.

'Listen to the great Stilgar!' Alia said, keeping her back to them, aware of a shrewish quality in her voice and unable to hide it. 'Advice to maidens from Stilgar, the Fremen!'

'As I love you both, I must speak,' Stilgar said, a profound dignity in his tone. 'I did not become a chieftain among the Fremen by being blind to what moves men and women together. One needs no mysterious powers for this.'

Paul weighed Stilgar's meaning, reviewed what they had seen here and his own undeniable male reaction to his own sister. Yes – there'd been a ruttish air about Alia, something wildly wanton. What had made her enter the practice floor in the nude? And risking her life in that foolhardy way! Eleven lights in the fencing prisms! That brainless automaton loomed in his mind with all the aspects of an ancient horror creature. Its possession was the shibboleth of this age, but it carried also the taint of old immorality. Once, they'd been guided by an artificial intelligence, computer brains. The Butlerian Jihad had ended that, but it hadn't ended the aura of aristocratic vice which enclosed such things.

Stilgar was right, of course. They must find a mate for Alia.

'I will see to it,' Paul said. 'Alia and I will discuss this later – privately.'

Alia turned around, focused on Paul. Knowing how his mind worked, she realised she'd been the subject of a mentat decision, uncounted bits falling together in that human-computer analysis. There was an inexorable quality to this realisation – a movement like the movement of planets. It carried something of the order of the universe in it, inevitable and terrifying.

'Sire,' Stilgar said, 'perhaps we'd –'

'Not now!' Paul snapped. 'We've other problems at the moment.'

Aware that she dared not try to match logic with her brother, Alia put the past few moments aside, Bene Gesserit fashion, said: 'Irulan sent you ?' She found herself experiencing menace in that thought.

'Indirectly,' Paul said. 'The information she gives us confirms our suspicion that the Guild is about to try for a sandworm.'

'They'll try to capture a small one and attempt to start the spice cycle on some other world,' Stilgar said. 'It means they've found a world they consider suitable.'

'It means they have Fremen accomplices!' Alia argued. 'No offworlder could capture a worm!'

'That goes without saying,' Stilgar said.

'No, it doesn't,' Alia said. She was outraged by such obtuseness. 'Paul, certainly you . . .'

'The rot is setting in,' Paul said. 'We've known that for quite some time. I've never *seen* this other world, though, and that bothers me. If they –'

'*That* bothers you ?' Alia demanded. 'It means only that they've clouded its location with Steersmen the way they hide their sanctuaries.'

Stilgar opened his mouth, closed it without speaking. He had the overwhelming sensation that his idols had admitted blasphemous weakness.

Paul, sensing Stilgar's disquiet, said: 'We've an immediate

problem! I want your opinion, Alia. Stilgar suggests we expand our patrols in the open bled and reinforce the sietch. It's just just possible we could spot a landing party and prevent the –'

'With a Steersman guiding them?' Alia asked.

'They *are* desperate, aren't they?' Paul agreed. '*That* is why I'm here.'

'What've they *seen* that we haven't?' Alia asked.

'Precisely.'

Alia nodded, remembering her thoughts about the new Dune Tarot. Quickly, she recounted her fears.

'Throwing a blanket over us,' Paul said.

'With adequate patrols,' Stilgar ventured, 'we might prevent the –'

'We prevent nothing . . . forever,' Alia said. She didn't like the *feel* of the way Stilgar's mind was working now. He had narrowed his scope, eliminated obvious essentials. This was not the Stilgar she remembered.

'We must count on their getting a worm,' Paul said. 'Whether they can start the melange cycle on another planet is a different question. They'll need more than a worm.'

Stilgar looked from brother to sister. Out of ecological thinking that had been ground into him by sietch life, he grasped their meaning. A captive worm couldn't live except within a bit of Arrakis – sand plankton, Little Makers and all. The Guild's problem was large, but not impossible. His own growing uncertainty lay in a different area.

'Then your visions do not detect the Guild at its work?' he asked.

'Damnation!' Paul exploded.

Alia studied Stilgar, sensing the savage sideshow of ideas taking place in his mind. He was hung on a rack of enchantment. Magic! Magic! To glimpse the future was to steal terrifying fire from a sacred flame. It held the attraction of ultimate peril, souls ventured and lost. One brought back from the formless, dangerous distances something with form and power. But Stilgar was beginning to sense other forces, perhaps greater powers beyond that unknown horizon. His Queen Witch and Sorcerer Friend betrayed dangerous weaknesses.

'Stilgar,' Alia said, fighting to hold him, 'you stand in a valley between dunes. I stand on the crest. I see where you do not see. And, among other things, I see mountains which conceal the distances.'

'There are things hidden from you,' Stilgar said. 'This you've always said.'

'All power is limited,' Alia said.

'And danger may come from behind the mountains,' Stilgar said.

'It's *something* on that order,' Alia said.

Stilgar nodded, his gaze fastened on Paul's face. 'But whatever comes from behind the mountains must cross the dunes.'

*The most dangerous game in the universe is to govern from an oracular base. We do not consider ourselves wise enough or brave enough to play that game. The measures detailed here for regulation in lesser matters are as near as we dare venture to the brink of government. For our purposes, we borrow a definition from the Bene Gesserit and we consider the various worlds as gene pools, sources of teachings and teachers, sources of the possible. Our goal is not to rule, but to tap these gene pools, to learn, and to free ourselves from all restraints imposed by dependency and government.*

— 'The Orgy as a Tool of Statecraft,'
Chapter Three of The Steersman's Guide

'Is that where your father died?' Edric asked, sending a beam pointer from his tank to a jeweled marker on one of the relief maps adorning a wall of Paul's reception salon.

'That's the shrine of his skull,' Paul said. 'My father died a prisoner on a Harkonnen frigate in the sink below us.'

'Oh, yes: I recall the story now,' Edric said. 'Something about killing the old Baron Harkonnen, his mortal enemy.' Hoping he didn't betray too much of the terror which small enclosures such as this room imposed upon him, Edric rolled over in the orange gas, directed his gaze at Paul, who sat alone on a long divan of striped gray and black.

'My sister killed the Baron,' Paul said, voice and manner dry, 'just before the battle of Arrakeen.'

84

And why, he wondered, did the Guild man-fish reopen old wounds in this place and at this time?

The Steersman appeared to be fighting a losing battle to contain his nervous energies. Gone were the languid fish motions of their earlier encounter. Edric's tiny eyes jerked here . . . there, questing and measuring. The one attendant who had accompanied him in here stood apart near the line of houseguards ranging the end wall at Paul's left. The attendant worried Paul – hulking, thick-necked, blunt and vacant face. The man had entered the salon, nudging Edric's tank along on its supporting field, walking with a strangler's gait, arms akimbo.

*Scytale*, Edric had called him. *Scytale, an aide.*

The aide's surface shouted stupidity, but the eyes betrayed him. They laughed at everything they saw.

'Your concubine appeared to enjoy the performance of the Face Dancers,' Edric said. 'It pleases me that I could provide that small entertainment. I particularly enjoyed her reaction to seeing her own features simultaneously repeated by the whole troupe.'

'Isn't there a warning against Guildsmen bearing gifts?' Paul asked.

And he thought of the performance out there in the Great Hall. The dancers had entered in the costumes and guise of the Dune Tarot, flinging themselves about in seemingly random patterns that devolved into fire eddies and ancient prognostic designs. Then had come the rulers – a parade of kings and emperors like faces on coins, formal and stiff in outline, but curiously fluid. And the jokes: a copy of Paul's own face and body. Chani repeated across the floor of the Hall, even Stilgar, who had grunted and shuddered while others laughed.

'But our gifts have the kindest intent,' Edric protested.

'How kindly can you be?' Paul asked. 'The ghola you gave us believes he was designed to destroy us.'

'Destroy you, Sire?' Edric asked, all bland attention. 'Can one destroy a god?'

Stilgar, entering on the last words, stopped, glared at the guards. They were much farther from Paul than he liked. Angrily he motioned them closer.

'It's all right, Stil,' Paul said, lifting a hand. 'Just a friendly discussion. Why don't you move the Ambassador's tank over by the end of my divan?'

Stilgar, weighing the order, saw that it would put the Steersman's tank between Paul and the hulking aide, much too close to Paul, but . . .

'It's all right, Stil,' Paul repeated, and he gave the private hand-signal which made the order an imperative.

Moving with obvious reluctance, Stilgar pushed the tank closer to Paul. He didn't like the feel of the container or the heavily perfumed smell of melange around it. He took up a position at the corner of the tank beneath the orbiting device through which the Steersman spoke.

'To kill a god,' Paul said. 'That's very interesting. But who says I'm a god?'

'Those who worship you,' Edric said, glancing pointedly at Stilgar.

'Is that what you believe?' Paul asked.

'What I believe is of no moment, Sire,' Edric said. 'It seems to most observers, however, that you conspire to make a god of yourself. And one might ask if that is something any mortal can do . . . safely?'

Paul studied the Guildsman. Repellent creature, but perceptive. It was a question Paul had asked himself time and again. But he had seen enough alternate Timelines to know of worse possibilities than accepting godhead for himself. Much worse. These were not, however, the normal avenues for a Steersman to probe. Curious. Why had that question been asked? What could Edric hope to gain by such effrontery? Paul's thoughts went *flick* (the association of Tleilaxu would be behind this move) – *flick* (the Jihad's recent Sembou victory would bear on Edric's action) – *flick* (various Bene Gesserit credos showed themselves here) *flick* . . .

A process involving thousands of information bits poured flickering through his computational awareness. It required perhaps three seconds.

'Does a Steersman question the guidelines of prescience?' Paul asked, putting Edric on the weakest ground.

This disturbed the Steersman, but he covered well, coming up with what sounded like a long aphorism: 'No man of intelligence questions the fact of prescience, Sire. Oracular vision has been known to men since most ancient times. It has a way of entangling us when we least suspect. Luckily, there are other forces in our universe.'

'Greater than prescience?' Paul asked, pressing him.

'If prescience alone existed and did everything, Sire, it would annihilate itself. Nothing but prescience? Where could it be applied except to its own degenerating movements?'

'There's always the human situation,' Paul agreed.

'A precarious thing at best,' Edric said, 'without confusing it by hallucinations.'

'Are my visions no more than hallucinations?' Paul asked, mock sadness in his voice. 'Or do you imply that my worshippers hallucinate?'

Stilgar, sensing the mounting tensions, moved a step nearer Paul, fixed his attention on the Guildsman reclining in the tank.

'You twist my words, Sire,' Edric protested. An odd sense of violence lay suspended in the words.

*Violence here?* Paul wondered. *They wouldn't dare! Unless* (and he glanced at his guards) *the forces which protected him were to be used in replacing him.*

'But you accuse me of conspiring to make a god of myself,' Paul said, pitching his voice that only Edric and Stilgar might hear. 'Conspire?'

'A poor choice of word, perhaps, my Lord,' Edric said.

'But significant,' Paul said. 'It says you expect the worst of me.'

Edric arched his neck, stared sideways at Stilgar with a look of apprehension. 'People always expect the worst of the rich and powerful, Sire. It is said one can always tell an aristocrat: he reveals only those of his vices which will make him popular.'

A tremor passed across Stilgar's face.

Paul looked up at the movement, sensing the thoughts and angers whispering in Stilgar's mind. How dared this Guildsman talk thus to Muad'dib?

'You're not joking, of course,' Paul said.

'Joking, Sire?'

Paul grew aware of dryness in his mouth. He felt that there were too many people in this room, that the air he breathed had passed through too many lungs. The taint of melange from Edric's tank felt threatening.

'Who might be accomplices be in such a conspiracy?' Paul asked presently. 'Do you nominate the Qizarate?'

Edric's shrug stirred the orange gas around his head. He no longer appeared concerned by Stilgar, although the Fremen continued to glare at him.

'Are you suggesting that my missionaries of the Holy Orders, *all of them,* are preaching subtle falsehood?' Paul insisted.

'It could be a question of self-interest and sincerity,' Edric said.

Stilgar put a hand to the crysknife beneath his robe.

Paul shook his head, said: 'Then you accuse me of insincerity.'

'I'm not sure that *accuse* is the proper word, Sire.'

*The boldness of this creature!* Paul thought. And he said: 'Accused or not, you're saying my bishops and I are no better than power-hungry brigands.'

'Power-hungry, Sire?' Again, Edric looked at Stilgar. 'Power tends to isolate those who hold too much of it. Eventually, they lose touch with reality . . . and fall.'

'M'Lord,' Stilgar growled, 'you've had men executed for less!'

'Men, yes,' Paul agreed. 'But this is a Guild Ambassador.'

'He accuses you of an unholy fraud!' Stilgar said.

'His thinking interests me, Stil,' Paul said. 'Contain your anger and remain alert.'

'As Muad'dib commands.'

'Tell me, Steersman,' Paul said, 'how could we maintain this hypothetical fraud over such enormous distances of space and time without the means to watch every missionary, to examine every nuance in every Qizarate priory and temple?'

'What is time to you?' Edric asked.

Stilgar frowned in obvious puzzlement. And he thought: *Muad'dib has often said he sees past the veils of time. What is the Guildsman really saying?*

'Wouldn't the structure of such a fraud begin to show holes?' Paul asked. 'Significant disagreements, schisms . . . doubts, confessions of guilt – surely fraud could not suppress all these.'

'What religion and self-interest cannot hide, governments can,' Edric said.

'Are you testing the limits of my tolerance?' Paul asked.

'Do my arguments lack all merit?' Edric countered.

*Does he want us to kill him?* Paul wondered. *Is Edric offering himself as a sacrifice?*

'I prefer the cynical view,' Paul said, testing. 'You obviously are trained in all the lying tricks of statecraft, the double meanings and the power words. Language is nothing more than a weapon to you and, thus, you test my armor.'

'The cynical view,' Edric said, a smile stretching his mouth. 'And rulers are notoriously cynical where religions are concerned. Religion, too, is a weapon. What manner of weapon is religion when it becomes the government?'

Paul felt himself go inwardly still, a profound caution gripping him. To whom was Edric speaking? Damnable clever words, heavy with manipulation leverages – that undertone of comfortable humor, the unspoken air of shared secrets: his manner said he and Paul were two sophisticates, men of a wider universe who understood things not granted common folk. With a feeling of shock, Paul realised that he had not been the main target for all this rhetoric. This affliction visited upon the court had been speaking for the benefit of others – speaking to Stilgar, to the household guards . . . perhaps even to the hulking aide.

'Religious *mana* was thrust upon me,' Paul said. 'I did not seek it.' And he thought: *There ! Let this manfish think himself victorious in our battle of words !*

'Then why have you not disavowed it, Sire ?' Edric asked.

'Because of my sister Alia,' Paul said, watching Edric carefully. 'She is a goddess. Let me urge caution where Alia is concerned lest she strike you dead with her glance.'

A gloating smile began forming on Edric's mouth, was replaced by a look of shock.

'I am deadly serious,' Paul said, watching the shock spread, seeing Stilgar nod.

In a bleak voice, Edric said: 'You have mauled my confidence in you, Sire. And no doubt that was your intent.'

'Do not be certain you know my intent,' Paul said, and he signalled Stilgar that the audience was at an end.

To Stilgar's questioning gesture asking if Edric were to be assassinated, Paul gave a negative hand-sign, amplified it with an imperative lest Stilgar take matters into his own hands.

Scytale, Edric's aide, moved to the rear corner of the tank, nudged it toward the door. When he came opposite Paul, he stopped, turned that laughing gaze on Paul, said: 'If my Lord permits ?'

'Yes, what is it ?' Paul asked, noting how Stilgar moved close in answer to the implied menace from this man.

'Some say,' Scytale said, 'that people cling to Imperial leadership because space is infinite. They feel lonely without a unifying symbol. For a lonely people, the Emperor is a definite place. They can turn toward him and say: 'See, there He is. He makes us one.' Perhaps religion serves the same purpose, m'Lord.'

Scytale nodded pleasantly, gave Edric's tank another nudge. They moved out of the salon, Edric supine in his tank, eyes closed. The Steersman appeared spent, all his nervous energies exhausted.

Paul stared after the shambling figure of Scytale, wondering at the man's words. A peculiar fellow, that Scytale, he thought. While he was speaking, he had radiated a feeling of many people – as though his entire genetic inheritance lay exposed on his skin.

'That was odd,' Stilgar said, speaking to no one in particular.

Paul arose from the divan as a guard closed the door behind Edric and the escort.

'Odd,' Stilgar repeated. A vein throbbed at his temple.

Paul dimmed the salon's lights, moved to a window which opened onto the angled cliff of his Keep. Lights glittered far below – pigmy movement. A work gang moved down there bring ing giant plasmeld blocks to repair a facade of Alia's temple, which had been damaged by a freak twisting of a sandblast wind.

'That was a foolish thing, Usul, inviting that creature into these chambers,' Stilgar said.

*Usul*, Paul thought. *My sietch name. Silgar reminds me that he ruled over me once, that he saved me from the desert.*

'Why did you do it?' Stilgar asked, speaking from close behind Paul.

'Data,' Paul said. 'I need more data.'

'Is it not dangerous to try meeting this threat *only* as a mentat? *That was perceptive*, Paul thought.

Mentat computation remained finite. You couldn't say something boundless within the boundaries of any language. Mentat abilities had their uses, though. He said as much now, daring Stilgar to refute his argument.

'There's always something outside,' Stilgar said. 'Some things best *kept* outside.'

'Or inside,' Paul said. And he accepted for a monent his own oracular/mentat summation. Outside, yes. And inside: here lay the true horror. How could he protect himself from himself? They certainly were setting him up to destroy himself, but this was a position hemmed in by even more terrifying possibilities.

His reverie was broken by the sound of rapid footsteps. The figure of Korba the Qizara surged through the doorway back-lighted by the brilliant illumination in the hallways. He entered as though hurled by an unseen force and came to an almost immediate halt when he encountered the salon's gloom. His hands appeared to be full of shigawire reels. They glittered in the light from the hall, strange little round jewels that were extinguished as a guardsman's hand came into view, closed the door.

'Is that you, m'Lord?' Korba asked, peering into the shadows.

'What is it?' Stilgar asked.

'Stilgar?'

'We're both here. What is it?'

'I'm disturbed by this reception for the Guildsman.'

'Disturbed?' Paul asked.

'The people say, m'Lord, that you honor our enemies.'

'Is that all?' Paul said. 'Are those the reels I asked you to bring earlier?' He indicated the shigawire orbs in Korba's hands.

'Reels . . . oh! Yes, m'Lord. These are the histories. Will you view them here?'

'I've viewed them. I want them for Stilgar here.'

'For me?' Stilgar asked. He felt resentment grow at what he interpreted as caprice on Paul's part. Histories! Stilgar had sought out Paul earlier to discuss the logistics computations for the Zabulon conquest. The Guild Ambassador's presence had intervened. And now – Korba with histories!

'How much history do you know?' Paul mused aloud, studying the shadowy figure beside him.

'M'Lord, I can name every world our people touched in their migrations. I know the reaches of Imperial . . .'

'The Golden Age of Earth, have you ever studied that?'

'Earth? Golden Age?' Stilgar was irritated and puzzled. Why would Paul wish to discuss myths from the dawn of time? Stilgar's mind still felt crammed with Zabulon data – computations from the staff mentats: two hundred and five attack frigates with thirty legions, support battalions, pacification cadres, Qizarate missionaries . . . the food requirements (he had the figures right here in his mind) and melange . . . weaponry, uniforms, medals . . . urns for the ashes of the dead . . . the number of specialists – men to produce raw materials of propaganda, clerks, accountants . . . spies . . . and spies upon the spies . . .

'I brought the pulse-synchroniser attachment, also, m'Lord,' Korba ventured. He obviously sensed the tensions building between Paul and Stilgar and was disturbed by them.

Stilgar shook his head from side to side. *Pulse-synchroniser?* Why would Paul wish him to use a mnemonic flutter-system on a shigawire projector? Why scan for specific data in histories? This was mentat work! As usual, Stilgar found he couldn't escape a deep suspicion at the thought of using a projector and attachments. The thing always immersed him in disturbing sensations, an overwhelming shower of data which his mind sorted out later, surprising him with information he had not known he possessed.

'Sire, I came with the Zabulon computations,' Stilgar said.

'Dehydrate the Zabulon computations!' Paul snapped, using the obscene Fremen term which meant that here was moisture no man could demean himself by touching.

'M'Lord!'

'Stilgar,' Paul said, 'you urgently need a sense of balance which can come only from an understanding of long term effects. What little information we have about the old times, the pittance of data which the Butlerians left us, Korba has brought it for you. Start with the Genghis Khan.'

'Genghis . . . Khan ? Was he of the Sardaukar, m'Lord ?'

'Oh, long before that. He killed . . . perhaps four million.'

'He must've had formidable weaponry to kill that many, Sire. Lasbeams, perhaps, or . . .'

'He didn't kill them himself, Stil. He killed the way I kill, by sending out his legions. There's another emperor I want you to note in passing – a Hitler. He killed more than six million. Pretty good for those days.'

'Killed . . . by his legions ?' Stilgar asked.

'Yes.'

'Not very impressive statistics, m'Lord.'

'Very good, Stil.' Paul glanced at the reels in Korba's hands. Korba stood with them as though he wished he could drop them and flee. 'Statistics: at a conservative estimate, I've killed sixty-one billion, sterilised ninety planets, completely demoralised five hundred others. I've wiped out the followers of forty religions which had existed since –'

'Unbelievers!' Korba protested. 'Unbelievers all!'

'No,' Paul said. 'Believers.'

'My Liege makes a joke,' Korba said, voice trembling. 'The Jihad has brought ten thousand worlds into the shining light of –'

'Into the darkness,' Paul said. 'We'll be a hundred generations recovering from Muad'dib's Jihad. I find it hard to imagine that anyone will ever surpass this.' A barking laugh erupted from his throat.

'What amuses Muad'dib ?' Stilgar asked.

'I am not amused. I merely had a sudden vision of the Emperor Hitler saying something similar. No doubt he did.'

'No other ruler ever had your powers,' Korba argued. 'Who

would dare challenge you? Your legions control the known universe and all the –'

'The legions control,' Paul said. 'I wonder if they know this?'

'You control your legions, Sire,' Stilgar interrupted, and it was obvious from the tone of his voice that he suddenly felt his own position in that chain of command, his own hand guiding all that power.

Having set Stilgar's thoughts in motion along the track he wanted, Paul turned his full attention to Korba, said: 'Put the reels here on the divan.' As Korba obeyed, Paul said: 'How goes the reception, Korba? Does my sister have everything well in hand?'

'Yes, m'Lord.' Korba's tone was wary. 'And Chani watches from the spy hole. She suspects there may be Sardaukar in the Guild entourage.'

'No doubt she's correct,' Paul said. 'The jackals gather.'

'Bannerjee,' Stilgar said, naming the chief of Paul's Security detail, 'was worried earlier that some of them might try to penetrate the private areas of the Keep.'

'Have they?'

'Not yet.'

'But there was some confusion in the formal gardens,' Korba said.

'What sort of confusion?' Stilgar demanded.

Paul nodded.

'Strangers coming and going,' Korba said, 'trampling the plants, whispered conversations – I heard reports of some disturbing remarks.'

'Such as?' Paul asked.

'*Is this the way our taxes are spent?* I'm told the Ambassador himself asked that question.'

'I don't find that surprising,' Paul said. 'Were there many strangers in the gardens?'

'Dozens, m'Lord.'

'Bannerjee stationed picked troopers at the vulnerable doors, m'Lord,' Stilgar said. He turned as he spoke, allowing the salon's single remaining light to illuminate half his face. The peculiar lighting, the face, all touched a node of memory in Paul's mind – something from the desert. Paul didn't bother bringing it to full recall, his attention being focused on how Stilgar had pulled back mentally. The Fremen had a tight-skinned forehead which mirrored almost every thought flickering across his mind. He was suspicious now, profoundly suspicious of his Emperor's odd behaviour.

'I don't like the intrusion into the gardens,' Paul said. 'Courtesy to guests is one thing, and the formal necessities of greeting an envoy, but this . . .'

'I'll see to removing them,' Korba said. 'Immediately.'

'Wait!' Paul ordered as Korba started to turn.

In the abrupt stillness of the moment, Stilgar edged himself into a position where he could study Paul's face. It was deftly done. Paul admired the way of it, an achievement devoid of any forwardness. It was a Fremen thing: slyness touched by respect for another's privacy, a movement of necessity.

'What time is it ?' Paul asked.

'Almost midnight, Sire,' Korba said.

'Korba, I think you may be my finest creation,' Paul said.

'Sire!' There was injury in Korba's voice.

'Do you feel awe of me ?' Paul asked.

'You are Paul-Muad'dib who was Usul in our sietch,' Korba said. 'You know my devotion to –'

'Have you ever felt like an apostle ?' Paul asked.

Korba obviously misunderstood the words, but correctly interpreted the tone. 'My Emperor knows I have a clean conscience!'

'Shai-hulud save us,' Paul murmured.

The questioning silence of the moment was broken by the sound of someone whistling as he walked down the outer hall. The whistling was stilled by a guardsman's barked command as it came opposite the door.

'Korba, I think you may survive all this,' Paul said. And he read the growing light of understanding on Stilgar's face.

'The strangers in the gardens, Sire ?' Stilgar asked.

'Ahh, yes,' Paul said. 'Have Bannerjee put them out, Stil. Korba will assist.'

'Me, Sire ?' Korba betrayed deep disquiet.

'Some of my friends have forgotten they once were Fremen,' Paul said, speaking to Korba, but designing his words for Stilgar. 'You will mark down the ones Chani identifies as Sardaukar and you will have them killed. Do it yourself. I want it done quietly and without undue disturbance. We must keep in mind that there's more to religion and government than approving treaties and sermons.'

'I obey the order of Muad'dib,' Korba whispered.

94

'The Zabulon computations?' Stilgar asked.

'Tomorrow,' Paul said. 'And when the strangers are removed from the gardens, announce that the reception is ended. The party's over, Stil.'

'I understand, my Lord.'

'I'm sure you do,' Paul said.

*Here lies a toppled god –*
*His fall was not a small one.*
*We did but build his pedestal,*
*A narrow and a tall one.*
                    *– Tleilaxu Epigram*

Alia crouched, resting elbows on knees, chin on fists, stared at the body on the dune – a few bones and some tattered flesh that once had been a young woman. The hands, the head, most of the upper torso were gone – eaten by the coriolis wind. The sand all around bore the tracks of her brother's medics and questors. They were gone now, all excepting the mortuary attendants who stood to one side with Hayt, the ghola, waiting for her to finish her mysterious perusal of what had been written here.

A wheat-colored sky enfolded the scene in the glaucous light common to midafternoon for these latitudes.

The body had been discovered several hours earlier by a low-flying courier whose instruments had detected a faint water trace where none should be. His call had brought the experts. And they had learned – what? That this had been a woman of about twenty years, Fremen, addicted to semuta . . . and she had died here in the crucible of the desert from the effects of a subtle poison of Tleilaxu origin.

To die in the desert was a common enough occurrence. But a Fremen addicted to semuta, this was such a rarity that Paul had sent her to examine the scene in the ways their mother had taught them.

Alia felt that she had accomplished nothing here except to cast her own aura of mystery about a scene that was already mysterious enough. She heard the ghola's feet stir the sand, looked at him. His attention rested momentarily upon the escort 'thopters circling overhead like a flock of ravens.

*Beware of the Guild bearing gifts*, Alia thought.

The mortuary 'thopter and her own craft stood on the sand near a rock outcropping behind the ghola. Focusing on the grounded 'thopters filled Alia with a craving to be airborne and away from here.

But Paul had thought she might see something here which others would miss. She squirmed in her stillsuit. It felt raspingly unfamiliar after all the suitless months of city life. She studied the ghola, wondering if he might know something important about this peculiar death. A lock of his black-goat hair, she saw, had escaped his stillsuit hood. She sensed her hand longing to tuck that hair back into place.

As though lured by this thought, his gleaming gray metal eyes turned toward her. The eyes set her trembling and she tore her gaze away from him.

A Fremen woman had died here from a poison called 'the throat of hell.'

A Fremen addicted to semuta.

She shared Paul's disquiet at this conjunction.

The mortuary attendants waited patiently. This corpse contained not enough water for them to salvage. They felt no need to hurry. And they'd believe that Alia, through some glyptic art, was reading a strange truth in these remains.

No strange truth came to her.

There was only a distant feeling of anger deep within her at the obvious thoughts in the attendants' minds. It was a product of the damned religious mystery. She and her brother could not be *people*. They had to be something more. The Bene Gesserit had seen to that by manipulating Atreides ancestry. Their mother had contributed to it by thrusting them onto the path of witchery.

And Paul perpetuated the difference.

The Reverend Mother encapsulated in Alia's memories stirred restlessly, provoking adab flashes of thought: *'Peace, Little One ! You are what you are. There are compensations.'*

Compensations !

She summoned the ghola with a gesture.

He stopped beside her, attentive, patient.

'What do you see in this ?' she asked.

'We may never learn who it was died here,' he said. 'The head, the teeth are gone. The hands . . . Unlikely such a one had a genetic record somewhere to which her cells could be matched.'

'Tleilaxu poison,' she said. 'What do you make of that ?'

'Many people buy such poisons.'

'True enough. And this flesh is too far gone to be regrown as was done with your body.'

'Even if you could trust the Tleilaxu to do it,' he said.

She nodded, stood. 'You will fly me back to the city now.'

When they were airborne and pointed north, she said: 'You fly exactly as Duncan Idaho did.'

He cast a speculative glance at her. 'Others have told me this.'

'What are you thinking now ?' she asked.

'Many things.'

'Stop dodging my question, damn you!'

'Which question ?'

She glared at him.

He saw the glare, shrugged.

How like Duncan Idaho, that gesture, she thought. Accusingly, her voice thick and with a catch in it, she said: 'I merely wanted your reactions voiced to play my own thoughts against them. That young woman's death bothers me.'

'I was not thinking about that.'

'What were you thinking about ?'

'About the strange emotions I feel when people speak of the one I may have been.'

'May have been ?'

'The Tleilaxu are very clever.'

'Not that clever. You were Duncan Idaho.'

'Very likely. It's the prime computation.'

'So you get emotional ?'

'To a degree. I feel eagerness. I'm uneasy. There's a tendency to tremble and I must devote effort to controlling it. I get . . . flashes of imagery.'

'What imagery ?'

'It's too rapid to recognise. Flashes. Spasms . . . almost memories.'

'Aren't you curious about such memories ?'

'Of course. Curiosity urges me forward, but I move against a heavy reluctance. I think: 'What if I'm not the one they believe me to be?' I don't like that thought.'

'And this is all you were thinking?'

'You know better than that, Alia.'

*How dare he use my given name?* She felt anger rise and go down beneath the memory of the way he'd spoken: softly throbbing undertones, casual male confidence. A muscle twitched along her jaw. She clenched her teeth.

'Isn't that El Kuds down there?' he asked, dipping a wing briefly, causing a sudden flurry in their escort.

She looked down at their shadows rippling across the promontory above Harg Pass, at the cliff and the rock pyramid containing the skull of her father. *El Kuds – the Holy Place.*

'That's the Holy Place,' she said.

'I must visit that place one day,' he said. 'Nearness to your father's remains may bring memories I can capture.'

She saw suddenly how strong must be this need to know who he'd been. It was a central compulsion with him. She looked back at the rocks, the cliff with its base sloping into a dry beach and a sea of sand – cinnamon rock lifting from the dunes like a ship breasting waves.

'Circle back,' she said.

'The escort . . .'

'They'll follow. Swing under them.'

He obeyed.

'Do you truly serve my brother?' she asked, when he was on the new course, the escort following.

'I serve the Atreides,' he said, his tone formal.

And she saw his right hand lift, fall – almost the old salute of Caladan. A pensive look came over his face. She watched him peer down at the rock pyramid.

'What bothers you?' she asked.

His lips moved. A voice emerged, brittle, tight: 'He was . . . he was . . . ' A tear slid down his cheek.

Alia found herself stilled by Fremen awe. He gave water to the dead! Compulsively, she touched a finger to his cheek, felt the tear.

'Duncan,' she whispered.

He appeared locked to the 'thopter's controls, gaze fastened to the tomb below.

She raised her voice: 'Duncan!'

He swallowed, shook his head, looked at her, the metal eyes glistening. 'I . . . felt . . . an arm . . . on my shoulders,' he

99

whispered. 'I felt it! An arm.' His throat worked. 'It was . . . a friend. It was . . . my friend.'

'Who?'

'I don't know. I think it was . . . I don't know.'

The call light began flashing in front of Alia, their escort captain wanting to know why they returned to the desert. She took the microphone, explained that they had paid a brief homage to her father's tomb. The captain reminded her that it was late.

'We will go to Arrakeen now,' she said, replacing the microphone.

Hayt took a deep breath, banked their 'thopter around to the north.

'It was my father's arm you felt, wasn't it?' she asked.

'Perhaps.'

His voice was that of the mentat computing probabilities, and she saw he had regained his composure.

'Are you aware of how I know my father?' she asked.

'I have some idea.'

'Let me make it clear,' she said. Briefly, she explained how she had awakened to Reverend Mother awareness before birth, a terrified fetus with the knowledge of countless lives embedded in her nerve cells – and all this after the death of her father.

'I know my father as my mother knew him,' she said. 'In every last detail of every experience she shared with him. In a way, I am my mother. I have all her memories up to the moment when she drank the Water of Life and entered the trance of transmigration.'

'Your brother explained something of this.'

'He did? Why?'

'I asked.'

'Why?'

'A mentat requires data.'

'Oh.' She looked down at the flat expanse of the Shield Wall – tortured rock, pits and crevices.

He saw the direction of her gaze, said: 'A very exposed place, that down there.'

'But an easy place to hide,' she said. She looked at him. 'It reminds me of a human mind . . . with all its concealments.'

'Ahhh,' he said.

'Ahhh? What does that mean – ahhh?' She was suddenly angry with him and the reason for it escaped her.

'You'd like to know what my mind conceals,' he said. It was a statement, not a question.

'How do you know I haven't exposed you for what you are by my powers of prescience?' she demanded.

'Have you?' He seemed genuinely curious.

'No!'

'Sibyls have limits,' he said.

He appeared to be amused and this reduced Alia's anger. 'Amused? Have you no respect for my powers?' she asked. The question sounded weakly argumentative even to her own ears.

'I respect your omens and portents perhaps more than you think,' he said. 'I was in the audience for your Morning Ritual.'

'And what does that signify?'

'You've great ability with symbols,' he said, keeping his attention on the 'thopter's controls. 'That's a Bene Gesserit thing, I'd say. But, as with many witches, you've become careless of your powers.'

She felt a spasm of fear, blared: 'How dare you?'

'I dare much more than my makers anticipated,' he said. 'Because of that rare fact, I remain with your brother.'

Alia studied the steel balls which were his eyes: no human expression there. The stillsuit hood concealed the line of his jaw. His mouth remained firm, though. Great strength in it . . . and determination. His words had carried a reassuring intensity. ' . . . dare much more . . . ' That was a thing Duncan Idaho might have said. Had the Tleilaxu fashioned their ghola better than they knew – or was this mere sham, part of his conditioning?

'Explain yourself, ghola,' she commanded.

'Know thyself, is that thy commandment?' he asked.

Again, she felt that he was amused. 'Don't bandy words with me, you . . . you *thing!*' she said. She put a hand to the crysknife in its throat sheath. 'Why were you given to my brother?'

'Your brother tells me that you watched the presentation,' he said. 'You've heard me answer that question for him.'

'Answer it again . . . for me!'

'I am intended to destroy him.'

'Is that the mentat speaking?'

'You knew the answer to that without asking,' he chided. 'And you know, as well, that such a gift wasn't necessary. Your brother already was destroying himself quite adequately.'

She weighed these words, her hand remaining on the haft of her knife. A tricky answer, but there was sincerity in the voice.

'Then why such a gift?' she probed.

'It may have amused the Tleilaxu. And, it is true, that the Guild asked for me as a gift.'

'Why?'

'Same answer.'

'How am I careless of my powers?'

'How are you employing them?' he countered.

His question slashed through to her own misgivings. She took her hand away from the knife, asked: 'Why do you say my brother was destroying himself?'

'Oh, come now, child! Where are these vaunted powers? Have you no ability to reason?'

Controlling anger, she said: 'Reason *for* me, mentat.'

'Very well.' He glanced around at their escort, returned his attention to their course. The plain of Arrakeen was beginning to show beyond the northern rim of the Shield Wall. The pattern of the pan and graben villages remained indistinct beneath a dust pall, but the distant gleam of Arrakeen could be discerned.

'Symptoms,' he said. 'Your brother keeps an official Panegyrist who – '

'Who was a gift of the Fremen Naibs!'

'An odd gift from friends,' he said. 'Why would they surround him with flattery and servility? Have you really listened to this Panegyrist? "*The people are illuminated by Muad'dib. The Umma Regent, our Emperor, came out of darkness to shine resplendently upon all men. He is our Sire. He is precious water from an endless fountain. He spills joy for all the universe to drink.*" Pah!'

Speaking softly, Alia said: 'If I but repeated your words for our Fremen escort, they'd hack you into bird feed.'

'Then tell them.'

'My brother rules by the natural law of heaven!'

'You don't believe that, so why say it?'

'How do you know what I believe?' She experienced trembling that no Bene Gesserit powers could control. This ghola was having an effect she hadn't anticipated.

'You commanded me to reason as a mentat,' he reminded her.

'No mentat knows what I believe!' She took two deep, shuddering breaths. 'How dare you judge us?'

'Judge you? I don't judge.'

'You've no idea how we were taught!'

'Both of you were taught to govern,' he said. 'You were conditioned to an overweening thirst for power. You were imbued with a shrewd grasp of politics and a deep understanding for the uses of war and ritual. Natural law? What natural law? That myth haunts human history. Haunts! It's a ghost. It's insubstantial, unreal. Is your Jihad a natural law?'

'Mentat jabber,' she sneered.

'I'm a servant of the Atreides and I speak with candor,' he said.

'Servant? We've no servants; only disciples.'

'And I am a disciple of awareness,' he said. 'Understand that, child, and you –'

'Don't call me child!' she snapped. She slipped her crysknife half out of its sheath.

'I stand corrected.' He glanced at her, smiled, returned his attention to piloting the 'thopter. The cliff-sided structure of the Atreides Keep could be made out now, dominating the northern suburbs of Arrakeen. 'You are something ancient in flesh that is little more than a child,' he said. 'And the flesh is disturbed by its new womanhood.'

'I don't know why I listen to you,' she growled, but she let the crysknife fall back into its sheath, wiped her palm on her robe. The palm, wet with perspiration, disturbed her sense of Fremen frugality. Such a waste of the body's moisture!

'You listen because you know I'm devoted to your brother,' he said. 'My actions are clear and easily understood.'

'Nothing about you is clear and easily understood. You're the most complex creature I've ever seen. How do I know what the Tleilaxu built into you?'

'By mistake or intent,' he said, 'they gave me freedom to mold myself.'

'You retreat into Zensunni parables,' she accused. 'The wise man molds himself – the fool lives only to die.' Her voice was heavy with mimicry. 'Disciple of awareness!'

'Men cannot separate means and enlightenment,' he said.

'You speak riddles!'

'I speak to the opening mind.'

'I'm going to repeat all this to Paul.'

'He's heard most of it already.'

She found herself overwhelmed by curiosity. 'How is it you're still alive . . . and free? What did he say?'

'He laughed. And he said, "People don't want a bookkeeper for an Emperor; they want a master, someone who'll protect them from change." But he agreed that destruction of his Empire arises from himself.'

'Why would he say such things?'

'Because I convinced him I understand his problem and will help him.'

'What could you possibly have said to do that?'

He remained silent, banking the 'thopter into the downwind leg for a landing at the guard complex on the roof of the Keep.

'I demand you tell me what you said!'

'I'm not sure you could take it.'

'I'll be the judge of that! I command you to speak at once!'

'Permit me to land us first,' he said. And not waiting for her permission, he turned onto the base leg, brought the wings into optimum lift, settled gently onto the bright orange pad atop the roof.

'Now,' Alia said. 'Speak.'

'I told him that to endure oneself may be the hardest task in the universe.'

She shook her head. 'That's ... that's ...'

'A bitter pill,' he said, watching the guards run toward them across the roof, taking up their escort positions.

'Bitter nonsense!'

'The greatest palatinate earl and the lowliest stipendiary serf share the same problem. You cannot hire a mentat or any other intellect to solve it for you. There's no writ of inquest or calling of witnesses to provide answers. No servant – or disciple – can dress the wound. You dress it yourself or continue bleeding for all to see.'

She whirled away from him, realising in the instant of action what this betrayed about her own feelings. Without wile of voice or witch-wrought trickery, he had reached into her psyche once more. How did he do this?

'What have you told him to do?' she whispered.

'I told him to judge, to impose order.'

Alia stared out at the guard, marking how patiently they waited – how orderly. 'To dispense justice,' she murmured.

'Not that!' he snapped. 'I suggested that he judge, no more, guided by one principle, perhaps ...'

'And that?'

'To keep his friends and destroy his enemies.'

'To judge unjustly, then.'

'What is justice? Two forces collide. Each may have the right in his own sphere. And here's where an Emperor commands orderly solutions. Those collisions he cannot prevent – he solves.'

'How?'

'In the simplest way: he decides.'

'Keeping his friends and destroying his enemies.'

'Isn't that stability? People want order, this kind or some other. They sit in the prison of their hungers and see that war has become the sport of the rich. That's a dangerous form of sophistication. It's disorderly.'

'I will suggest to my brother that you are much too dangerous and must be destroyed,' she said, turning to face him.

'A solution I've already suggested,' he said.

'And that's why you are dangerous,' she said, measuring out her words. 'You've mastered your passions.'

'That is *not* why I'm dangerous.' Before she could move, he leaned across, gripped her chin in one hand, planted his lips on hers.

It was a gentle kiss, brief. He pulled away and she stared at him with a shock leavened by glimpses of spasmodic grins on the faces of her guardsmen still standing at orderly attention outside.

Alia put a finger to her lips. There'd been such a sense of familiarity about that kiss. His lips had been flesh of a future she'd seen in some prescient byway. Breast heaving, she said: 'I should have you flayed.'

'Because I'm dangerous?'

'Because you presume too much!'

'I presume nothing. I take nothing which is not first offered to me. Be glad I did not take all that was offered.' He opened his door, slid out. 'Come along. We've dallied too long on a fool's errand.' He strode toward the entrance dome beyond the pad.

Alia leaped out, ran to match his stride. 'I'll tell him everything you've said and everything you did,' she said.

'Good.' He held the door for her.

'He will order you executed,' she said, slipping into the dome.

'Why? Because I took the kiss I wanted?' He followed her, his movement forcing her back. The door slid closed behind him.

'The kiss *you* wanted!' Outrage filled her.

'All right, Alia. The kiss you wanted, then.' He started to move around her toward the drop field.

As though his movement had propelled her into heightened awareness, she realised his candor – the utter truthfulness of him. *The kiss I wanted*, she told herself. *True.*

'Your truthfulness, that's what's dangerous,' she said, following him.

'You return to the ways of wisdom,' he said, not breaking his stride. 'A mentat could not've stated the matter more directly. Now: what is it you saw in the desert?'

She grabbed his arm, forcing him to a halt. He'd done it again: shocked her mind into sharpened awareness.

'I can't explain it,' she said, 'but I keep thinking of the Face Dancers. Why is that?'

'That is why you brother sent you to the desert,' he said, nodding. 'Tell him of this persistent thought.'

'But why?' She shook her head. 'Why Face Dancers?'

'There's a young woman dead out there,' he said. 'Perhaps no young woman is reported missing among the Fremen.'

*I think what a joy it is to be alive, and I wonder if I'll ever leap inward to the root of this flesh and know myself as once I was. The root is there. Whether any act of mine can find it, that remains tangled in the future. But all things a man can do are mine. Any act of mine may do it.*

> – The Ghola Speaks
> Alia's Commentary

As he lay immersed in the screaming odor of the spice, staring inward through the oracular trance, Paul saw the moon become an elongated sphere. It rolled and twisted, hissing – the terrible hissing of a star being quenched in an infinite sea – down . . . down . . . down . . . like a ball thrown by a child.

It was gone.

This moon had not set. Realisation engulfed him. It was gone: no moon. The earth quaked like an animal shaking its skin. Terror swept over him.

Paul jerked upright on his pallet, eyes wide open, staring. Part of him looked outward, part inward. Outwardly, he saw the plasmeld grillwork which vented his private room, and he knew he lay beside a stonelike abyss of his Keep. Inwardly, he continued to see the moon fall.

*Out ! Out !*

His grillwork of plasmeld looked onto the blazing light of noon across Arrakeen. Inward – there lay blackest night. A shower of sweet odors from a garden roof nibbled at his senses, but no floral perfume could roll back that fallen moon.

Paul swung his feet to the cold surface of the floor, peered through the grillwork. He could see directly across to the gentle arc of a footbridge constructed of crystal-stabilised gold and platinum. Fire jewels from far Cedon decorated the bridge. It led to the galleries of the inner city across a pool and fountain filled with waterflowers. If he stood, Paul knew, he could look down into petals as clean and red as fresh blood whirling, turning there – disks of ambient color tossed on an emerald freshet.

His eyes absorbed the scene without pulling him from spice thralldom.

*That terrible vision of a lost moon.*

The vision suggested a monstrous loss of individual security. Perhaps he'd seen his civilisation fall, toppled by its own pretensions.

*A moon . . . a moon . . . a falling moon*

It had taken a massive dose of the spice essence to penetrate the mud thrown up by the tarot. All it had shown him was a falling moon and the hateful way he'd known from the beginning. To buy an end for the Jihad, to silence the volcano of butchery, he must discredit himself.

*Disengage . . . disengage . . . disengage . . .*

Floral perfume from the garden roof reminded him of Chani. He longed for her arms now, for the clinging arms of love and forgetfulness. But even Chani could not exorcise this vision. What would Chani say if he went to her with the statement that he had a particular death in mind? Knowing it to be inevitable, why not choose an aristocrat's death, ending life on a secret flourish, squandering any years that might have been? To die before coming to the end of willpower, was that not an aristocrat's choice?

He stood, crossed to the lapped opening in the grillwork, went out onto a balcony which looked upward to flowers and vines trailing from the garden. His mouth held the dryness of a desert march.

*Moon . . . moon – where is that moon?*

He thought of Alia's description, the young woman's body found in the dunes. A Fremen addicted to semuta! Everything fitted the hateful pattern.

*You do not take from this universe,* he thought. *It grants what it will.*

The remains of a conch shell from the seas of Mother Earth lay on a low table beside the balcony rail. He took its lustrous smoothness into his hands, tried to feel backward in Time. The pearl surface reflected glittering moons of light. He tore his gaze from it, peered upward past the garden to a sky become a conflagration – trails of rainbow dust shining in the silver sun.

*My Fremen call themselves 'Children of the Moon,'* he thought.

He put down the conch, strode along the balcony. Did that terrifying moon hold out hope of escape? He probed for meaning in the region of mystic communion. He felt weak, shaken, still gripped by the spice.

At the north end of his plasmeld chasm, he came in sight of the lower buildings of the government warren. Foot traffic thronged the roof walks. He felt that the people moved there like a frieze against a background of doors, walls, tile designs. The people were tiles! When he blinked, he could hold them frozen in his mind. A frieze.

*A moon falls and is gone.*

A feeling came over him that the city out there had been translated into an odd symbol for his universe. The buildings he could see had been erected on the plain where his Fremen had obliterated the Sardaukar legions. Ground once trampled by battles rang now to the rushing clamor of business.

Keeping to the balcony's outer edge, Paul strode around the corner. Now, his vista was a suburb where city structures lost themselves in rocks and the blowing sand of the desert. Alia's temple dominated the foreground; green and black hangings along its two-thousand-meter sides displayed the moon symbol of Muad'dib.

*A falling moon.*

Paul passed a hand across his forehead and eyes. The symbol-metropolis oppressed him. He despised his own thoughts. Such vacillation in another would have aroused his anger.

He loathed his city!

Rage rooted in boredom flickered and simmered deep within him, nurtured by decisions that couldn't be avoided. He knew which path his feet must follow. He'd seen it enough times, hadn't he? *Seen* it! Once . . . long ago, he'd thought of himself as an inventor of government. But the invention had fallen into old patterns. It was like some hideous contrivance with plastic memory. Shape it any way you wanted, but relax for a moment, and it snapped into the ancient forms. Forces at work beyond his reach in human breasts eluded and defied him.

Paul stared out across the rooftops. What treasures of untrammeled life lay beneath those roofs? He glimpsed leaf-green places, open plantings amidst the chalk-red and gold of the roofs. Green, the gift of Muad'dib and his water. Orchards and groves lay within his view – open plantings to rival those of fabled Lebanon.

'Muad'dib spends water like a madman,' Fremen said.

Paul put his hands over his eyes.

*The moon fell.*

He dropped his hands, stared at his metropolis with clarified vision. Buildings took on an aura of monstrous imperial barbarity. They stood enormous and bright beneath the northern sun. Colossi! Every extravagance of architecture a demented history could produce lay within his view: terraces of mesa proportion, squares as large as some cities, parks, premises, bits of cultured wilderness.

Superb artistry abutted inexplicable prodigies of dismal tastelessness. Details impressed themselves upon him: a postern out of most ancient Baghdad . . . a dome dreamed in mythical Damascus . . . an arch from the low gravity of Atar . . . harmonious elevations and queer depths. All created an effect of unrivaled magnificence.

*A moon! A moon! A moon!*

Frustration tangled him. He felt the pressure of mass-unconscious, that burgeoning sweep of humankind across his universe. They rushed upon him with a force like a gigantic tidal bore. He sensed the vast migrations at work in human affairs: eddies, currents, gene flows No dams of abstinence, no seizures of impotence nor maledictions could stop it.

Muad'dib's Jihad was less than an eye-blink in his larger movement. The Bene Gesserit swimming in this tide, that corporate entity trading in genes, was trapped in the torrent as he was. Visions of a falling moon must be measured against other legends, other visions in a universe where even the seemingly eternal stars waned flickered, died . . .

What mattered a single moon in such a universe?

Far within his fortress citadel, so deep within that the sound sometimes lost itself in the flow of city noises, a ten-string rebaba tinkled with a song of the Jihad, a lament for a woman left behind on Arrakis:

*Her hips are dunes curved by the wind,*
*Her eyes shine like summer heat.*
*Two braids of hair hang down her back –*
*Rich with water rings, her hair !*
*My hands remembered her skin,*
*Fragrant as amber, flower-scented.*
*Eyelids tremble with memories . . .*
*I am stricken by love's white flame !*

The song sickened him. A tune for stupid creatures lost in sentimentality ! As well sing to the dune-impregnated corpse Alia had seen.

A figure moved in shadows of the balcony's grillwork. Paul whirled.

The ghola emerged into the sun's full glare. His metal eyes glittered.

'Is it Duncan Idaho or the man called Hayt ?' Paul asked.

The ghola came to a stop two paces from him. 'Which would my Lord prefer ?'

The voice carried a soft ring of caution.

'Play the Zensunni,' Paul said bitterly. *Meanings within meanings !* What could a Zensunni philosopher say or do to change one jot of the reality unrolling before them at this instant ?

'My Lord is troubled.'

Paul turned away, stared at the Shield Wall's distant scarp, saw wind-carved arches and buttresses, terrible mimicry of his city. Nature playing a joke on him ! *See what I can build !* He recognized a slash in the distant massif, a place where sand spilled from a crevasse, and thought: *There ! Right there, we fought Sardaukar !*

'What troubles my Lord ?' the ghola asked.

'A vision,' Paul whispered.

'Ahhhhh, when the Tleilaxu first awakened me, I had visions. I was restless, lonely . . . not really knowing I was lonely. Not then. My visions revealed nothing ! The Tleilaxu told me it was an intrusion of the flesh which men and gholas all suffer, a sickness, no more.'

Paul turned, studied the ghola's eyes, those pitted, steely balls without expression. What visions did those eyes see ?

'Duncan . . . Duncan . . . ' Paul whispered.

'I am called Hayt.'

'I saw a moon fall,' Paul said. 'It was gone, destroyed. I heard a great hissing. The earth shook.'

'You are drunk on too much time,' the ghola said.

'I ask for the Zensunni and get the mentat!' Paul said. 'Very well! Play my vision through your logic, mentat. Analyse it and reduce it to mere words laid out for burial.'

'Burial, indeed,' the ghola said. 'You run from death. You strain at the next instant, refuse to live here and now. Augury! What a crutch for an Emperor?'

Paul found himself fascinated by a well-remembered mole on the ghola's chin.

'Trying to live in this future,' the ghola said, 'do you give substance to such a future? Do you make it real?'

'If I go the way of my vision-future, I'll be alive *then*,' Paul muttered. 'What makes you think I want to live there?'

The ghola shrugged. 'You asked me for a substantial answer.'

'Where is there substance in a universe composed of events?' Paul asked. 'Is there a final answer? Doesn't each solution produce new questions?'

'You've digested so much time you have delusions of immortality,' the ghola said. 'Even *your* Empire, my Lord, must live its time and die.'

'Don't parade smoke-blackened altars before me,' Paul growled. 'I've heard enough sad histories of gods and messiahs. Why should I need special powers to forecast ruins of my own like all those others? The lowliest servant of my kitchens could do this.' He shook his head. 'The moon fell!'

'You've not brought your mind to rest at its beginning,' the ghola said.

'Is that how you destroy me?' Paul demanded. 'Prevent me from collecting my thoughts?'

'Can you collect chaos?' the ghola asked. 'We Zensunni say: "not collecting, that is the ultimate gathering." What can you gather without gathering yourself?'

'I'm deviled by a vision and you spew nonsense!' Paul raged. 'What do you know of prescience?'

'I've seen the oracle at work,' the ghola said. 'I've seen those who seek signs and omens for their individual destiny. They fear what they seek.'

'My falling moon is real,' Paul whispered. He took a trembling breath. 'It moves. It moves.'

'Men always fear things which move by themselves,' the ghola said. 'You fear your own powers. Things fall into your head from nowhere. When they fall out, where do they go?'

'You comfort me with thorns,' Paul growled.

An inner illumination came over the ghola's face. For a moment, he became pure Duncan Idaho. 'I give you what comfort I can,' he said.

Paul wondered at the momentary spasm. Had the ghola felt grief which his mind rejected? Had Hayt put down a vision of his own?

'My moon has a name,' Paul whispered.

He let the vision flow over him then. Though his whole being shrieked, no sound escaped him. He was afraid to speak, fearful that his voice might betray him. The air of this terrifying future was thick with Chani's absence. Flesh that had cried in ecstasy, eyes that had burned him with their desire, the voice that had charmed him because it played no tricks of subtle control – all gone, back into the water and the sand.

Slowly, Paul turned away, looked out at the present and the plaza before Alia's temple. Three shaven-headed pilgrims entered from the processional avenue. They wore grimy yellow robes and hurried with their heads bent against the afternoon's wind. One walked with a limp, dragging his left foot. They beat their way against the wind, rounded a corner and were gone from his sight.

Just as his moon would go, they were gone. Still, his vision lay before him. Its terrible purpose gave him no choice.

*The flesh surrenders itself,* he thought. *Eternity takes back its own. Our bodies stirred these waters briefly, danced with a certain intoxication before the love of life and self, dealt with a few strange ideas, then submitted to the instruments of Time. What can we say of this? I occurred. I am not ... yet, I occurred.*

*'You do not beg the sun for mercy.'*
— Muad'dib's Travail
from The Stilgar Commentary

One moment of incompetence can be fatal, the Reverend Mother Gaius Helen Mohiam reminded herself.

She hobbled along, apparently unconcerned, within a ring of Fremen guards. One of those behind her, she knew, was a deaf-mute immune to any wiles of Voice. No doubt he'd been charged to kill her at the slightest provocation.

Why had Paul summoned her ? she wondered. Was he about to pass sentence ? She remembered the day long ago when she'd tested him . . . the child kwisatz haderach. He was a deep one.

Damn his mother for all eternity ! It was her fault the Bene Gesserit had lost their hold on this gene line.

Silence surged along the vaulted passages ahead of her entourage. She sensed the word being passed. Paul would hear the silence. He'd know of her coming before it was announced. She didn't delude herself with ideas that her powers exceeded his.

Damn him !

She begrudged the burdens age had imposed on her; the aching joints, responses not as quick as once they'd been, muscles not as elastic as the whipcords of her youth. A long day lay behind her and a long life. She'd spent this day with the Dune Tarot in a fruitless search for some clue to her own fate. But the cards were sluggish.

114

The guards herded her around a corner into another of the seemingly endless vaulted passages. Triangular metaglass windows on her left gave a view upward to trellised vines and indigo flowers in deep shadows cast by the afternoon sun. Tiles lay underfoot – figures of water creatures from exotic planets. Water reminders everywhere. Wealth . . . riches.

Robed figures passed across another hall in front of her, cast covert glances at the Reverend Mother. Recognition was obvious in their manner – and tension.

She kept her attention on the sharp hairline of the guard immediately in front: young flesh, pink creases at the uniform collar.

The immensity of this ighir citadel began to impress her. Passages . . . passages . . . They passed an open doorway from which emerged the sound of timbur and flute playing soft, elder music. A glance showed her blue-in-blue Fremen eyes staring from the room. She sensed in them the ferment of legendary revolts stirring in wild genes.

There lay the measure of her personal burden, she knew. A Bene Gesserit could not escape awareness of the genes and their possibilities. She was touched by a feeling of loss: that stubborn fool of an Atreides! How could he deny the jewels of posterity within his loins ? A kwisatz haderach! Born out of his time, true, but real – as his abomination of a sister . . . and there lay a dangerous unknown. A wild Reverend Mother spawned without Bene Gesserit inhibitions, holding no loyalty to orderly development of the genes. She shared her brother's powers, no doubt – and more.

The size of the citadel began to oppress her. Would the passages never end ? The place reeked of terrifying physical power. No planet, no civilisation in all human history had ever before seen such man-made immensity. A dozen ancient cities could be hidden in its walls!

They passed oval doors with winking lights. She recognised them for Ixian handiwork: pneumatic transport orifices. Why was she being marched all this distance, then ? The answer began to shape itself in her mind: to oppress her in preparation for this audience with the Emperor.

A small clue, but it joined other subtle indications – the relative suppression and selection of words by her escort, the traces of primitive shyness in their eyes when they called her *Reverend Mother*, the cold and bland, essentially odorless nature of these halls – all combined to reveal much that a Bene Gesserit could interpret.

Paul wanted something from her!

She concealed a feeling of elation. A bargaining lever existed. It remained only to find the nature of that lever and test its strength. Some levers had moved things greater than this citadel. A finger's touch had been known to topple civilisations.

The Reverend Mother reminded herself then of Scytale's assessment: *When a creature has developed into one thing, he will choose death rather than change into his opposite.*

The passages through which she was being escorted grew larger by subtle stages – tricks of arching, graduated amplification of pillared supports, displacement of the triangular windows by larger, oblong shapes. Ahead of her, finally, loomed double doors centered in the far wall of a tall ante chamber. She sensed that the doors were *very* large, and was forced to suppress a gasp as her trained awareness measured out the true proportions. The doorway stood at least eighty meters high, half that in width.

As she approached with her escort, the door swung inward – an immense and silent movement of hidden machinery. She recognised more Ixian handiwork. Through that towering doorway she marched with her guards into the Grand Reception Hall of the Emperor Paul Atreides – 'Muad'dib, before whom all people are dwarfed.' Now, she saw the effect of that popular saying at work.

As she advanced toward Paul on the distant throne, the Reverend Mother found herself more impressed by the architectural subtleties of her surroundings than she was by the immensities. The space was large: it could've housed the entire citadel of any ruler in human history. The open sweep of the room said much about hidden structural forces balanced with nicety. Trusses and supporting beams behind these walls and the faraway domed ceiling must surpass anything ever before attempted. Everything spoke of engineering genius.

Without seeming to do so, the hall grew smaller at its far end, refusing to dwarf Paul on his throne centered on a dais. An untrained awareness, shocked by surrounding proportions, would see him at first as many times larger than his actual size. Colors played upon the unprotected psyche: Paul's green throne had been cut from a single Hagar emerald. It suggested growing things and, out of the Fremen mythos, reflected the mourning color. It whispered that here sat he who could make you mourn –

life and death in one symbol, a clever stress of opposites. Behind the throne, draperies cascaded in burnt orange, curried gold of Dune earth, and cinnamon flecks of melange. To a trained eye, the symbolism was obvious, but it contained hammer blows to beat down the uninitiated.

Time played its role here.

The Reverend Mother measured the minutes required to approach the Imperial Presence at her hobbling pace. You had time to be cowed. Any tendency toward resentment would be squeezed out of you by the unbridled power which focused down upon your person. You might start the long march toward that throne as a human of dignity, but you ended the march as a gnat.

Aides and attendants stood around the Emperor in a curiously ordered sequence – attentive household guardsmen along the draped back wall, that abomination, Alia, two steps below Paul and on his left hand; Stilgar, the Imperial lackey, on the step directly below Alia; and on the right, one step up from the floor of the hall, a solitary figure: the fleshy revenant of Duncan Idaho, the ghola. She marked older Fremen among the guardsmen, bearded Naibs with stillsuit scars on their noses, sheathed crysknives at their waists, a few maula pistols, even some lasguns. Those must be trusted men, she thought, to carry lasguns in Paul's presence when he obviously wore a shield generator. She could see the shimmering of its field around him. One burst of a lasgun into that field and the entire citadel would be a hole in the ground.

Her guard stopped ten paces from the foot of the dais, parted to open an unobstructed view of the Emperor. She noted now the absence of Chani and Irulan, wondered at it. He held no important audience without them, so it was said.

Paul nodded to her, silent, measuring.

Immediately, she decided to take the offensive, said: 'So, the great Paul Atreides deigns to see the one he banished.'

Paul smiled wryly, thinking: *She knows I want something from her.* That knowledge had been inevitable, she being who she was. He recognised her powers. The Bene Gesserit didn't become Reverend Mothers by chance.

'Shall we dispense with fencing?' he asked.

Would it be this easy? she wondered. And she said: 'Name the thing you want.'

Stilgar stirred, cast a sharp glance at Paul. The Imperial lackey didn't like her tone.

'Stilgar wants me to send you away,' Paul said.

'Not kill me?' she asked. 'I would've expected something more direct from a Fremen Naib.'

Stilgar scowled, said: 'Often, I must speak otherwise than I think. That is called diplomacy.'

'Then let us dispense with diplomacy as well,' she said. 'Was it necessary to have me walk all that distance. I am an old woman.'

'You had to be shown how callous I can be,' Paul said. 'That way, you'll appreciate magnanimity.'

'You dare such gaucheries with a Bene Gesserit?' she asked.

'Gross actions carry their own messages,' Paul said.

She hesitated, weighed his words. So – he might yet dispense with her . . . grossly, obviously, if she . . . if she what?

'Say what it is you want from me,' she muttered.

Alia glanced at her brother, nodded toward the draperies behind the throne. She knew Paul's reasoning in this, but disliked it all the same. Call it *wild prophecy:* She felt pregnant with reluctance to take part in this bargaining.

'You must be careful how you speak to me, old woman,' Paul said.

*He called me old woman when he was a stripling*, the Reverend Mother thought. *Does he remind me now of my hand in his past? The decision I made then, must I remake it here?* She felt the weight of decision, a physical thing that set her knees to trembling. Muscles cried their fatigue.

'It was a long walk,' Paul said, 'and I can see that you're tired. We will retire to my private chamber behind the throne. You may sit there.' He gave a hand-signal to Stilgar, arose.

Stilgar and the ghola converged on her, helped her up the steps, followed Paul through a passage concealed by the draperies She realised then why he had greeted her in the hall: a dumb-show for the guards and Naibs. He feared them, then. And now – now, he displayed kindly benevolence, daring such wiles on a Bene Gesserit. Or was it daring? She sensed another presence behind, glanced back to see Alia following. The younger woman's eyes held a brooding, baleful cast. The Reverend Mother shuddered.

The private chamber at the end of the passage was a twenty-meter cube of plasmeld, yellow glowglobes for light, the deep orange hangings of a desert stilltent around the walls. It contained divans, soft cushions, a faint odor of melange, crystal water flagons on a low table. It felt cramped, tiny after the outer hall.

Paul seated her on a divan, stood over her, studying the ancient face – steely teeth, eyes that hid more than they revealed, deeply wrinkled skin. He indicated a water flagon. She shook her head, dislodging a wisp of gray hair.

In a low voice, Paul said: 'I wish to bargain with you for the life of my beloved.'

Stilgar cleared his throat.

Alia fingered the handle of the crysknife sheathed at her neck.

The ghola remained at the door, face impassive, metal eyes pointed at the air above the Reverend Mother's head.

'Have you had a vision of my hand in her death ?' the Reverend Mother asked. She kept her attention on the ghola, oddly disturbed by him. Why should she feel threatened by the ghola ? He was a tool of the conspiracy.

'I know what it is you want from me,' Paul said, avoiding her question.

*Then he only suspects,* she thought. The Reverend Mother looked down at the tips of her shoes exposed by a fold of her robe. Black . . . black . . . shoes and robe showed marks of her confinement: stains, wrinkles. She lifted her chin, met an angry glare in Paul's eyes. Elation surged through her, but she hid the emotion behind pursed lips, slitted eyelids.

'What coin do you offer ?' she asked.

'You may have my seed, but not my person,' Paul said. 'Irulan banished and inseminated by artificial –'

'You dare !' the Reverend Mother flared, stiffening.

Stilgar took a half step forward.

Disconcertingly, the ghola smiled, And now Alia was studying him.

'We'll not discuss the things your Sisterhood forbids,' Paul said. 'I will listen to no talk of sins, abominations or the beliefs left from past Jihads. You may have my seed for your plans, but no child of Irulan's will sit on my throne.'

'Your throne,' she sneered.

'*My* throne.'

'Then who will bear the Imperial heir ?'

'Chani.'

'She is barren.'

'She is with child.'

An involuntary indrawn breath exposed her shock. 'You lie!' she snapped.

**Paul held up a restraining hand as Stilgar surged forward.**

'We've known for two days that she carries my child.'

'But Irulan . . .'

'By artificial means only. That's my offer.'

The Reverend Mother closed her eyes to hide his face. Damnation! To cast the genetic dice in such a way! Loathing boiled in her breast. The teaching of the Bene Gesserit, the lessons of the Butlerian Jihad – all proscribed such an act. One did not demean the highest aspirations of humankind. No machine could function in the way of a human mind. No word or deed could imply that men might be bred on the level of animals.

'Your decision,' Paul said.

She shook her head. The genes, the precious Atreides genes – only these were important. Need went deeper than proscription. For the Sisterhood, mating mingled more than sperm and ovum. One aimed to capture the psyche.

The Reverend Mother understood now the subtle depths of Paul's offer. He would make the Bene Gesserit party to an act which would bring down popular wrath . . . were it ever discovered. They could not admit such paternity if the Emperor denied it. This coin might save the Atreides genes for the Sisterhood, but it would never buy a throne.

She swept her gaze around the room, studying each face: Stilgar, passive and waiting now; the ghola frozen at some inward place; Alia watching the ghola . . . and Paul – wrath beneath a shallow veneer.

'This is your only offer?' she asked.

'My only offer.'

She glanced at the ghola, caught by a brief movement of muscles across his cheeks. Emotion? 'You, ghola,' she said. 'Should such an offer be made? Having been made, should it be accepted? Function as the mentat for us.'

The metallic eyes turned to Paul.

'Answer as you will,' Paul said.

The ghola returned his gleaming attention to the Reverend Mother, shocked her once more by smiling. 'An offer is only as good as the real thing it buys,' he said. 'The exchange offered here is life-for-life, a high order of business.'

Alia brushed a strand of coppery hair from her forehead, said: 'And what else is hidden in this bargain?'

The Reverend Mother refused to look at Alia, but the words burned in her mind. Yes, far deeper implications lay here. The sister was an abomination, true, but there could be no denying

120

her status as a Reverend Mother with all the title implied. Gaius Helen Mohiam felt herself in this instant to be not one single person, but all the others who sat like tiny congeries in her memory. They were alert, every Reverend Mother she had absorbed in becoming a Priestess of the Sisterhood. Alia would be standing in the same situation here.

'What else?' the ghola asked. 'One wonders why the witches of the Bene Gesserit have not used Tleilaxu methods.'

Gaius Helen Mohiam and all the Reverend Mothers within her shuddered. Yes, the Tleilaxu did loathsome things. If one let down the barriers to artificial insemination, was the next step a Tleilaxu one – controlled mutation?

Paul, observing the play of emotion around him, felt abruptly that he no longer knew these people. He could see only strangers. Even Alia was a stranger.

Alia said: 'If we set the Atreides genes adrift in a Bene Gesserit river, who knows what may result?'

Gaius Helen Mohiam's head snapped around, and she met Alia's gaze. For a flashing instant, they were two Reverend Mothers together, communing on a single thought: *What lay behind any Tleilaxu action? The ghola was a Tleilaxu thing. Had he put this plan into Paul's mind? Would Paul attempt to bargain directly with the Bene Tleilax?*

She broke her gaze from Alia's, feeling her own ambivalence and inadequacies. The pitfall of Bene Gesserit training, she reminded herself, lay in the powers granted: such powers predisposed one to vanity and pride. But power deluded those who used it. One tended to believe power could overcome any barrier . . . including one's own ignorance.

Only one thing stood paramount here for the Bene Gesserit, she told herself. That was the pyramid of generations which had reached an apex in Paul Atreides . . . and in his abomination of a sister. A wrong choice here and the pyramid would have to be rebuilt . . . starting generations back in the parallel lines and with breeding specimens lacking the choicest characteristics.

*Controlled mutation,* she thought. *Did the Tleilaxu really practice it? How tempting!* She shook her head, the better to rid it of such thoughts.

'You reject my proposal?' Paul asked.

'I'm thinking,' she said.

And again, she looked at the sister. The optimum cross for this female Atreides had been lost . . . killed by Paul. Another possibility remained, however – one which would *cement* the desired characteristic into an offspring. Paul dared offer animal breeding to the Bene Gesserit! How much was he really prepared to pay for this Chani's life? Would he accept a cross with his own sister?

Sparring for time, the Reverend Mother said: 'Tell me, oh flawless exemplar of all that's holy, has Irulan anything to say of your proposal?'

'Irulan will do what you tell her to do,' Paul growled.

*True enough*, Mohiam thought. She firmed her jaw, offered a new gambit: 'There are two Atreides.'

Paul, sensing something of what lay in the old witch's mind, felt blood darken his face. 'Careful what you suggest,' he said.

'You'd just *use* Irulan to gain your own ends, eh?' she asked.

'Wasn't she trained to be used?' Paul asked.

*And we trained her, that's what he's saying*, Mohiam thought. *Well . . . Irulan's a divided coin. Was there another way to spend such a coin?*

'Will you put Chani's child on the throne?' the Reverend Mother asked.

'On *my* throne,' Paul said. He glanced at Alia, wondering suddenly if she knew the divergent possibilities in this exchange. Alia stood with eyes closed, an odd stillness-of-person about her. With what inner force did she commune? Seeing his sister thus, Paul felt he'd been cast adrift. Alia stood on a shore that was receding from him.

The Reverend Mother made her decision, said: 'This is too much for one person to decide. I must consult with my Council on Wallach. Will you permit a message?'

*As though she needed my permission!* Paul thought.

He said: 'Agreed, then. But don't delay too long. I will not sit idly by while you debate.'

'Will you bargain with the Bene Tleilax?' the ghola asked, his voice a sharp intrusion.

Alia's eyes popped open and she stared at the ghola as though she'd been wakened by a dangerous intruder.

'I've made no such decision,' Paul said. 'What I will do is go into the desert as soon as it can be arranged. Our child will be born in sietch.'

'A wise decision,' Stilgar intoned.

Alia refused to look at Stilgar. It was a wrong decision. She could feel this in every cell. Paul *must* know it. Why had he fixed himself upon such a path?

'Have the Bene Tleilax offered their services?' Alia asked. She saw Mohiam hanging on the answer.

Paul shook his head. 'No.' He glanced at Stilgar. 'Stil, arrange for the message to be sent to Wallach.'

'At once, m'Lord.'

Paul turned away, waited while Stilgar summoned guards, left with the old witch. He sensed Alia debating whether to confront him with more questions. She turned, instead, to the ghola.

'Mentat,' she said, 'will the Tleilaxu bid for favor with my brother?'

The ghola shrugged.

Paul felt his attention wander. *The Tleilaxu? No ... not in the way Alia meant.* Her question revealed, though, that she had not seen the alternatives here. Well ... vision varied from sibyl to sibyl. Why not a variance from brother to sister? Wandering ... wandering ... He came back from each thought with a start to pick up shards of the nearby conversation.

'... must know what the Tleilaxu ...'

'... the fullness of data is always ...'

'... healthy doubts where ...'

Paul turned, looked at his sister, caught her attention. He knew she would see tears on his face and wonder at them. Let her wonder. Wondering was a kindness now. He glanced at the ghola, seeing only Duncan Idaho despite the metallic eyes. Sorrow and compassion warred in Paul. What might those metal eyes record?

*There are many degrees of sight and many degrees of blindness,* Paul thought. His mind turned to a paraphrase of the passage from the Orange Catholic Bible: *What senses do we lack that we cannot see another world all around us?*

Were those metal eyes another sense than sight?

Alia crossed to her brother, sensing his utter sadness. She touched a tear on his cheek with a Fremen gesture of awe, said: 'We must not grieve for those dear to us before their passing.'

'Before their passing,' Paul whispered. 'Tell me, little sister, what is *before?*'

*'I've had a bellyful of the god and priest business ! You think
I don't see my own mythos ? Consult your data once more,
Hayt. I've insinuated my rites into the most elementary human
acts. The people eat in the name of Muad'dib ! They make love
in my name, are born in my name — cross the street in my name.
A roof beam cannot be raised in the lowest hovel of far Gangi-
shree without invoking the blessing of Muad'dib !'*

— Book of Diatribes
from The Hayt Chronicle

'You risk much leaving your post and coming to me here at this
time,' Edric said, glaring through the walls of his tank at the
Face Dancer.

'How weak and narrow is your thinking,' Scytale said. 'Who
is it who comes to visit you ?'

Edric hesitated, observing the hulk shape, heavy eyelids, blunt
face. It was early in the day and Edric's metabolism had not yet
cycled from night repose into full melange consumption.

'This is not the shape which walked the streets ?' Edric asked.

'One would not look twice at some of the figures I have been
today,' Scytale said.

*The chameleon thinks a change of shape will hide him from any-
thing.* Edric thought with rare insight. And he wondered if his
presence in the conspiracy truly hid them from all oracular
powers. The Emperor's sister, now . . .

Edric shook his head, stirring the orange gas of his tank, said: 'Why are you here ?'

'The gift must be prodded to swifter action,' Scytale said.

'That cannot be done.'

'A way must be found,' Scytale insisted.

'Why ?'

'Things are not to my liking. The Emperor is trying to split us. Already he has made his bid to the Bene Gesserit.'

'Oh, *that*.'

'That! You must prod the ghola to . . .'

'You fashioned him, Tleilaxu,' Edric said. 'You know better than to ask this.' He paused, moved closer to the transparent wall of his tank. 'Or did you lie to us about this gift ?'

'Lie ?'

'You said the weapon was to be aimed and released, nothing more. Once the ghola was given we could not tamper.'

'Any ghola can be disturbed,' Scytale said. 'You need do nothing more than question him about his original being.'

'What will this do ?'

'It will stir him to actions which will serve our purposes.'

'He is a mentat with powers of logic and reason,' Edric objected. 'He may guess what I'm doing . . . or the sister. If her attention is focused upon –'

'Do you hide us from the sibyl or don't you ?' Scytale asked.

'I'm not afraid of oracles,' Edric said. 'I'm concerned with logic, with real spies, with the physical powers of the Imperium, with the control of the spice, with –'

'One can contemplate the Emperor and his powers comfortably if one remembers that all things are finite,' Scytale said.

Oddly, the Steersman recoiled in agitation, threshing his limbs like some weird newt. Scytale fought a sense of loathing at the sight. The Guild Navigator wore his usual dark leotard bulging at the belt with various containers. Yet . . . he gave the impression of nakedness when he moved. It was the swimming, reaching movements. Scytale decided, and he was struck once more by the delicate linkages of their conspiracy. They were not a compatible group. That was weakness.

Edric's agitation subsided. He stared out at Scytale, vision colored by the orange gas which sustained him. What plot did the Face Dancer hold in reserve to save himself ? Edric wondered The Tleilaxu was not acting in a predictable fashion. Evil omen.

Something in the Navigator's voice and actions told Scytale

that the Guildsman feared the sister more than the Emperor. This was an abrupt thought flashed on the screen of awareness. Disturbing. Had they overlooked something important about Alia? Would the ghola be sufficient weapon to destroy both?

'You know what is said of Alia?' Scytale asked, probing.

'What do you mean?' Again, the fish-man was agitated.

'Never have philosophy and culture had such a patroness,' Scytale said. 'Pleasure and beauty unite in –'

'What is enduring about beauty and pleasure?' Edric demanded. 'We will destroy both Atreides. Culture! They dispense culture the better to rule. Beauty! They promote the beauty which enslaves. They create a literate ignorance – easiest thing of all. They leave nothing to chance. Chains! Everything they do forges chains, enslaves. But slaves always revolt.'

'The sister may wed and produce offspring,' Scytale said.

'Why do you speak of the sister?' Edric asked.

'The Emperor may choose a mate for her,' Scytale said.

'Let him choose. Already, it is too late.'

'Even you cannot invent the next moment,' Scytale warned. 'You are not a creator . . . any more than are the Atreides.' He nodded. 'We must not presume too much.'

'We aren't the ones to flap our tongues about creation.' Edric protested. 'We aren't the rabble trying to make a messiah out of Muad'dib. What is this nonsense? Why are you raising such questions?'

'It's this planet,' Scytale said. '*It* raises questions.'

'Planets don't speak!'

'This one does.'

'Oh?'

'It speaks of creation. Sand blowing in the night, that is creation.'

'Sand blowing . . .'

'When you awaken, the first light shows you the new world – all fresh and ready for your tracks.'

*Untracked sand?* Edric thought. *Creation?* He felt knotted with sudden anxiety. The confinement of his tank, the surrounding room, everything closed in upon him, constricted him.

*Tracks in sand.*

'You talk like a Fremen,' Edric said.

'This is a Fremen thought and it's instructive,' Scytale agreed. 'They speak of Muad'dib's Jihad as leaving tracks in the universe in the same way that a Fremen tracks new sand. They've marked out a trail in men's lives.'

'So ?'

'Another night comes,' Scytale said. 'Winds blow.'

'Yes,' Edric said, 'the Jihad is finite. Muad'dib has used his Jihad and –'

'He didn't use the Jihad,' Scytale said. 'The Jihad used him. I think he would've stopped it if he could.'

'If he could ? All he had to do was –'

'Oh, be still!' Scytale barked. 'You can't stop a mentat epidemic. It leaps from person to person across parsecs. It's overwhelmingly contagious. It strikes at the unprotected side, in the place where we lodge the fragments of other such plagues. Who can stop such a thing ? Muad'dib hasn't the antidote. The thing has roots in chaos. Can orders reach there ?'

'Have you been infected, then ?' Edric asked. He turned slowly in the orange gas, wondering why Scytale's words carried such a tone of fear. Had the Face Dancer broken from the conspiracy ? There was no way to peer into the future and examine this now. The future had become a muddy stream, clogged with prophets.

'We're all contaminated,' Scytale said, and he reminded himself that Edric's intelligence had severe limits. How could this point be made that the Guildsman would understand it ?

'But when we destroy him,' Edric said, 'the contag –'

'I should leave you in this ignorance,' Scytale said. 'But my duties will not permit it. Besides, it's dangerous to all of us.'

Edric recoiled, steadied himself with a kick of one webbed foot which sent the orange gas whipping around his legs. 'You speak strangely,' he said.

'This whole thing is explosive,' Scytale said in a calmer voice. 'It's ready to shatter. When it goes, it will send bits of itself out through the centuries. Don't you see this ?'

'We've dealt with religions before,' Edric protested. 'If this new –'

'It is *not* just a religion!' Scytale said, wondering what the Reverend Mother would say to this harsh education of their fellow conspirator. 'Religious government is something else. Muad'dib has crowded his Qizarate in everywhere, displaced the old functions of government. But he has no permanent civil service, no interlocking embassies. He has bishoprics, islands of authority. At the center of each island is a man. Men learn how to gain and hold personal power. Men are jealous.'

'When they're divided, we'll absorb them one by one,' Edric said with a complacent smile. 'Cut off the head and the body will fall to —'

'This body has two heads,' Scytale said.

'The sister . . . who may wed.'

'Who will certainly wed.'

'I don't like your tone, Scytale.'

'And I don't like your ignorance.'

'What if she does wed? Will that shake our plans?'

'It will shake the universe.'

'But they're not unique. I, myself, possess powers which —'

'You're an infant. You toddle where they stride.'

'They are *not* unique!'

'You forget, Guildsman, that we once made a kwisatz haderach. This is a being filled by the spectacle of Time. It is a form of existence which cannot be threatened without enclosing yourself in the identical threat. Muad'dib knows we would attack his Chani. We must move faster than we have. You must get the ghola, prod him as I have instructed.'

'And if I do not?'

'We will feel the thunderbolt.'

*Oh, worm of many teeth,*
*Canst thou deny what has no cure ?*
*The flesh and breath which lure thee*
*To the ground of all beginnings*
*Feed on monsters twisting in a door of fire !*
*Thou hast no robe in all thy attire*
*To cover intoxications of divinity*
*Or hide the burnings of desire !*

– Wormsong
from The Dunebook

Paul had worked up a sweat on the practice floor using crysknife and short sword against the ghola. He stood now at a window looking down into the temple plaza, tried to imagine the scene with Chani at the clinic. She'd been taken ill at midmorning, the sixth week of her pregnancy. The medics were the best. They'd call when they had news.

Murky afternoon sandclouds darkened the sky over the plaza. Fremen called such weather 'dirty air'.

Would the medics never call ? Each second struggled past, reluctant to enter his universe.

Waiting . . . waiting . . . The Bene Gesserit sent no word from Wallach. Deliberately delaying, of course.

Prescient vision had recorded these moments, but he shielded his awareness from the oracle, preferring the role here of a Time-fish swimming not where he willed, but where the currents carried him. Destiny permitted no struggles now.

The ghola could be heard racking weapons, examining the equipment. Paul sighed, put a hand to his own belt, deactivated his shield. The tingling passage of its field ran down against his skin.

He'd face events when Chani came, Paul told himself. Time enough then to accept the fact that what he'd concealed from her had prolonged her life. Was it evil, he wondered, to prefer Chani to an heir ? By what right did he make her choice for her ? Foolish thoughts! Who could hesitate, given the alternatives – slave pits, torture, agonising sorrow . . . and worse.

He heard the door open, Chani's footsteps.

Paul turned.

Murder sat on Chani's face. The wide Fremen belt which gathered the waist of her golden robe, the water rings worn as a necklace, one hand at her hip (never far from the knife), the trenchant stare which was her first inspection of any room – everything about her stood now only as a background for violence.

He opened his arms as she came to him, gathered her close.

'Someone,' she rasped, speaking against his breast, 'has been feeding me a contraceptive for a long time . . . before I began the new diet. There'll be problems with this birth because of it.'

'But there are remedies ?' he asked.

'Dangerous remedies. I know the source of that poison! I'll have her blood.'

'My Sihaya,' he whispered, holding her close to calm a sudden trembling. 'You'll bear the heir we want. Isn't that enough ?'

'My life burns faster,' she said, pressing against him. 'The birth now controls my life. The medics told me it goes at a terrible pace. I must eat and eat . . . and take more spice, as well . . . eat it, drink it. I'll kill her for this!'

Paul kissed her cheek. 'No, my Sihaya. You'll kill no one.' And he thought: *Irulan prolonged your life, beloved. For you, the time of birth is the time of death.*

He felt hidden grief drain his marrow then, empty his life into a black flask.

Chani pushed away from him. 'She cannot be forgiven!'

'Who said anything about forgiving ?'

'Then why shouldn't I kill her ?'

It was such a flat, Fremen question that Paul felt himself

almost overcome by a hysterical desire to laugh. He covered it by saying: 'It wouldn't help.'

'You've *seen* that?'

Paul felt his belly tighten with vision-memory.

'What I've seen . . . what I've seen . . . ' he muttered. Every aspect of surrounding events fitted a present which paralysed him. He felt chained to a future which, exposed too often, had locked onto him like a greedy succubus. Tight dryness clogged his throat. Had he followed the witchcall of his own oracle, he wondered, until it'd spilled him into a merciless present?

'Tell me what you've *seen*,' Chani said.

'I can't.'

'Why mustn't I kill her?'

'Because I ask it.'

He watched her accept this. She did it the way sand accepted water: absorbing and concealing. Was there obedience beneath that hot, angry surface? he wondered. And he realised then that life in the royal Keep had left Chani unchanged. She'd merely stopped here for a time, inhabited a way station on a journey with her man. Nothing of the desert had been taken from her.

Chani stepped away from him then, glanced at the ghola who stood waiting near the diamond circle of the practice floor.

'You've been crossing blades with him?' she asked.

'And I'm better for it.'

Her gaze went to the circle on the floor, back to the ghola's metallic eyes.

'I don't like it,' she said.

'He's not intended to do me violence,' Paul said.

'You've seen *that?*'

'I've not *seen* it!'

'Then how do you know?'

'Because he's more than ghola; he's Duncan Idaho.'

'The Bene Tleilaxu made him.'

'They made more than they intended.'

She shook her head. A corner of her nezhoni scarf rubbed the collar of her robe. 'How can you change the fact that he is ghola?'

'Hayt,' Paul said, 'are you the tool of my undoing?'

'If the substance of here and now is changed, the future is changed,' the ghola said.

'That is no answer!' Chani objected.

Paul raised his voice: 'How will I die, Hayt?'

Light glinted from the artificial eyes. 'It is said, m'Lord, that you will die of money and power.'

Chani stiffened. 'How dare he speak thus to you?'

'The mentat is truthful,' Paul said.

'Was Duncan Idaho a real friend?' she asked.

'He gave his life for me.'

'It is said,' Chani whispered, 'that a ghola cannot be restored to his original being.'

'Would you convert me?' the ghola asked, directing his gaze to Chani.

'What does he mean?' Chani asked.

'To be converted is to be turned around,' Paul said. 'But there's no going back.'

'Every man carries his own past with him,' Hayt said.

'And every ghola?' Paul asked.

'In a way, m'Lord.'

'Then what of that past in your secret flesh?' Paul asked.

Chani saw how the question disturbed the ghola. His movements quickened, hands clenched into fists. She glanced at Paul, wondering why he probed thus. Was there a way to restore this creature to the man he'd been?

'Has a ghola ever remembered his real past?' Chani asked.

'Many attempts have been made,' Hayt said, his gaze fixed on the floor near his feet. 'No ghola has ever been restored to his former being.'

'But you long for this to happen,' Paul said.

The blank surfaces of the ghola's eyes came up to center on Paul with a pressing intensity. 'Yes!'

Voice soft, Paul said: 'If there's a way . . .'

'This flesh,' Hayt said, touching left hand to forehead in a curious saluting movement, 'is not the flesh of my original birth. It is . . . reborn. Only the shape is familiar. A Face Dancer might do as well.'

'Not as well,' Paul said. 'And you're not a Face Dancer.'

'That is true, m'Lord.'

'Whence comes your shape?'

'The genetic imprint of the original cells.'

'Somewhere,' Paul said, 'there's a plastic something which remembers the shape of Duncan Idaho. It's said the ancients probed this region before the Butlerian Jihad. What's the extent of this memory, Hayt? What did it learn from the original?'

The ghola shrugged.

'What if he wasn't Idaho?' Chani asked.

'He was.'

'Can you be certain?' she asked.

'He is Duncan in every aspect. I cannot imagine a force strong enough to hold that shape thus without any relaxation or any deviation.'

'M'Lord!' Hayt objected. 'Because we cannot imagine a thing, that doesn't exclude it from reality. There are things I must do as a ghola that I would not do as a man.'

Keeping his attention on Chani, Paul said: 'You see?'

She nodded.

Paul turned away, fighting deep sadness. He crossed to the balcony windows, drew the draperies. Lights came on in the sudden gloom. He pulled the sash of his robe tight, listened for sound behind him.

Nothing.

He turned, Chani stood as though entranced, her gaze centered on the ghola.

Hayt, Paul saw, had retreated to some inner chamber of his being – had gone back to the ghola place.

Chani turned at the sound of Paul's return. She still felt the thralldom of the instant Paul had precipitated. For a brief moment, the ghola had been an intense, vital human being. For that moment, he had been someone she did not fear – indeed, someone she liked and admired. Now, she understood Paul's purpose in this probing. He had wanted her to see the *man* in the ghola flesh.

She stared at Paul. 'That man was that Duncan Idaho?'

'That was Duncan Idaho. He is still there.'

'Would *he* have allowed Irulan to go on living?' Chani asked.

*The water didn't sink too deep*, Paul thought. And he said: 'If I commanded it.'

'I don't understand,' she said. 'Shouldn't you be angry?'

'I am angry.'

'You don't sound . . . angry. You sound sorrowful.'

He closed his eyes. 'Yes. That, too.'

'You're my man,' she said. 'I know this, but suddenly I don't understand you.'

Abruptly, Paul felt that he walked down a long cavern. His flesh moved – one foot and then another – but his thoughts went elsewhere. 'I don't understand myself,' he whispered. When he opened his eyes, he found that he had moved away from Chani.

She spoke from somewhere behind him. 'Beloved, I'll not ask

again what you've *seen*. I only know I'm to give you the heir we want.'

He nodded, then: 'I've known that from the beginning.' He turned, studied her. Chani seemed very far away.

She drew herself up, placed a hand on her abdomen. 'I'm hungry. The medics tell me I must eat three or four times what I ate before. I'm frightened, beloved. It goes too fast.'

*Too fast*, he agreed. *This fetus knows the necessity for speed.*

*The audacious nature of Muad'dib's actions may be seen in the fact that He knew from the beginning whither He was bound, yet not once did He step aside from that path. He put it clearly when He said: 'I tell you that I come now to my time of testing when it will be shown that I am the Ultimate Servant.' Thus He weaves all into One, that both friend and foe may worship Him. It is for this reason and this reason only that His Apostles prayed: 'Lord, save us from the other paths which Muad'dib covered with the Waters of His Life.' Those 'other paths' may be imagined only with the deepest revulsion.*

— from The Yiam-el-Din
(Book of Judgement)

The messenger was a young woman – her face, name and family known to Chani – which was how she'd penetrated Imperial Security.

Chani had done no more than identify her for a Security Officer named Bannerjee, who then arranged the meeting with Muad'-dib. Bannerjee acted out of instinct and the assurance that the young woman's father had been a member of the Emperor's Death Commandos, the dreaded Fedaykin, in the days before the Jihad. Otherwise, he might have ignored her plea that her message was intended only for the ears of Muad'dib.

She was, of course, screened and searched before the meeting in Paul's private office. Even so, Bannerjee accompanied her, hand on knife, other hand on her arm.

It was almost midday when they brought her into the room – an odd space, mixture of desert-Fremen and Family-Aristocrat. *Hiereg* hangings lined three walls: delicate tapestries adorned with figures out of Fremen mythology. A view screen covered the fourth wall, a silver-gray surface behind an oval desk whose top held only one object, a Fremen sandclock built into an *orrery*. The orrery, a suspensor mechanism from Ix, carried both moons of Arrakis in the classic Worm Trine aligned with the sun.

Paul, standing beside the desk, glanced at Bannerjee. The Security Officer was one of those who'd come up through the Fremen Constabulary, winning his place on brains and proven loyalty despite the smuggler ancestry attested by his name. He was a solid figure, almost fat, Wisps of black hair fell down over the dark, wet-appearing skin of his forehead like the crest of an exotic bird. His eyes were blue-blue and steady in a gaze which could look upon happiness or atrocity without change of expression. Both Chani and Stilgar trusted him. Paul knew that if he told Bannerjee to throttle the girl immediately, Bannerjee would do it.

'Sire, here is the messenger girl,' Bannerjee said. 'M'Lady Chani said she sent word to you.'

'Yes,' Paul nodded curtly.

Oddly, the girl didn't look at him. Her attention remained on the orrery. She was dark-skinned, of medium height, her figure concealed by a robe whose rich wine fabric and simple cut spoke of wealth. Her blue-black hair was held in a narrow band of material which matched the robe. The robe concealed her hands. Paul suspected that the hands were tightly clasped. It would be in character. Everything about her would be in character – including the robe: a last piece of finery saved for such a moment.

Paul motioned Bannerjee aside. He hesitated before obeying. Now, the girl moved – one step forward. When she moved there was grace. Still, her eyes avoided him.

Paul cleared his throat.

Now the girl lifted her gaze, the whiteless eyes widening with just the right shade of awe. She had an odd little face with delicate chin, a sense of reserve in the way she held her small mouth. The eyes appeared abnormally large above slanted cheeks. There was a cheerless air about her, something which said she seldom smiled. The corners of her eyes even held a faint yellow misting which could have been from dust irritation or the tracery of semuta.

Everything was in character.

'You asked to see me,' Paul said.

The moment of supreme test for this girl-shape had come. Scytale had put on the shape, the mannerisms, the sex, the voice – everything his abilities could grasp and assume. But this was a female known to Muad'dib in the sietch days. She'd been a child, then, but she and Muad'dib shared common experiences. Certain areas of memory must be avoided delicately. It was the most exacting part Scytale had ever attempted.

'I am Otheym's Lichna of Berk al Dib.'

The girl's voice came out small, but firm, giving name, father and pedigree.

Paul nodded. He saw how Chani had been fooled. The timbre of voice, everything reproduced with exactitude. Had it not been for his own Bene Gesserit training in voice and for the web of *dao* in which oracular vision enfolded him, this Face-Dancer disguise might have gulled even him.

Training exposed certain discrepancies: the girl was older than her known years; too much control tuned the vocal cords; set of neck and shoulders missed by a fraction the subtle hauteur of Fremen poise. But there were niceties, too: the rich robe had been patched to betray actual status . . . and the features were beautifully exact. They spoke a certain sympathy of this Face Dancer for the role being played.

'Rest in my home, daughter of Otheym,' Paul said in formal Fremen greeting. 'You are welcome as water after a dry crossing.'

The faintest of relaxations exposed the confidence this apparent acceptance had conveyed.

'I bring a message,' she said.

'A man's messenger is as himself,' Paul said.

Scytale breathed softly. It went well, but now came the crucial task: the Atreides must be guided onto that special path. He must lose his Fremen concubine in circumstances where no other shared the blame. The failure must belong only to the *omnipotent* Muad'dib. He had to be led into an ultimate realisation of his failure and thence to acceptance of the Tleilaxu alternative.

'I am the smoke which banishes sleep in the night,' Scytale said: employing a Fedaykin code phrase: *I bear bad tidings.*

Paul fought to maintain calmness. He felt naked, his soul abandoned in a groping-time concealed from every vision. Powerful oracles hid this Face Dancer. Only the edges of these moments were known to Paul. He knew only what he could *not* do. He could not slay this Face Dancer. That would precipitate the future which must be avoided at all cost. Somehow, a way must be found to reach into the darkness and change the terrifying pattern.

'Give me your message,' Paul said.

Bannerjee moved to place himself where he could watch the girl's face. She seemed to notice him for the first time and her gaze went to the knife handle beneath the Security Officer's hand.

'The innocent do not believe in evil,' she said, looking squarely at Bannerjee.

*Ahhh, well done*, Paul thought. It was what the real Lichna would've said. He felt a momentary pang for the real daughter of Otheym – dead now, a corpse in the sand. There was no time for such emotions, though. He scowled.

Bannerjee kept his attention on the girl.

'I was told to deliver my message in secret,' she said.

'Why ?' Bannerjee demanded, voice harsh, probing.

'Because it is my father's wish.'

'This is my friend,' Paul said. 'Am I not a Fremen ? Then my friend may hear anything I hear.'

Scytale composed the girl-shape. Was this a true Fremen custom . . . or was it a test ?

'The Emperor may make his own rules,' Scytale said. 'This is the message: My father wishes you to come to him, bringing Chani.'

'Why must I bring Chani ?'

'She is your woman and a Sayyadina. This is a Water matter, by the rules of our tribes. She must attest it that my father speaks according to the Fremen Way.'

*There truly are Fremen in the conspiracy*, Paul thought. This moment fitted the shape of things to come for sure. And he had no alternative but to commit himself to this course.

'Of what will your father speak ?' Paul asked.

'He will speak of a plot against you – a plot among the Fremen.'

'Why doesn't he bring that message in person ?' Bannerjee demanded.

She kept her gaze on Paul. 'My father cannot come here. The plotters suspect him. He'd not survive the journey.'

'Could he not divulge the plot to you ?' Bannerjee asked. 'How came he to risk his daughter on such a mission ?'

'The details are locked in a distrans carrier that only Muad'dib may open,' she said. 'This much I know.'

'Why not send the distrans, then?' Paul asked.

'It is a human distrans,' she said.

'I'll go, then,' Paul said. 'But I'll go alone.'

'Chani must come with you!'

'Chani is with child.'

'When has a Fremen woman refused to . . .'

'My enemies fed her a subtle poison,' Paul said. 'It will be a difficult birth. Her health will not permit her to accompany me now.'

Before Scytale could still them, strange emotions passed over the girl-features; frustration, anger. Scytale was reminded that every victim must have a way of escape – even such a one as Muad'dib. The conspiracy had not failed, though. This Atreides remained in the net. He was a creature who had developed firmly into one pattern. He'd destroy himself before changing into the opposite of that pattern. That had been the way with the Tleilaxu kwisatz haderach. It'd be the way with this one. And then . . . the ghola.

'Let me ask Chani to decide this,' she said.

'I have decided it,' Paul said. 'You will accompany me in Chani's stead.'

'It requires a Sayyadina of the Rite!'

'Are you not Chani's friend?'

*Boxed!* Scytale thought. *Does he suspect? No. He's being Fremen-cautious. And the contraceptive is a fact. Well – there are other ways.*

'My father told me I was not to return,' Scytale said, 'that I was to seek asylum with you. He said you'd not risk me.'

Paul nodded. It was beautifully in character. He couldn't deny this asylum. She'd plead Fremen obedience to a father's command.

'I'll take Stilgar's wife, Harah,' Paul said. 'You'll tell us the way to your father.'

'How do you know you can trust Stilgar's wife?'

'I know it.'

'But I don't.'

Paul pursed his lips, then: 'Does you mother live?'

'My true mother has gone to Shai-hulud. My second mother still lives and cares for my father. Why?'

'She's of Sietch Tabr?'

'Yes.'

'I remember her,' Paul said. 'She will serve in Chani's place.'

He motioned to Bannerjee. 'Have attendants take Otheym's Lichna to suitable quarters.'

Bannerjee nodded. *Attendants*. The key word meant that this messenger must be put under special guard. He took her arm. She resisted.

'How will you go to my father?' she pleaded.

'You'll describe the way to Bannerjee,' Paul said. 'He is my friend.'

'No! My father has commanded it! I cannot!'

'Bannerjee?' Paul said.

Bannerjee paused. Paul saw the man searching that encyclopedic memory which had helped bring him to his position of trust. 'I know a guide who can take you to Otheym,' Bannerjee said.

'Then I'll go alone,' Paul said.

'Sire, if you . . . '

'Otheym wants it this way,' Paul said, barely concealing the irony which consumed him.

'Sire, it's too dangerous,' Bannerjee protested.

'Even an Emperor must accept some risks,' Paul said. 'The decision is made. Do as I've commanded.'

Reluctantly, Bannerjee led the Face Dancer from the room.

Paul turned toward the blank screen behind his desk. He felt that he waited for the arrival of a rock on its blind journey from some height.

Should he tell Bannerjee about the messenger's true nature? he wondered. No! Such an incident hadn't been written on the screen of his vison. Any deviation here carried precipitate violence. A moment of fulcrum had to be found, a place where he could will himself out of the vision.

*If such a moment existed . . .*

recent devising, but there was something about this setting in a desert sink at the edge of Arrakeen – something in the way wind-driven sand had begun to weather stones and plastene, something in the haphazard way buildings had gone up around the Fane. Everything conspired to produce the impression that this was a very old place full of traditions and mystery.

He was down into the press of people now – committed. The only guide his Security force could find had insisted it be done this way. Security hadn't liked Paul's ready agreement. Stilgar had liked it even less. And Chani had objected most of all.

The crowd round him, even while its members brushed against him, glanced his way unseeing and passed on, gave him a curious freedom of movement. It was the way they'd been conditioned to treat a Fremen, he knew. He carried himself like a man of the inner desert. Such men were quick to anger.

As he moved into the quickening flow to the temple steps, the crush of people became even greater. Those all around could not help but press against him now, but he found himself the target for ritual apologies: 'Your pardon, noble sir. I cannot prevent this discourtesy.' 'Pardon, sir; this crush of people is the worst I've ever seen.' 'I abase myself, holy citizen. A lout shoved me.'

Paul ignored the words after the first few. There was no feeling in them except a kind of ritual fear. He found himself, instead, thinking that he had come a long way from his boyhood days in Caladan Castle. Where had he put his foot on the path that led to this journey across a crowded square on a planet so far from Caladan? Had he really put his foot on a path? He could not say he had acted at any point in his life for one specific reason. The motives and impinging forces had been complex – more complex possibly than any other set of goads in human history. He had the heady feeling here that he might still avoid the fate he could see so clearly along this path. But the crowd pushed him forward and he experienced the dizzy sense that he had lost his way, lost personal direction over his life.

The crowd flowed with him up the steps now into the temple portico. Voices grew hushed. The smell of fear grew stronger – acrid, sweaty.

Acolytes had already begun the service within the temple. Their plain chant dominated the other sounds – whispers, rustle of garments, shuffling feet, coughs – telling the story of the Far Places visited by the Priestess in her holy trance.

'She rides the sandworms of space!
She guides through all storms
Into the land of gentle winds.
Though we sleep by the snake's den,
She guards our dreaming souls.
Shunning the desert heat,
She hides us in a cool hollow.
The gleaming of her white teeth
Guides us in the night.
By the braids of her hair
We are lifted up to heaven!
Sweet fragrance, flower-scented,
Surrounds us in her presence.'

*Balak!* Paul thought, thinking in Fremen. *Look out! She can be filled with angry passion, too.*

The temple portico was lined with tall, slender glowtubes simulating candle flame. They flickered. The flickering stirred ancestral memories in Paul even while he knew that was the intent. This setting was an atavism, subtly contrived, effective. He hated his own hand in it.

The crowd flowed with him through tall metal doors into the gigantic nave, a gloomy place with the flickering lights far away overhead, a brilliantly illuminated altar at the far end. Behind the altar, a deceptively simple affair of black wood encrusted with sand patterns from the Fremen mythology, hidden lights played on the field of a pru-door to create a rainbow borealis. The seven rows of chanting acolytes ranked below that spectral curtain took on an eerie quality: black robes, white faces, mouths moving in unison.

Paul studied the pilgrims around him, suddenly envious of their intentness, their air of listening to truths he could not hear. It seemed to him that they gained something here which was denied to him, something mysteriously healing.

He tried to inch his way closer to the altar, was stopped by a hand on his arm. Paul whipped his gaze around, met the probing stare of an ancient Fremen – blue-blue eyes beneath overhanging brows, recognition in them. A name flashed into Paul's mind: Rasir, a companion from the sietch days.

In the press of the crowd, Paul knew he was completely vulnerable if Rasir planned violence.

The old man pressed close, one hand beneath a sand-grimed

144

robe – grasping the hilt of a crysknife, no doubt. Paul set himself as best he could to resist attack. The old man moved his head towards Paul's ear, whispered: 'We will go with the others.'

It was the signal to identify his guide. Paul nodded.

Rasir drew back, faced the altar.

'She comes from the east,' the acolytes chanted. 'The sun stands at her back. All things are exposed. In the full glare of light – her eyes miss nothing, neither light nor dark.'

A wailing rebaba jarred across the voices, stilled them, receded into silence. With an electric abruptness, the crowd surged forward several meters. They were packed into a tight mass of flesh now, the air heavy with their breathing and the scent of spice.

'Shai-hulud writes on clean sand!' the acolytes shouted.

Paul felt his own breath catch in unison with those around him. A feminine chorus began singing faintly from the shadows behind the shimmering pru-door: 'Alia ... Alia ... Alia ...' It grew louder and louder, fell to a sudden silence.

Again – voices beginning vesper-soft:

> 'She stills all storms –
> Her eyes kill our enemies,
> And torment the unbelievers.
> From the spires of Tuono
> Where dawnlight strikes
> And clear water runs,
> You see her shadow.
> In the shining summer heat
> She serves us bread and milk –
> Cool, fragrant with spices.
> Her eyes melt our enemies,
> Torment our oppressors
> And pierce all mysteries.
> She is Alia ... Alia ... Alia ... Alia ...'

Slowly, the voices trailed off.

Paul felt sickened. *What are we doing?* he asked himself. Alia was a child witch, but she was growing older. And he thought: *Growing older is to grow more wicked.*

The collective mental atmosphere of the temple ate at his psyche. He could sense that element of himself which was one with those all around him, but the differences formed a deadly contradiction. He stood immersed, isolated in a personal sin which he could never expiate. The immensity of the universe outside the temple flooded his awareness. How could one man, one ritual, hope to knit such immensity into a garment fitted to all men?

Paul shuddered.

The universe opposed him at every step. It eluded his grasp, conceived countless disguises to delude him. That universe would never agree with any shape he gave it.

A profound hush spread through the temple.

Alia emerged from the darkness behind the shimmering rainbows. She wore a yellow robe trimmed in Atreides green — yellow for sunlight, green for the death which produced life. Paul experienced the sudden surprising thought that Alia had emerged here just for him, for him alone. He stared across the mob in the temple at his sister. She *was* his sister. He knew her ritual and its roots, but he had never before stood out here with the pilgrims, watched her through their eyes. Here, performing the mystery of this place, he saw that she partook of the universe which opposed him.

Acolytes brought her a golden chalice.

Alia raised the chalice.

With part of his awareness, Paul knew that the chalice contained the unaltered melange, the subtle poison, her sacrament of the oracle.

Her gaze on the chalice, Alia spoke. Her voice caressed the ears, flower sound, flowing and musical:

'In the beginning, we were empty,' she said.

'Ignorant of all things,' the chorus sang.

'We did not know the Power that abides in every place,' Alia said.

'And in every Time,' the chorus sang.

'Here is the Power,' Alia said, raising the chalice slightly.

'It brings us joy,' sang the chorus.

*And it brings us distress*, Paul thought.

'It awakens the soul,' Alia said.

'It dispels all doubts,' the chorus sang.

'In words, we perish,' Alia said.

'In the Power, we survive,' sang the chorus.

Alia put the chalice to her lips, drank.

To his astonishment, Paul found he was holding his breath like the meanest pilgrim of this mob. Despite every shred of personal knowledge about the experience Alia was undergoing, he had been caught in the tao-web. He felt himself remembering how that fiery poison coursed into the body. Memory unfolded the time-stopping when awareness became a mote which changed the poison. He reexperienced the awakening into timelessness where all things were possible. He *knew* Alia's present experience, yet he saw now that he did not know it. Mystery blinded the eyes.

Alia trembled, sank to her knees.

Paul exhaled with the enraptured pilgrims. He nodded. Part of the veil began to lift from him. Absorbed in the bliss of a vision, he had forgotten that each vision belonged to all those who were still on-the-way, still to become. In the vision, one passed through a darkness, unable to distinguish reality from insubstantial accident. One hungered for absolutes which could never be.

Hungering, one lost the present.

Alia swayed with the rapture of spice change.

Paul felt that some transcendental presence spoke to him, saying: 'Look! See there! See what you've ignored?' In that instant, he thought he looked through other eyes, that he saw an imagery and rhythm in this place which no artist or poet could reproduce. It was vital and beautiful, a glaring light that exposed all power-gluttony . . . even his own.

Alia spoke. Her amplified voice boomed across the nave.

'Luminous night,' she cried.

A moan swept like a wave through the crush of pilgrims.

'Nothing hides in such a night!' Alia said. 'What rare light is this darkness? You cannot fix your gaze upon it! Senses cannot record it. No words describe it.' Her voice lowered. 'The abyss remains. It is pregnant with all the things yet to be. Ahhhhh, what gentle violence!'

Paul felt that he waited for some private signal from his sister. It could be any action or word, something of wizardry and mystical processes, an outward streaming that would fit him like an arrow into a cosmic bow. This instant lay like quivering mercury in his awareness.

'There will be sadness,' Alia intoned. 'I remind you that all things are but a beginning, forever beginning. Worlds wait to be conquered. Some within the sound of my voice will attain exalted destinies. You will sneer at the past, forgetting what I tell you now; within all differences there is unity.'

Paul suppressed a cry of disappointment as Alia lowered her head. She had not said the thing he waited to hear. His body felt like a dry shell, a husk abandoned by some desert insect.

Others must feel something similar, he thought. He sensed the restlessness about him. Abruptly, a woman in the mob, someone far down in the nave to Paul's left, cried out, a wordless noise of anguish.

Alia lifted her head and Paul had the giddy sensation that the distance between them collapsed, that he stared directly into her glazed eyes only inches away from her.

'Who summons me?' Alia asked.

'I do,' the woman cried. 'I do, Alia. Oh, Alia, help me. They say my son was killed on Muritan. Is he gone? Will I never see my son again . . . never?'

'You try to walk backward in the sand,' Alia intoned. 'Nothing is lost. Everything returns later, but you may not recognise the changed form that returns.'

'Alia, I don't understand!' the woman wailed.

'You live in the air but you do not see it,' Alia said, sharpness in her voice. 'Are you a lizard? Your voice has the Fremen accent. Does a Fremen try to bring back the dead? What do we need from our dead except their water?'

Down in the center of the nave, a man in a rich red cloak lifted both hands, the sleeves falling to expose white-clad arms. 'Alia,' he shouted, 'I have had a business proposal. Should I accept?'

'You come here like a beggar,' Alia said. 'You look for the golden bowl but you will find only a dagger.'

'I have been asked to kill a man!' a voice shouted from off to the right — a deep voice with sietch tones. 'Should I accept? Accepting, would I succeed?'

'Beginning and end are a single thing,' Alia snapped. 'Have I not told you this before? You didn't come here to ask that question. What is it you cannot believe that you must come here and cry out against it?'

'She's in a fierce mood tonight,' a woman near Paul muttered. 'Have you ever seen her this angry?'

*She knows I'm out here*, Paul thought. *Did she see something in the vision that angered her? Is she raging at me?*

'Alia,' a man directly in front of Paul called. 'Tell these businessmen and faint-hearts how long your brother will rule!'

'I permit you to look around that corner by yourself,' Alia snarled. 'You carry your prejudice in your mouth! It is because my brother rides the worm of chaos that you have roof and water!'

With a fierce gesture, clutching her robe, Alia whirled away, strode through the shimmering ribbons of light, was lost in the darkness behind.

Immediately, the acolytes took up the closing chant, but their rhythm was off. Obviously, they'd been caught by the unexpected ending of the rite. An incoherent mumbling arose on all sides of the crowd. Paul felt the stirring around him – restless, dissatisfied.

'It was that fool with his stupid question about business,' a woman near Paul muttered. 'The hypocrite!'

What had Alia seen? What track through the future?

Something had happened here tonight, souring the rite of the oracle. Usually, the crowd clamored for Alia to answer their pitiful questions. They came as beggars to the oracle, yes. He had heard them thus many times as he'd watched, hidden in the darkness behind the altar. What had been different about this night?

The old Fremen tugged Paul's sleeve, nodded toward the exit. The crowd already was beginning to push in that direction. Paul allowed himself to be pressed along with them, the guide's hand upon his sleeve. There was the feeling in him then that his body had become the manifestation of some power he could no longer control. He had become a non-being, a stillness which moved itself. At the core of the non-being, there he existed, allowing himself to be led through the streets of his city, following a track so familiar to his visions that it froze his heart with grief.

*I should know what Alia saw*, he thought. *I have seen it enough times myself. And she didn't cry out against it . . . she saw the alternatives, too.*

*Production growth and income growth must not get out of step in my Empire. That is the substance of my command. There are to be no balance-of-payment difficulties between the different spheres of influence. And the reason for this is simply because I command it. I want to emphasise my authority in this area. I am the supreme energy-eater of this domain, and will remain so, alive or dead. My Government is the economy.*

– Order in Council
The Emperor Paul Muad'dib

'I will leave you here,' the old man said, taking his hand from Paul's sleeve. 'It is on the right, second door from the far end. Go with Shai-hulud, Muad'dib . . . and remember when you were Usul.'

Paul's guide slipped away into the darkness.

There would be Security men somewhere out there waiting to grab the guide and take the man to a place of questioning. Paul knew. But Paul found himself hoping the old Fremen would escape.

There were stars overhead and the distant light of First Moon somewhere beyond the Shield Wall. But this place was not the open desert where a man could sight on a star to guide his course. The old man had brought him into one of the new suburbs; this much Paul recognised.

This street now was thick with sand blown in from encroaching dunes. A dim light glowed from a single public suspensor globe far down the street. It gave enough illumination to show that this was a dead-end street.

The air around him was thick with the smell of a reclamation still. The thing must be poorly capped for its fetid odors to escape, loosing a dangerously wasteful amount of moisture into the night air. How careless his people had grown, Paul thought. They were millionaires of water – forgetful of the days when a man on Arrakis could have been killed for just an eighth share of the water in his body.

*Why am I hesitating?* Paul wondered. *It is the second door from the far end. I knew that without being told. But this thing must be played out with precision. So . . . I hesitate.*

The noise of an argument arose suddenly from the corner house on Paul's left. A woman there berated someone: the new wing of their house leaked dust, she complained. Did he think water fell from heaven? If dust came in, moisture got out.

*Some remember*, Paul thought.

He moved down the street and the quarrel faded away behind.

*Water from heaven!* he thought.

Some Fremen had seen that wonder on other worlds. He had seen it himself, had ordered it for Arrakis, but the memory of it felt like something that had occurred to another person. Rain, it was called. Abruptly, he recalled a rainstorm on his birthworld – clouds thick and gray in the sky of Caladan, an electric storm presence, moist air, the big wet drops drumming on skylights. It ran in rivulets off the eaves. Storm drains took the water away to a river which ran muddy and turgid past the Family orchards . . . trees there with their barren branches glistening wetly.

Paul's foot caught in a low drift of sand across the street. For an instant, he felt mud clinging to the shoes of his childhood. Then he was back in the sand, in the dust-clotted, wind-muffled darkness with the Future hanging over him, taunting. He could feel the aridity of life around him like an accusation. *You did this!* They'd become a civilisation of dry-eyed watchers and tale-tellers, people who solved all problems with power . . . and more power . . . and still more power – hating every erg of it.

Rough stones came underfoot. His vision remembered them. The dark rectangle of a doorway appeared on his right – black in black: Otheym's house, Fate's house, a place different from the ones around it only in the role Time had chosen for it. It was a strange place to be marked down in history.

The door opened to his knock. The gap revealed the dull green light of an atrium. A dwarf peered out, ancient face on a child's body, an apparition prescience had never seen.

'You've come then,' the apparition said. The dwarf stepped aside, no awe in his manner, merely the gloating of a slow smile. 'Come in! Come in!'

Paul hesitated. There'd been no dwarf in the vision, but all else remained identical. Visions could contain such disparities and still hold true to their original plunge into infinity. But the difference dared him to hope. He glanced back up the street at the creamy pearl glistening of his moon swimming out of jagged shadows. The moon haunted him. How did it fall?

'Come in,' the dwarf insisted.

Paul entered, heard the door thud into its moisture seals behind. The dwarf passed him, led the way, enormous feet slapping the floor, opened the delicate lattice gate into the roofed central courtyard, gestured. 'They await, Sire.'

*Sire*, Paul thought. *He knows me, then.*

Before Paul could explore this discovery, the dwarf slipped away down a side passage. Hope was a dervish wind whirling, dancing in Paul. He headed across the courtyard. It was a dark and gloomy place, the smell of sickness and defeat in it. He felt daunted by the atmosphere. Was it defeat to choose a lesser evil? he wondered. How far down this track had he come?

Light poured from a narrow doorway in the far wall. He put down the feeling of watchers and evil smells, entered the doorway into a small room. It was a barren place by Fremen standards with heireg hangings on only two walls. Opposite the door, a man sat on carmine cushions beneath the best hanging. A feminine figure hovered in shadows behind another doorway in a barren wall to the left.

Paul felt vision-trapped. This was the way it'd gone. Where was the dwarf? Where was the difference?

His senses absorbed the room in a single gestalten sweep. The place had received painstaking care despite its poor furnishings. Hooks and rods across the barren walls showed where hangings had been removed. Pilgrims paid enormous prices for authentic Fremen artifacts, Paul reminded himself. Rich pilgrims counted desert tapestries as treasures, true marks of a hajj.

Paul felt that the barren walls accused him with their fresh gypsum wash. The threadbare condition of the two remaining hangings amplified the sense of guilt.

A narrow shelf occupied the wall on his right. It held a row of portraits – mostly bearded Fremen, some in stillsuits with their catchtubes dangling, some in Imperial uniforms posed against exotic offworld backgrounds. The most common scene was a seascape.

The Fremen on the cushions cleared his throat, forcing Paul to look at him. It was Otheym precisely as the vision had revealed him: neck grown scrawny, a bird thing which appeared too weak to support the large head. The face was a lopsided ruin – networks of crisscrossed scars on the left cheek below a drooping, wet eye, but clear skin on the other side and a straight, blue-in-blue Fremen gaze. A long kedge of a nose bisected the face.

Otheym's cushion sat in the center of a threadbare rug, brown with maroon and gold threads. The cushion fabric betrayed splotches of wear and patching, but every bit of metal around the seated figure shone from polishing – the portrait frames, shelf lip and brackets, the pedestal of a low table on the right.

Paul nodded to the clear half of Otheym's face, said: 'Good luck to you and your dwelling place.' It was the greeting of an old friend and sietch mate.

'So I see you once more, Usul.'

The voice speaking his tribal name whined with an old man's quavering. The dull drooping eye on the ruined side of the face moved above the parchment skin and scars. Gray bristles stubbed that side and the jawline there hung with scabrous peelings. Otheym's mouth twisted as he spoke, the gap exposing silvery metal teeth.

'Muad'dib always answers the call of a Fedaykin,' Paul said.

The woman in the doorway shadows moved, said: 'So Stilgar boasts.'

She came forward into the light, an older version of the Lichna which the Face Dancer had copied. Paul recalled then that Otheym had married sisters. Her hair was gray, nose grown witch-sharp. Weavers' calluses ran along her forefingers and thumbs. A Fremen woman would've displayed such marks proudly in the sietch days, but she saw his attention on her hands, hid them under a fold of her pale blue robe.

Paul remembered her name then – Dhuri. The shock was he remembered her as a child, not as she'd been in his vision of these moments. It was the whine that edged her voice, Paul told himself. She'd whined even as a child.

'You see me here,' Paul said. 'Would I be here if Stilgar hadn't approved ? He turned toward Otheym. 'I carry your water burden, Otheym. Command me.'

This was the straight Fremen talk of sietch brothers.

Otheym produced a shaky nod, almost too much for that thin neck. He lifted a liver-marked left hand, pointed to the ruin of his face. 'I caught the splitting disease on Tarahell, Usul,' he wheezed. 'Right after the victory when we'd all . . . ' A fit of coughing stopped his voice.

'The tribe will collect his water soon,' Dhuri said. She crossed to Otheym, propped pillows behind him, held his shoulder to steady him until the coughing passed. She wasn't really very old, Paul saw, but a look of lost hopes ringed her mouth, bitterness lay in her eyes.

'I'll summon doctors,' Paul said.

Dhuri turned, hand on hip. 'We've had medical men, as good as any you could summon.' She sent an involuntary glance to the barren wall on her left.

*And the medical men were costly*, Paul thought.

He felt edgy, constrained by the vision but aware that minor differences had crept in. How could he exploit the differences ? Time came out of its skein with subtle changes, but the background fabric held oppressive sameness. He knew with terrifying certainty that if he tried to break out of the enclosing pattern here, It'd become a thing of terrible violence. The power in this deceptively gentle flow of Time oppressed him.

'Say what you want of me,' he growled.

'Couldn't it be that Otheym needed a friend to stand by him in this time ?' Dhuri asked. 'Does a Fedaykin have to consign his flesh to strangers ?'

*We shared Sietch Tabr*, Paul reminded himself. *She has the right to berate me for apparent callousness.*

'What I can do I will do,' Paul said.

Another fit of coughing shook Otheym. When it had passed, he gasped: 'There's treachery, Usul. Fremen plot against you.' His mouth worked then without sound. Spittle escaped his lips. Dhuri wiped his mouth with a corner of her robe, and Paul saw how her face betrayed anger at such waste of moisture.

Frustrated rage threatened to overwhelm Paul then. *That Otheymn should be spent thus ! A Fedaykin deserved better.* But no choice remained – not for a Death Commando or his Emperor. They walked occam's razor in this room. The slightest misstep multiplied horrors – not just for themselves, but for all human-kind, even for those who would destroy them.

Paul squeezed calmness into his mind, looked at Dhuri. The expression of terrible longing with which she gazed at Otheym strengthened Paul. *Chani must never look at me that way,* he told himself.

'Lichna spoke of a message,' Paul said.

'My dwarf,' Otheym wheezed. 'I bought him on . . . on . . . on a world . . . I forget. He's a human distrans, a toy discarded by the Tleilaxu. He's recorded all the names . . . the traitors . . .'

Otheym fell silent, trembling.

'You speak of Lichna,' Dhuir said. 'When you arrived, we knew she'd reached you safely. If you're thinking of this new burden Otheym places upon you, Lichna is the sum of that burden. An even exchange, Usul: take the dwarf and go.'

Paul suppressed a shudder, closed his eyes. *Lichna !* The real daughter had perished in the desert, a semuta-wracked body abandoned to the sand and the wind.

Opening his eyes, Paul said: 'You could've come to me at any time for . . .'

'Otheym stayed away that he might be numbered among those who hate you, Usul,' Dhuri said. 'The house to the south of us at the end of the street, that is a gathering place for your foes. It's why we took this hovel.'

'Then summon the dwarf and we'll leave,' Paul said.

'You've not listened well,' Dhuri said.

'You must take the dwarf to a safe place,' Otheym said, an odd strength in his voice. 'He carries the only record of the traitors. No one suspects his talent. They think I keep him for amuse-ment.'

'We cannot leave,' Dhuri said. 'Only you and the dwarf. It's known . . . how poor we are. We've said we're selling the dwarf. They'll take you for the buyer. It's your only chance.'

Paul consulted his memory of the vision: in it, he'd left here with names of the traitors, but never seeing how those names were carried. The dwarf obviously moved under the protection of another oracle. It occurred to Paul then that all creatures must carry some kind of destiny stamped out by purposes of varying strengths, by the fixation of training and disposition. From the moment the Jihad had chosen him, he'd felt himself hemmed in by the forces of a multitude. Their fixed purposes demanded and controlled his course. Any delusions of Free Will he harbored now must be merely the prisoner rattling his cage. His curse lay in the fact that he *saw* the cage. He *saw* it?

He listened now to the emptiness of this house: only the four of them in it – Dhuri, Otheym, the dwarf and himself. He inhaled the fear and tension of his companions, sensed the watchers – his own force hovering in 'thopters far overhead ... and those others ... next door.

*I was wrong to hope*, Paul thought. But thinking of hope brought him a twisted *sense* of hope, and he felt that he might yet seize his moment.

'Summon the dwarf,' he said.

'Bijaz!' Dhuri called.

'You call me?' The dwarf stepped into the room from the courtyard, an alert expression of worry on his face.

'You have a new master, Bijaz,' Dhuri said. She stared at Paul. 'You may call him ... Usul.'

'Usul, that's the base of the pillar,' Bijaz said, translating. 'How can Usul be base when I'm the basest thing living?'

'He always speaks thus,' Otheym apologised.

'I don't speak,' Bijaz said. 'I operate a machine called language. It creaks and groans, but is mine own.'

*A Tleilaxu toy, learned and alert*, Paul thought. *The Bene Tleilax never threw away something this valuable.* He turned, studied the dwarf. Round melange eyes returned his stare.

'What other talents have you, Bijaz?' Paul asked.

'I know when we should leave,' Bijaz said. 'It's a talent few men have. There's a time for endings – and that's a good beginning. Let us begin to go, Usul.'

Paul examined his vision memory: no dwarf, but the little man's words fitted the occasion.

'At the door, you called me Sire,' Paul said. 'You know me, then?'

'You've sired, Sire,' Bijaz said, grinning. 'You are much more than the base Usul. You're the Atreides Emperor, Paul Muad'dib. And you are my finger.' He held up the index finger of his right hand.

'Bijaz!' Dhuri snapped. 'You tempt fate.'

'I tempt my finger,' Bijaz protested, voice squeaking. He pointed at Usul. 'I point at Usul. Is my finger not Usul himself? Or is it a reflection of something more base?' He brought the finger close to his eyes, examined it with a mocking grin, first one side then the other. 'Ahhh, it's merely a finger, after all.'

'He often rattles on thus,' Dhuri said, worry in her voice. 'I think it's why he was discarded by the Tleilaxu.'

'I'll not be patronised,' Bijaz said, 'yet I have a new patron. How strange the workings of the finger.' He peered at Dhuri and Otheym, eyes oddly bright. 'A weak glue bound us, Otheym. A few tears and we part.' The dwarf's big feet rasped on the floor as he whirled completely around, stopped facing Paul. 'Ahhh, patron! I came the long way around to find you.'

Paul nodded.

'You'll be kind, Usul?' Bijaz asked. 'I'm a person, you know. Persons come in many shapes and sizes. This be but one of them. I'm weak of muscle, but strong of mouth; cheap to feed, but costly to fill. Empty me as you will, there's still more in me than men put there.'

'We've no time for your stupid riddles,' Dhuri growled. 'You should be gone.'

'I'm riddled with conundrums,' Bijaz said, 'but not all of them stupid. To be gone, Usul, is to be a bygone. Yes? Let us let bygones be bygones. Dhuri speaks truth, and I've the talent for hearing that, too.'

'You've truthsense?' Paul asked, determined now to wait out the clockwork of his vision. Anything was better than shattering these moments and producing the new consequences. There remained things for Otheym to say lest Time be diverted into even more horrifying channels.

'I've *now*-sense,' Bijaz said.

Paul noted that the dwarf had grown more nervous. Was the little man aware of things about to happen? Could Bijaz be his own oracle?

'Did you inquire of Lichna?' Otheym asked suddenly, peering up at Dhuri with his one good eye.

'Lichna is safe,' Dhuri said.

Paul lowered his head, lest his expression betray the lie. *Safe!* Lichna was ashes in a secret grave.

'That's good then,' Otheym said, taking Paul's lowered head for a nod of agreement. 'One good thing among the evils, Usul. I don't like the world we're making, you know that? It was better when we were alone in the desert with only the Harkonnens for enemy.'

'There's but a thin line between many an enemy and many a

friend,' Bijaz said. 'Where that line stops, there's no beginning and no end. Let's end it, my friends.' He moved to Paul's side, jittered from one foot to the other.

'What's *now*-sense ?' Paul asked, dragging out these moments, goading the dwarf.

'Now!' Bijaz said, trembling. 'Now! Now!' He tugged at Paul's robe. 'Let us go now!'

'His mouth rattles, but there's no harm in him.' Otheym said, affection in his voice, the one good eye staring at Bijaz.

'Even a rattle can signal departure,' Bijaz said. 'And so can tears. Let's be gone while there's time to begin.'

'Bijaz, what do you fear ?' Paul asked.

'I fear the spirit seeking me now,' Bijaz muttered. Perspiration stood out on his forehead. His cheeks twitched. 'I fear the one who thinks not and will have no body except mine – and that one gone back into itself! I fear the things I see and the things I do not see.'

*This dwarf does possess the power of prescience*, Paul thought. Bijaz shared the terrifying oracle. Did he share the oracle's fate, as well ? How potent was the dwarf's power ? Did he have the little prescience of those who dabbled in the Dune Tarot ? Or was it something greater ? How much had he seen ?

'Best you go,' Dhuri said. 'Bijaz is right.'

'Every minute we linger,' Bijaz said, 'prolongs . . . prolongs the present!'

*Every minute I linger defers my guilt*, Paul thought. A worm's poisonous breath, its teeth dripping dust, had washed over him. It had happened long ago, but he inhaled the memory of it now – spice and bitterness. He could sense his own worm waiting – 'the urn of the desert.'

'These are troubled times,' he said, addressing himself to Otheym's judgement of their world.

'Fremen know what to do in time of trouble,' Dhuri said.

Otheym contributed a shaky nod.

Paul glanced at Dhuri. He'd not expected gratitude, would have been burdened by it more than he could bear, but Otheym's bitterness and the passionate resentment he saw in Dhuri's eyes shook his resolve. Was *anything* worth this price ?

'Delay serves no purpose,' Dhuri said.

'Do what you must, Usul,' Otheym wheezed.

Paul sighed. The words of the vision had been spoken. 'There'll be an accounting,' he said to complete it. Turning, he strode from the room, heard Bijaz foot-slapping behind.

'Bygones, bygones,' Bijaz muttered as they went. 'Let bygones fall where they may. This has been a dirty day.'

*The convoluted wording of legalisms grew up around the
necessity to hide from ourselves the violence we intend toward
each other. Between depriving a man of one hour from his life
and depriving him of his life there exists only a difference of
degree. You have done violence to him, consumed his energy.
Elaborate euphemisms may conceal your intent to kill, but
behind any use of power over another the ultimate assumption
remains: 'I feed on your energy.'*

> — Addenda to Orders in Council
> The Emperor Paul Muad'dib

First Moon stood high over the city as Paul, his shield activated
and shimmering around him, emerged from the cul-de-sac. A
wind off the massif whirled sand and dust down the narrow
street, causing Bijaz to blink and shield his eyes.

'We must hurry,' the dwarf muttered. 'Hurry! Hurry!'

'You sense danger?' Paul asked, probing.

'I *know* danger!'

An abrupt sense of peril very near was followed almost immediately by a figure joining them out of a doorway.

Bijaz crouched and whimpered.

It was only Stilgar moving like a war machine, head thrust
forward, feet striking the street solidly.

Swiftly, Paul explained the value of the dwarf, handed Bijaz
over to Stilgar. The pace of the vision moved here with great
rapidity. Stilgar sped away with Bijaz. Security Guards enveloped

Paul. Orders were given to send men down the street toward the house beyond Otheym's. The men hurried to obey, shadows among shadows.

*More sacrifices*, Paul thought.

'We want live prisoners,' one of the guard officers hissed.

The sound was a vision-echo in Paul's ears. It went with solid precision here – vision/reality, tick for tick. Ornithopters drifted down across the moon.

The night was full of Imperial troopers attacking.

A soft hiss grew out of the other sounds, climbed to a roar while they still heard the sibilance. It picked up a terra-cotta glow that hid the stars, engulfed the moon.

Paul, knowing that sound and glow from the earliest nightmare glimpses of his vision, felt an odd sense of fulfillment. It went the way it must.

'Stone burner!' someone screamed.

'Stone burner!' The cry was all around him. 'Stone burner ... stone burner ...'

Because it was required of him, Paul threw a protective arm across his face, dove for the low lip of a curb. It already was too late, of course.

Where Otheym's house had been there stood now a pillar of fire, a blinding jet roaring at the heavens. It gave off a dirty brilliance which threw into sharp relief every ballet movement of the fighting and fleeing men, the tipping retreat of ornithopters.

For every member of this frantic throng it was too late.

The ground grew hot beneath Paul. He heard the sound of running stop. Men threw themselves down all around him, every one of them aware that there was no point in running. The first damage had been done; and now they must wait out the extent of the stone burner's potency. The thing's radiation, which no man could outrun, already had penetrated their flesh. The peculiar result of stone-burner radiation already was at work in them. What else this weapon might do now lay in the planning of the men who had used it, the men who had defied the Great Convention to use it.

'Gods ... a stone burner,' someone whimpered. 'I ... don't ... want ... to ... be ... blind.'

'Who does ?' The harsh voice of a trooper far down the street.

'The Tleilaxu will sell many eyes here,' someone near Paul growled. 'Now, shut up and wait!'

They waited.

Paul remained silent, thinking what this weapon implied. Too much fuel in it and it'd cut its way into the planet's core. Dune's molten level lay deep, but the more dangerous for that. Such pressures released and out of control might split a planet, scattering lifeless bits and pieces through space.

'I think it's dying down a bit,' someone said.

'It's just digging deeper,' Paul cautioned. 'Stay put, all of you. Stilgar will be sending help.'

'Stilgar got away?'

'Stilgar got away.'

'The ground's hot,' someone complained.

'They dared use atomics!' a trooper near Paul protested.

'The sound's diminishing,' someone down the street said.

Paul ignored the words, concentrated on his fingertips against the street. He could feel the rolling-rumbling of the thing – deep ... deep ...

'My eyes!' someone cried. 'I can't see!'

*Someone closer to it than I was,* Paul thought. He still could see to the end of the cul-de-sac when he lifted his head, although there was a mistiness across the scene. A red-yellow glow filled the area where Otheym's house and its neighbor had been. Pieces of adjoining buildings made dark patterns as they crumbled into the glowing pit.

Paul climbed to his feet. He felt the stone burner die, silence beneath him. His body was wet with perspiration against the stillsuit's slickness – too much for the suit to accommodate. The air he drew into his lungs carried the heat and sulfur stench of the burner.

As he looked at the troopers beginning to stand up around him, the mist on Paul's eyes faded into darkness. He summoned up his oracular vision of these moments, then, turned and strode along the track that Time had carved for him, fitting himself into the vision so tightly that it could not escape. He felt himself grow aware of this place as a multitudinous possession, reality welded to prediction.

Moans and groans of his troopers arose all around him as the men realised their blindness.

'Hold fast!' Paul shouted. 'Help is coming!' And, as the complaints persisted, he said: 'This is Muad'dib! I command you to hold fast! Help comes!'

Silence.

Then, true to his vision, a nearby guardsman said: 'Is it truly the Emperor? Which of you can see? Tell me.'

'None of us has eyes,' Paul said. 'They have taken my eyes, as well, but not my vision. I can *see* you standing there, a dirty wall within touching distance on your left. Now wait bravely. Stilgar comes with our friends.'

The thwock-thwock of many 'thopters grew louder all around There was the sound of hurrying feet. Paul *watched* his friends come, matching their sounds to his oracular vision.

'Stilgar!' Paul shouted, waving an arm. 'Over here!'

'Thanks to Shai-hulud,' Stilgar cried, running up to Paul. 'You're not . . . ' In the sudden silence, Paul's vision showed him Stilgar staring with an expression of agony at the ruined eyes of his friend and Emperor. 'Oh, m'Lord,' Stilgar groaned. 'Usul . . . Usul . . . Usul . . . '

'What of the stone burner?' one of the newcomers shouted.

'It's ended,' Paul said, raising his voice. He gestured. 'Get up there now and rescue the ones who were closest to it. Put up barriers. Lively now!' He turned back to Stilgar.

'Do you *see*, m'Lord?' Stilgar asked, wonder in his tone. 'How can you see?'

'For answer, Paul put a finger out to touch Stilgar's cheek above the stillsuit mouthcap, felt tears. 'You need give no moisture to me, old friend,' Paul said. 'I am not dead.'

'But your eyes!'

'They've blinded my body, but not my vision,' Paul said. 'Ah, Stil, I live in an apocalyptic dream. My steps fit into it so precisely that I fear most of all I will grow bored reliving the thing so exactly.'

'Usul, I don't, I don't . . . '

'Don't try to understand it. Accept it. I am in the world beyond this world here. For me, they are the same. I need no hand to guide me. I see every movement all around me. I see every expression on your face. I have no eyes, yet I see.'

Stilgar shook his head sharply. 'Sire, we must conceal your affliction from –'

'We hide it from no man,' Paul said.

'But the law . . . '

'We live by the Atreides Law now, Stil. The Fremen Law that the blind should be abandoned in the desert applies only to the blind. I am not blind. I live in the cycle of being where the war of good and evil has its arena. We are at a turning point in the succession of ages and we have our parts to play.'

In a sudden stillness, Paul heard one of the wounded being led past him. 'It was terrible,' the man groaned, 'a great fury of fire.'

'None of these men shall be taken into the desert,' Paul said. 'You hear me, Stil?'

'I hear you, m'Lord.'

'They are to be fitted with new eyes at my expense.'

'It will be done, m'Lord.'

Paul, hearing the awe grow in Stilgar's voice, said: 'I will be at the Command 'thopter. Take charge here.'

'Yes, m'Lord.'

Paul stepped around Stilgar, strode down the street. His vision told him every movement, every irregularity beneath his feet, every face he encountered. He gave orders as he moved, pointing to men of his personal entourage, calling out names, summoning to himself the ones who represented the intimate apparatus of government. He could feel the terror grow behind him, the fearful whispers.

'His eyes!'

'But he looked right at you, called you by name!'

At the Command 'thopter, he deactivated his personal shield, reached into the machine and took the microphone from the hand of a startled communications officer, issued a swift string of orders, thrust the microphone back into the officer's hand. Turning, Paul summoned the weapons specialist, one of the eager and brilliant new breed who remembered sietch life only dimly.

'They used a stone burner,' Paul said.

After the briefest pause, the man said: 'So I was told, Sire.'

'You know what that means, of course.'

'The fuel could only have been atomic.'

Paul nodded, thinking of how this man's mind must be racing. Atomics. The Great Convention prohibited such weapons. Discovery of the perpetrator would bring down the combined retributive assault of the Great Houses. Old feuds would be forgotten, discarded in the face of this threat and the ancient fears it aroused.

'It cannot have been manufactured without leaving some traces,' Paul said. 'You will assemble the proper equipment and search out the place where the stone burner was made.'

'At once, Sire,' With one last fearful glance, the man sped away.

'M'Lord,' the communications officer ventured from behind him. 'Your eyes...'

Paul turned, reached into the 'thopter, returned the command set to his personal band. 'Call Chani,' he ordered. 'Tell her . . . tell her I am alive and will be with her soon.'

*Now the forces gather*, Paul thought. And he noted how strong was the smell of fear in the perspiration all around.

*He has gone from Alia,*
*The womb of heaven!*
*Holy, holy, holy!*
*Fire-sand leagues*
*Confront our Lord.*
*He can see*
*Without eyes!*
*A demon upon him!*
*Holy, holy, holy*
*Equation:*
*He solved for*
*Martyrdom!*

– The Moon Falls Down
Songs of Muad'dib

After seven days of radiating fevered activity, the Keep took on an unnatural quiet. On this morning, there were people about, but they spoke in whispers, heads close together, and they walked softly. Some scurried with an oddly furtive gait. The sight of a guard detail coming in from the forecourt drew questioning looks and frowns at the noise which the newcomers brought with their tramping about and stacking of weapons. The newcomers caught the mood of the interior, though, and began moving in that furtive way.

Talk of the stone burner still floated around: 'He said the fire had blue-green in it and a smell out of hell.'

166

'Elpa is a fool! He says he'll commit suicide rather than take Tleilaxu eyes.'

'I don't like talk of eyes.'

'Muad'dib passed me and called me by name!'

'How does *He* see without eyes?'

'People are leaving, had you heard? There's great fear. The Naibs say they'll go to Sietch Makab for a Grand Council.'

'What've they done with the Panegyrist?'

'I saw them take him into the chamber where the Naibs are meeting. Imagine Korba a prisoner!'

Chani had arisen early, awakened by a stillness in the Keep. Awakening, she'd found Paul sitting up beside her, his eyeless sockets aimed at some formless place beyond the far wall of their bedchamber. What the stone burner had done with its peculiar affinity for eye tissue, all that ruined flesh had been removed. Injections and unguents had saved the stronger flesh around the sockets, but she felt that the radiation had gone deeper.

Ravenous hunger seized her as she sat up. She fed on the food kept by the bedside – spicebread, a heavy cheese.

Paul gestured at the food. 'Beloved, there was no way to spare you this. Believe me.'

Chani stilled a fit of trembling when he aimed those empty sockets at her. She'd given up asking him to explain. He spoke so oddly: '*I was baptised in sand and it cost me the knack of believing. Who trades in faiths anymore? Who'll buy? Who'll sell?*'

What could he mean by such words?

He refused even to consider Tleilaxu eyes, although he bought them with a lavish hand for the men who'd shared his affliction.

Hunger satisfied, Chani slipped from bed, glanced back at Paul, noted his tiredness. Grim lines framed his mouth. The dark hair stood up, mussed from a sleep that hadn't healed. He appeared so saturnine and remote. The back and forth of waking and sleeping did nothing to change this. She forced herself to turn away, whispered: 'My love ... my love ...'

He leaned over, pulled her back into the bed, kissed her cheeks. 'Soon we'll go back to our desert,' he whispered. 'Only a few things remain to be done here.'

She trembled at the finality of his voice.

He tightened his arms around her, murmured: 'Don't fear me, my Sihaya. Forget mystery and accept love. There's no mystery about love. It comes from life. Can't you feel that?'

'Yes.'

She put a palm against his chest, counting his heartbeats. His love cried out to the Fremen spirit in her – torrential, outpouring, savage. A magnetic power enveloped her.

'I promise you a thing, beloved,' he said. 'A child of ours will rule such an empire that mine will fade in comparison. Such achievements of living and art and sublime –'

'We're here now!' she protested, fighting a dry sob. 'And . . . I feel we have so little . . . time.'

'We have eternity, beloved.'

'*You* may have eternity. I have only now.'

'But this *is* eternity.' He stroked her forehead.

She pressed against him, lips on his neck. The pressure agitated the life in her womb. She felt it stir.

Paul felt it, too. He put a hand on her abdomen, said: 'Ahh, little ruler of the universe, wait your time. This moment is mine.'

She wondered then why he always spoke of the life within her as singular. Hadn't the medics told him? She searched back in her own memory, curious that the subject had never arisen between them. Surely, he must know she carried twins. She hesitated on the point of raising this question. He *must* know. He knew everything. He knew all the things that were herself. His hands, his mouth – all of him knew her.

Presently, she said: 'Yes, love. This is forever . . . this is real.' And she closed her eyes tightly lest sight of his dark sockets stretched her soul from paradise to hell. No matter the *rihani* magic in which he'd enciphered their lives, his flesh remained real, his caresses could not be denied.

When they arose to dress for the day, she said: 'If the people only knew your love . . .'

But his mood had changed. 'You can't build politics on love,' he said. 'People aren't concerned with love; it's too disordered. They prefer despotism. Too much freedom breeds chaos. We can't have that, can we? And how do you make despotism lovable?'

'You're not a despot!' she protested, tying her scarf. 'Your laws are just.'

'Ahh. laws,' he said. He crossed to the window, pulled back the draperies as though he could look out. 'What's law? Control? Law filters chaos and what drips through? Serenity? Law – our highest ideal and our basest nature. Don't look too closely at the law. Do, and you'll find the rationalised interpretations, the legal casuistry, the precedents of convenience. You'll find the serenity, which is just another word for death.'

Chani's mouth drew into a tight line. She couldn't deny his wisdom and sagacity, but these moods frightened her. He turned upon himself and she sensed internal wars. It was as though he took the Fremen maxim, *'Never to forgive – never to forget,'* and whipped his own flesh with it.

She crossed to his side, stared past him at an angle. The growing heat of the day had begun pulling the north wind out of these protected latitudes. The wind painted a false sky full of ochre plumes and sheets of crystal, strange designs in rushing gold and red. High and cold, the wind broke against the Shield Wall with fountains of dust.

Paul felt Chani's warmth beside him. Momentarily, he lowered a curtain of forgetfulness across his vision. He might just be standing here with his eyes closed. Time refused to stand still for him, though. He inhaled darkness – starless, tearless. His affliction dissolved substance until all that remained was astonishment at the way sounds condensed his universe. Everything around him leaned on his lonely sense of hearing, falling back only when he touched objects: the drapery, Chani's hand . . . He caught himself listening for Chani's breaths.

Where was the insecurity of things that were only probable? he asked himself. His mind carried such a burden of mutilated memories. For every instant of reality there existed countless projections, things fated never to be. An invisible self within him remembered the false pasts, their burden threatening at times to overwhelm the present.

Chani leaned against his arm.

He felt his body through her touch: dead flesh carried by time eddies. He reeked of memories that had glimpsed eternity. To see eternity was to be exposed to eternity's whims, oppressed by endless dimensions. The oracle's false immortality demanded retribution: Past and Future became simultaneous.

Once more, the vision arose from its black pit, locked onto him. It was his eyes. It moved his muscles. It guided him into the next moment, the next hour, the next day . . . until he felt himself to be always *there!*

'It's time we were going,' Chani said. 'The Council . . .'

'Alia will be there to stand in my place.'

'Does she know what to do?'

'She knows.'

Alia's day began with a guard squadron swarming into the parade yard below her quarters. She stared down at a scene of frantic confusion, clamorous and intimidating babble. The scene became intelligible only when she recognised the prisoner they'd brought: Korba, the Panegyrist.

She made her morning toilet, moving occasionally to the window, keeping watch on the progress of impatience down there. Her gaze kept straying to Korba. She tried to remember him as the rough and bearded commander of the third wave in the battle of Arrakeen. It was impossible. Korba had become an immaculate fop dressed now in a Parato silk robe of exquisite cut. It lay open to the waist, revealing a beautifully laundered ruff and embroidered undercoat set with green gems. A purple belt gathered the waist. The sleeves poking through the robe's armhole slits had been tailored into rivulet ridges of dark green and black velvet.

A few Naibs had come out to observe the treatment accorded a fellow Fremen. They'd brought on the clamor, exciting Korba to protest his innocence. Alia moved her gaze across the Fremen faces, trying to recapture memories of the original men. The present blotted out the past. They'd all become hedonists, samplers of pleasures most men couldn't even imagine.

Their uneasy glances, she saw, strayed often to the doorway into the chamber where they would meet. They were thinking o Muad'dib's blind-sight, a new manifestation of mysterious powers. By their law, a blind man should be abandoned in the desert, his water given up to Shai-hulud. But eyeless Muad'dib saw them. They disliked buildings, too, and felt vulnerable in space built above the ground. Give them a proper cave cut from rock, then they could relax – but not here, not with this new Muad'dib waiting *inside*.

As she turned to go down to the meeting, she saw the letter where she'd left it on a table by the door: the latest message from their mother. Despite the special reverence held for Caladan as the place of Paul's birth, the Lady Jessica had emphasised her refusal to make her planet a stop on the hajj.

'No doubt my son is an epochal figure of history,' she'd written, 'but I cannot see this as an excuse for submitting to a rabble invasion.'

Alia touched the letter, experienced an odd sensation of mutual contact. This paper had been in her mother's hands. Such an archaic device, the letter – but personal in a way no recording could achieve. Written in the Atreides Battle Tongue, it represented an almost invulnerable privacy of communication.

Thinking of her mother afflicted Alia with the usual inward burning. The spice change that had mixed the psyches of mother and daughter forced her at times to think of Paul as a son to whom she had given birth. The capsule-complex of oneness could present her own father as a lover. Ghost shadows cavorted in her mind, people of possibility.

Alia reviewed the letter as she walked down the ramp to the antechamber where her guard amazons waited.

'You produce a deadly paradox,' Jessica had written. 'Government cannot be religious and self-assertive at the same time. Religious experience needs a spontaneity which laws inevitably suppress. And you cannot govern without laws. Your laws eventually must replace morality, replace conscience, replace even the religion by which you think to govern. Sacred ritual must spring from praise and holy yearnings which hammer out a significant morality. Government, on the other hand, is a cultural organism particularly attractive to doubts, questions and contentions. I see the day coming when ceremony must take the place of faith and symbolism replaces morality.'

The smell of spice-coffee greeted Alia in the antechamber. Four guard amazons in green watchrobes came to attention as she entered. They fell into step behind her, striding firmly in the bravado of their youth, eyes alert for trouble. They had zealot faces untouched by awe. They radiated that special Fremen quality of violence: they could kill casually with no sense of guilt.

*In this, I am different,* Alia thought. *The Atreides name has enough dirt on it without that.*

Word preceded her. A waiting page darted off as she entered the lower hall, running to summon the full guard detail. The hall stretched out windowless and gloomy, illuminated only by a few subdued glowglobes. Abruptly, the doors to the parade yard opened wide at the far end to admit a glaring shaft of daylight. The guard with Korba in their midst wavered into view from the outside with the light behind them.

'Where is Stilgar?' Alia demanded.

'Already inside,' one of her amazons said.

Alia led the way into the chamber. It was one of the Keep's more pretentious meeting places. A high balcony with rows of soft seats occupied one side. Across from the balcony, orange draperies had been pulled back from tall windows. Bright sunlight poured through from an open space with a garden and a fountain. At the rear end of the chamber on her right stood a dais with a single massive chair.

Moving to the chair, Alia glanced back and up, saw the gallery filled with Naibs.

Household guardsmen packed the open space beneath the gallery, Stilgar moving among them with a quiet word here, a command there. He gave no sign that he'd seen Alia enter.

Korba was brought in, seated at a low table with cushions beside it on the chamber floor below the dais. Despite his finery, the Panegyrist gave the appearance now of a surly, sleepy old man huddled up in his robes as against the outer cold. Two guardsmen took up positions behind him.

Stilgar approached the dais as Alia seated herself.

'Where is Muad'dib?' he asked.

'My brother has delegated me to preside as Reverend Mother,' Alia said.

Hearing this, the Naibs in the gallery began raising their voices in protest.

'Silence!' Alia commanded. In the abrupt quiet, she said: 'Is it not Fremen law that a Reverend Mother presides when life and death are at issue?'

As the gravity of her statement penetrated, stillness came over the Naibs, but Alia marked angry stares across the rows of faces. She named them in her mind for discussion in Council – Hobars, Rajifiri, Tasmin, Saajid, Umbu, Legg . . . The names carried pieces of Dune in them: Umbu Sietch, Tasmin Sink, Hobars Gap . . .

She turned her attention to Korba.

Observing her attention, Korba lifted his chin, said: 'I protest my innocence.'

'Stilgar, read the charges,' Alia said.

Stilgar produced a brown spicepaper scroll, stepped forward. He began reading, a solemn flourish in his voice as though to hidden rhythms. He gave the words an incisive quality, clear and full of probity:

' . . . that you did conspire with traitors to accomplish the destruction of our Lord and Emperor; that you did meet in vile secrecy with diverse enemies of the realm; that you . . . '

Korba kept shaking his head with a look of pained anger.

Alia listened broodingly, chin planted on her left fist, head cocked to that side, the other arm extended along the chair arm. Bits of the formal procedure began dropping out of her awareness, screened by her own feelings of disquiet.

'... venerable tradition ... support of the legions and all Fremen everywhere ... violence met with violence according to the Law ... majesty of the Imperial Person ... forfeit all rights to ...'

It was nonsense, she thought. Nonsense! All of it – nonsense ... nonsense ... nonsense ...

Stilgar finished: 'Thus the issue is brought to judgement.'

In the immediate silence, Korba rocked forward, hands gripping his knees, veined neck stretched as though he were preparing to leap. His tongue flicked between his teeth as he spoke.

'Not by word or deed have I been traitor to my Fremen vows! I demand to confront my accuser!'

*A simple enough protest,* Alia thought.

And she saw that it had produced a considerable effect on the Naibs. They knew Korba. He was one of them. To become a Naib, he'd proved his Fremen courage and caution. Not brilliant, Korba, but reliable. Not one to lead a Jihad, perhaps, but a good choice as supply officer. Not a crusader, but one who cherished the old Fremen virtues: *The Tribe is paramount.*

Otheym's bitter words as Paul had recited them swept through Alia's mind. She scanned the gallery. Any of those men might see himself in Korba's place – some for good reason. But an innocent Naib was as dangerous as a guilty one here.

Korba felt it, too. 'Who accuses me?' he demanded. 'I have a Fremen right to confront my accuser.'

'Perhaps you accuse yourself,' Alia said.

Before he could mask it, mystical terror lay briefly on Korba's face. It was there for anyone to read: *With her powers, Alia had but to accuse him herself, saying she brought the evidence from the shadow region, the* alam al-mythal.

'Our enemies have Fremen allies,' Alia pressed. 'Water traps have been destroyed, qanats blasted, plantings poisoned and storage basins plundered ...'

'And now – they've stolen a worm from the desert, taken it to another world!'

The voice of this intrusion was known to all of them – Muad'dib. Paul came through the doorway from the hall, pressed through the guard ranks and crossed to Alia's side. Chani, accompanying him, remained on the sidelines.

'M'Lord,' Silgar said, refusing to look at Paul's face.

Paul aimed his empty sockets at the gallery, then down to Korba. 'What, Korba – no words of praise?'

Muttering could be heard in the gallery. It grew louder, isolated words and phrases audible: ' . . . law for the blind . . . Fremen way . . . in the desert . . . who breaks . . . '

'Who says I'm blind?' Paul demanded. He faced the gallery. 'You, Rajifiri? I see you're wearing gold today, and that blue shirt beneath it which still has dust on it from the streets. You always were untidy.'

Rajifiri made a warding gesture, three fingers against evil.

'Point those fingers at yourself!' Paul shouted. 'We know where the evil is!' He turned back to Korba. 'There's guilt on your face, Korba.'

'Not my guilt! I may've associated with the guilty, but no . . . ' He broke off, shot a frightened look at the gallery.

Taking her cue from Paul, Alia arose, stepped down to the floor of the chamber, advanced to the edge of Korba's table. From a range of less than a meter, she stared down at him, silent and intimidating.

Korba cowered under the burden of eyes. He fidgeted, shot anxious glances at the gallery.

'Whose eyes do you seek up there?' Paul asked.

'You cannot see!' Korba blurted.

Paul put down a momentary feeling of pity for Korba. The man lay trapped in the vision's snare as securely as any of those present. He played a part, no more.

'I don't need eyes to see you,' Paul said. And he began describing Korba, every movement, every twitch, every alarmed and pleading look at the gallery.

Desperation grew in Korba.

Watching him, Alia saw he might break any second. Someone in the gallery must realise how near he was to breaking, she thought. Who? She studied the faces of the Naibs, noting small betrayals in the masked faces . . . angers, fears, uncertainties . . . guilts.

Paul fell silent.

Korba mustered a pitiful air of pomposity to plead: 'Who accuses me?'

'Otheym accuses you,' Alia said.

'But Otheym's dead!' Korba protested.

'How did you know that?' Paul asked. 'Through your spy system? Oh, yes! We know about your spies and couriers. We know who brought the stone burner here from Tarahell.'

'It was for the defense of the Qizarate!' Korba blurted.

'Is that how it got into traitorous hands?' Paul asked.

'It was stolen and we . . .' Korba fell silent, swallowed. His gaze darted left and right. 'Everyone knows I've been the voice of love for Muad'dib.' He stared at the gallery. 'How can a dead man accuse a Fremen?'

'Otheym's voice isn't dead,' Alia said. She stopped as Paul touched her arm.

'Otheym sent us his voice,' Paul said. 'It gives the names, the acts of treachery, the meeting places and the times. Do you miss certain faces in the Council of Naibs, Korba? Where are Merkur and Fash? Keke the Lame isn't with us today. And Takim, where is he?'

Korba shook his head from side to side.

'They've fled Arrakis with the stolen worm,' Paul said. 'Even if I freed you now, Korba, Shai-hulud would have your water for your part in this. Why don't I free you, Korba? Think of all those men whose eyes were taken, the men who cannot see as I see. They have families and friends, Korba. Where could you hide from them?'

'It was an accident,' Korba pleaded. 'Anyway, they're getting Tleilaxu . . .' Again, he subsided.

'Who knows what bondage goes with metal eyes?' Paul asked.

The Naibs in their gallery began exchanging whispered comments, speaking behind raised hands. They gazed coldly at Korba now.

'Defense of the Qizarate,' Paul murmured, returning to Korba's plea. 'A device which either destroys a plane or produces J-rays to blind those too near it. Which effect, Korba, did you conceive as a defense? Does the Qizarate rely on stopping the eyes of all observers?'

'It was a curiosity, m'Lord,' Korba pleaded. 'We knew the Old Law said that only Families could possess atomics, but the Qizarate obeyed . . . obeyed . . .'

'Obeyed you,' Paul said. 'A curiosity, indeed.'

'Even if it's only the voice of my accuser, you must face me with it!' Korba said. 'A Fremen has rights.'

'He speaks truth, Sire,' Stilgar said.

Alia glanced sharply at Stilgar.

'The law is the law,' Stilgar said, sensing Alia's protest. He began quoting Fremen Law, interspersing his own comments on how the Law pertained.

Alia experienced the odd sensation she was hearing Stilgar's words before he spoke them. How could he be this credulous?

175

Stilgar had never appeared more official and conservative, more intent on adhering to the Dune Code. His chin was outthrust, aggressive. His mouth chopped. Was there really nothing in him but this outrageous pomposity?

'Korba is a Fremen and must be judged by Fremen Law,' Stilgar concluded.

Alia turned away, looked out at the day shadows dropping down the wall across from the garden. She felt drained by frustration. They'd dragged this thing along well into midmorning. Now what? Korba had relaxed. The Panegyrist's manner said he'd suffered an unjust attack, that everything he'd done had been for love of Muad'dib. She glanced at Korba, surprised a look of sly self-importance sliding across his face.

He might almost have received a message, she thought. He acted the part of a man who'd heard friends shout: '*Hold fast! Help is on its way!*'

For an instant, they'd held this thing in their hands – the information out of the dwarf, the clues that others were in the plot, the names of informants. But the critical moment had flown. *Stilgar? Surely not Stilgar.* She turned, stared at the old Fremen. Stilgar met her gaze without flinching.

'Thank you, Stil,' Paul said, 'for reminding us of the Law.'

Stilgar inclined his head. He moved close, shaped silent words in a way he knew both Paul and Alia could read. *I'll wring him dry and then take care of the matter.*

Paul nodded, signaled the guardsmen behind Korba.

'Remove Korba to a maximum security cell,' Paul said. 'No visitors except counsel. As counsel, I appoint Stilgar.'

'Let me choose my own counsel!' Korba shouted.

Paul whirled. 'You deny the fairness and judgement of Stilgar?'

'Oh, no, m'Lord, but . . . '

'Take him away!' Paul barked.

The guardsmen lifted Korba off the cushions, herded him out. With new mutterings, the Naibs began quitting their gallery. Attendants came from beneath the gallery, crossed to the windows and drew the orange draperies. Orange gloom took over the chamber.

'Paul,' Alia said.

'When we precipitate violence,' Paul said, 'it'll be when we have full control of it. Thank you, Stil; you played your part well. Alia, I'm certain, has identified the Naibs who were with him. They couldn't help giving themselves away.'

'You cooked this up between you?' Alia demanded.

'Had I ordered Korba slain out of hand, the Naibs would have understood,' Paul said. 'But this formal procedure without strict adherence to Fremen Law – they felt their own rights threatened Which Naibs were with him, Alia?'

'Rajifiri for certain,' she said, voice low. 'And Saajid, but . . . '

'Give Stilgar the complete list,' Paul said.

Alia swallowed in a dry throat, sharing the general fear of Paul in this moment. She knew how he moved among them without eyes, but the delicacy of it daunted her. To see their forms in the air of his vision! She sensed her person shimmering for him in a sidereal time whose accord with reality depended entirely on his words and actions. He held them all in the palm of his vision!

'It's past time for your morning audience, Sire,' Stilgar said. 'Many people – curious . . . afraid . . . '

'Are you afraid, Stil?'

It was barely a whisper: 'Yes.'

'You're my friend and have nothing to fear from me,' Paul said.

Stilgar swallowed. 'Yes, m'Lord.'

'Alia, take the morning audience,' Paul said. 'Stilgar, give the signal.'

Stilgar obeyed.

A flurry of movement erupted at the great doors. A crowd was pressed back from the shadowy room to permit entrance of officials. Many things began happening all at once: the household guard elbowing and shoving back the press of Supplicants, garishly robed Pleaders trying to break through, shouts, curses. Pleaders waved the papers of their calling. The Clerk of the Assemblage strode ahead of them through the opening cleared by the guard. He carried the List of Preferences, those who'd be permitted to approach the Throne. The Clerk, a wiry Fremen named Tecrube, carried himself with weary cynicism, flaunting his shaven head, clumped whiskers.

Alia moved to intercept him, giving Paul time to slip away with Chani through the private passage behind the dais. She experienced a momentary distrust of Tecrube at the prying curiosity in the stare he sent after Paul.

'I speak for my brother today,' she said. 'Have the Supplicants approach one at a time.'

'Yes, m'Lady.' He turned to arrange his throng.

'I can remember a time when you wouldn't have mistaken

your brother's purpose here,' Stilgar said.

'I was distracted,' she said. 'There's been a dramatic change in you, Stil. What is it?'

Stilgar drew himself up, shocked. One changed, of course. But dramatically? This was a particular view of himself that he'd never encountered. Drama was a questionable thing. Imported entertainers of dubious loyalty and more dubious virtue were dramatic. Enemies of the Empire employed drama in their attempts to sway the fickle populace. Korba had slipped away from Fremen virtues to employ drama for the Qizarate. And he'd die for that.

'You're being perverse,' Stilgar said. 'Do you distrust me?'

The distress in his voice softened her expression, but not her tone. 'You *know* I don't distrust you. I've always agreed with my brother that once matters were in Stilgar's hands we could safely forget them.'

'Then why do you say I've . . . changed?'

'You're preparing to disobey my brother,' she said. 'I can read it in you. I only hope it doesn't destroy you both.'

The first of the Pleaders and Supplicants were approaching now. She turned away before Stilgar could respond. His face, though, was filled with the things she'd sensed in her mother's letter – the replacement of morality and conscience with law.

'*You produce a deadly paradox.*'

*Tibana was an apologist for Socratic Christianity, probably a native of IV Anbus who lived between the eighth and ninth centuries before Corrino, likely in the second reign of Dalamak. Of his writings, only a portion survives from which this fragment is taken: 'The hearts of all men dwell in the same wilderness.'*

— from The Dunebuk of Irulan

'You are Bijaz,' the ghola said, entering the small chamber where the dwarf was held under guard. 'I am called Hayt.'

A strong contingent of the household guard had come in with the ghola to take over the evening watch. Sand carried by the sunset wind had stung their cheeks while they crossed the outer yard, made them blink and hurry. They could be heard in the passage outside now exchanging the banter and ritual of their tasks.

'You are not Hayt,' the dwarf said. 'You are Duncan Idaho. I was there when they put your dead flesh into the tank and I was there when they removed it, alive and ready for training.'

The ghola swallowed in a throat suddenly dry. The bright glow-globes of the chamber lost their yellowness in the room's green hangings. The light showed beads of perspiration on the dwarf's forehead. Bijaz seemed a creature of odd integrity, as though the purpose fashioned into him by the Tleilaxu were projected out through his skin. There was power beneath the dwarf's mask of cowardice and frivolity.

179

'Muad'dib has charged me to question you to determine what it is the Tleilaxu intend you to do here,' Hayt said.

'Tleilaxu, Tleilaxu,' the dwarf sang. 'I am the Tleilaxu, you dolt! For that matter so are you.'

Hayt stared at the dwarf. Bijaz radiated a charismatic alertness that made the observer think of ancient idols.

'You hear that guard outside?' Hayt asked. 'If I gave them the order, they'd strangle you.'

'Hai! Hai!' Bijaz cried. 'What a callous lout you've become. And you said you came seeking truth.'

Hayt found he didn't like the look of secret repose beneath the dwarf's expression. 'Perhaps I only seek the future,' he said.

'Well spoken,' Bijaz said. 'Now we know each other. When two thieves meet they need no introduction.'

'So we're thieves,' Hayt said. 'What do we steal?'

'Not thieves, but dice,' Bijaz said. 'And you came here to read my spots. I, in turn, read yours. And lo! You have two faces!'

'Did you really see me go into the Tleilaxu tanks?' Hayt asked, fighting an odd reluctance to ask that question.

'Did I not say it?' Bijaz demanded. The dwarf bounced to his feet. 'We had a terrific struggle with you. The flesh did not want to come back.'

Hayt felt suddenly that he existed in a dream controlled by some other mind, and that he might momentarily forget this to become lost in the convolutions of that mind.

Bijaz tipped his head slyly to one side, walked all around the ghola, staring up at him. 'Excitement kindles old patterns in you,' Bijaz said. 'You are the pursuer who doesn't want to find what he pursues.'

'You're a weapon aimed at Muad'dib,' Hayt said, swivelling to follow the dwarf. 'What is it you're to do?'

'Nothing!' Bijaz said, stopping. 'I give you a common answer to a common question.'

'Then you were aimed at Alia,' Hayt said. 'Is she your target?'

'They call her Hawt, the Fish Monster, on the outworlds,' Bijaz said. 'How is it I hear your blood boiling when you speak of her?'

'So they call her Hawt,' the ghola said, studying Bijaz for any clue to his purpose. The dwarf made such odd responses.

'She is the virgin-harlot,' Bijaz said. 'She is vulgar, witty, knowledgeable to a depth that terrifies, cruel when she is most kind, unthinking while she thinks, and when she seeks to build

180

she is as destructive as a coriolis storm.'

'So you came here to speak out against Alia,' Hayt said.

'Against her?' Bijaz sank to a cushion against the wall. 'I came here to be captured by the magnetism of her physical beauty.' He grinned, a saurian expression in the big-featured face.

'To attack Alia is to attack her brother,' Hayt said.

'That is so clear it is difficult to see,' Bijaz said. 'In truth, Emperor and sister are one person back to back, one being half male and half female.'

'That is a thing we've heard said by the Fremen of the deep desert,' Hayt said. 'And those are the ones who've revived the blood sacrifice to Shai-hulud. How is it you repeat their non-sense?'

'You dare say nonsense?' Bijaz demanded. 'You, who are both man and mask? Ahh, but the dice cannot read their own spots. I forget this. And you are doubly confused because you serve the Atreides double-being. Your senses are not as close to the answer as your mind is.'

'Do you preach that false ritual about Muad'dib to your guards?' Hayt asked, his words low. He felt his mind being tangled by the dwarf's words.

'They preach to me!' Bijaz said. 'And they pray. Why should they not? All of us should pray. Do we not live in the shadow of the most dangerous creation the universe has ever seen?'

'Dangerous creation . . .'

'Their own mother refuses to live on the same planet with them!'

'Why don't you answer me straight out?' Hayt demanded. 'You know we have other ways of questioning you. We'll get our answers . . . one way or another.'

'But I have answered you! Have I not said the myth is real? Am I the wind that carries death in it belly? No! I am words! Such words as the lightning which strikes from the sand in a dark sky. I have said: "Blow out the lamp! Day is here!" And you keep saying: "Give me a lamp so I can find the day."'

'You play a dangerous game with me,' Hayt said. 'Did you think I could not understand these Zensunni ideas? You leave tracks as clear as those of a bird in mud.'

Bijaz began to giggle.

'Why do you laugh?' Hayt demanded.

'Because I have teeth and wish I had not,' Bijaz managed between giggles. 'Having no teeth, I could not gnash them.'

'And now I know your target,' Hayt said. 'You were aimed at me.'

'And I've hit it right on!' Bijaz said. 'You made such a big target, how could I miss?' He nodded as though to himself. 'Now I will sing to you.' He began to hum, a keening, whining monotonous theme, repeated over and over.

Hayt stiffened, experiencing odd pains that played up and down his spine. He stared at the face of the dwarf, seeing youthful eyes in an old face. The eyes were the center of a network of knobby white lines which ran to the hollows below his temples. Such a large head! Every feature focused on the pursed-up mouth from which that monotonous noise issued. The sound made Hayt think of ancient rituals, folk memories, old words and customs, half-forgotten meanings in lost mutterings. Something vital was happening here – a bloody play of ideas across Time. Elder ideas lay tangled in the dwarf's singing. It was like a blazing light in the distance, coming nearer and nearer, illuminating life across a span of centuries.

'What are you doing to me?' Hayt gasped.

'You are the instrument I was taught to play,' Bijaz said. 'I am playing you. Let me tell you the names of the other traitors among the Naibs. They are Bikouros and Cahueit. There is Djedida, who was secretary to Korba. There is Abumojandis, the aide to Bannerjee. Even now, one of them could be sinking a blade into your Muad'dib.'

Hayt shook his head from side to side. He found it too difficult to talk.

'We are like brothers,' Bijaz said, interrupting his monotonous hum once more. 'We grew in the same tank: I first and then you.'

Hayt's metal eyes inflicted him with a sudden burning pain. Flickering red haze surrounded everything he saw. He felt he had been cut away from every immediate sense except the pain, and he experienced his surroundings through a thin separation like windblown gauze. All had become accident, the chance involvement of inanimate matter. His own will was no more than a subtle, shifting thing. It lived without breath and was intelligible only as an inward illumination.

With a clarity born of desperation, he broke through the gauze curtain with the lonely sense of sight. His attention focused like a blazing light under Bijaz. Hayt felt that his eyes cut through layers of the dwarf, seeing the little man as a hired intellect, and beneath that, a creature imprisoned by hungers and cravings which lay huddled in the eyes – layer after layer, until finally, there was only an entity-aspect being manipulated by symbols.

'We are upon a battleground,' Bijaz said. 'You may speak of it.'

His voice freed by the command, Hayt said: 'You cannot force me to slay Muad'dib.'

'I have heard the Bene Gesserit say,' Bijaz said, 'that there is nothing firm, nothing balanced, nothing durable in all the universe – that nothing remains in its state, that each day, sometimes each hour, brings change.'

Hayt shook his head dumbly from side to side.

'You believed the silly Emperor was the prize we sought,' Bijaz said. 'How little you understand our masters, the Tleilaxu. The Guild and Bene Gesserit believe we produce artifacts. In reality, we produce tools and services. Anything can be a tool – poverty, war. War is useful because it is effective in so many areas. It stimulates the metabolism. It enforces government. It diffuses genetic strains. It possesses a vitality such as nothing else in the universe. Only those who recognise the value of war and exercise it have any degree of self-determination.'

In an oddly placid voice, Hayt said: 'Strange thoughts coming from you, almost enough to make me believe in a vengeful Providence. What restitution was exacted to create you? It would make a fascinating story, doubtless with an even more extraordinary epilogue.'

'Magnificent!' Bijaz chortled. 'You attack – therefore you have will power and exercise self-determination.'

'You're trying to awaken violence in me,' Hayt said in a panting voice.

Bijaz denied this with a shake of the head. 'Awaken, yes; violence, no. You are a disciple of awareness by training, so you have said. I have an awareness to awaken in you, Duncan Idaho.'

'Hayt!'

'Duncan Idaho. Killer extraordinary. Lover of many women. swordsman soldier. Atreides field-hand on the field of battle. Duncan Idaho.'

'The past cannot be awakened.'

'Cannot?'

'It has never been done!'

'True, but our masters defy the idea that something cannot be done. Always, they seek the proper tool, the right application of effort, the services of the proper –'

'You hide your real purpose! You throw up a screen of words and they mean nothing!'

'There is a Duncan Idaho in you,' Bijaz said. 'It will submit to emotion or to dispassionate examination, but submit it will. This awareness will rise through a screen of suppression and selection out of the dark past which dogs your footsteps. It goads you even now while it holds you back. There exists that being within you upon which awareness must focus and which you will obey.'

'The Tleilaxu think I'm still their slave, but I –'

'Quiet, slave!' Bijaz said in that whining voice.

Hayt found himself frozen in silence.

'Now we are down to bedrock,' Bijaz said. 'I know you feel it. And these are the power-words to manipulate you . . . I think they will have sufficient leverage.'

Hayt felt the perspiration pouring down his cheeks, the trembling of his chest and arms, but he was powerless to move.

'One day,' Bijaz said, 'the Emperor will come to you. He will say: "She is gone." The grief mask will occupy his face. He will give water to the dead, as they call their tears hereabouts. And you will say, using my voice: "Master! Oh, Master!"'

Hayt's jaw and throat ached with the locking of his muscles. He could only twist his head in a brief arc from side to side.

'You will say, "I carry a message from Bijaz."' The dwarf grimaced. 'Poor Bijaz, who has no mind . . . poor Bijaz, a drum stuffed with messages, an essence for others to use . . . pound on Bijaz and he produces a noise . . . ' Again, he grimaced. 'You think me a hypocrite, Duncan Idaho! I am not! I can grieve, too. But the time has come to substitute swords for words.'

A hiccup shook Hayt.

Bijaz giggled, then: 'Ah, thank you. Duncan, thank you. The demands of the body save us. As the Emperor carries the blood of the Harkonnens in his veins, he will do as we demand. He will turn into a spitting machine, a biter of words that ring with a lovely noise to our masters.'

Hayt blinked, thinking how the dwarf appeared like an alert little animal, a thing of spite and rare intelligence. *Harkonnen blood in the Atreides?*

'You think of Beast Rabban, the vile Harkonnen, and you glare,' Bijaz said. 'You are like the Fremen in this. When words fail, the sword is always at hand, eh? You think of the torture inflicted upon your family by the Harkonnens. And, through his mother, your precious Paul is a Harkonnen! You would not find it difficult to slay a Harkonnen, now would you?'

Bitter frustration coursed through the ghola. Was it anger? Why should this cause anger?

'Ohhh,' Bijaz said, and: 'Ahhhh, hah! Click-click. There is more to the message. It is a trade the Tleilaxu offer your precious Paul Atreides. Our masters will restore his beloved. A sister to yourself – another ghola.'

Hayt felt suddenly that he existed in a universe occupied only by his own heartbeats.

'A ghola,' Bijaz said. 'It will be the flesh of his beloved. She will bear his children. She will love only him. We can even improve on the original if he so desires. Did ever a man have greater opportunity to regain what he'd lost? It is a bargain he will leap to strike.'

Bijaz nodded, eyes drooping as though tiring. Then: 'He will be tempted . . . and in his distraction, you will move close. In the instant, you will strike! Two gholas, not one! That is what our masters demand!' The dwarf cleared his throat, nodded once more, said: 'Speak.'

'I will not do it,' Hayt said.

'But Duncan Idaho would,' Bijaz said. 'It will be the moment of supreme vulnerability for this descendant of the Harkonnens. Do not forget this. You will suggest improvements to his beloved – perhaps a deathless heart, gentler emotions. You will offer asylum as you move close to him – a planet of his choice somewhere beyond the Imperium. Think of it! His beloved restored. No more need for tears, and a place of idyls to live out his years.'

'A costly package,' Hayt said, probing. 'He'll ask the price.'

'Tell him he must renounce his godhead and discredit the Qizarate. He must discredit himself, his sister.'

'Nothing more?' Hayt asked, sneering.

'He must relinquish his CHOAM holdings, naturally.'

'Naturally.'

'And if you're not yet close enough to strike, speak of how much the Tleilaxu admire what he has taught them about the possibilities of religion. Tell him the Tleilaxu have a department of religious engineering, shaping religions to particular needs.'

'How very clever,' Hayt said.

'You think yourself free to sneer and disobey me,' Bijaz said. He cocked his head slyly to one side. 'Don't deny it . . . '

'They made you well, little animal,' Hayt said.

'And you as well,' the dwarf said. 'You will tell him to hurry.

Flesh decays and her flesh must be preserved in a cryological tank.'

Hayt felt himself floundering, caught in a matrix of objects he could not recognise. The dwarf appeared so sure of himself! There had to be a flaw in the Tleilaxu logic. In making their ghola, they'd keyed him to the voice of Bijaz, but . . . But what? Logic/matrix/object . . . How easy it was to mistake clear reasoning for correct reasoning! Was Tleilaxu logic distorted?

Bijaz smiled, listened as though to a hidden voice. 'Now, you will forget,' he said. 'When the moment comes, you will remember. He will say: "She is gone." Dundan Idaho will awaken then.'

The dwarf clapped his hands together.

Hayt grunted, feeling that he had been interrupted in the middle of a thought . . . or perhaps in the middle of a sentence. What was it? Something about . . . targets?

'You think to confuse me and manipulate me,' he said.

'How is that?' Bijaz asked.

'I am your target and you can't deny it,' Hayt said.

'I would not think of denying it.'

'What is it you'd try to do with me?'

'A kindness,' Bijaz said. 'A simple kindness.'

*The sequential nature of actual events is not illuminated with lengthy precision by the powers of prescience except under the most extraordinary circumstances. The oracle grasps incidents cut out of the historic chain. Eternity moves. It inflicts itself upon the oracle and the supplicant alike. Let Muad'dib's subjects doubt his majesty and his oracular visions. Let them deny his powers. Let them never doubt Eternity.*

— The Dune Gospels

Hayt watched Alia emerge from her temple and cross the plaza. Her guard was bunched close, fierce expressions on their faces to mask the lines molded by good living and complacency.

A heliograph of 'thopter wings flashed in the bright afternoon sun above the temple, part of the Royal Guard with Muad'dib's fist-symbol on its fuselage.

Hayt returned his gaze to Alia. She looked out of place here in the city, he thought. Her proper setting was the desert – open, untrammeled space. An odd thing about her came back to him as he watched her approach: Alia appeared thoughtful only when she smiled. It was a trick of the eyes, he decided, recalling a cameo memory of her as she'd appeared at the reception for the Guild Ambassador: haughty against a background of music and brittle conversation among extravagant gowns and uniforms. And Alia had been wearing white, dazzling, a bright garment of chastity. He had looked down upon her from a window as she crossed an inner garden with its formal pond, its fluting fountains

187

fonds of pampas grass and a white belvedere.

Entirely wrong . . . all wrong. She belonged in the desert.

Hayt drew in a ragged breath. Alia had moved out of his view then as she did now. He waited, clenching and unclenching his fists. The interview with Bijaz had left him uneasy.

He heard Alia's entourage pass outside the room where he waited. She went into the Family quarters.

Now he tried to focus on the thing about her which troubled him. The way she'd walked across the plaza ? Yes. She'd moved like a hunted creature fleeing some predator. He stepped out onto the connecting balcony, walked along it behind the plasmeld sunscreen, stopped while still in concealing shadows. Alia stood at the balustrade overlooking her temple.

He looked where she was looking – out over the city. He saw rectangles, blocks of color, creeping movements of life and sound. Structures gleamed, shimmered. Heat patterns spiraled off the rooftops. There was a boy across the way bouncing a ball in a cul-de-sac formed by a buttressed massif at a corner of the temple Back and forth the ball went.

Alia, too, watched the ball. She felt a compelling identity with that ball – back and forth . . . back and forth. She sensed herself bouncing through corridors of Time.

The potion of melange she'd drained just before leaving the temple was the largest she'd ever attempted – a massive overdose. Even before beginning to take effect, it had terrified her.

*Why did I do it ?* she asked herself.

One made a choice between dangers. Was that it ? This was the way to penetrate the fog spread over the future by that damnable Dune Tarot. A barrier existed. It must be breached. She had acted out of a necessity to see where it was her brother walked with his eyeless stride.

The familiar melange fugue state began creeping into her awareness. She took a deep breath, experienced a brittle form of calm, poised and selfless.

*Possession of second sight has a tendency to make one a dangerous fatalist,* she thought. Unfortunately, there existed no abstract leverage, no calculus of prescience. Visions of the future could not be manipulated as formulas. One had to enter them, risking life and sanity.

A figure moved from the harsh shadows of the adjoining balcony. The ghola! In her heightened awareness, Alia saw him with intense clarity – the dark, lively features dominated by those glistening metal eyes. He was a union of terrifying opposites, something put together in a shocking, linear way. He was shadow and blazing light, a product of the process which had revived his dead flesh . . . and of something intensely pure . . . innocent.

He was innocence under siege!

'Have you been there all along, Duncan?' she asked.

'So I'm to be Duncan,' he said. 'Why?'

'Don't question me,' she said.

And she thought, looking at him, that the Tleilaxu had left no corner of their ghola unfinished.

'Only gods can safely risk perfection,' she said. 'It's a dangerous thing for a man.'

'Duncan died,' he said, wishing she would not call him that. 'I am Hayt.'

She studied his artificial eyes, wondering what they saw. Observed closely, they betrayed tiny black pockmarks, little wells of darkness in the glittering metal. Facets! The universe shimmered around her and lurched. She steadied herself with a hand on the sun-warmed surface of the balustrade. Ahhh, the melange moved swiftly.

'Are you ill?' Hayt asked. He moved closer, the steely eyes opened wide, staring.

*Who spoke?* she wondered. Was it Duncan Idaho? Was it the mentat-ghola or the Zensunni philosopher? Or was it a Tleilaxu pawn more dangerous than any Guild Steersman? Her brother knew.

Again, she looked at the ghola. There was something inactive about him now, a latent something. He was saturated with waiting and with powers beyond their common life.

'Out of my mother, I am like the Bene Gesserit,' she said. 'Do you know that?'

'I know it.'

'I use their powers, think as they think. Part of me knows the sacred urgency of the breeding program . . . and its products.'

She blinked, feeling part of her awareness begin to move freely in Time.

'It's said that the Bene Gesserit never let go,' he said. And he watched her closely, noting how white her knuckles were where she gripped the edge of the balcony.

'Have I stumbled?' she asked.

He marked how deeply she breathed, with tension in every movement, the glazed appearance of her eyes.

'When you stumble,' he said, 'you may regain your balance by jumping beyond the thing that tripped you.'

'The Bene Gesserit stumbled,' she said. 'Now they wish to regain their balance by leaping beyond my brother. They want Chani's baby . . . or mine.'

'Are you with child?'

She struggled to fix herself in a timespace relationship to this question. With child? When? Where?

'I see . . . my child,' she whispered.

She moved away from the balcony's edge, turned her head to look at the ghola. He had a face of salt, bitter eyes – two circles of glistening lead . . . and, as he turned away from the light to follow her movement, blue shadows.

'What . . . do you see with such eyes?' she whispered.

'What other eyes see,' he said.

His words rang in her ears, stretching her awareness. She felt that she reached across the universe – such a stretching . . . out . . . out. She lay intertwined with all Time.

'You've taken the spice, a large dose,' he said.

'Why can't I see him?' she muttered. The womb of all creation held her captive. 'Tell me, Duncan, why I cannot see him.'

'Who can't you see?'

'I cannot see the father of my children. I'm lost in a Tarot fog. Help me.'

Mentat logic offered its prime computation, and he said: 'The Bene Gesserit want a mating between you and your brother. It would lock the genetic . . .'

A wail escaped her. 'The egg in the flesh,' she gasped. A sensation of chill swept over her, followed by intense heat. The unseen mate of her darkest dreams! Flesh of her flesh that the oracle could not reveal – would it come to that?

'Have you risked a dangerous dose of the spice?' he asked. Something within him fought to express the utmost terror at the thought that an Atreides woman might die, that Paul might face him with the knowledge that a female of the royal family had . . . gone.

'You don't know what it's like to hunt the future,' she said. 'Sometimes I glimpse myself . . . but I get in my own way. I cannot see through myself.' She lowered her head, shook it from side to side.

'How much of the spice did you take?' he asked.

'Nature abhors prescience,' she said, raising her head. 'Did

190

you know that, Duncan?'

He spoke softly, reasonably, as to a small child: 'Tell me how much of the spice you took.' He took hold of her shoulder with his left hand.

'Words are such gross machinery, so primitive and ambiguous,' she said. She pulled away from his hand.

'You must tell me,' he said.

'Look at the Shield Wall,' she commanded, pointing. She sent her gaze along her own outstretched hand, trembled as the landscape crumbled in an overwhelming vision – a sandcastle destroyed by invisible waves. She averted her eyes, was transfixed by the appearance of the ghola's face. His features crawled, became aged, then young . . . aged . . . young. He was life itself, assertive, endless . . . She turned to flee, but he grabbed her left wrist.

'I am going to summon a doctor,' he said.

'No! You must let me have the vision! I have to know!'

'You are going inside now,' he said.

She stared down at his hand. Where their flesh touched, she felt an electric presence that both lured and frightened her. She jerked free, gasped: 'You can't hold the whirlwind!'

'You must have medical help!' he snapped.

'Don't you understand?' she demanded. 'My vision's incomplete, just fragments. It flickers and jumps. I have to remember the future. Can't you see that?'

'What is the future if you die?' he asked, forcing her gently into the Family chambers.

'Words . . . words,' she muttered. 'I can't explain it. One thing is the occasion of another thing, but there's no cause . . . no effect. We can't leave the universe as it was. Try as we may, there's a gap.'

'Stretch out here,' he commanded.

*He is so dense!* she thought.

Cool shadows enveloped her. She felt her own muscles crawling like worms – a firm bed that she knew to be insubstantial. Only space was permanent. Nothing else had substance. The bed flowed with many bodies, all of them her own. Time became a multiple sensation, overloaded. It presented no single reaction for her to abstract. It was Time. It moved. The whole universe slipped backward, forward, sideways.

'It has no thing-aspect,' she explained. 'You can't get under it or around it. There's no place to get leverage.'

There came a fluttering of people all around her. Many some-ones held her left hand. She looked at her own moving flesh, followed a twining arm out to a fluid mask of face: Duncan Idaho! His eyes were . . . wrong, but it was Duncan – child-man-adole-scent-child-man-adolescent . . . Every line of his features be-trayed concern for her.

'Duncan, don't be afraid,' she whispered.

He squeezed her hand, nodded. 'Be still,' he said.

And he thought: *She must not die! She must not! No Atreides woman can die!* He shook his head sharply. Such thoughts defied mentat logic. Death was a necessity that life might continue.

*The ghola loves me*, Alia thought.

The thought became bedrock to which she might cling. He was a familiar face with a solid room behind him. She recognised one of the bedrooms in Paul's suite.

A fixed, immutable person did something with a tube in her throat. She fought against retching.

'We got her in time,' a voice said, and she recognised the tones of a Family medic. 'You should've called me sooner.' There was suspicion in the medic's voice. She felt the tube slide out of her throat – a snake, a shimmering cord.

'The slapshot will make her sleep,' the medic said. 'I'll send one of her attendants to –'

'I will stay with her,' the ghola said.

'That is not seemly!' the medic snapped.

'Stay . . . Duncan,' Alia whispered.

He stroked her hand to tell her he'd heard.

'M'Lady,' the medic said, 'it'd be better if . . . '

'You do not tell me what is best,' she rasped. Her throat ached with each syllable.

'M'Lady,' the medic said, voice accusing, '*you* know the dangers of consuming too much melange. I can only assume someone gave it to you without –'

'You are a fool,' she rasped. 'Would you deny me my visions? I knew what I took and why.' She put a hand to her throat. 'Leave us. At once!'

The medic pulled out of her field of vision, said: 'I will send word to your brother.'

She felt him leave, turned her attention to the ghola. The vision lay clearly in her awareness now, a culture medium in which the present grew outward. She sensed the ghola move in that play of Time, no longer cryptic, fixed now against a recognisable background.

*He is the crucible*, she thought. *He is danger and salvation.*

And she shuddered, knowing she saw the vision her brother had seen. Unwanted tears burned her eyes. She shook her head sharply. No tears! They wasted moisture and, worse, distracted the harsh flow of vision. Paul must be stopped! Once, just once, she had bridged Time to place her voice where he would pass. But stress and mutability would not permit that here. The web of Time passed through her brother now like rays of light through a lens. He stood at the focus and he knew it. He had gathered all the lines to himself and would not permit them to escape or change.

'Why?' she muttered. 'Is it hate? Does he strike out at Time itself because it hurt him? Is that it ... hate?'

Thinking he heard her speak his name, the ghola said: 'M'Lady?'

'If I could only burn this thing out of me!' she cried. 'I didn't want to be different.'

'Please, Alia,' he murmured. 'Let yourself sleep.'

'I wanted to be able to laugh,' she whispered. Tears slid down her cheeks. 'But I'm sister to an Emperor who's worshipped as a god. People fear me. I never wanted to be feared.'

He wiped the tears from her face.

'I don't want to be part of history,' she whispered. 'I just want to be loved ... and to love.'

'You are loved,' he said.

'Ahhh, loyal, loyal Duncan,' she said.

'Please, don't call me that,' he pleaded.

'But you are,' she said. 'And loyalty is a valued commodity. It can be sold ... not bought, but sold.'

'I don't like your cynicism,' he said.

'Damn your logic! It's true!'

'Sleep,' he said.

'Do you love me, Duncan?' she asked.

'Yes.'

'Is that one of those lies,' she asked, 'one of the lies that are easier to believe than the truth? Why am I afraid to believe you?'

'You fear my differences as you fear your own.'

'Be a man, not a mentat!' she snarled.

'I am a mentat and a man.'

'Will you make me your woman, then?'

'I will do what love demands.'

'And loyalty?'

'And loyalty.'

'That's where you're dangerous,' she said.

Her words disturbed him. No sign of the disturbance arose to his face, no muscle trembled – but she knew it. Vision-memory exposed the disturbance. She felt she had missed part of the vision, though, that she should remember something else from the future. There existed another perception which did not go precisely by the senses, a thing which fell into her head from nowhere the way prescience did. It lay in the Time shadows – infinitely painful.

Emotion! That was it – emotion! It had appeared in the vision, not directly, but as a product from which she could infer what lay behind. She had been possessed by emotion – a single constriction made up of fear, grief and love. They lay there in the vision, all collected into a single epidemic body, overpowering and primordial.

'Duncan, don't let me go,' she whispered.

'Sleep,' he said. 'Don't fight it.'

'I must . . . I must. He's the bait in his own trap. He's the servant of power and terror. Violence . . . deification is a prison enclosing him. He'll lose . . . everything. It'll tear him apart.'

'You speak of Paul?'

'They drive him to destroy himself,' she gasped, arching her back. 'Too much weight, too much grief. They seduce him away from love.' She sank back to the bed. 'They're creating a universe where he won't permit himself to live.'

'Who is doing this?'

'He is! Ohhh, you're so dense. He's part of the pattern. And it's too late . . . too late . . . too late . . . '

As she spoke, she felt her awareness descend, layer by layer. It came to rest directly behind her navel. Body and mind separated and merged in a storehouse of relic visions – moving, moving . . . She heard a fetal heartbeat, a child of the future. The melange still possessed her, then, setting her adrift in Time. She knew she had tasted the life of a child not yet conceived. One thing certain about this child – it would suffer the same awakening she had suffered. It would be an aware, thinking entity before birth.

*There exists a limit to the force even the most powerful may apply without destroying themselves. Judging this limit is the true artistry of government. Misuse of power is the fatal sin. The law cannot be a tool of vengeance, never a hostage, nor a fortification against the martyrs it has created. You cannot threaten any individual and escape the consequences.*

— Muad'dib on Law
The Stilgar Commentary

Chani stared out at the morning desert framed in the fault cleft below Sietch Tabr. She wore no stillsuit, and this made her feel unprotected here in the desert. The sietch grotto's entrance lay hidden in the buttressed cliff above and behind her.

The desert . . . the desert . . . She felt that the desert had followed her wherever she had gone. Coming back to the desert was not so much a homecoming as a turning around to see what had always been there.

A painful constriction surged through her abdomen. The birth would be soon. She fought down the pain, wanting this moment alone with her desert.

Dawn stillness gripped the land. Shadows fled among the dunes and terraces of the Shield Wall all around. Daylight lunged over the high scarp and plunged her up to her eyes in a bleak landscape stretching beneath a washed blue sky. The scene matched the feeling of dreadful cynicism which had tormented her since the moment she'd learned of Paul's blindness.

*Why are we here?* she wondered.

It was not a hajra, a journey of seeking. Paul sought nothing here except, perhaps, a place for her to give birth. He had summoned odd companions for this journey, she thought – Bijaz, the Tleilaxu dwarf: the ghola, Hayt, who might be Duncan Idaho's revenant; Edric, the Guild Steersman-Ambassador; Gaius Helen Mohiam, the Bene Gesserit Reverend Mother he so obviously hated; Lichna, Otheym's strange daughter, who seemed unable to move beyond the watchful eyes of guards; Stilgar, her uncle of the Naibs, and his favorite wife, Harah . . . and Irulan . . . Alia . . .

The sound of wind through the rocks accompanied her thoughts. The desert day had become yellow on yellow, tan on tan, gray on gray.

Why such a strange mixture of companions?

'We have forgotten,' Paul had said in response to her question, 'that the word "company" originally meant traveling companions. We are a company.'

'But what value are they?'

'There!' he'd said, turning his frightful sockets toward her. 'We've lost that clear, single-note of living. If it cannot be bottled, beaten, pointed or hoarded, we give it no value.'

Hurt, she'd said: 'That's not what I meant.'

'Ahhh, dearest one,' he'd said, soothing, 'we are so money-rich and so life-poor. I am evil, obstinate, stupid . . . '

'You are not!'

'That, too, is true. But my hands are blue with time. I think . . . I think I tried to invent life, not realising it'd already been invented.'

And he'd touched her abdomen to feel the new life there.

Remembering, she placed both hands over her abdomen and trembled, sorry that she'd asked Paul to bring her here.

The desert wind had stirred up evil odors from the fringe plantings which anchored the dunes at the cliff base. Fremen superstition gripped her: *evil odors, evil times.* She faced into the wind, saw a worm appear outside the plantings. It arose like the prow of a demon ship out of the dunes, threshed sand, smelled the water deadly to its kind, and fled beneath a long, burrowing mound.

She hated the water then, inspired by the worm's fear. Water, once the spirit-soul of Arrakis, had become a poison. Water brought pestilence. Only the desert was clean.

Below her, a Fremen work gang appeared. They climbed to the sietch's middle entrance, and she saw that they had muddy feet.

*Fremen with muddy feet!*

The children of the sietch began singing to the morning above her, their voices piping from the upper entrance. The voices made her feel time fleeing from her like hawks before the wind. She shuddered.

What storms did Paul *see* with his eyeless vision?

She sensed a vicious madman in him, someone weary of songs and polemics.

The sky, she noted, had become crystal gray filled with alabaster rays, bizarre designs etched across the heavens by windborne sand. A line of gleaming white in the south caught her attention. Eyes suddenly alerted, she interpreted the sign: White sky in the south: Shai-hulud's mouth. A storm came, big wind. She felt the warning breeze, a crystal blowing of sand against her cheeks. The incense of death came on the wind: odors of water flowing in qanats, sweating sand, flint. The water – that was why Shai-hulud sent his coriolis wind.

Hawks appeared in the cleft where she stood, seeking safety from the wind. They were brown as the rocks and with scarlet in their wings. She felt her spirit go out to them: they had a place to hide; she had none.

'M'Lady, the wind comes!'

She turned, saw the ghola calling to her outside the upper entrance to the sietch. Fremen fears gripped her. Clean death and the body's water claimed for the tribe, these she understood. But . . . something brought back from death . . .

Windblown sand whipped at her, reddened her cheeks. She glanced over her shoulder at the frightful band of dust across the sky. The desert beneath the storm had taken on a tawny, restless appearance as though dune waves beat on a tempest shore the way Paul had once described a sea. She hesitated, caught by a feeling of the desert's transience. Measured against eternity, this was not more than a caldron. Dune surf thundered against cliffs.

The storm out there had become a universal thing for her – all the animals hiding from it . . . nothing left of the desert but its own private sounds: blown sand scraping along rock, a wind-surge whistling, the gallop of a boulder tumbled suddenly from its hill – then! somewhere out of sight, a capsized worm thumping its idiot way aright and slithering off to its dry depths.

It was only a moment as her life measured time, but in that moment she felt this planet being swept away – cosmic dust, part of other waves.

'We must hurry,' the ghola said from right beside her.

She sensed fear in him then, concern for her safety.

'It'll shred the flesh from your bones,' he said, as though he needed to explain such a storm to *her*.

Her fear of him dispelled by his obvious concern, Chani allowed the ghola to help her up the rock stairway to the sietch. They entered the twisting baffle which protected the entrance. Attendants opened the moisture seals, closed them behind.

Sietch odors assaulted her nostrils. The place was a ferment of nasal memories – the warren closeness of bodies, rank ester of the reclamation stills, familiar food aromas, the flinty burning of machines at work . . . and through it all, the omnipresent spice: melange everywhere.

She took a deep breath. 'Home.'

The ghola took his hand from her arm, stood aside, a patient figure now, almost as though turned off when not in use. Yet . . . he watched.

Chani hesitated in the entrance chamber, puzzled by something she could not name. This was truly her home. As a child, she'd hunted scorpions here by glowglobe light. Something was changed, though . . .

'Shouldn't you be going to your quarters, m'Lady ?' the ghola asked.

As though ignited by his words, a rippling birth constriction seized her abdomen. She fought against revealing it.

'M'Lady ?' the ghola said.

'Why is Paul afraid for me to bear our children ?' she asked.

'It is a natural thing to fear for your safety,' the ghola said.

She put a hand to her cheek where the sand had reddened it. 'And he doesn't fear for the children ?'

'M'Lady, he cannot think of a child without remembering that your firstborn was slain by the Sardaukar.'

She studied the ghola – flat face, unreadable mechanical eyes. Was he truly Duncan Idaho, this creature ? Was he friend to anyone ? Had he spoken truthfully now ?

'You should be with the medics,' the ghola said.

Again, she heard the fear for her safety in his voice. She felt abruptly that her mind lay undefended, ready to be invaded by shocking perceptions.

'Hayt, I'm afraid,' she whispered. 'Where is my Usul?'

'Affairs of state detain him,' the ghola said.

She nodded, thinking of the government apparatus which had accompanied them in a great flight of ornithopters. Abruptly, she realised what puzzled her about the sietch: outworld odors. The clerks and aides had brought their own perfumes into this environment, aromas of diet and clothing, of exotic toiletries. They were an undercurrent of odors here.

Chani shook herself, concealing an urge to bitter laughter. Even the smells changed in Muad'dib's presence!

'There were pressing matters which he could not defer,' the ghola said, misreading her hesitation.

'Yes . . . yes, I understand. I came with that swarm, too.'

Recalling the flight from Arrakeen, she admitted to herself now that she had not expected to survive it. Paul had insisted on piloting his own 'thopter. Eyeless, he had guided the machine here. After that experience, she knew nothing he did could surprise her.

Another pain fanned out through her abdomen.

The ghola saw her indrawn breath, the tightening of her cheeks, said: 'Is it your time?'

'I . . . yes, it is.'

'You must not delay,' he said. He grasped her arm, hurried her down the hall.

She sensed panic in him, said: 'There's time.'

He seemed not to hear. 'The Zensunni approach to birth,' he said, urging her even faster, 'is to wait without purpose in the state of highest tension. Do not compete with what is happening. To compete is to prepare for failure. Do not be trapped by the need to achieve anything. This way, you achieve everything.'

While he spoke, they reached the entrance to her quarters. He thrust her through the hangings, cried out: 'Harah! Harah! It is Chani's time. Summon the medics!'

His call brought attendants running. There was a great bustling of people in which Chani felt herself an isolated island of calm . . . until the next pain came.

Hayt, dismissed to the outer passage, took time to wonder at his own actions. He felt fixated at some point of time where all truths were only temporary. Panic lay beneath his actions, he realised. Panic centered not on the possibility that Chani might die, but that Paul should come to him afterward . . . filled with grief . . . his loved one . . . gone . . . gone . . .

*Something cannot emerge from nothing*, the ghola told himself. *From what does this panic emerge?*

He felt that his mentat faculties had been dulled, let out a long, shuddering breath. A psychic shadow passed over him. In the emotional darkness of it, he felt himself waiting for some absolute sound – the snap of a branch in a jungle.

A sigh shook him. Danger had passed without striking.

Slowly, marshaling his powers, shedding bits of inhibition, he sank into mentat awareness. He forced it – not the best way – but somehow necessary. Ghost shadows moved within him in place of people. He was a transshipping station for every datum he had ever encountered. His being was inhabited by creatures of possibility. They passed in revue to be compared, judged.

Perspiration broke out on his forehead.

Thoughts with fuzzy edges feathered away into darkness – unknown. Infinite systems! A mentat could not function without realising he worked in infinite systems. Fixed knowledge could not surround the infinite. *Everywhere* could not be brought into finite perspective Instead, he must *become* the infinite – momentarily.

In one gestalten spasm, he had it, seeing Bijaz seated before him blazing from some inner fire.

*Bijaz!*

The dwarf had done something to him!

Hayt felt himself teetering on the lip of a deadly pit. He projected the mentat computation line forward, seeing what could develop out of his own actions.

'A compulsion!' he gasped. 'I've been rigged with a compulsion!'

A blue-robed courier, passing as Hayt spoke, hesitated. 'Did you say something, sirra?'

Not looking at him, the ghola nodded. 'I said everything.'

> *There was a man so wise,*
> *He jumped into*
> *A sandy place*
> *And burnt out both his eyes !*
> *And when he knew his eyes were gone,*
> *He offered no complaint.*
> *He summoned up a vision*
> *And made himself a saint.*
>
> — Children's Verse
> from History of Muad'dib

Paul stood in darkness outside the sietch. Oracular vision told him it was night, that moonlight silhouetted the shrine atop Chin Rock high on his left. This was a memory-saturated place, his first sietch, where he and Chani . . .

*I must not think of Chani,* he told himself.

The thinning cup of his vision told him of changes all around — a cluster of palms far down to the right, the black-silver line of a qanat carrying water through dunes piled up by that morning's storm.

*Water flowing in the desert !* He recalled another kind of water flowing in a river of his birthworld, Caladan. He hadn't realised then the treasure of such a flow, even the murky slithering in a qanat across a desert basin. Treasure.

With a delicate cough, an aide came up from behind.

Paul held out his hands for a magnaboard with a single sheet of metallic paper on it. He moved as sluggishly as the qanat's water. The vision flowed, but he found himself increasingly reluctant to move with it.

'Pardon, Sire,' the aide said. 'The Semboule Treaty – your signature?'

'I can read it!' Paul snapped. He scrawled 'Atreides Imper.' in the proper place, returned the board, thrusting it directly into the aide's outstretched hand, aware of the fear this inspired.

The man fled.

Paul turned away. *Ugly, barren land!* He imagined it sunsoaked and monstrous with heat, a place of sandslides and the drowned darkness of dust pools, blowdevils unreeling tiny dunes across the rocks, their narrow bellies full of ochre crystals. But it was a rich land, too; big, exploding out of narrow places with vistas of storm-trodden emptiness, rampart cliffs and tumbledown ridges.

All it required was water . . . and love.

Life changed those irascible wastes into shapes of grace and movement, he thought. That was the message of the desert. Contrast stunned him with realisation. He wanted to turn to the aides massed in the sietch entrance, shout at them: If you need something to worship, then worship life – all life, every last crawling bit of it! We're all in this beauty together!

They wouldn't understand. In the desert, they were endlessly desert. Growing things performed no green ballet for them.

He clenched his fists at his sides, trying to halt the vision. He wanted to flee from his own mind. It was a beast come to devour him! Awareness lay in him, sodden, heavy with all the living it had sponged up, saturated with too many experiences.

Desperately, Paul squeezed his thoughts outward.

*Stars!*

Awareness turned over at the thought of all those stars above him – an infinite volume. A man must be half mad to imagine he could rule even a teardrop of that volume. He couldn't begin to imagine the number of subjects his Imperium claimed.

Subjects? Worshippers and enemies, more likely. Did any among them see beyond rigid beliefs? Where was one man who'd escaped the narrow destiny of his prejudices? Not even an Emperor escaped. He'd lived a take-everything life, tried to create a universe in his own image. But the exultant universe was breaking him at last with its silent waves.

*I spit on Dune! he thought. I give it my moisture!*

This myth he'd made out of intricate movements and imagination, out of moonlight and love, out of prayers older than Adam, and gray cliffs and crimson shadows, laments and rivers of martyrs – what had it come to at last ? When the waves receded the shores of Time would spread out there clean, empty, shining with infinite grains of memory and little else. Was this the golden genesis of man ?

Sand scuffed against rocks told him that the ghola had joined him.

'You've been avoiding me today, Duncan,' Paul said.

'It's dangerous for you to call me that,' the ghola said.

'I know.'

'I . . . came to warn you, m'Lord.'

'I know.'

The story of the compulsion Bijaz had put on him poured from the ghola then.

'Do you know the nature of the compulsion ?' Paul asked.

'Violence.'

Paul felt himself arriving at a place which had claimed him from the beginning. He stood suspended. The Jihad had seized him, fixed him onto a glidepath from which the terrible gravity of the Future would never release him.

'There'll be no violence from Duncan,' Paul whispered.

'But, Sire . . . '

'Tell me what you see around us,' Paul said.

'M'Lord ?'

'The desert – how is it tonight ?'

'Don't you *see* it ?'

'I have no eyes, Duncan.'

'But . . . '

'I've only my vision,' Paul said, 'and wish I didn't have it. I'm dying of prescience, did you know that, Duncan ?'

'Perhaps . . . what you fear won't happen,' the ghola said.

'What ? Deny my own oracle ? How can I when I've seen it fulfilled thousands of time ? People call it a power, a gift. It's an affliction ! It won't let me leave my life where I found it !'

'M'Lord,' the ghola muttered, 'I . . . it isn't . . . young master, you don't . . . I . . . ' He fell silent.

Paul sensed the ghola's confusion, said: 'What'd you call me, Duncan ?'

'What ? What ? I . . . for a moment, I . . . '

'You called me "young master". '

'I did, yes.'

'That's what Duncan always called me.' Paul reached out, touched the ghola's face. 'Was that part of your Tleilaxu training?'

'No.'

Paul lowered his hand. 'What, then?'

'It came from . . . me.'

'Do you serve two masters?'

'Perhaps.'

'Free yourself from the ghola, Duncan.'

'How?'

'You're human. Do a human thing.'

'I'm a ghola!'

'But your flesh is human. Duncan's in there.'

'*Something's* in there.'

'I care not how you do it,' Paul said, 'but you'll do it.'

'You've foreknowledge?'

'Foreknowledge be damned!' Paul turned away. His vision hurtled forward now, gaps in it, but it wasn't a thing to be stopped.

'M'Lord, if you've –'

'Quiet!' Paul held up a hand. 'Did you hear that?'

'Hear what, m'Lord?'

Paul shook his head. Duncan hadn't heard it. Had he only imagined the sound? It'd been his tribal name called from the desert – far away and low: 'Usul . . . Uuuussssuuuullll . . . '

'What is it, m'Lord?'

Paul shook his head. He felt watched. Something out there in the night shadows knew he was here. Something? No – some*one*.

'It was mostly sweet,' he whispered, 'and you were the sweetest of all.'

'What'd you say, m'Lord?'

'It's the future,' Paul said.

That amorphous human universe out there had undergone a spurt of motion, dancing to the tune of his vision. It had struck a powerful note then. The ghost-echoes might endure.

'I don't understand, m'Lord,' the ghola said.

'A Fremen dies when he's too long from the desert,' Paul said. 'They call it the "water sickness". Isn't that odd?'

'That's very odd.'

Paul strained at memories, tried to recall the sound of Chani breathing beside him in the night. *Where is there comfort?* he wondered. All he could remember was Chani at breakfast the day they'd left for the desert. She'd been restless, irritable.

'Why do you wear that old jacket?' she'd demanded, eyeing the black uniform coat with its red hawk crest beneath his Fremen robes. 'You're an Emperor!'

'Even an Emperor has his favorite clothing,' he'd said.

For no reason he could explain, this had brought real tears to Chani's eyes – the second time in her life when Fremen inhibitions had been shattered.

Now, in the darkness, Paul rubbed his own cheeks, felt moisture there. *Who gives moisture to the dead?* he wondered. It was his own face, yet not his. The wind chilled the wet skin. A frail dream formed, broke. What was this swelling in his breast? Was it something he'd eaten? How bitter and plaintive was this other self, giving moisture to the dead. The wind bristled with sand. The skin, dry now, was his own. But whose was the quivering which remained?

They heard the wailing then, far away in the sietch depths. It grew louder ... louder ...

The ghola whirled at a sudden glare of light, someone flinging wide the entrance seals. In the light, he saw a man with a raffish grin – no! Not a grin, but a grimace of grief! It was a Fedaykin lieutenant named Tandis. Behind him came a press of many people, all fallen silent now that they saw Muad'dib.

'Chani ...' Tandis said.

'Is dead,' Paul whispered. 'I heard her call.'

He turned toward the sietch. He knew this place. It was a place where he could not hide. His onrushing vision illuminated the entire Fremen mob. He *saw* Tandis, felt the Fedaykin's grief, the fear and anger.

'She is gone,' Paul said.

The ghola heard the words out of a blazing corona. They burned his chest, his backbone, the sockets of his metal eyes. He felt his right hand move toward the knife at his belt. His own thinking became strange, disjointed. He was a puppet held fast by strings reaching down from that awful corona. He moved to another's commands, to another's desires. The strings jerked his arms, his legs, his jaw. Sounds came squeezing out of his mouth, a terrifying repetitive noise –

'Hrrak! Hraak! Hraak!'

The knife came up to strike. In that instant, he grabbed his own voice, shaped rasping words: 'Run! Young master, run!'

'We will not run,' Paul said. 'We'll move with dignity. We'll do what must be done.'

The ghola's muscles locked. He shuddered, swayed.

' . . . *what must be done* !' The words rolled in his mind like a great fish surfacing. ' . . . *what must be done* !' Ahhh, that had sounded like the old Duke, Paul's grandfather. The young master had some of the old man in him. ' . . . *what must be done* !'

The words began to unfold in the ghola's consciousness. A sensation of living two lives simultaneously spread out through his awareness: Hayt/Idaho/Hayt/Idaho . . . He became a motionless chain of relative existence, singular, alone. Old memories flooded his mind. He marked them, adjusted them to new understandings, made a beginning at the integration of a new awareness. A new *persona* achieved a temporary form of internal tyranny. The masculating synthesis remained charged with potential disorder, but events pressed him to the temporary adjustment. The young master needed him.

It was done then. He knew himself as Duncan Idaho, remembering everything of Hayt as though it had been stored secretly in him and ignited by a flaming catalyst. The corona dissolved. He shed the Tleilaxu compulsions.

'Stay close to me, Duncan,' Paul said. 'I'll need to depend on you for many things.' And, as Idaho continued to stand entranced: 'Duncan!'

'Yes, I am Duncan.'

'Of course you are! This was the moment when you came back. We'll go inside now.'

Idaho fell into step beside Paul. It was like the old times, yet not like them. Now that he stood free of the Tleilaxu, he could appreciate what they had given him. Zensunni training permitted him to overcome the shock of events. The mentat accomplishment formed a counterbalance. He put off all fear, standing above the source. His entire consciousness looked outward from a position of infinite wonder: he had been dead; he was alive.

'Sire,' the Fedaykin Tandis said as they approached him, 'the woman, Lichna, says she must see you. I told her to wait.'

'Thank you,' Paul said. 'The birth . . . '

'I spoke to the medics,' Tandis said, falling into step. 'They said you have two children, both of them alive and sound.'

'Two?' Paul stumbled, caught himself on Idaho's arm.

'A boy and a girl,' Tandis said. 'I saw them. They're good Fremen babies.'

'How . . . how did she die?' Paul whispered.

'M'Lord?' Tandis bent close.

'Chani?' Paul said.

'It was the birth, m'Lord,' Tandis husked. 'They said her body was drained by the speed of it. I don't understand, but that is what they said.'

'Take me to her,' Paul whispered.

'M'Lord?'

'Take me to her!'

'That's where we're going, m'Lord.' Again, Tandis bent close to Paul. 'Why does your ghola carry a bared knife?'

'Duncan, put away your knife,' Paul said. 'The time for violence is past.'

As he spoke, Paul felt closer to the sound of his voice than to the mechanism which had created the sound. Two babies! The vision had contained but one. Yet, these moments went as the vision went. There was a person here who felt grief and anger. Someone. His own awareness lay in the grip of an awful tread-mill, replaying his life from memory.

*Two babies?*

Again he stumbled. *Chani, Chani*, he thought. *There was no other way. Chani, beloved, believe me that this death was quicker for you . . . and kinder. They'd have held our children hostage, displayed you in a cage and slave pits, reviled you with the blame for my death. This way . . . this way we destroy them and save our children.*

*Children?*

Once more, he stumbled.

*I permitted this*, he thought. *I should feel guilty.*

The sound of noisy confusion filled the cavern ahead of them. It grew louder precisely as he remembered it growing louder. Yes, this was the pattern, the inexorable pattern, even with two children.

*Chani is dead*, he told himself.

At some faraway instant in a past which he had shared with others, this future had reached down to him. It had chivvied him and herded him into a chasm whose walls grew narrower and narrower. He could feel them closing in on him. This was the way the vision went.

*Chani is dead. I should abandon myself to grief.*

But that was *not* the way the vision went.

'Has Alia been summoned?' he asked.

'She is with Chani's friends,' Tandis said.

Paul sensed the mob pressing back to give him passage. Their silence moved ahead of him like a wave. The noisy confusion began dying down. A sense of congested emotion filled the sietch. He wanted to remove the people from his vision, found it impossible. Every face turning to follow him carried its special imprint. They were pitiless with curiosity, those faces. They felt grief, yes, but he understood the cruelty which drenched them. They were watching the articulate become dumb, the wise become a fool. Didn't the clown always appeal to cruelty?

This was more than a deathwatch, less than a wake.

Paul felt his soul begging for respite, but still the vison moved him. *Just a little farther now*, he told himself. Black, visionless dark awaited him just ahead. There lay the place ripped out of the vision by grief and guilt, the place where the moon fell.

He stumbled into it, would've fallen had Idaho not taken his arm in a fierce grip, a solid presence knowing how to share his grief in silence.

'Here is the place,' Tandis said.

'Watch your step, Sire,' Idaho said, helping him over an entrance lip. Hangings brushed Paul's face. Idaho pulled him to a halt. Paul felt the room then, a reflection against his cheeks and ears. It was a rock-walled space with the rock hidden behind tapestries.

'Where is Chani?' Paul whispered.

Harah's voice answered him: 'She is right here, Usul.'

Paul heaved a trembling sigh. He had feared her body already had been removed to the stills where Fremen reclaimed the water of the tribe. Was that the way the vision went? He felt abandoned in his blindness.

'The children?' Paul asked.

'They are here, too, m'Lord,' Idaho said.

'You have beautiful twins, Usul,' Harah said, 'a boy and a girl. See? We have them here in a creche.'

*Two children*, Paul thought wonderingly. The vision had contained only a daughter. He cast himself adrift from Idaho's arm, moved toward the place where Harah had spoken, stumbled into a hard surface. His hands explored it: the metaglass outlines of a creche.

Someone took his left arm. 'Usul?' It was Harah. She guided his hand into the creche. He felt soft-soft flesh. It was so warm! He felt ribs, breathing.

'That is your son,' Harah whispered. She moved his hand.

208

'And this is your daughter.' Her hand tightened on his. 'Usul, are you truly blind now?'

He knew what she was thinking. *The blind must be abandoned in the desert.* Fremen tribes carried no dead weight.

'Take me to Chani,' Paul said, ignoring her question.

Harah turned him, guided him to the left.

Paul felt himself accepting now the fact that Chani was dead. He had taken his place in a universe he did not want, wearing flesh that did not fit. Every breath he drew bruised his emotions. *Two children!* He wondered if he had committed himself to a passage where his vision would never return. It seemed unimportant.

'Where is my brother?'

It was Alia's voice behind him. He heard the rush of her, the overwhelming presence as she took his arm from Harah.

'I must speak to you!' Alia hissed.

'In a moment,' Paul said.

'Now! It's about Lichna.'

'I know,' Paul said. 'In a moment.'

'You don't have a moment!'

'I have many moments.'

'But Chani doesn't!'

'Be still!' he ordered. 'Chani is dead.' He put a hand across her mouth as she started to protest. 'I order you to be still!' He felt her subside and removed his hand. 'Describe what you see,' he said.

'Paul!' Frustration and tears battled in her voice.

'Never mind,' he said. And he forced himself to inner stillness, opened the eyes of his vision to this moment. Yes – it was still here. Chani's body lay on a pallet within a ring of light. Someone had straightened her white robe, smoothed it trying to hide the blood from the birth. No matter; he could not turn his awareness from the vision of her face: such a mirror of eternity in the still features!

He turned away, but the vision moved with him. She was gone . . . never to return. The air, the universe, all vacant – everywhere vacant. Was this the essence of his penance? he wondered. He wanted tears, but they would not come. Had he lived too long a Fremen? This death demanded its moisture!

Nearby, a baby cried and was hushed. The sound pulled a curtain on his vision. Paul welcomed the darkness. *This is another world*, he thought. *Two children.*

The thought came out of some lost oracular trance. He tried to recapture the timeless mind-dilation of the melange, but awareness fell short. No burst of the future came into his new consciousness. He felt himself rejecting the future – any future.

'Goodbye, my Sihaya,' he whispered.

Alia's voice, harsh and demanding, came from somewhere behind him. 'I've brought Lichna!'

Paul turned. 'That's not Lichna,' he said. 'That's a Face Dancer. Lichna's dead.'

'But here what she says,' Alia said.

Slowly, Paul moved toward his sister's voice.

'I'm not surprised to find you alive, Atreides.' The voice was like Lichna's, but with subtle differences, as though the speaker used Lichna's vocal chords, but no longer bothered to control them sufficiently. Paul found himself struck by an odd note of honesty in the voice.

'Not surprised?' Paul asked.

'I am Scytale, a Tleilaxu of the Face Dancers, and I would know a thing before we bargain. Is that a ghola I see behind you or Duncan Idaho?'

'It's Duncan Idaho,' Paul said. 'And I will not bargain with you.'

'I think you'll bargain,' Scytale said.

'Duncan,' Paul said, speaking over his shoulder, 'will you kill this Tleilaxu if I ask it?'

'Yes, m'Lord.' There was the suppressed rage of a berserker in Idaho's voice.

'Wait!' Alia said. 'You don't know what you're rejecting.'

'But I do know,' Paul said.

'So it's truly Duncan Idaho of the Atreides,' Scytale said. 'We found the lever! A ghola *can* regain his past.' Paul heard footsteps. Someone brushed past him on the left. Scytale's voice came from behind him now. 'What do you remember of your past, Duncan?'

'Everything. From my childhood on. I even remember you at the tank when they removed me from it,' Idaho said.

'Wonderful,' Scytale breathed. 'Wonderful.'

Paul heard the voice moving. *I need a vison*, he thought. Darkness frustrated him. Bene Gesserit training warned him of terrifying menace in Scytale, yet the creature remained a voice, a shadow of movement – entirely beyond him.

'Are these the Atreides babies?' Scytale asked.

'Harah!' Paul cried. 'Get her away from there!'

'Stay where you are!' Scytale shouted. 'All of you! I warn you, a Face Dancer can move faster than you suspect. My knife can have both these lives before you touch me.'

Paul felt someone touch his right arm, then move off to the right.

'That's far enough, Alia,' Scytale said.

'It's my fault,' Alia groaned. 'My fault!'

'Atreides,' Scytale said, 'shall we bargain now?'

Behind him, Paul heard a single hoarse curse. His throat constricted at the suppressed violence in Idaho's voice. Idaho must not break! Scytale would kill the babies!

'To strike a bargain, one requires a thing to sell,' Scytale said. 'Not so, Atreides? Will you have your Chani back? We can restore her to you. A ghola. Atreides. A ghola *with full memory*! But we must hurry. Call your friends to bring a cryologic tank to preserve the flesh.'

*To hear Chani's voice once more,* Paul thought. *To feel her presence beside me, Ahhh, that's why they gave me Idaho as a ghola, to let me discover how much the re-creation is like the original. But now – full restoration . . . at their price. I'd be a Tleilaxu tool forevermore. And Chani . . . chained to the same fate by a threat to our children, exposed once more to the Qizarate's plotting . . .*

'What pressures would you use to restore Chani's memory to her?' Paul asked, fighting to keep his voice calm. 'Would you condition her to . . . to kill one of her own children?'

'We use whatever pressures we need,' Scytale said. 'What say you, Atreides?'

'Alia,' Paul said, 'bargain with this *thing*. I cannot bargain with what I cannot see.'

'A wise choice,' Scytale gloated. 'Well, Alia, what do you offer me as your brother's agent?'

Paul lowered his head, bringing himself to stillness within stillness. He'd glimpsed something just then – like a vision, but not a vision. It had been a knife close to him. There!

'Give me a moment to think,' Alia said.

'My knife is patient,' Scytale said, 'but Chani's flesh is not. Take a *reasonable* amount of time.'

Paul felt himself blinking. It could not be . . . but it was! He felt eyes! Their vantage point was odd and they moved in an erratic way. *There !* The knife swam into his view. With a breath-stilling shock, Paul recognised the viewpoint. It was that of

211

one of his children! He was seeing Scytale's knife hand from within the creche! It glittered only inches from him. Yes – and he could see himself across the room, as well – head down, standing quietly, a figure of no menace, ignored by the others in this room.

'To begin, you might assign us all your CHOAM holdings,' Scytale suggested.

'All of them?' Alia protested.

'All.'

Watching himself through the eyes in the creche, Paul slipped his crysknife from its belt sheath. The movement produced a strange sensation of duality. He measured the distance, the angle. There'd be no second chance. He prepared his body then in the Bene Gesserit way, armed himself like a cocked spring for a single concentrated movement, a *prajna* thing requiring all his muscles balanced in one exquisite unity.

The crysknife leaped from his hand. The milky blur of it flashed into Scytale's right eye, jerked the Face Dancer's head back. Scytale threw both hands up and staggered backward against the wall. His knife clattered off the ceiling, to hit the floor. Scytale rebounded from the wall; he fell face forward, dead before he touched the floor.

Still through the eyes in the creche, Paul watched the faces in the room turn toward his eyeless figure, read the combined shock. Then Alia rushed to the creche, bent over it and hid the view from him.

'Oh, they're safe,' Alia said. 'They're safe.'

'M'Lord,' Idaho whispered, 'was *that* part of your vision?'

'No.' He waved a hand in Idaho's direction. 'Let it be.'

'Forgive me, Paul,' Alia said. 'But when that creature said they could ... revive ...'

'There are some prices an Atreides cannot pay,' Paul said. 'You know that.'

'I know,' she sighed. 'But I was tempted ...'

'Who was not tempted?' Paul asked.

He turned away from them, groped his way to a wall, leaned against it and tried to understand what he had done. *How? How? The eyes in the creche!* He felt poised on the brink of terrifying revelation.

'*My eyes, father.*'

The word-shapings shimmered before his sightless vision.

'My son!' Paul whispered, too low for any to hear. 'You're ... aware.'

'Yes, father. Look!'

Paul sagged against the wall in a spasm of dizziness. He felt that he'd been upended and drained. His own life whipped past him. He saw his father. He *was* his father. And the grandfather, and the grandfathers before that. His awareness tumbled through a mind-shattering corridor of his whole male line.

'How?' he asked silently.

Faint word-shapings appeared, faded and were gone, as though the strain was too great. Paul wiped saliva from the corner of his mouth. He remembered the awakening of Alia in the Lady Jessica's womb. But there had been no Water of Life, no overdose of melange this time . . . or had there? Had Chani's hunger been for that? Or was this somehow the genetic product of his line, foreseen by the Reverend Mother Gaius Helen Mohiam?

Paul felt himself in the creche then, with Alia cooing over him. Her hands soothed him. Her face loomed, a giant thing directly over him. She turned him then and he saw his creche companion – a girl with that bony-ribbed look of strength which came from a desert heritage. She had a full head of tawny red hair. As he stared, she opened her eyes. Those eyes! Chani peered out of her eyes . . . and the Lady Jessica. A multitude peered out of those eyes.

'Look at that,' Alia said. 'They're staring at each other.'

'Babies can't focus at this age.' Harah said.

'I could,' Alia said.

Slowly, Paul felt himself being disengaged from that endless awareness. He was back at his own wailing wall then, leaning against it. Idaho shook his shoulder gently.

'M'Lord?'

'Let my son be called Leto for my father,' Paul said, straightening.

'At the time of naming,' Harah said, 'I will stand beside you as a friend of the mother and give that name.'

'And my daughter,' Paul said. 'Let her be called Ghanima.'

'Usul!' Harah objected. 'Ghanima's an ill-omened name.'

'It saved your life,' Paul said. 'What matter that Alia made fun of you with that name? My daughter is Ghanima, a spoil of war.'

Paul heard wheels squeak behind him then – the pallet with Chani's body being moved. The chant of the Water Rite began.

'Hal yawm!' Harah said. 'I must leave now if I am to be the observer of the holy truth and stand beside my friend for the last time. Her water belongs to the tribe.'

'Her water belongs to the tribe,' Paul murmured. He heard Harah leave. He groped outward and found Idaho's sleeve. 'Take me to my quarters, Duncan.'

Inside his quarters, he shook himself free gently. It was a time to be alone. But before Idaho could leave there was a disturbance at the door.

'Master!' It was Bijaz calling from the doorway.

'Duncan,' Paul said, 'let him come two paces forward. Kill him if he comes farther.'

'Ayyah,' Idaho said.

'Duncan is it?' Bijaz asked. 'Is it *truly* Duncan Idaho?'

'It is,' Idaho said. 'I remember.'

'Then Scytale's plan succeeded!'

'Scytale is dead,' Paul said.

'But I am not and the plan is not,' Bijaz said. 'By the tank in which I grew! It can be done! I shall have my pasts – all of them. It needs only the right trigger.'

'Trigger?' Paul asked.

'The compulsion to kill you.' Idaho said rage thick in his voice. 'Mentat computation: They found that I thought of you as the son I never had. Rather than slay you, the true Duncan Idaho would take over the ghola body. But . . . it might have failed. Tell me, dwarf, if your plan had failed, if I'd killed him, what then?'

'Oh . . . then we'd have bargained with the sister to save her brother. But this way the bargaining is better.'

Paul took a shuddering breath. He could hear the mourners moving down the last passage now toward the deep rooms and the water stills.

'It's not too late, m'Lord,' Bijaz said. 'Will you have your love back? We can restore her to you. A ghola, yes. But now – we hold out the full restoration. Shall we summon servants with a cryological tank, preserve the flesh of your beloved . . .'

It was harder now, Paul found. He had exhausted his powers in the first Tleilaxu temptation. And now all that was for nothing! To feel Chani's presence once more . . .

'Silence him,' Paul told Idaho, speaking in Atreides battle tongue. He heard Idaho move toward the door.

'Master!' Bijaz squeaked.

'As you love me,' Paul said, still in battle tongue, 'do me this favor: Kill him before I succumb!'

'Noooooo . . .' Bijaz screamed.

The sound stopped abruptly with a frightened grunt.

'I did him the kindness,' Idaho said.

Paul bent his head, listening. He no longer could hear the mourners. He thought of the ancient Fremen rite being performed now deep in the sietch, far down in the room of the death-still where the tribe recovered its water.

'There was no choice,' Paul said. 'You understand that, Duncan?'

'I understand.'

'There are some things no one can bear. I meddled in all the possible futures I could create until, finally, they created me.'

'M'Lord, you shouldn't . . . '

'There are problems in this universe for which there are no answers,' Paul said. 'Nothing. Nothing can be done.'

As he spoke, Paul felt his link with the vision shatter. His mind cowered, overwhelmed by infinite possibilities. His lost vision became like the wind, blowing where it willed.

*We say of Muad'dib that he has gone on a journey into that land where we walk without footprints.*
— Preamble to the Qizarate Creed

There was a dike of water against the sand, an outer limit for the plantings of the sietch holding. A rock bridge came next and then the open desert beneath Idaho's feet. The promontory of Sietch Tabr dominated the night sky behind him. The light of both moons frosted its high rim. An orchard had been brought right down to the water.

Idaho paused on the desert side and stared back at flowered branches over silent water – reflections and reality – four moons. The stillsuit felt greasy against his skin. Wet flint odors invaded his nostrils past the filters. There was a malignant simpering to the wind through the orchard. He listened for night sounds. Kangaroo mice inhabited the grass at the water verge; a hawk owl bounced its droning call into the cliff shadows; the wind-broken hiss of a sandfall came from the open bled.

Idaho turned toward the sound.

He could see no movement out there on the moonlit dunes.

It was Tandis who had brought Paul this far. Then the man had returned to tell his account. And Paul had walked out into the desert – like a Fremen.

'He was blind – truly blind,' Tandis had said, as though that explained it. 'Before that, he had the vision which he told to us ... but ...'

A shrug. Blind Fremen were abandoned in the desert. Muad'-dib might be Emperor, but he was also Fremen. Had he not made provision that Fremen guard and raise his children? He was Fremen.

It was a skeleton desert here, Idaho saw. Moon-silvered ribs of rock showed through the sand; then the dunes began.

*I should not have left him alone, not even for a minute,* Idaho thought. *I knew what was in his mind.*

'He told me the future no longer needed his physical presence,' Tandis had reported. 'When he left me, he called back. "Now I am free" were his words.'

*Damn them!* Idaho thought.

The Fremen had refused to send 'thopters or searchers of any kind. Rescue was against their ancient customs.

'There will be a worm for Muad'dib,' they said. And they began the chant for those committed to the desert, the ones whose water went to Shai-hulud: 'Mother of sand, father of Time, beginning of Life, grant him passage.'

Idaho seated himself on a flat rock and stared at the desert. The night out there was filled with camouflage patterns. There was no way to tell where Paul had gone.

'Now I am free.'

Idaho spoke the words aloud, surprised by the sound of his own voice. For a time, he let his mind run, remembering a day when he'd taken the child Paul to the sea market on Caladan, the dazzling glare of a sun on water, the sea's riches brought up dead, there to be sold. Idaho remembered Gurney Halleck playing music of the baliset for them – pleasure, laughter. Rhythms pranced in his awareness, leading his mind like a thrall down channels of remembered delight.

Gurney Halleck. Gurney would blame him for this tragedy.

Memory music faded.

He recalled Paul's words: '*There are problems in this universe for which there are no answers.*'

Idaho began to wonder how Paul would die out there in the desert. Quickly, killed by a worm? Slowly, in the sun? Some of the Fremen back there in the sietch had said Muad'dib would never die, that he had entered the ruh-world where all possible futures existed, that he would be present henceforth in the *alam al-mythal*, wandering there endlessly even after his flesh had ceased to be.

*He'll die and I'm powerless to prevent it,* Idaho thought.

217

He began to realise that there might be a certain fastidious courtesy in dying without a trace – no remains, nothing, and an entire planet for a tomb.

*Mentat, solve thyself,* he thought.

Words intruded on his memory – the ritual words of the Fedaykin lieutenant, posting a guard over Muad'dib's children: 'It shall be the solemn duty of the officer in charge . . .'

The plodding, self-important language of government enraged him. It had seduced the Fremen. It had seduced everyone. A man, a great man, was dying out there, but language plodded on . . . and on . . . and on . . .

What had happened, he wondered, to all the clean meanings that screened out nonsense? Somewhere, in some lost *where* which the Imperium had created, they'd been walled off, sealed against chance rediscovery. His mind quested for solutions, mentat fashion. Patterns of knowledge glistened there. Lorelei hair might shimmer thus, beckoning . . . beckoning the enchanted seaman into emerald caverns . . .

With an abrupt start, Idaho drew back from catatonic forgetfulness.

*So!* he thought. *Rather than face my failure, I would disappear within myself!*

The instant of that almost-plunge remained in his memory. Examining it, he felt his life stretch out as long as the existence of universe. Real flesh lay condensed, finite in its emerald cavern of awareness, but infinite life had shared his being.

Idaho stood up, feeling cleansed by the desert. Sand was beginning to chatter in the wind, pecking at the surfaces of leaves in the orchard behind him. There was the dry and abrasive smell of dust in the night air. His robe whipped to the pulse of a sudden gust.

Somewhere far out in the bled, Idaho realised, a mother storm raged, lifting vortices of winding dust in hissing violence – a giant worm of sand powerful enough to cut flesh from bones.

*He will become one with the desert,* Idaho thought. *The desert will fulfill him.*

It was a Zensunni thought washing through his mind like clear water. Paul would go on marching out there, he knew. An Atreides would not give himself up completely to destiny, not even in the full awareness of the inevitable.

A touch of prescience came over Idaho then, and he saw that people of the future would speak of Paul in terms of seas. Despite

a life soaked in dust, water would follow him. 'His flesh foun-
dered,' they would say, 'but he swam on.'

Behind Idaho, a man cleared his throat.

Idaho turned to discern the figure of Stilgar standing on the
bridge over the qanat.

'He will not be found,' Stilgar said. 'Yet all men will find him.'

'The desert takes him – and deifies him,' Idaho said. 'Yet he
was an interloper here. He brought an alien chemistry to this
planet – water.'

'The desert imposes its own rhythms,' Stilgar said. 'We welcomed him, called him our Mahdi, our Muad'dib, and gave him
his secret name, Base of the Pillar: Usul.'

'Still, he was not born a Fremen.'

'And that does not change the fact that we claimed him . . .
and have claimed him finally.' Stilgar put a hand on Idaho's
shoulder. 'All men are interlopers, old friend.'

'You're a deep one, aren't you, Stil?'

'Deep enough. I can see how we clutter the universe with our
migrations. Muad'dib gave us something uncluttered. Men will
remember his Jihad for that, at least.'

'He won't give up to the desert,' Idaho said. 'He's blind, but
he won't give up. He's a man of honor and principle. He was
Atreides-trained.'

'And his water will be poured on the sand,' Stilgar said.
'Come.' He pulled gently at Idaho's arm. 'Alia is back and is
asking for you.'

'She was with you at Sietch Makab?'

'Yes – she helped whip those soft Naibs into line. They take
her orders now . . . as I do.'

'What orders?'

'She commanded the execution of the traitors.'

'Oh,' Idaho suppressed a feeling of vertigo as he looked up at
the promontory. 'Which traitors?'

'The Guildsman, the Reverend Mother Mohiam, Korba . . . a
few others.'

'You slew a Reverend Mother?'

'I did. Muad'dib left word that it would not be done. He
shrugged. 'But I disobeyed him, as Alia knew I would.'

Idaho stared again into the desert, feeling himself become
whole, one person capable of seeing the pattern of what Paul had
created. *Judgement strategy*, the Atreides called it in their training
manuals. *People are subordinate to government, but the ruled in-*

*fluence the rulers*. Did the ruled have any concept, he wondered, of what they had helped create here?

'Alia . . . ' Stilgar said, clearing his throat. He sounded embarrassed. 'She needs the comfort of your presence.'

'And she is the government,' Idaho murmured.

'A regency, no more.'

'Fortune passes everywhere, as her father often said,' Idaho muttered.

'We make our bargain with the future,' Stilgar said. 'Will you come now? We need you back there.' Again, he sounded embarrassed. 'She is . . . distraught. She cries out against her brother one moment, mourns him the next.'

'Presently,' Idaho promised. He heard Stilgar leave. He stood facing into the rising wind, letting the grains of sand rattle against the stillsuit.

Mentat awareness projected the outflowing patterns into the future. The possibilities dazzled him. Paul had set in motion a whirling vortex and nothing could stand in its path.

The Bene Tleilax and the Guild had overplayed their hands and had lost, were discredited. The Qizarate was shaken by the treason of Korba and others high within it. And Paul's final voluntary act, his ultimate acceptance of their customs, had ensured the loyalty of the Fremen to him and to his house. He was one of them forever now.

'Paul is gone!' Alia's voice was choked. She had come up almost silently to where Idaho stood and was now beside him. 'He was a fool, Duncan!'

'Don't say that!' he snapped.

'The whole universe will say it before I'm through,' she said.

'Why, for the love of heaven?'

'For the love of my brother, not of heaven.'

Zensunni insight dilated his awareness. He could sense that there was no vision in her – had been none since Chani's death. 'You practice an odd love,' he said.

'Love? Duncan, he had but to step off the track! What matter that the rest of the universe would have come shattering down behind him? He'd have been safe . . . and Chani with him!'

'Then . . . why didn't he?'

'For the love of heaven,' she whispered. Then, more loudly, she said: 'Paul's entire life was a struggle to escape his Jihad and its deification. At least, he's free of it. He chose this!'

'Ah, yes – the oracle.' Idaho shook his head in wonder. 'Even

Chani's death. His moon fell.'

'He *was* a fool, wasn't he, Duncan?'

Idaho's throat tightened with suppressed grief.

'Such a fool!' Alia gasped, her control breaking. 'He'll live forever while we must die!'

'Alia, don't . . .'

'It's just grief,' she said, voice low. 'Just grief. Do you know what I must do for him? I must save the life of the Princess Irulan. That one! You should hear *her* grief. Wailing, giving moisture to the dead; she swears she loved him and knew it not. She reviles her Sisterhood, says she'll spend her life teaching Paul's children.'

'You trust her?'

'She reeks of trustworthiness!'

'Ahhh,' Idaho murmured. The final pattern unreeled before his awareness like a design on fabric. The defection of the Princess Irulan was the last step. It left the Bene Gesserit with no remaining lever against the Atreides heirs.

Alia began to sob, leaned against him, face pressed into his chest. 'Ohhh, Duncan, Duncan! He's gone!'

Idaho put his lips against her hair. 'Please,' he whispered. He felt her grief mingling with his like two streams entering the same pool.

'I need you Duncan,' she sobbed. 'Love me!'

'I do,' he whispered.

She lifted her head, peered at the moon-frosted outline of his face. 'I know, Duncan. Love knows love.'

Her words sent a shudder through him, a feeling of estrangement from his old self. He had come out here looking for one thing and had found another. It was as though he'd lurched into a room full of familiar people only to realise too late that he knew none of them.

She pushed away from him, took his hand. 'Will you come with me, Duncan?'

'Wherever you lead,' he said.

She led him back across the qanat into the darkness at the base of the massif and its Place of Safety.

## EPILOGUE

No bitter stench of funeral-still for Muad'dib.
No knell nor solemn rite to free the mind
From avaricious shadows.
He is the fool saint,
The golden stranger living forever
On the edge of reason.
Let your guard fall and he is there!
His crimson peace and sovereign pallor
Strike into our universe on prophetic webs
To the verge of a quiet glance – there!
Out of bristling star-jungles;
Mysterious, lethal, an oracle without eyes,
Catspaw of prophecy, whose voice never dies!
Shai-hulud, he awaits thee upon a strand
Where couples walk and fix, eye to eye,
The delicious ennui of love.
He strides through the long cavern of time,
Scattering the fool-self of his dream.
                                    – The Ghola's Hymn

# DUNE
# by Frank Herbert

DUNE is the finest, most widely acclaimed science fiction novel of this century. Huge in scope, towering in concept, it is a work which will live in the reader's imagination for the rest of his life.

'DUNE seems to me unique among science fiction novels in the depth of its characterisation and the extra-ordinary detail of the world it creates. I know nothing comparable to it except THE LORD OF THE RINGS.'
—*Arthur C. Clarke*

'Certainly one of the landmarks of modern science fiction . . . an amazing feat of creation.'     —**Analog**

**NEW ENGLISH LIBRARY**

# CHILDREN OF DUNE
## by Frank Herbert

Frank Herbert's *Dune*, winner of both the Hugo and Nebula Awards, was one of the most famous and widely read science fiction novels ever written. It was followed by the equally acclaimed *Dune Messiah* and now, with *Children of Dune*, comes the magnificent finale to this epic series.

Old Paul Atreides, who led the Fremen to domination of the human galaxy, is gone now, and Arrakis itself is slowly changing; ecological change has brought vast areas of greenery and even open water to the desert planet. But all is not well; the altered climate is threatening extinction to the sandworms which are essential to the planet's economy, and the continued rule of the Atreides family is being challenged by fanatics and their worst enemy, Baron Vladimir Harkonnen.

These are problems potentially far more deadly than any Paul had had to contend with. How the Children of Dune faced up to them creates an impressive climax to one of science fiction's greatest achievements.

**NEW ENGLISH LIBRARY**

# ON LIBERTY

# JOHN STUART MILL

# ON LIBERTY

Introduction by
Russell Kirk

## A GATEWAY EDITION

HENRY REGNERY COMPANY   CHICAGO

Fourth Printing

# CONTENTS

# INTRODUCTION

Some books form the character of their age; others reflect it; and Mill's *Liberty* is of the latter order. This is not to say that it was uninfluential nor that it is quite irrelevant to our time. *On Liberty* has been kept in print ever since it was published in 1859, and is the most widely-read of all liberal tracts. But the little book is a product of the tranquillity and optimism of Victorian England; quite literally, it is *dated*; written at the summit of what Bagehot calls the Age of Discussion, it is a voice from out the vanished past of nineteenth-century meliorism. The future, after all, was not to the school of Mill. Thus the essay lacks the energetic and prophetic qualities of Calvin's *Institutes*, or Rousseau's *Social Contract*, or Burke's *Reflections*, or Marx's *Capital*, each of which helped to shape the age that was dawning, and all of which probably contain greater meaning for us nowadays than John Stuart Mill's work. As Mill himself was the last of the distinguished line of British empiricists, so his *Liberty*, with its foreboding remarks on the despotism of the masses, was more an epilogue to middle-class liberalism than a rallying-cry.

The younger Mill was born in 1806, the son of the austere and indefatigable James Mill; and by his doctrinaire father he was subjected to a rigorous course of private study which is understated, rather than exaggerated, in the son's famous *Autobiog-*

*raphy.* By the time he was eight, he knew nearly everything that a doctor of philosophy knows nowadays, to put the matter mildly; but what his intellectual training lacked was the higher imagination, and for that he groped in vain all his life long. J. S. Mill became all head and no heart, in which character he represents Jeremy Bentham; but in truth it was Mill himself, rather than Bentham, who was turned into defecated intellect. Lacking the poetic fancy and the warmth of strong affections, this "saint of rationalism" (as Gladstone called him) could not be expected to live a very interesting life. He spent his best years in the London offices of the East India Company, and exhibited but one failing, and that not an uncommon one—being too fond of another man's wife. This was Harriet Taylor, a dismaying bluestocking, whom he married at last in 1851. He was devoted to her, and she was devoted to humanitarian abstractions. Under her influence, he moved back toward the Benthamite dogmas from which he had endeavored to emancipate himself, and toward the end she made of him a socialist of sorts.[1] It was under her tutelage that he wrote *On Liberty,* which he published shortly after her death, dedicating the little book by which he is best known to the woman of whose talents he entertained so extravagant an opinion.

From Bentham and his father, J. S. Mill had learnt—indeed, these doctrines were impressed upon

---

[1] A learned old friend of mine maintains, I know not how playfully, that it was not the negligent parlor-maid, but Mrs. Mill herself (who hated Carlyle) that threw into the fire the manuscript of *The French Revolution.*

him as if they were the laws of the Medes and the Persians, immutable—that the object of all existence is to attain the greatest happiness of the greatest number, and that this happiness will be obtained by methods strictly utilitarian, wholly rational, and described by a few simple social principles. But as he entered upon manhood, the younger Mill suffered indescribably from melancholy and apathy, and commenced to ask himself if, after all, Utilitarianism could cure all the ills to which flesh is heir, for certainly it had not brought him happiness, though he knew more about the happiness-principle than anyone else. Thus he turned, for a time, to the Romantics, and sought in Wordsworth's nature-poetry some relief from the bleak materialism of his father's philosophical system, and in Coleridge's imaginative conservatism an antidote to Bentham's arrogant rationalism. Yet (as Mr. R. J. White observes)[2] he did not understand either Bentham or Coleridge very well, and vacillated unhappily between them for years, until Mrs. Taylor made up his mind for him. Miss Ruth Borchard has given us the most succinct description of this philosopher's struggle against reality:

"Compared to the grand domain of ideas, abstractions and universal laws in which he tried to live with his strong father, everything which is psychologically represented by a man's mother seemed petty and futile, in his own nature as well as outside. Personal feelings, attachments, physical sensations, pleasures and pains, seemed to him like so many senseless and mostly inconvenient or em-

[2] R. J. White, "John Stuart Mill," *Cambridge Journal*, November, 1951.

barrassing trifles. Weakness set him on edge and
provoked the worst in him. He had no pity or
tolerance for it, either in himself or in others. Char-
acteristically, his reform ideals did not spring as
with so many Victorian reformers from pity for
the poor but wholly from abstract ideas. While all
his aspirations were for the betterment of humanity
he loathed everything human, most of all his own
human nature. It required his utmost in will power
to submit his natural impulses and urges, particularly towards day-dreaming, to the constant discipline of work and thought. Especially as a child
and youth he would frequently be overcome, in the
midst of a purposeful intellectual pursuit, by sullen
moodiness, despondency, irritation. He suffered,
and made those around him suffer, a great deal
under these emotional upsets. He realised so little
of his own inner life that he hardly realised when
(let alone why) such moods laid hold of him. By
slaying all his animal spirits he was utterly cut off
from his instincts—instincts for life, instinctive understanding of nature, of human nature in general
and of his own in particular." [3]

It might be interesting to examine here how these
traits, in considerable degree, characterized and
vitiated the whole liberal movement in English and
American thought, at length exposing the liberals
naked unto their enemies, who did not leave the
passions out of *their* reckonings; but we must pass
on, remarking only that this imperfect apprehension
of human nature is easily discerned in the pages
of his *Liberty*. That book displays a strong power

[3] Ruth Borchard, "Mill: the Man and the Thinker," *Contemporary
Review,* February, 1954.

of logic, and some eloquence; but there runs through it Mill's error that the tranquil English society of his own day was destined to become the universal pattern for all mankind, and Mill's curious assumption that most men, if only they were properly schooled, would think and act precisely as John Stuart Mill did.

Now the younger Mill, in his essays on Coleridge and Bentham, had remarked quite truly that the cardinal error of Bentham was his supposition that the affairs of men may be reduced to a few simple formulas, to be applied universally and inflexibly —when in truth the great mysterious incorporation of the human race is infinitely subtle and complex, not to be governed by neat little abstractions. Yet into precisely this same pit Mill falls in his *Liberty*. In his introductory chapter, he declares his object to be the assertion of "one very simple principle, as entitled to govern absolutely the dealings of society with the individual in the way of compulsion and control, whether the means used be physical force in the form of legal penalties, or the moral coercion of public opinion. That principle is, that the sole end for which mankind are warranted, individually or collectively, in interfering with the liberty of action of any of their number, is self-protection. That the only purpose for which power can be rightfully exercised over any member of a civilised community, against his will, is to prevent harm to others." This is a very attractive solitary simple principle; but the trouble with it is that solitary simple principles, however tidy, really do not describe human behavior, and certainly cannot govern it.

James Fitzjames Stephen, a wonderfully forthright man of affairs and scholar of high attainment, preceived with great irritation the fallacy which makes Mill's *Liberty* a frail reed in troubled times; and in *Liberty, Equality, Fraternity,* which Stephen published in 1873, he set upon poor Mill with a whip of scorpions. That book, long out of print, really demolished Mill's latter-day Utilitarianism, so that if one takes up the two tracts nowadays, it is scarcely possible to understand how Mill's essay became almost holy writ for all liberals in the English-speaking world. Yet so long as material progress seemed to be the wave of the future, and so long as representative government and humanitarian reform seemed destined to subdue the dark passions of the human heart in every corner of the modern world, Stephen's gloomy vaticinations were derided as the fancies of obscurantism. We are compelled to look upon matters in another light today, a century after Mill wrote. J. S. Mill, in Stephen's eyes, was hopelessly naïve.

"To me the question whether liberty is a good or bad thing appears as irrational as the question whether fire is a good or a bad thing? It is both good and bad according to time, place, and circumstance, and a complete answer to the question, In what cases is liberty good and in what cases is it bad? would involve not merely a universal history of mankind, but a complete solution of the problems which such a history would offer. I do not believe that the state of our knowledge is such as to enable us to enunciate any 'very simple principle as entitled to govern absolutely the dealings of society with the individual in the way of compulsion and control.' We must proceed in a far more cautious way, and confine ourselves to such remarks as experience suggests about the advantages and disadvantages of compulsion and liberty respectively in particular cases."

In every principal premise of his argument, Stephen declared, Mill suffered from an inadequate understanding of human nature and history. All the great movements of humankind, Stephen said, have been achieved by force, not by free discussion; and if we leave force out of our calculations, very soon we will be subject to the intolerant wills of men who have no scruples about employing force against us. It is consummate folly to tolerate every variety of opinion, on every topic, out of devotion to an abstract "liberty"; for opinion soon finds its expression in action, and the fanatics whom we tolerated will not tolerate us when they have power. The fierce current of events, in our century, has supplied the proof for Stephen's case. Was the world improved by free discussion of the Nazis' thesis that Jews ought to be treated as less than human? Just this subject was presented to the population of one of the most advanced and most thoroughly schooled nations of the modern world; and then that nation, or rather the crew of adventurers who had contrived to win the argument, acted after the fashion with which we are now dreadfully familiar. We have come to understand, to our cost, what Burke meant by a "licentious toleration." Kerensky, when he hesitated to suppress the Kronstadt mutineers because that would be an illiberal resort to force, was a perfect pupil of J. S. Mill; but we all know the consequences

An incessant zeal for repression is not the answer to the complex problems of liberty, either. What Stephen was saying, however, and what we realize now, is that liberty cannot be maintained or extended by an abstract appeal to free discussion, sweet reasonableness, and solitary simple principle.

Yet though Mill now seems perplexingly short-sighted in some particulars, in other things he touches upon difficulties which are become more important today than they were in his time. In Chapter III, "Of Individuality," he discusses the menace of mass-opinion, the deadening influence of conformity to a dreary mediocrity, which impends in our age over every nation which still retains some measure of freedom. Tocqueville analyzes this problem more cogently than does Mill; nevertheless, Mill's observations have relevance for us. Even here, though, *On Liberty* has an old-fangled flavor: Mill argues that this peril is an unthinking obedience to the dictates of custom; while in actuality, a century later, the real danger is that custom and tradition and prescription will be overthrown utterly by neoterism, the lust after novelty, and that men will be no better than the flies of a summer, oblivious to the wisdom of their ancestors, and forming every opinion solely under the influence of the passion of the hour. Mill's projected check upon this deadening conformity of the mass-age is a deliberate encouragement of eccentricity; but that erratic remedy was exposed for what it is by Stephen, and is similarly torn to pieces by the best recent critic of Mill's thought, Mr. R. P. Anschutz:

"This is simply to substitute one error for another—bohemian nonsense for bourgeois nonsense.

Whatever the capacities of any man, in any walk of life, he will necessarily spend a large part of this time in assimilating the traditions of his calling. After that he is usually engaged in a perpetual struggle to be equal to them. It is this which provides the content of his individuality. The assumption of the sort of self-sufficiency that Mill recommends will prevent him from attaining any individuality at all." [4]

But whatever the deficiencies of *Liberty*, it remains a book to rouse our minds to the complexities of that enormous subject. In the modern age, Dean Inge once remarked, freedom survives only in the shadow-world of the intellectuals. If liberty is to be restored to the mass of humanity, the intellectuals, whom Coleridge called the clerisy, must do the work—though they will require imagination of a higher order than Mill himself possessed, if they are to succeed. Various sophisticated definitions of liberty are in fashion just now, particularly among collectivists of one variety or another: Mr. P. C. Gordon Walker, for instance, informs us that liberty is "an activity, an arduous pursuit of a goal that is never reached," and is to be pursued by a gigantic extension of the powers of the state, reaching omnipotently into every household concern. Thinkers of this description share Humpty

---

[4] R. P. Anschutz, *The Philosophy of J. S. Mill* (Oxford: the Clarendon Press, 1953). For an interesting modern adaptation of Mill, particularly on the topic of the "autonomous" individual, see David Riesman, *Individualism Reconsidered* (Glencoe, Illinois: Free Press, 1954). Two recent valuable contributions to the understanding of Mill are F. A. Hayek's *John Stuart Mill and Harriet Taylor* (Chicago: University of Chicago Press, 1950) and Michael St. John Packe's *The Life of John Stuart Mill* (London: Secker and Warburg, 1954).

Dumpty's conviction that when one deals with words, the question is simply who's to be master, that's all: and "liberty" can be made to mean whatever they want it to mean, by rewriting the dictionary.[5] John Stuart Mill, valuing truth and accuracy above all else, never allowed himself to sink into this treacherous game, which George Orwell calls "Newspeak." His little book, though hedged by many limitations and refuted in part by the return of Chaos and old Night, is an honest and high-minded endeavor to examine one quality which lifts man above the brutes.

RUSSELL KIRK

[5] A truly perceptive re-examination of "liberty" is Bertrand de Jouvenel's "A Discussion of Freedom," *Cambridge Journal*, September, 1953.

# ON LIBERTY

# CHAPTER I

## INTRODUCTORY

THE SUBJECT OF THIS ESSAY IS NOT THE so-called Liberty of the Will, so unfortunately opposed to the misnamed doctrine of Philosophical Necessity; but Civil, or Social Liberty: the nature and limits of the power which can be legitimately exercised by society over the individual. A question seldom stated, and hardly ever discussed, in general terms, but which profoundly influences the practical controversies of the age by its latent presence, and is likely soon to make itself recognised as the vital question of the future. It is so far from being new, that, in a certain sense, it has divided mankind, almost from the remotest ages; but in the stage of progress into which the more civilised portions of the species have now entered, it presents itself under new conditions, and requires a different and more fundamental treatment.

The struggle between Liberty and Authority is the most conspicuous feature in the portions of history with which we are earliest familiar, particularly in that of Greece, Rome, and England. But in old times this contest was between subjects, or some classes of subjects, and the Government. By liberty, was meant protection against the tyranny of the political rulers. The rulers were conceived (except in some of the popular governments of Greece) as in a necessarily antagonistic position to the people whom they ruled. They consisted of a governing One, or a governing tribe or caste, who derived their authority from inheritance or conquest, who, at all events, did not hold it at the pleasure of the governed, and whose supremacy men did not venture, perhaps did not desire, to contest, whatever precautions might be taken against its oppressive exercise. Their power was regarded as necessary, but also as highly dangerous; as a weapon which they would attempt to use against their subjects, no less than against external enemies. To prevent the weaker members of the community from being preyed upon by innumerable vultures, it was needful that there should be an animal of prey stronger than the rest, commissioned to keep them down. But as the king of the vultures would be no less bent upon preying on the flock than any of the minor harpies, it was indispensable to be in a perpetual attitude of defence against his beak and claws. The aim, therefore, of patriots was to set limits to the power which the ruler should be suffered to exercise over the community; and this limitation was what they meant by liberty. It was attempted in two ways. First, by obtaining a recognition of certain immunities, called political liberties or rights, which it was to be regarded as a breach of duty in the ruler to infringe, and which if he did infringe, specific resistance, or general rebellion, was held to be justifiable. A second, and generally a later expedient, was the establishment of constitutional checks, by which the consent of the community, or of a body of some sort, supposed to represent its interests, was made a necessary condition to some of the more important acts of the governing power. To the first of these modes of limitation, the ruling power, in most European countries, was compelled, more or less, to submit. It was not so with the second; and, to attain this, or when already in some degree possessed, to attain it more completely, became everywhere the principal object of the lovers of liberty. And so long as mankind were content to combat one enemy by another, and to be ruled by a master, on condition of being guaranteed more or less efficaciously against his tyranny, they did not carry their aspirations beyond this point.

A time, however, came, in the progress of human affairs, when men ceased to think it a necessity of nature that their governors should be an independent power, opposed in interest to themselves. It appeared to them much better that the various magistrates of the State should be their tenants or delegates, revocable at their pleasure. In that way alone, it seemed, could they have complete security that the powers of government would never be abused to their disadvantage. By degrees this new demand for elective and temporary rulers became the prominent object of the exertions of the popular party, wherever any such party existed; and superseded, to a considerable extent, the previous efforts to limit the power of rulers. As the struggle proceeded for making the ruling power emanate from the periodical choice of the ruled,

some persons began to think that too much importance had been attached to the limitation of the
power itself. *That* (it might seem) was a resource
against rulers whose interests were habitually opposed to those of the people. What was now wanted
was, that the rulers should be identified with the
people; that their interest and will should be the
interest and will of the nation. The nation did not
need to be protected against its own will. There
was no fear of its tyrannising over itself. Let the
rulers be effectually responsible to it, promptly
removable by it, and it could afford to trust them
with power of which it could itself dictate the use
to be made. Their power was but the nation's own
power, concentrated, and in a form convenient for
exercise. This mode of thought, or rather perhaps
of feeling, was common among the last generation
of European liberalism, in the Continental section
of which it still apparently predominates. Those
who admit any limit to what a government may do,
except in the case of such governments as they
think ought not to exist, stand out as brilliant exceptions among the political thinkers of the Continent. A similar tone of sentiment might by this
time have been prevalent in our own country, if
the circumstances which for a time encouraged it,
had continued unaltered.

But, in political and philosophical theories, as
well as in persons, success discloses faults and in-
firmities which failure might have concealed from
observation. The notion, that the people have no
need to limit their power over themselves, might
seem axiomatic, when popular government was a
thing only dreamed about, or read of as having

existed at some distant period of the past. Neither was that notion necessarily disturbed by such temporary aberrations as those of the French Revolution, the worst of which were the work of a usurping few, and which, in any case, belonged, not to the permanent working of popular institutions, but to a sudden and convulsive outbreak against monarchical and aristocratic despotism. In time, however, a democratic republic came to occupy a large portion of the earth's surface, and made itself felt as one of the most powerful members of the community of nations; and elective and responsible government became subject to the observations and criticisms which wait upon a great existing fact. It was not perceived that such phrases as "self-government," and "the power of the people over themselves," do not express the true state of the case. The "people" who exercise the power are not always the same people with those over whom it is exercised; and the "self-government" spoken of is not the government of each by himself, but of each by all the rest. The will of the people, moreover, practically means the will of the most numerous or the most active *part* of the people; the majority, or those who succeed in making themselves accepted as the majority; the people, consequently *may* desire to oppress a part of their number; and precautions are as much needed against this as against any other abuse of power. The limitation, therefore, of the power of government over individuals loses none of its importance when the holders of power are regularly accountable to the community, that is, to the strongest party therein. This view of things, recommending itself equally to the intelligence of thinkers and to the inclination of those important classes in European society to whose real or supposed interests democracy is adverse, has had no difficulty in establishing itself; and in political speculations "the tyranny of the majority" is now generally included among the evils against which society requires to be on its guard.

Like other tyrannies, the tyranny of the majority was at first, and is still vulgarly, held in dread, chiefly as operating through the acts of the public authorities. But reflecting persons perceived that when society is itself the tyrant—society collectively over the separate individuals who compose it—its means of tyrannising are not restricted to the acts which it may do by the hands of its political functionaries. Society can and does execute its own mandates: and if it issues wrong mandates instead of right, or any mandates at all in things with which it ought not to meddle, it practises a social tyranny more formidable than many kinds of political oppression, since, though not usually upheld by such extreme penalties, it leaves fewer means of escape, penetrating much more deeply into the details of life, and enslaving the soul itself. Protection, therefore, against the tyranny of the magistrate is not enough: there needs protection also against the tyranny of the prevailing opinion and feeling; against the tendency of society to impose, by other means than civil penalties, its own ideas and practices as rules of conduct on those who dissent from them; to fetter the development, and if possible, prevent the formation, of any individuality not in harmony with its ways, and compel all characters to fashion themselves upon the model of its own. There is a limit to the legitimate interference of collective opinion with individual independence: and to find that limit, and maintain it against encroachment, is as indispensable to a good condition of human affairs, as protection against political despotism.

But though this proposition is not likely to be contested in general terms, the practical question, where to place the limit—how to make the fitting adjustment between individual independence and social control—is a subject on which nearly everything remains to be done. All that makes existence valuable to any one, depends on the enforcement of restraints upon the actions of other people. Some rules of conduct, therefore, must be imposed by law in the first place, and by opinion on many things which are not fit subjects for the operation of law. What these rules should be is the principal question in human affairs; but if we except a few of the most obvious cases, it is one of those which least progress has been made in resolving. No two ages, and scarcely any two countries, have decided it alike; and the decision of one age or country is a wonder to another. Yet the people of any given age and country no more suspect any difficulty in it, than if it were a subject on which mankind has always been agreed. The rules which obtain among themselves appear to them self-evident and self-justifying. This all but universal illusion is one of the examples of the magical influence of custom, which is not only, as the proverb says, a second nature, but is continually mistaken for the first. The effect of custom, in preventing any misgiving respecting the rules of conduct which mankind impose on one another, is all the more complete because the subject is one on which it is not generally considered necessary that reasons should be given, either by one person to others or by each to himself. People are accustomed to believe, and have been encouraged in the belief by some who aspire to the character of philosophers, that their feelings, on subjects of this nature, are better than reasons, and render reasons unnecessary. The practical principle which guides them to their opinions on the regulation of human conduct, is the feeling in each person's mind that everybody should be required to act as he, and those with whom he sympathises, would like them to act. No one, indeed, acknowledges to himself that his standard of judgment is his own liking; but an opinion on a point of conduct, not supported by reasons, can only count as one person's preference; and if the reasons, when given, are a mere appeal to a similar preference felt by other people, it is still only many people's liking instead of one. To an ordinary man, however, his own preference, thus supported, is not only a perfectly satisfactory reason, but the only one he generally has for any of his notions of morality, taste, or propriety, which are not expressly written in his religious creed; and his chief guide in the interpretation even of that. Men's opinions, accordingly, on what is laudable or blamable, are affected by all the multifarious causes which influence their wishes in regard to the conduct of others, and which are as numerous as those which determine their wishes on any other subject. Some times their reason—at other times their prejudices or superstitions: often their social affections, not seldom their antisocial ones, their envy or jealousy, their arrogance or contemptuousness: but most commonly their desires or fears for themselves— their legitimate or illegitimate self-interest. Wherever there is an ascendant class, a large portion of the morality of the country emanates from its class interests, and its feelings of class superiority. The morality between Spartans and Helots, between planters and negroes, between princes and subjects, between nobles and roturiers, between men and women, has been for the most part the creation of these class interests and feelings: and the sentiments thus generated react in turn upon the moral feelings of the members of the ascendant class, in their relations among themselves. Where, on the other hand, a class, formerly ascendant, has lost its ascendancy, or where its ascendancy is unpopular, the prevailing moral sentiments frequently bear the impress of an impatient dislike of superiority. Another grand determining principle of the rules of conduct, both in act and forbearance, which have been enforced by law or opinion, has been the servility of mankind towards the supposed preferences or aversions of the temporal masters or of their gods. This servility, though essentially selfish, is not hypocrisy; it gives rise to perfectly genuine sentiments of abhorrence; it made men burn magicians and heretics. Among so many baser influences, the general and obvious interests of society have of course had a share, and a large one, in the direction of the moral sentiments: less, however, as a matter of reason, and on their own account, than as a consequence of the sympathies

9

and antipathies which grew out of them: and sympathies and antipathies which had little or nothing to do with the interests of society, have made themselves felt in the establishment of moralities with quite as great force.

The likings and dislikings of society, or of some powerful portion of it, are thus the main thing which has practically determined the rules laid down for general observance, under the penalties of law or opinion. And in general, those who have been in advance of society in thought and feeling, have left this condition of things unassailed in principle, however they may have come into conflict with it in some of its details. They have occupied themselves rather in inquiring what things society ought to like or dislike, than in questioning whether its likings or dislikings should be a law to individuals. They preferred endeavouring to alter the feelings of mankind on the particular points on which they were themselves heretical, rather than make common cause in defence of freedom, with heretics generally. The only case in which the higher ground has been taken on principle and maintained with consistency, by any but an individual here and there, is that of religious belief: a case instructive in many ways, and not least so as forming a most striking instance of the fallibility of what is called the moral sense: for the *odium theologicum*, in a sincere bigot, is one of the most unequivocal cases of moral feeling. Those who first broke the yoke of what called itself the Universal Church, were in general as little willing to permit difference of religious opinion as that church itself. But when the heat of the conflict was over, without giving a complete victory to any party, and each church or sect was reduced to limit its hopes to retaining possession of the ground it already occupied; minorities, seeing that they had no chance of becoming majorities, were under the necessity of pleading to those whom they could not convert, for permission to differ. It is accordingly on this battle field, almost solely, that the rights of the individual against society have been asserted on broad grounds of principle, and the claim of society to exercise authority over dissentients openly controverted. The great writers to whom the world owes what religious liberty it possesses, have mostly asserted freedom of conscience as an indefeasible right, and denied absolutely that a human being is accountable to others for his religious beliefs. Yet so natural to mankind is intolerance in whatever they really care about, that religious freedom has hardly anywhere been practically realised, except where religious indifference, which dislikes to have its peace disturbed by theological quarrels, has added its weight to the scale. In the minds of almost all religious persons, even in the most tolerant countries, the duty of toleration is admitted with tacit reserves. One person will bear with dissent in matters of church government, but not of dogma; another can tolerate everybody, short of a Papist or a Unitarian; another everyone who believes in revealed religion; a few extend their charity a little further, but stop at the belief in a God and in a future state. Wherever the sentiment of the majority is still genuine and intense, it is found to have abated little of its claim to be obeyed.

In England, from the peculiar circumstances of

our political history, though the yoke of opinion is perhaps heavier, that of law is lighter, than in most other countries of Europe; and there is considerable jealousy of direct interference, by the legislative or the executive power with private conduct; not so much from any just regard for the independence of the individual, as from the still subsisting habit of looking on the government as representing an opposite interest to the public. The majority have not yet learnt to feel the power of the government their power, or its opinions their opinions. When they do so, individual liberty will probably be as much exposed to invasion from the government, as it already is from public opinion. But, as yet, there is a considerable amount of feeling ready to be called forth against any attempt of the law to control individuals in things in which they have not hitherto been accustomed to be controlled by it; and this with very little discrimination as to whether the matter is, or is not, within the legitimate sphere of legal control; insomuch that the feeling, highly salutary on the whole, is perhaps quite as often misplaced as well grounded in the particular instances of its application. There is, in fact, no recognised principle by which the propriety or impropriety of government interference is customarily tested. People decide according to their personal preferences. Some, whenever they see any good to be done, or evil to be remedied, would willingly instigate the government to undertake the business; while others prefer to bear almost any amount of social evil rather than add one to the departments of human interests amenable to governmental control. And men range themselves on one or the other side in any particular case, according to this general direction of their sentiments; or according to the degree of interest which they feel in the particular thing which it is proposed that the government should do, or according to the belief they entertain that the government would, or would not, do it in the manner they prefer; but very rarely on account of any opinion to which they consistently adhere, as to what things are fit to be done by a government. And it seems to me that in consequence of this absence of rule or principle, one side is at present as often wrong as the other; the interference of government is, with about equal frequency, improperly invoked and improperly condemned.

The object of this Essay is to assert one very simple principle, as entitled to govern absolutely the dealings of society with the individual in the way of compulsion and control, whether the means used be physical force in the form of legal penalties, or the moral coercion of public opinion. That principle is, that the sole end for which mankind are warranted, individually or collectively, in interfering with the liberty of action of any of their number, is self-protection. That the only purpose for which power can be rightfully exercised over any member of a civilised community, against his will, is to prevent harm to others. His own good, either physical or moral, is not a sufficient warrant. He cannot rightfully be compelled to do or forbear because it will be better for him to do so, because it will make him happier, because, in the opinions of others, to do so would be wise, or even right. These are good reasons for remonstrating with him, or reasoning with him, or persuading him, or entreating him, but not for compelling him, or visiting him with any evil in case he do otherwise. To justify that, the conduct from which it is desired to deter him must be calculated to produce evil to someone else. The only part of the conduct of anyone, for which he is amenable to society, is that which concerns others. In the part which merely concerns himself, his independence is, of right, absolute. Over himself, over his own body and mind, the individual is sovereign.

It is, perhaps, hardly necessary to say that this doctrine is meant to apply only to human beings in the maturity of their faculties. We are not speaking of children, or of young persons below the age which the law may fix as that of manhood or womanhood. Those who are still in a state to require being taken care of by others, must be protected against their own actions as well as against external injury. For the same reason, we may leave out of consideration those backward states of society in which the race itself may be considered as in its nonage. The early difficulties in the way of spontaneous progress are so great, that there is seldom any choice of means for overcoming them; and a ruler full of the spirit of improvement is warranted in the use of any expedients that will attain an end, perhaps otherwise unattainable. Despotism is a legitimate mode of government in dealing with barbarians, provided the end be their improvement, and the means justified by actually effecting that end. Liberty, as a principle, has no application to any state of things anterior to the time when mankind have become capable of being improved by free and equal discussion. Until then, there is nothing for them but implicit obedience to an Akbar or a Charlemagne, if they are so fortunate as to find one. But as soon as mankind have attained the capacity of being guided to their own improvement by conviction or persuasion (a period long since reached in all nations with whom we need here concern ourselves), compulsion, either in the direct form or in that of pains and penalties for non-compliance, is no longer admissible as a means to their own good, and justifiable only for the security of others.

It is proper to state that I forego any advantage which could be derived to my argument from the idea of abstract right, as a thing independent of utility. I regard utility as the ultimate appeal on all ethical questions; but it must be utility in the largest sense, grounded on the permanent interests of a man as a progressive being. Those interests, I contend, authorise the subjection of individual spontaneity to external control, only in respect to those actions of each which concern the interest of other people. If any one does an act hurtful to others, there is a *prima facie* case for punishing him, by law, or, where legal penalties are not safely applicable, by general disapprobation. There are also many positive acts for the benefit of others, which he may rightfully be compelled to perform; such as to give evidence in a court of justice; to bear his fair share in the common defence, or in any other joint work necessary to the interest of the society of which he enjoys the protection; and to perform certain acts of individual

15

beneficence, such as saving a fellow-creature's life, or interposing to protect the defenceless against ill-usage, things which whenever it is obviously a man's duty to do, he may rightfully be made responsible to society for not doing. A person may cause evil to others not only by his actions but by his inaction, and in either case he is justly accountable to them for the injury. The latter case, it is true, requires a much more cautious exercise of compulsion than the former. To make any one answerable for doing evil to others is the rule; to make him answerable for not preventing evil is, comparatively speaking, the exception. Yet there are many cases clear enough and grave enough to justify that exception. In all things which regard the external relations of the individual, he is *de jure* amenable to those whose interests are concerned, and, if need be, to society as their protector. There are often good reasons for not holding him to the responsibility; but these reasons must arise from the special expediencies of the case: either because it is a kind of case in which he is on the whole likely to act better, when left to his own discretion, than when controlled in any way in which society have it in their power to control him; or because the attempt to exercise control would produce other evils, greater than those which it would prevent. When such reasons as these preclude the enforcement of responsibility, the conscience of the agent himself should step into the vacant judgment seat, and protect those interests of others who have no external protection; judging himself all the more rigidly, because the case does not admit of his being made accountable to the judgment of his fellow-creatures.

But there is a sphere of action in which society, as distinguished from the individual, has, if any, only an indirect interest; comprehending all that portion of a person's life and conduct which affects only himself, or if it also affects others, only with their free, voluntary, and undeceived consent and participation. When I say only himself, I mean directly, and in the first instance; for whatever affects himself, may affect others through himself; and the objection which may be grounded on this contingency, will receive consideration in the sequel. This, then, is the appropriate region of human liberty. It comprises, first, the inward domain of consciousness; demanding liberty of conscience in the most comprehensive sense; liberty of thought and feeling; absolute freedom of opinion and sentiment on all subjects, practical or speculative, scientific, moral, or theological. The liberty of expressing and publishing opinions may seem to fall under a different principle, since it belongs to that part of the conduct of an individual which concerns other people; but, being almost of as much importance as the liberty of thought itself, and resting in great part on the same reasons, is practically inseparable from it. Secondly, the principle requires liberty of tastes and pursuits; of framing the plan of our life to suit our own character; of doing as we like, subject to such consequences as may follow: without impediment from our fellow-creatures, so long as what we do does not harm them, even though they should think our conduct foolish, perverse, or wrong. Thirdly, from this liberty of each individual, follows the liberty, within the same limits, of combination among individuals; freedom to unite, for any purpose not involving harm to others: the persons combining being supposed to be of full age, and not forced or deceived.

No society in which these liberties are not, on the whole, respected, is free, whatever may be its form of government; and none is completely free in which they do not exist absolute and unqualified. The only freedom which deserves the name, is that of pursuing our own good in our own way, so long as we do not attempt to deprive others of theirs, or impede their efforts to obtain it. Each is the proper guardian of his own health, whether bodily, *or* mental and spiritual. Mankind are greater gainers by suffering each other to live as seems good to themselves, than by compelling each to live as seems good to the rest.

Though this doctrine is anything but new, and, to some persons, may have the air of a truism, there is no doctrine which stands more directly opposed to the general tendency of existing opinion and practice. Society has expended fully as much effort in the attempt (according to its lights) to compel people to conform to its notions of personal as of social excellence. The ancient commonwealths thought themselves entitled to practise, and the ancient philosophers countenanced, the regulation of every part of private conduct by public authority, on the ground that the State had a deep interest in the whole bodily and mental discipline of every one of its citizens; a mode of thinking which may have been admissible in small republics surrounded by powerful enemies, in constant peril of being subverted by foreign attack or internal commotion, and to which even a short interval of relaxed energy and self-command might so easily be fatal that they could not afford to wait for the salutary permanent effects of freedom. In the modern world, the greater size of political communities, and, above all, the separation between spiritual and temporal authority (which placed the direction of men's consciences in other hands than those which controlled their worldly affairs), prevented so great an interference by law in the details of private life; but the engines of moral repression have been wielded more strenuously against divergence from the reigning opinion in self-regarding, than even in social matters; religion, the most powerful of the elements which have entered into the formation of moral feeling, having almost always been governed either by the ambition of a hierarchy, seeking control over every department of human conduct, or by the spirit of Puritanism. And some of those modern reformers who have placed themselves in strongest opposition to the religions of the past, have been noway behind either churches or sects in their assertion of the right of spiritual domination: M. Comte, in particular, whose social system, as unfolded in his *Système de Politique Positive,* aims at establishing (though by moral more than by legal appliances) a despotism of society over the individual, surpassing anything contemplated in the political ideal of the most rigid disciplinarian among the ancient philosophers.

Apart from the peculiar tenets of individual

thinkers, there is also in the world at large an increasing inclination to stretch unduly the powers of society over the individual, both by the force of opinion, and even by that of legislation; and as the tendency of all the changes taking place in the world is to strengthen society, and diminish the power of the individual, this encroachment is not one of the evils which tend spontaneously to disappear, but, on the contrary, to grow more and more formidable. The disposition of mankind, whether as rulers or as fellow-citizens, to impose their own opinions and inclinations as a rule of conduct on others, is so energetically supported by some of the best and by some of the worst feelings incident to human nature, that it is hardly ever kept under restraint by anything but want of power; and as the power is not declining, but growing, unless a strong barrier of moral conviction can be raised against the mischief, we must expect, in the present circumstances of the world to see it increase.

It will be convenient for the argument, if, instead of at once entering upon the general thesis, we confine ourselves in the first instance to a single branch of it, on which the principle here stated is, if not fully, yet to a certain point, recognised by the current opinions. This one branch is the Liberty of Thought: from which it is impossible to separate the cognate liberty of speaking and of writing. Although these liberties, to some considerable amount, form part of the political morality of all countries which profess religious toleration and free institutions, the grounds, both philosophical and practical, on which they rest, are perhaps not so familiar to the general mind, nor so thoroughly appreciated by many even of the leaders of opinion, as might have been expected. Those grounds, when rightly understood, are of much wider application than to only one division of the subject, and a thorough consideration of this part of the question will be found the best introduction to the remainder. Those to whom nothing which I am about to say will be new, may therefore, I hope, excuse me, if on a subject which for now three centuries has been so often discussed, I venture on one discussion more.

# CHAPTER II

## OF THE LIBERTY OF THOUGHT
## AND DISCUSSION

THE TIME, IT IS TO BE HOPED, IS GONE BY, WHEN
any defence would be necessary of the "liberty of
the press" as one of the securities against corrupt
or tyrannical government. No argument, we may
suppose, can now be needed, against permitting a
legislature or an executive, not identified in interest with the people, to prescribe opinions to
them, and determine what doctrines or what arguments they shall be allowed to hear. This aspect
of the question, besides, has been so often and so
triumphantly enforced by preceding writers, that
it needs not be specially insisted on in this place.
Though the law of England, on the subject of the
press, is as servile to this day as it was in the time
of the Tudors, there is little danger of its being
actually put in force against political discussion,
except during some temporary panic, when fear of
insurrection drives ministers and judges from their
propriety;[1] and, speaking generally, it is not, in

[1] These words had scarcely been written, when, as if to give
them an emphatic contradiction, occurred the Government Press
Prosecutions of 1858. That ill-judged interference with the liberty

22

constitutional countries, to be apprehended, that the government, whether completely responsible to the people or not, will often attempt to control the expression of opinion, except when in doing so it makes itself the organ of the general intolerance of the public. Let us suppose, therefore, that the government is entirely at one with the people, and never thinks of exerting any power of coercion unless in agreement with what it conceives to be their voice. But I deny the right of the people to exercise such coercion, either by themselves or by their government. The power itself is illegitimate. The best government has no more title to it than

of public discussion has not, however, induced me to alter a single word in the text, nor has it at all weakened my conviction that, moments of panic excepted, the era of pains and penalties for political discussion, has in our own country, passed away. For, in the first place the prosecutions were not persisted in; and, in the second, they were never, properly speaking, political prosecutions. The offence charged was not that of criticising institutions, or the acts or persons of rulers, but of circulating what was deemed an immoral doctrine, the lawfulness of Tyrannicide.

If the arguments of the present chapter are of any validity, there ought to exist the fullest liberty of professing and discussing, as a matter of ethical conviction, any doctrine, however immoral it may be considered. It would, therefore, be irrelevant and out of place to examine here, whether the doctrine of Tyrannicide deserves that title. I shall content myself with saying that the subject has been at all times one of the open questions of morals; that the act of a private citizen in striking down a criminal, who, by raising himself above the law, has placed himself beyond the reach of legal punishment or control, has been accounted by whole nations, and by some of the best and wisest of men, not a crime, but an act of exalted virtue; and that, right or wrong, it is not of the nature of assassination, but of civil war. As such, I hold that the instigation to it, in a specific case, may be a proper subject of punishment, but only if an overt act has followed, and at least a probable connection can be established between the act and the instigation. Even then, it is not a foreign government, but the very government assailed, which alone, in the exercise of self-defence, can legitimately punish attacks directed against its own existence.

the worst. It is as noxious, or more noxious, when exerted in accordance with public opinion, than when in opposition to it. If all mankind minus one were of one opinion, and only one person were of the contrary opinion, mankind would be no more justified in silencing that one person, than he, if he had the power, would be justified in silencing mankind. Were an opinion a personal possession of no value except to the owner; if to be obstructed in the enjoyment of it were simply a private injury, it would make some difference whether the injury was inflicted only on a few persons or on many. But the peculiar evil of silencing the expression of an opinion is, that it is robbing the human race: posterity as well as the existing generation; those who dissent from the opinion, still more than those who hold it. If the opinion is right, they are deprived of the opportunity of exchanging error for truth: if wrong, they lose, what is almost as great a benefit, the clearer perception and livelier impression of truth, produced by its collision with error.

It is necessary to consider separately these two hypotheses, each of which has a distinct branch of the argument corresponding to it. We can never be sure that the opinion we are endeavouring to stifle is a false opinion; and if we were sure, stifling it would be an evil still.

First: the opinion which it is attempted to suppress by authority may possibly be true. Those who desire to suppress it, of course deny its truth; but they are not infallible. They have no authority to decide the question for all mankind, and exclude every other person from the means of judging. To refuse a hearing to an opinion, because they are sure that it is false, is to assume that *their* certainty is the same thing as *absolute* certainty. All silencing of discussion is an assumption of infallibility. Its condemnation may be allowed to rest on this common argument, not the worse for being common.

Unfortunately for the good sense of mankind, the fact of their fallibility is far from carrying the weight in their practical judgment which is always allowed to it in theory; for while every one well knows himself to be fallible, few think it necessary to take any precautions against their own fallibility, or admit the supposition that any opinion, of which they feel very certain, may be one of the examples of the error to which they acknowledge themselves to be liable. Absolute princes, or others who are accustomed to unlimited deference, usually feel this complete confidence in their own opinions on nearly all subjects. People more happily situated, who sometimes hear their opinions disputed, and are not wholly unused to be set right when they are wrong, place the same unbounded reliance only on such of their opinions as are shared by all who surround them, or to whom they habitually defer; for in proportion to a man's want of confidence in his own solitary judgment, does he usually repose, with implicit trust, on the infallibility of "the world" in general. And the world, to each individual, means the part of it with which he comes in contact: his party, his sect, his church, his class of society; the man may be called, by comparison, almost liberal and large-minded to whom it means anything so comprehensive as his own country or his own age. Nor is his faith in this collective authority at all shaken by his being aware that other ages, countries, sects, churches, classes, and parties have thought, and even now think, the exact reverse. He devolves upon his own world the responsibility of being in the right against the dissentient worlds of other people; and it never troubles him that mere accident has decided which of these numerous worlds is the object of his reliance, and that the same causes which make him a Churchman in London, would have made him a Buddhist or a Confucian in Pekin. Yet it is as evident in itself, as any amount of argument can make it, that ages are no more infallible than individuals; every age having held many opinions which subsequent ages have deemed not only false but absurd; and it is as certain that many opinions now general will be rejected by future ages, as it is that many, once general, are rejected by the present.

The objection likely to be made to this argument would probably take some such form as the following. There is no greater assumption of infallibility in forbidding the propagation of error, than in any other thing which is done by public authority on its own judgment and responsibility. Judgment is given to men that they may use it. Because it may be used erroneously, are men to be told that they ought not to use it all? To prohibit what they think pernicious, is not claiming exemption from error, but fulfilling the duty incumbent on them, although fallible, of acting on their conscientious conviction. If we were never to act on our opinions, because those opinions may be wrong, we should leave all our interest uncared for, and all our duties unperformed. An objection which applies to all conduct can be no valid objection to conduct in particular. It is the duty of governments and of individuals, to form the truest opinions they can; to form them carefully, and never impose them upon others unless they are quite sure of being right. But when they are sure (such reasoners may say), it is not conscientiousness but cowardice to shrink from acting on their opinions, and allow doctrines which they honestly think dangerous to the welfare of mankind, either in this life or in another, to be scattered abroad without restraint, because other people, in less enlightened times, have persecuted opinions now believed to be true. Let us take care, it may be said, not to make the same mistake; but governments and nations have made mistakes in other things, which are not denied to be fit subjects for the exercise of authority: they have laid on bad taxes, made unjust wars. Ought we therefore to lay on no taxes, and, under whatever provocation, make no wars? Men, and governments, must act to the best of their ability. There is no such thing as absolute certainty, but there is assurance sufficient for the purposes of human life. We may, and must, assume our opinion to be true for the guidance of our own conduct: and it is assuming no more when we forbid bad men to pervert society by the propagation of opinions which we regard as false and pernicious.

I answer, that it is assuming very much more. There is the greatest difference between presuming an opinion to be true, because, with every opportunity for contesting it, it has not been refuted, and assuming its truth for the purpose of not permitting its refutation. Complete liberty of contra-condition which justifies us in assuming its truth dicting and disproving our opinion is the very for purposes of action; and on no other terms can a being with human faculties have any rational assurance of being right.

When we consider either the history of opinion, or the ordinary conduct of human life, to what is it to be ascribed that the one and the other are no worse than they are? Not certainly to the inherent force of the human understanding; for, on any matter not self-evident, there are ninety-nine persons totally incapable of judging of it for one who is capable; and the capacity of the hundredth person is only comparative; for the majority of the eminent men of every past generation held many opinions now known to be erroneous, and did or approved numerous things which no one will now justify. Why is it, then, that there is on the whole a preponderance among mankind of rational opinions and rational conduct? If there really is this preponderance—which there must be unless human affairs are, and have always been, in an almost desperate state—it is owing to a quality of the human mind, the source of everything respectable in man either as an intellectual or as a moral being, namely, that his errors are corrigible. He is capable of rectifying his mistakes, by discussion and experience. Not by experience alone. There must be discussion, to show how experience is to be interpreted. Wrong opinions and practices gradually yield to fact and argument; but facts and arguments, to produce any effect on the mind, must be brought before it. Very few facts are able to tell their own story, without comments to bring out their meaning. The whole strength and value, then, of human judgment, depending on the one property, that it can be set right when it is wrong, reliance can be placed on it only when the means of setting it right are kept constantly at hand. In the case of any person whose judgment is really deserving of confidence, how has it become so? Because he has kept his mind open to criticism of his opinions and conduct. Because it has been his practice to listen to all that could be said against him; to profit by as much of it as was just, and expound to himself, and upon occasion to others, the fallacy of what was fallacious. Because he has felt, that the only way in which a human being can make some approach to knowing the whole of a subject, is by hearing what can be said about it by persons of every variety of opinion, and studying all modes in which it can be looked at by every character of mind. No wise man ever acquired his wisdom in any mode but this; nor is it in the nature of human intellect to become wise in any other manner. The steady habit of correcting and completing his own opinion by collating it with those of others, so far from causing doubt and hesitation in carrying it into practice, is the only stable foundation for a just reliance on it: for, being cognisant of all that can, at least obviously, be said against him, and having taken up his position against all gainsayers—knowing that he has sought for objections and difficulties, instead of avoiding them, and has shut out no light which can be thrown upon the subject from any quarter—he has a right to think his judgment better than that of any person, or any multitude, who have not gone through a similar process.

It is not too much to require that what the wisest of mankind, those who are best entitled to trust their own judgment, find necessary to warrant their relying on it, should be submitted to by that miscellaneous collection of a few wise and many foolish individuals, called the public. The most intolerant of churches, the Roman Catholic Church, even at the canonisation of a saint, admits, and listens patiently to, a "devil's advocate." The holiest of men, it appears, cannot be admitted to posthumous honours, until all that the devil could say against him is known and weighed. If even the Newtonian philosophy were not permitted to be questioned, mankind could not feel as complete assurance of its truth as they now do. The beliefs which we have most warrant for have no safeguard to rest on but a standing invitation to the whole world to prove them unfounded. If the challenge is not accepted, or is accepted and the attempt fails, we are far enough from certainty still; but we have done the best that the existing state of human reason admits of; we have neglected nothing that could give the truth a chance of reaching us: if the lists are kept open, we may hope that if there be a better truth, it will be found when the human mind is capable of receiving it; and in the meantime we may rely on having attained such approach to truth as is possible in our own way. This is the amount of certainty attainable by a fallible being, and this the sole way of attaining it.

Strange it is, that men should admit the validity of the arguments for free discussion, but object to their being "pushed to an extreme"; not seeing that unless the reasons are good for an extreme case, they are not good for any case. Strange that they should imagine that they are not assuming infallibility, when they acknowledge that there should be free discussion on all subjects which can possibly be *doubtful*, but think that some particular principle or doctrine should be forbidden to be questioned because it is so *certain*, that is, because *they are certain* that it is certain. To call any proposition certain, while there is any who would deny its certainty if permitted, but who is not permitted, is to assume that we ourselves and those who agree with us, are the judges of certainty, and judges without hearing the other side.

In the present age—which has been described as "destitute of faith, but terrified at skepticism"— in which people feel sure, not so much that their opinions are true, as that they should not know what to do without them—the claims of an opinion to be protected from public attack are rested not so much on its truth, as on its importance to society. There are, it is alleged, certain beliefs so useful, not to say indispensable, to well-being that it is as much the duty of governments to uphold those beliefs, as to protect any other of the interests of society. In a case of such necessity, and so directly in the line of their duty, something less than infallibility may, it is maintained, warrant, and even bind, governments to act on their own opinion, confirmed by the general opinion of mankind. It is also often argued, and still oftener thought, that none but bad men would desire to weaken these salutary beliefs; and there can be nothing wrong, it is thought, in restraining bad men, and prohibiting what only such men would wish to practise. This mode of thinking makes the justification of restraints on discussion not a question of the truth of doctrines, but of their usefulness; and flatters itself by that means to escape the responsibility of claiming to be an infallible judge of opinions. But those who thus satisfy themselves, do not perceive that the assumption of infallibility is merely shifted from one point to another. The usefulness of an opinion is itself a matter of opinion: as disputable, as open to discussion, and requiring discussion as much as the opinion itself. There is the same need of an infallible judge of opinions to decide an opinion to be noxious, as to decide it to be false, unless the opinion condemned has full opportunity of defending itself. And it will not do to say that the heretic may be allowed to maintain the utility or harmlessness of his opinion, though forbidden to maintain its truth. The truth of an opinion is part of its utility. If we would know whether or not it is desirable that a proposition should be believed, is it possible to exclude the consideration of whether or not it is true? In the opinion, not of bad men, but of the best men, no belief which is contrary to truth can be really useful: and can you prevent such men from urging that plea, when they are charged with culpability for denying some doctrine which they are told is useful, but which they believe to be false? Those who are on the side of received opinions never fail to take all possible advantage of this plea; you do not find *them* handling the question of utility as if it could be completely abstracted from that of truth: on the contrary, it is, above all, because their doctrine is "the truth," that the knowledge or the belief of it is held to be so indispensable. There can be no fair discussion of the question of usefulness when an argument so vital may be employed on one side, but not on the other. And in point of fact, when law or public feeling do not permit the truth of an opinion to be disputed, they are just as little tolerant of a denial of its usefulness. The utmost they allow is an extenuation of its absolute necessity, or of the positive guilt of rejecting it.

In order more fully to illustrate the mischief of denying a hearing to opinions because we, in our own judgment, have condemned them, it will be desirable to fix down the discussion to a concrete case; and I choose, by preference, the cases which are least favourable to me—in which the argument against freedom of opinion, both on the score of truth and on that of utility, is considered the strongest. Let the opinions impugned be the belief in a God and in a future state, or any of the commonly received doctrines of morality. To fight the battle on such ground gives a great advantage to an unfair antagonist; since he will be sure to say (and many who have no desire to be unfair will say it internally), Are these the doctrines which you do not deem sufficiently certain to be taken under the protection of the law? Is the belief in a God one of the opinions to feel sure of which you hold to be assuming infallibility? But I must be permitted to observe, that it is not the feeling sure of a doctrine (be it what it may) which I call an assumption of infallibility. It is the undertaking to decide that question *for others,* without allowing them to hear what can be said on the contrary side. And I denounce and reprobate this pretension not the less, if put forth on the side of my solemn convictions. However positive any one's persuasion may be, not only of the falsity but of the pernicious consequences, not only of the pernicious consequences, but (to adopt expressions which I altogether condemn) the immorality and impiety of an opinion; yet, if, in pursuance of that private judgment though backed by the public judgment of his country or his contemporaries, he prevents the opinion from being heard in its defence, he assumes infallibility. And so far from the assumption being less objectionable or less dangerous because the opinion is called immoral or impious, this is the case of all others in which it is most fatal. These are exactly the occasions on which men of one generation commit those dreadful mistakes which excite the astonishment and horror of posterity. It is among such that we find the instances memorable in history, when the arm of the law has been employed to root out the best men and the noblest doctrines; with deplorable success as to the men, though some of the doctrines have survived to be (as if in mockery) invoked in defence of similar conduct towards those who dissent from *them,* or from their received interpretation.

Mankind can hardly be too often reminded, that there was once a man named Socrates, between whom and the legal authorities and public opinion of his time there took place a memorable collision. Born in an age and country abounding in individual greatness, this man has been handed down to us by those who best knew both him and the age, as the most virtuous man in it; while *we* know him as the head and prototype of all subsequent teachers of virtue, the source equally of the lofty inspiration of Plato and the judicious utilitarianism of Aristotle, *"i maëstri di color che sanno,"* the two headsprings of ethical as of all other philosophy. This acknowledged master of all the eminent thinkers who have since lived—whose fame, still growing after more than two thousand years, all but outweighs the whole remainder of the names which make his native city illustrious—was put to death by his countrymen, after a judicial conviction, for impiety and immorality. Impiety, in denying the gods recognised by the State; indeed his accuser asserted (see the "Apologia") that he believed in no gods at all. Immorality, in being, by his doctrines and instructions, a "corruptor of youth." Of these charges the tribunal, there is every ground for believing, honestly found him guilty, and condemned the man who probably of all then born had deserved best of mankind to be put to death as a criminal.

To pass from this to the only other instance of judicial iniquity, the mention of which, after the condemnation of Socrates, would not be an anti-climax: the event which took place on Calvary rather more than eighteen hundred years ago. The man who left on the memory of those who witnessed his life and conversation such an impression of his moral grandeur that eighteen subsequent centuries have done homage to him as the Almighty in person, was ignominiously put to death, as what?

As a blasphemer. Men did not merely mistake their benefactor; they mistook him for the exact contrary of what he was, and treated him as that prodigy of impiety which they themselves are now held to be for their treatment of him. The feelings with which mankind now regard these lamentable transactions, especially the later of the two, render them extremely unjust in their judgment of the unhappy actors. These were, to all appearance, not bad men—not worse than men commonly are, but rather the contrary; men who possessed in a full, or somewhat more than a full measure, the religious, moral, and patriotic feelings of their time and people: the very kind of men who, in all times, our own included, have every chance of passing through life blameless and respected. The highpriest who rent his garments when the words were pronounced, which, according to all the ideas of his country, constituted the blackest guilt, was in all probability quite as sincere in his horror and indignation as the generality of respectable and pious men now are in the religious and moral sentiments they profess; and most of those who now shudder at his conduct, if they had lived in his time, and been born Jews, would have acted precisely as he did. Orthodox Christians who are tempted to think that those who stoned to death the first martyrs must have been worse men than they themselves are, ought to remember that one of those persecutors was Saint Paul.

Let us add one more example, the most striking of all, if the impressiveness of an error is measured by the wisdom and virtue of him who falls into it. If ever any one, possessed of power, had grounds for thinking himself the best and most enlightened among his contemporaries, it was the Emperor Marcus Aurelius. Absolute monarch of the whole civilized world, he preserved through life not only the most unblemished justice, but what was less to be expected from his Stoical breeding, the tenderest heart. The few failings which are attributed to him were all on the side of indulgence: while his writings, the highest ethical product of the ancient mind, differ scarcely perceptibly, if they differ at all, from the most characteristic teachings of Christ. This man, a better Christian in all but the dogmatic sense of the word than almost any of the ostensibly Christian sovereigns who have since reigned, persecuted Christianity. Placed at the summit of all the previous attainments of humanity, with an open, unfettered intellect, and a character which led him of himself to embody in his moral writings the Christian idea, he yet failed to see that Christianity was to be a good and not an evil to the world, with his duties to which he was so ˙eeply penetrated. Existing society he knew to be n a deplorable state. But such as it was, he saw, or thought he saw, that it was held together, and prevented from being worse, by belief and reverence of the received divinities. As a ruler of mankind, he deemed it his duty not to suffer society to fall in pieces; and saw not how, if its existing ties were removed, any others could be formed which could again knit it together. The new religion openly aimed at dissolving these ties: unless, therefore, it was his duty to adopt that religion, it seemed to be his duty to put it down. Inasmuch then as the theology of Christianity did not appear to him true or of divine origin; inasmuch as this strange history of a crucified God was not credible to him, and a system which purported to rest entirely upon a foundation to him so wholly unbelievable, could not be foreseen by him to be that renovating agency which, after all abatements, it has in fact proved to be; the gentlest and most amiable of philosophers and rulers, under a solemn sense of duty, authorised the persecution of Christianity. To my mind this is one of the most tragical facts in all history. It is a bitter thought, how different a thing the Christianity of the world might have been, if the Christian faith had been adopted as the religion of the empire under the auspices of Marcus Aurelius instead of those of Constantine. But it would be equally unjust to him and false to truth to deny, that no one plea which can be urged for punishing anti-Christian teaching was wanting to Marcus Aurelius for punishing, as he did, the propagation of Christianity. No Christian more firmly believes that Atheism is false, and tends to the dissolution of society, than Marcus Aurelius believed the same things of Christianity; he who, of all men then living, might have been thought the most capable of appreciating it. Unless any one who approves of punishment for the promulgation of opinions, flatters himself that he is a wiser and better man than Marcus Aurelius—more deeply versed in the wisdom of his time, more elevated in his intellect above it—more earnest in his search for truth, or more single-minded in his devotion to it when found; let him abstain from that assumption of the joint infallibility of himself and

the multitude, which the great Antoninus made
with so unfortunate a result.

Aware of the impossibility of defending the use
of punishment for restraining irreligious opinions
by any argument which will not justify Marcus
Antoninus, the enemies of religious freedom, when
hard pressed, occasionally accept this consequence,
and say, with Dr. Johnson, that the persecutors of
Christianity were in the right; that persecution is
an ordeal through which truth ought to pass, and
always passes successfully, legal penalties being, in
the end, powerless against truth, though sometimes
beneficially effective against mischievous errors.
This is a form of the argument for religious intolerance sufficiently remarkable not to be passed without notice.

A theory which maintains that truth may justifiably be persecuted because persecution cannot
possibly do it any harm, cannot be charged with
being intentionally hostile to the reception of new
truths; but we cannot commend the generosity of
its dealing with the persons to whom mankind are
indebted for them. To discover to the world something which deeply concerns it, and of which it was
previously ignorant; to prove to it that it had been
mistaken on some vital point of temporal or
spiritual interest, is as important a service as a
human being can render to his fellow-creatures,
and in certain cases, as in those of the early Christians and of the Reformers, those who think with
Dr. Johnson believe it to have been the most precious gift which could be bestowed on mankind.
That the authors of such splendid benefits should

be requited by martyrdom; that their reward should be to be dealt with as the vilest of criminals, is not, upon this theory, a deplorable error and misfortune, for which humanity should mourn in sackcloth and ashes, but the normal and justifiable state of things. The propounder of a new truth, according to this doctrine, should stand, as stood, in the legislation of the Locrians, the proposer of a new law, with a halter round his neck, to be instantly tightened if the public assembly did not, on hearing his reasons, then and there adopt his proposition. People who defend this mode of treating benefactors cannot be supposed to set much value on the benefit; and I believe this view of the subject is mostly confined to the sort of persons who think that new truths may have been desirable once, but that we have had enough of them now.

But, indeed, the dictum that truth always triumphs over persecution is one of those pleasant falsehoods which men repeat after one another till they pass into common-places, but which all experience refutes. History teems with instances of truth put down by persecution. If not suppressed for ever, it may be thrown back for centuries. To speak only of religious opinions: the Reformation broke out at least twenty times before Luther, and was put down. Arnold of Brescia was put down. Fra Dolcino was put down. Savonarola was put down. The Albigeois were put down. The Vaudois were put down. The Lollards were put down. The Hussites were put down. Even after the era of Luther, wherever persecution was persisted in, it was successful. In Spain, Italy, Flanders, the Austrian empire, Protestantism was rooted out; and, most likely, would have been so in England, had Queen Mary lived, or Queen Elizabeth died. Persecution has always succeeded, save where the heretics were too strong a party to be effectually persecuted. No reasonable person can doubt that Christianity might have been extirpated in the Roman Empire. It spread, and became predominant, because the persecutions were only occasional, lasting but a short time, and separated by long intervals of almost undisturbed propagandism. It is a piece of idle sentimentality that truth, merely as truth, has any inherent power denied to error of prevailing against the dungeon and the stake. Men are not more zealous for truth than they often are for error, and a sufficient application of legal or even of social penalties will generally succeed in stopping the propagation of either. The real advantage which truth has consists in that, that when an opinion is true, it may be extinguished once, twice, or many times, but in the course of ages there will generally be found persons to rediscover it, until some one of its reappearances falls on a time when from favourable circumstances it escapes persecution until it has made such head as to withstand all subsequent attempts to suppress it.

It will be said, that we do not now put to death the introducers of new opinions: we are not like our fathers who slew the prophets, we even build sepulchres to them. It is true we no longer put heretics to death; and the amount of penal infliction which modern feeling would probably tolerate, even against the most obnoxious opinions, is not sufficient to extirpate them. But let us not flatter ourselves that we are yet free from the stain of legal persecution. Penalties for opinion, or at least for its expression, still exist by law; and their enforcement is not, even in these times, so unexampled as to make it at all incredible that they may some day be revived in full force. In the year 1857, at the summer assizes of the county of Cornwall, an unfortunate man,[2] said to be of unexceptionable conduct in all relations of life, was sentenced to twenty-one months' imprisonment, for uttering, and writing on a gate, some offensive words concerning Christianity. Within a month of the same time, at Old Bailey, two persons, on two separate occasions,[3] were rejected as jurymen, and one of them grossly insulted by the judge and by one of the counsel, because they honestly declared that they had no theological belief; and a third, a foreigner,[4] for the same reason, was denied justice against a thief. This refusal of redress took place in virtue of the legal doctrine, that no person can be allowed to give evidence in a court of justice who does not profess belief in a God (any god is sufficient) and in a future state; which is equivalent to declaring such persons to be outlaws, excluded from the protection of the tribunals; who may not only be robbed or assaulted with impunity, if no one but themselves, or persons of similar opinions, be present, but any one else may be robbed or assaulted with impunity, if the proof of the fact depends on their evidence. The assumption on which

2. Thomas Pooley, Bodmin Assizes, July 31, 1857. In December following, he received a free pardon from the Crown.

3. George Jacob Holyoake, August 17, 1857; Edward Truelove, July, 1857.

4. Baron de Gleichen, Marlborough Street Police Court, August 4, 1857.

this is grounded is that the oath is worthless of a person who does not believe in a future state; a proposition which betokens much ignorance of history in those who assent to it (since it is historically true that a large proportion of infidels in all ages have been persons of distinguished integrity and honour); and would be maintained by no one who had the smallest conception how many of the persons in greatest repute with the world, both for virtues and attainments, are well known, at least to their intimates, to be unbelievers. The rule, besides, is suicidal, and cuts away its own foundation. Under pretence that atheists must be liars, it admits the testimony of all atheists who are willing to lie, and rejects only those who brave the obloquy of publicly confessing a detested creed rather than affirm a falsehood. A rule thus self-convicted of absurdity so far as regards its professed purpose, can be kept in force only as a badge of hatred, a relic of persecution; a persecution, too, having the peculiarity that the qualification for undergoing it is the being clearly proved not to deserve it. The rule, and the theory it implies, are hardly less insulting to believers than to infidels. For if he who does not believe in a future state necessarily lies, it follows that they who do believe are only prevented from lying, if prevented they are, by the fear of hell. We will not do the authors and abettors of the rule the injury of supposing that the conception which they have formed of Christian virtue is drawn from their own consciousness.

These, indeed, are but rags and remnants of persecution, and may be thought to be not so much an indication of the wish to persecute, as an example of that very frequent infirmity of English minds, which makes them take a preposterous pleasure in the assertion of a bad principle, when they are no longer bad enough to desire to carry it really into practice. But unhappily there is no security in the state of the public mind that the suspension of worse forms of legal persecution, which has lasted for about the space of a generation, will continue. In this age the quiet surface of routine is as often ruffled by attempts to resuscitate past evils, as to introduce new benefits. What is boasted of at the present time as the revival of religion, is always, in narrow and uncultivated minds, at least as much the revival of bigotry; and where there is the strong permanent leaven of intolerance in the feelings of a people, which at all times abides in the middle classes of this country, it needs but little to provoke them into actively persecuting those whom they have never ceased to think proper objects of persecution.[5] For it is this—it is the opinions men

5. Ample warning may be drawn from the large infusion of the passions of a persecutor, which mingled with the general display of the worst parts of our national character on the occasion of the Sepoy insurrection. The ravings of fanatics or charlatans from the pulpit may be unworthy of notice; but the heads of the Evangelical party have announced as their principle for the government of Hindoos and Mahomedans, that no schools be supported by public money in which the Bible is not taught, and by necessary consequence that no public employment be given to any but real or pretended Christians. An Under-Secretary of State, in a speech delivered to his constituents on the 12th of November, 1857, is reported to have said: "Toleration of their faith" (the faith of a hundred millions of British subjects), "the superstition which they called religion, by the British government, had had the effect of retarding the ascendancy of the British name, and preventing the salutary growth of Christianity. . . ." Toleration was the great corner-stone of the religious liberties of this country; but do not let them abuse that precious word toleration. As he understood it, it meant the complete liberty to all, freedom of worship,

entertain, and the feelings they cherish, respecting those who disown the beliefs they deem important, which makes this country not a place of mental freedom. For a long time past, the chief mischief of the legal penalties is that they strengthen the social stigma. It is that stigma which is really effective, and so effective is it, that the profession of opinions which are under the ban of society is much less common in England than is, in many other countries, the avowal of those which incur risk of judicial punishment. In respect to all persons but those whose pecuniary circumstances make them independent of the good will of other people, opinion, on this subject, is as efficacious as law; men might as well be imprisoned, as excluded from the means of earning their bread. Those whose bread is already secured, and who desire no favours from men in power, or from bodies of men, or from the public, have nothing to fear from the open avowal of any opinions, but to be ill-thought of and ill-spoken of, and this it ought not to require a very heroic mould to enable them to bear. There is no room for any appeal *ad misericordiam* in behalf of such persons. But though we do not now inflict so much evil on those who think differently from us as it was formerly our custom to do, it may be that we do ourselves as

---

among *Christians, who worshiped upon the same foundation.* It meant toleration of all sects and denominations of *Christians who believed in the one mediation.* I desire to call attention to the fact, that a man who has been deemed fit to fill a high office in the government of this country under a liberal ministry, maintains the doctrine that all who do not believe in the divinity of Christ are beyond the pale of toleration. Who, after this imbecile display, can indulge the illusion that religious persecution has passed away, never to return?

much evil as ever by our treatment of them. Socrates was put to death, but the Socratic philosophy rose like the sun in heaven, and spread its illumination over the whole intellectual firmament.
Christians were cast to the lions, but the Christian
church grew up a stately and spreading tree, over-
topping the older and less vigorous growths, and
stifling them by its shade. Our merely social intolerance kills no one, roots out no opinions, but
induces men to disguise them, or to abstain from
any active effort for their diffusion. With us, heretical opinions do not perceptibly gain, or even
lose, ground in each decade or generation; they
never blaze out far and wide, but continue to
smoulder in the narrow circles of thinking and
studious persons among whom they originate, without ever lighting up the general affairs of mankind
with either a true or a deceptive light. And thus is
kept up a state of things very satisfactory to some
minds, because, without the unpleasant process
of fining or imprisoning anybody, it maintains
all prevailing opinions outwardly undisturbed,
while it does not absolutely interdict the exercise
of reason by dissentients afflicted with the malady
of thought. A convenient plan for having peace in
the intellectual world, and keeping all things going
on therein very much as they do already. But the
price paid for this sort of intellectual pacification is
the sacrifice of the entire moral courage of the
human mind. A state of things in which a large
portion of the most active and inquiring intellects
find it advisable to keep the general principles and
grounds of their convictions within their own
breasts, and attempt, in what they address to the

public, to fit as much as they can of their own conclusions to premises which they have internally
renounced, cannot send forth the open, fearless
characters, and logical, consistent intellects who
once adorned the thinking world. The sort of men
who can be looked for under it, are either mere
conformers to commonplace, or time-servers for
truth, whose arguments on all great subjects are
meant for their hearers, and are not those which
have convinced themselves. Those who avoid this
alternative, do so by narrowing their thoughts and
interest to things which can be spoken of without
venturing within the region of principles, that is,
to small practical matters, which would come right
of themselves, if but the minds of mankind were
strengthened and enlarged, and which will never
be made effectually right until then; while that
which would strengthen and enlarge men's minds,
free and daring speculation on the highest subjects, is abandoned.

Those in whose eyes this reticence on the part of
heretics is no evil should consider, in the first place,
that in consequence of it there is never any fair
and thorough discussion of heretical opinions; and
that such of them as could not stand such a discussion, though they may be prevented from
spreading, do not disappear. But it is not the
minds of heretics that are deteriorated most by the
ban placed on all inquiry which does not end in
the orthodox conclusions. The greatest harm done
is to those who are not heretics, and whose whole
mental development is cramped, and their reason
cowed, by the fear of heresy. Who can compute
what the world loses in the multitude of promising

intellects combined with timid characters, who dare not follow out any bold, vigorous, independent train of thought, lest it should land them in something which would admit of being considered irreligious or immoral? Among them we may occasionally see some man of deep conscientiousness, and subtle and refined understanding, who spends a life in sophisticating with an intellect which he cannot silence, and exhausts the resources of ingenuity in attempting to reconcile the promptings of his conscience and reason with orthodoxy, which yet he does not, perhaps, to the end succeed in doing. No one can be a great thinker who does not recognize, that as a thinker it is his first duty to follow his intellect to whatever conclusions it may lead. Truth gains more even by the errors of one who, with due study and preparation, thinks for himself, than by the true opinions of those who only hold them because they do not suffer themselves to think. Not that it is solely, or chiefly, to form great thinkers, that freedom of thinking is required. On the contrary, it is as much and even more indispensable to enable average human beings to attain the mental stature which they are capable of. There have been, and may again be, great individual thinkers in a general atmosphere of mental slavery. But there never has been, nor ever will be, in that atmosphere an intellectually active people. Where any people has made a temporary approach to such a character, it has been because the dread of heterodox speculation was for a time suspended. Where there is a tacit convention that principles are not to be disputed; where the discussion of the greatest questions which can occupy humanity is considered to be closed, we cannot hope to find that generally high scale of mental activity which has made some periods of history so remarkable. Never when controversy avoided the subjects which are large and important enough to kindle enthusiasm, was the mind of a people stirred up from its foundations, and the impulse given which raised even persons of the most ordinary intellect to something of the dignity of thinking beings. Of such we have had an example in the condition of Europe during the times immediately following the Reformation; another, though limited to the Continent and to a more cultivated class, in the speculative movement of the latter half of the eighteenth century; and a third, of still briefer duration, in the intellectual fermentation of Germany during the Goethian and Fichtean period. These periods differed widely in the particular opinions which they developed; but were alike in this, that during all three the yoke of authority was broken. In each, an old mental despotism had been thrown off, and no new one had yet taken its place. The impulse given at these three periods has made Europe what it now is. Every single improvement which has taken place either in the human mind or in institutions, may be traced distinctly to one or other of them. Appearances have for some time indicated that all three impulses are well nigh spent; and we can expect no fresh start until we again assert our mental freedom.

Let us now pass to the second division of the argument, and dismissing the supposition that any of the received opinions may be false, let us assume

49

them to be true, and examine into the worth of the manner in which they are likely to be held, when their truth is not freely and openly canvassed. However unwillingly a person who has a strong opinion may admit the possibility that his opinion may be false, he ought to be moved by the consideration that, however true it may be, if it is not fully, frequently, and fearlessly discussed, it will be held as a dead dogma, not a living truth.

There is a class of persons (happily not quite so numerous as formerly) who think it enough if a person assents undoubtingly to what they think true, though he has no knowledge whatever of the grounds of the opinion, and could not make a tenable defence of it against the most superficial objections. Such persons, if they can once get their creed taught from authority, naturally think that no good, and some harm, comes of its being allowed to be questioned. Where their influence prevails, they make it nearly impossible for the received opinion to be rejected wisely and considerately, though it may still be rejected rashly and ignorantly; for to shut out discussion entirely is seldom possible, and when it once gets in, beliefs not grounded on convictions are apt to give way before the slightest semblance of an argument. Waiving, however, this possibility—assuming that the true opinion abides in the mind, but abides as a prejudice, a belief independent of, and proof against, argument—this is not the way in which truth ought to be held by a rational being. This is not knowing the truth. Truth, thus held, is but one superstition the more, accidently clinging to the words which enunciate a truth.

If the intellect and judgment of mankind ought to be cultivated, a thing which Protestants at least do not deny, on what can these faculties be more appropriately exercised by any one, than on the things which concern him so much that it is considered necessary for him to hold opinions on them? If the cultivation of the understanding consists in one thing more than in another, it is surely in learning the grounds of one's own opinions. Whatever people believe, on subjects on which it is of the first importance to believe rightly, they ought to be able to defend against at least the common objections. But, some one may say, "Let them be *taught* the grounds of their opinions. It does not follow that opinions must be merely parroted because they are never heard controverted. Persons who learn geometry do not simply commit the theorems to memory, but understand and learn likewise the demonstrations; and it would be absurd to say that they remain ignorant of the grounds of geometrical truths, because they never hear any one deny, and attempt to disprove them." Undoubtedly: and such teaching suffices on a subject like mathematics, where there is nothing at all to be said on the wrong side of the question. The peculiarity of the evidence of mathematical truths is that all the argument is on one side. There are no objections, and no answers to objections. But on every subject on which difference of opinion is possible, the truth depends on a balance to be struck between two sets of conflicting reasons. Even in natural philosophy, there is always some other explanation possible of the same facts: some geocentric theory instead of heliocentric, some phlogiston instead of oxygen; and it has to be shown why that other theory cannot be the true one; and until this is shown, and until we know how it is shown, we do not understand the grounds of our opinion. But when we turn to subjects infinitely more complicated, to morals, religion, politics, social relations, and the business of life, three-fourths of the arguments for every disputed opinion consist in dispelling the appearances which favour some opinion different from it. The greatest orator, save one, of antiquity, has left it on record that he always studied his adversary's case with as great, if not still greater, intensity than even his own. What Cicero practised as the means of forensic success requires to be imitated by all who study any subject in order to arrive at the truth. He who knows only his own side of the case, knows little of that. His reasons may be good, and no one may have been able to refute them. But if he is equally unable to refute the reasons on the opposite side; if he does not so much as know what they are, he has no ground for preferring either opinion. The rational position for him would be suspension of judgment, and unless he contents himself with that, he is either led by authority, or adopts, like the generality of the world, the side to which he feels most inclination. Nor is it enough that he should hear the arguments of adversaries from his own teachers, presented as they state them, and accompanied by what they offer as refutations. That is not the way to do justice to the arguments, or bring them into real contact with his own mind. He must be able to hear them from persons who actually believe them; who defend them in earnest, and do their very most for them. He must know them in their most plausible and persuasive form; he must feel the whole force of the difficulty which the true view of the subject has to encounter and dispose of; else he will never really possess himself of the portion of truth which meets and removes that difficulty. Ninety-nine in a hundred of what are called educated men are in this condition; even of those who can argue fluently for their opinions. Their conclusion may be true, but it might be false for anything they know: they have never thrown themselves into the mental position of those who think differently from them, and considered what such persons may have to say; and consequently they do not, in any proper sense of the word, know the doctrine which they themselves profess. They do not know those parts of it which explain and justify the remainder; the considerations which show that a fact which seemingly conflicts with another is reconcilable with it, or that, of two apparently strong reasons, one and not the other ought to be preferred. All that part of the truth which turns the scale, and decides the judgment of a completely informed mind, they are strangers to; nor is it ever really known, but to those who have attended equally and impartially to both sides, and endeavoured to see the reasons of both in the strongest light. So essential is this discipline to a real understanding of moral and human subjects, that if opponents of all important truths do not exist, it is indispensable to imagine them, and supply them with the strongest arguments which the most skillful devil's advocate can conjure up.

To abate the force of these considerations, an enemy of free discussion may be supposed to say, that there is no necessity for mankind in general to know and understand all that can be said against or for their opinions by philosophers and theologians. That it is not needful for common men to be able to expose all the misstatements or fallacies of an ingenious opponent. That it is enough if there is always somebody capable of answering them, so that nothing likely to mislead uninstructed persons remains unrefuted. That simple minds, having been taught the obvious grounds of the truths inculcated them, may trust to authority for the rest, and being aware that they have neither knowledge nor talent to resolve every difficulty which can be raised, many repose in the assurance that all those which have been raised have been or can be answered, by those who are specially trained to the task.

Conceding to this view of the subject the utmost that can be claimed for it by those most easily satisfied with the amount of understanding and truth which ought to accompany the belief of it; even so, the argument for free discussion is no way weakened. For even this doctrine acknowledges that mankind ought to have a rational assurance that all objections have been satisfactorily answered; and how are they to be answered if that which requires to be answered is not spoken? or how can the answer be known to be satisfactory, if the objectors have no opportunity of showing that it is unsatisfactory? If not the public, at least the philosophers and theologians who are to resolve the difficulties, must make themselves familiar with those difficulties in their most puzzling form; and this cannot be accomplished unless they are freely stated, and placed in the most advantageous light which they admit of. The Catholic Church has its own way of dealing with this embarrassing problem. It makes a broad separation between those who can be permitted to receive its doctrines on conviction, and those who must accept them on trust. Neither, indeed, are allowed any choice as to what they will accept; but the clergy, such at least as can be fully confided in, may admissibly and meritoriously make themselves acquainted with the arguments of opponents, in order to answer them, and may, therefore, read heretical books; the laity, not unless by special permission, hard to be obtained. This discipline recognises a knowledge of the enemy's case as beneficial to the teachers, but finds means, consistent with this, of denying it to the rest of the world: thus giving to the *élite* more mental culture, though not more mental freedom, than it allows to the mass. By this device it succeeds in obtaining the kind of mental superiority which its purposes require; for though culture without freedom never made a large and liberal mind, it can make a clever *nisi prius* advocate of a cause. But in countries professing Protestantism, this resource is denied: since Protestants hold, at least in theory, that the responsibility for the choice of a religion must be borne by each for himself, and cannot be thrown off upon teachers. Besides, in the present state of the world, it is practically impossible that writings which are read by the instructed can be kept from the uninstructed. If the teachers of mankind are to be cognisant of all that they ought to know, everything must be free to be written and published without restraint.

If, however, the mischievous operation of the absence of free discussion, when the received opinions are true, were confined to leaving men ignorant of the grounds of those opinions, it might be thought that this, if an intellectual, is no moral evil, and does not affect the worth of the opinions, regarded in their influence on the character. The fact, however, is, that not only the grounds of the opinion are forgotten in the absence of discussion, but too often the meaning of the opinion itself. The words which convey it cease to suggest ideas, or suggest only a small portion of those they were originally employed to communicate. Instead of a vivid conception and a living belief, there remain only a few phrases retained by rote; or, if any part, the shell and husk only of the meaning is retained, the finer essence being lost. The great chapter on human history which this fact occupies and fills, cannot be too earnestly studied and meditated on.

It is illustrated in the experience of almost all ethical doctrines and religious creeds. They are all full of meaning and vitality to those who originate them, and to the direct disciples of the originators. Their meaning continues to be felt in undiminished strength and is perhaps brought out into even fuller consciousness, so long as the struggle lasts to give the doctrine or creed an ascendancy over other creeds. At last it either prevails, and becomes the general opinion, or its progress stops; it keeps possession of the ground it has gained, but ceases to spread further. When either of these results has become apparent, controversy on the subject flags, and gradually dies away. The doctrine has taken its place if not as a received opinion, as one of the admitted sects or divisions of opinion: those who hold it have generally inherited, not adopted it; and conversion from one of these doctrines to another, being now an exceptional fact, occupies little place in the thoughts of their professors. Instead of being, as at first, constantly on the alert either to defend themselves against the world, or to bring the world over to them, they have subsided into acquiescence, and neither listen, when they can help it, to arguments against their creed, nor trouble dissentients (if there be such) with arguments in its favour. From this time may usually be dated the decline in the living power of the doctrine. We often hear the teachers of all creeds lamenting the difficulty of keeping up in the mind of believers a lively apprehension of the truth which they nominally recognize, so that it may penetrate the feelings, and acquire a real mastery over the conduct. No such difficulty is complained of while the creed is still fighting for its existence: even the weaker combatants then know and feel what they are fighting for, and the difference between it and other doctrines; and in that period of every creed's existence, not a few persons may be found, who have realized its fundamental principles in all the forms of thought, have weighed and considered them in all their important bearings, and have experienced the full effect on the character which belief in that creed ought to produce in a mind thoroughly imbued with it. But when it has come to be an hereditary creed, and to be received passively, not actively—when the mind is no longer compelled, in the same degree as at first, to exercise its vital powers on the questions which its belief presents to it, there is a progressive tendency to forget all of the belief except the formularies, or to give it a dull and torpid assent, as if accepting it on trust dispensed with the necessity of realising it in consciousness, or testing it by personal experience, until it almost ceases to connect itself at all with the inner life of the human being. Then are seen the cases, so frequent in this age of the world as almost to form the majority, in which the creed remains as it were outside the mind, incrusting and petrifying it against all other influences addressed to the higher parts of our nature; manifesting its power by not suffering any fresh and living conviction to get in, but itself doing nothing for the mind or heart, except standing sentinel over them to keep them vacant.

To what an extent doctrines intrinsically fitted to make the deepest impression upon the mind may remain in it as dead beliefs, without being ever realised in the imagination, the feelings, or the understanding, is exemplified by the manner in which the majority of believers hold the doctrines of Christianity. By Christianity I here mean what is accounted such by all churches and sects —the maxims and precepts contained in the New Testament. These are considered sacred, and accepted as laws, by all professing Christians. Yet it is scarcely too much to say that not one Christian in a thousand guides or tests his individual conduct by reference to those laws. The standard to which he does refer it, is the custom of his nation, his class, or his religious profession. He has thus, on the one hand, a collection of ethical maxims, which he believes to have been vouchsafed to him by infallible wisdom as rules for his government; and on the other a set of every-day judgments and practices, which go a certain length with some of those maxims, not so great a length with others, stand in direct opposition to some, and are, on the whole, a compromise between the Christian creed and the interests and suggestions of worldly life. To the first of these standards he gives his homage; to the other his real allegiance. All Christians believe that the blessed are the poor and humble, and those who are ill-used by the world; that it is easier for a camel to pass through the eye of a needle than for a rich man to enter the kingdom of heaven; that they should judge not, lest they be judged; that they should swear not at all; that they should love their neighbour as themselves; that if one take their cloak, they should give him their coat also; that they should take no thought for the morrow; that if they would be perfect they should sell all that they have and give it to the poor. They are not insincere when they say that they believe these things. They do believe them, as people believe what they have always heard lauded and never discussed. But in the sense of that living belief which regulates conduct, they believe these doctrines just up to the point to which it is usual to act upon them. The doctrines in their integrity are serviceable to pelt adversaries with; and it is understood that they are to be put forward (when possible) as the reasons for whatever people do that they think laudable. But any one who reminded them that the maxims require an infinity of things which they never even think of doing, would gain nothing but to be classed among those very unpopular characters who affect to be better than other people. The doctrines have no hold on ordinary believers—are not a power in their minds. They have an habitual respect for the sound of them, but no feeling which spreads from the words to the things signified, and forces the mind to take *them* in, and make them conform to the formula. Whenever conduct is concerned, they look round for Mr. A and B to direct them how far to go in obeying Christ.

Now we may be well assured that the case was not thus, but far otherwise, with the early Christians. Had it been thus, Christianity never would have expanded from an obscure sect of the despised Hebrews into the religion of the Roman empire. When their enemies said, "See how these Christians love one another" (a remark not likely to be made by anybody now), they assuredly had a much livelier feeling of the meaning of their creed than they have ever had since. And to this cause, probably, it is chiefly owing that Christianity now makes so little progress in extending its domain, and after eighteen centuries is still nearly confined to Europeans and the descendants of Europeans. Even with the strictly religious, who are much in earnest about their doctrines, and attach a greater amount of meaning to many of them than people in general, it commonly happens that the part which is thus comparatively active in their minds is that which was made by Calvin, or Knox, or some such person much nearer in character to themselves. The sayings of Christ coexist passively in their minds, producing hardly any effect beyond what is caused by mere listening to words so amiable and bland. There are many reasons, doubtless, why doctrines which are the badge of a sect retain more of their vitality than those common to all recognized sects, and why more pains are taken by teachers to keep their meaning alive; but one reason certainly is, that the peculiar doctrines are more questioned, and have to be oftener defended against open gain-sayers. Both teachers and learners go to sleep at their post, as soon as there is no enemy in the field.

The same thing holds true, generally speaking, of all traditional doctrines—those of prudence and knowledge of life, as well as of morals or religion. All languages and literatures are full of general observations on life, both as to what it is, and how to conduct oneself in it; observations which everybody knows, which everybody repeats, or hears with acquiescence, which are received as truisms, yet of which most people first truly learn the meaning when experience, generally of a painful kind, has made it a reality to them. How often, when smarting under some unforeseen misfortune or disappointment, does a person call to mind some proverb or common saying, familiar to him all his life, the meaning of which, if he had ever before felt it as he does now, would have saved him from the calamity. There are indeed reasons for this other than the absence of discussion; there are many truths of which the full meaning *cannot* be realised until personal experience has brought it home, but much more of the meaning even of these would have been understood, and what was understood would have been far more deeply impressed on the mind, if the man had been accustomed to hear it argued *pro* and *con* by people who did understand it. The fatal tendency of mankind to leave off thinking about a thing when it is no longer doubtful, is the cause of half their errors. A contemporary author has well spoken of "the deep slumber of a decided opinion."

But what! (it may be asked). Is the absence of unanimity an indispensable condition of true knowledge? Is it necessary that some part of mankind should persist in error to enable any to realise the truth? Does a belief cease to be real and vital as soon as it is generally received—and is a proposition never thoroughly understood and felt unless some doubt of it remains? As soon as mankind have unanimously accepted a truth, does the truth perish within them? The highest aim and best result of improved intelligence, it has hitherto been thought, is to unite mankind more and more in the acknowledgment of all important truths; and does the intelligence only last as long as it has not achieved its object? Do the fruits of conquest perish by the very completeness of the victory?

I affirm no such thing. As mankind improve, the number of doctrines which are no longer disputed or doubted will be constantly on the increase: and the well-being of mankind may almost be measured by the number and gravity of the truths which have reached the point of being uncontested. The cessation, on one question after another, of serious controversy, is one of the necessary incidents of the consolidation of opinion; a consolidation as salutary in the case of true opinions, as it is dangerous and noxious when the opinions are erroneous. But though this gradual narrowing of the bounds of diversity of opinion is necessary in both senses of the term, being at once inevitable and indispensable, we are not therefore obliged to conclude that all its consequences must be beneficial. The loss of so important an aid to the intelligent and living apprehension of a truth, as is afforded by the necessity of explaining it to, or defending it against, opponents though not sufficient to outweigh, is no trifling drawback from, the benefit of its universal recognition. Where this advantage can no longer be had, I confess I should like to see the teachers of mankind endeavouring to provide a substitute for it; some contrivance for making the difficulties of the question as present to the learner's consciousness, as if they were pressed upon him by a dissentient champion, eager for his conversion.

But instead of seeking contrivances for this purpose, they have lost those they formerly had. The Socratic dialectics, so magnificently exemplified in the dialogues of Plato, were a contrivance of this description. They were essentially a negative discussion of the great question of philosophy and life, directed with consummate skill to the purpose of convincing any who had merely adopted the commonplaces of received opinion that he did not understand the subject—that he as yet attached no definite meaning to the doctrines he professed; in order that, becoming aware of his ignorance, he might be put in the way to obtain a stable belief, resting on a clear apprehension both of the meaning of doctrines he professed; in order that, becoming aware of his ignorance, he might be put in the way to obtain a stable belief, resting on a clear apprehension both of the meaning of doctrines and of their evidence. The school disputations of the Middle Ages had a somewhat similar object. They were intended to make sure that the pupil understood his own opinion, and (by necessary correlation) the opinion opposed to it, and could enforce the grounds of the one and confute those of the other. These last-mentioned contests had indeed the incurable defect, that the premises appealed to were taken from authority, not from reason; and, as a discipline to the mind, they were in every respect inferior to the powerful dialectics which formed the intellects of the "Socratic viri"; but the modern mind owes far more to both than it is generally willing to admit, and the present modes of education contain nothing which in the smallest degree supplies the place either of the one or of the other. A person who derives all his instruction from teachers or books, even if he escape the besetting temptation of contenting himself with cram, is under no compulsion to hear both sides; accordingly it is far from a frequent accomplishment, even among thinkers, to know both sides; and the weakest part of what everybody says in defence of his opinion is what he intends as a reply to antagonists. It is the fashion of the present time to disparage negative logic—that which points out weaknesses in theory or errors in practice, without establishing positive truths. Such negative criticism would indeed be poor enough as an ultimate result; but as a means to attaining any positive knowledge or conviction worthy the name, it cannot be valued too highly; and until people are again systematically trained to it, there will be few great thinkers, and a low general average of intellect, in any but the mathematical and physical department of speculation. On any other subject no one's opinions deserve the name of knowledge, except so far as he has either had forced upon him by others, or gone through of himself, the same mental process which would have been required of him in carrying on an active controversy with opponents. That, therefore, which when absent, it is so indispensable, but so difficult, to create, how worse than absurd it is to forego, when spontaneously offering itself! If there are any persons who contest a received opinion or who will do so if law or opinion will let them, let us thank them for it, open our minds to listen to them and rejoice that there is some one to do for us what we otherwise ought, if we have any regard for either the certainty or the vitality of our convictions, to do with much greater labour for ourselves.

It still remains to speak of one of the principal causes which make diversity of opinion advantageous, and will continue to do so until mankind shall have entered a stage of intellectual advancement which at present seems at an incalculable distance. We have hitherto considered only two possibilities: that the received opinion may be false, and some other opinion, consequently, true; or that, the received opinion being true, a conflict with the opposite error is essential to a clear apprehension and deep feeling of its truth. But there is a commoner case than either of these; when the conflicting doctrines, instead of being one true and the other false, share the truth between them; and the nonconforming opinion is needed to supply the remainder of the truth, of which the received doctrine embodies only a part. Popular opinions, on subjects not palpable to sense, are often true, but seldom or never the whole truth. They are a part of the truth; sometimes a greater, sometimes a smaller part, but exaggerated, distorted, and disjointed from the truths by which they ought to be accompanied and limited. Heretical opinions, on the other hand, are generally some of these suppressed and neglected truths, bursting the bonds which kept them down, and either seeking reconciliation with the truth contained in the common opinion, or fronting it as enemies, and setting themselves up, with similar exclusiveness, as the whole truth. The latter case is hitherto the most frequent, as in the human mind, one-sidedness has always been the rule, and many-sidedness the exception. Hence, even in revolutions of opinion, one part of the truth usually sets while another rises. Even progress, which ought to superadd, for the most part only substitutes, one partial and incomplete truth for another; improvement consisting chiefly in this, that the new fragment of truth is more wanted, more adapted to the needs of the time, than that which it displaces. Such being the partial character of prevailing opinions, even when resting on a true foundation, every opinion which embodies somewhat of the portion of truth which the common opinion omits, ought to be considered precious, with whatever amount of error and confusion that truth may be blended. No sober judge of human affairs will feel bound to be indignant

because those who force on our notice truths which
we should otherwise have overlooked, overlook
some of those which we see. Rather, he will think
that so long as popular truth is one-sided, it is more
desirable than otherwise that unpopular truth
should have one-sided assertors too; such being
usually the most energetic, and the most likely to
compel reluctant attention to the fragment of wisdom which they proclaim as if it were the whole.

Thus, in the eighteenth century, when nearly all
the instructed, and all those of the uninstructed
who were led by them, were lost in admiration of
what is called civilisation, and of the marvels of
modern science, literature, and philosophy, and
while greatly overrating the amount of unlikeness
between the men of modern and those of ancient
times, indulged the belief that the whole of the
difference was in their own favour; with what a
salutary shock did the paradoxes of Rousseau ex-
plode like bombshells in the midst, dislocating the
compact mass of one-sided opinion, and forcing its
elements to recombine in a better form and with
additional ingredients. Not that the current opinions were on the whole farther from the truth than
Rousseau's were; on the contrary, they were nearer
to it; they contained more of positive truth, and
very much less of error. Nevertheless there lay in
Rousseau's doctrine, and has floated down the
stream of opinion along with it, a considerable
amount of exactly those truths which the popular
opinion wanted; and these are the deposit which
was left behind when the flood subsided. The superior worth of simplicity of life, the enervating
and demoralising effect of the trammels and hy-

pocrisies of artificial society, are ideas which have never been entirely absent from cultivated minds since Rousseau wrote; and they will in time produce their due effect, though at present needing to be asserted as much as ever, and to be asserted by deeds, for words, on this subject have nearly exhausted their power.

In politics, again, it is almost a commonplace, that a party of order or stability, and a party of progress or reform, are both necessary elements of a healthy state of political life; until the one or the other shall have so enlarged its mental grasp as to be a party equally of order and of progress, knowing and distinguishing what is fit to be preserved from what ought to be swept away. Each of these modes of thinking derives its utility from the deficiencies of the other; but it is in a great measure the opposition of the other that keeps each within the limits of reason and sanity. Unless opinions favourable to democracy and to aristocracy, to property and to equality, to co-operation and to competition, to luxury and to abstinence, to sociality and individuality, to liberty and discipline, and all the other standing antagonisms of practical life, are expressed with equal freedom, and enforced and defended with equal talent and energy, there is no chance of both elements obtaining their due; one scale is sure to go up, and the other down. Truth, in the great practical concerns of life, is so much a question of the reconciling and combining of opposites that very few have minds sufficiently capacious and impartial to make the adjustments with an approach to correctness, and it has to be made by the rough process of a struggle between combatants fighting under hostile banners. On any of the great open questions just enumerated, if either of the two opinions has a better claim than the other, not merely to be tolerated, but to be encouraged and countenanced, it is the one which happens at the particular time and place to be in a minority. That is the opinion which, for the time being, represents the neglected interests, the side of human well-being which is in danger of obtaining less than its share. I am aware that there is not, in this country, any intolerance of differences of opinion on most of these topics. They are adduced to show, by admitted and multiplied examples, the universality of the fact, that only through diversity of opinion is there, in the existing state of human intellect, a chance of fair play to all sides of the truth. When there are persons to be found who form an exception to the apparent unanimity of the world on any subject, even if the world is in the right, it is always probable that dissentients have something worth hearing to say for themselves, and that truth would lose something by their silence.

It may be objected, "But *some* received principles, especially on the highest and most vital subjects, are more than half-truths. The Christian morality, for instance, is the whole truth on that subject, and if any one teaches a morality which varies from it, he is wholly in error." As this is of all cases the most important in practice, none can be fitter to test the general maxim. But before pronouncing what Christian morality is or is not, it would be desirable to decide what is meant by Christian morality. If it means the morality of the

New Testament, I wonder that any one who derives his knowledge of this from the book itself, can suppose that it was announced, or intended as a complete doctrine of morals. The gospel always refers to a pre-existing morality, and confines its precepts to the particulars in which that morality was to be corrected, or superseded by a wider and higher; expressing itself, moreover, in terms most general, often impossible to be interpreted literally, and possessing rather the impressiveness of poetry or eloquence than the precision of legislation. To extract from it a body of ethical doctrine, has never been possible without eking it out from the Old Testament, that is, from a system elaborate indeed, but in many respects barbarous, and intended only for a barbarous people. St. Paul, a declared enemy to this Judaical mode of interpreting the doctrine and filling up the scheme of his Master, equally assumes a pre-existing morality, namely that of the Greeks and Romans; and his advice to Christians is in a great measure a system of accommodation to that; even to the extent of giving an apparent sanction to slavery. What is called Christian, but should rather be termed theological, morality, was not the work of Christ or the Apostles, but is of much later origin, having been gradually built up by the Catholic church of the first five centuries, and though not implicitly adopted by moderns and Protestants, has been much less modified by them than might have been expected. For the most part, indeed, they have contented themselves with cutting off the additions which had been made to it in the Middle Ages, each sect supplying the place by fresh additions, adapted to its own character and tendencies. That mankind owe a great debt to this morality, and to its early teachers, I should be the last person to deny; but I do not scruple to say of it that it is, in many important points, incomplete and one-sided, and that unless ideas and feelings, not sanctioned by it, had contributed to the formation of European life and character, human affairs would have been in a worse condition than they now are. Christian morality (so called) has all the characters of a reaction; it is, in great part, a protest against Paganism. Its ideal is negative rather than positive; passive rather than active; Innocence rather than Nobleness; Abstinence from Evil, rather than energetic Pursuit of Good; in its precepts (as has been well said) "thou shalt not" predominates unduly over "thou shalt." In its horror of sensuality, it made an idol of asceticism, which has been gradually compromised away into one of legality. It holds out the hope of heaven and the threat of hell, as the appointed and appropriate motives to a virtuous life: in this falling far below the best of the ancients, and doing what lies in it to give to human morality an essentially selfish character, by disconnecting each man's feelings of duty from the interests of his fellow-creatures, except so far as a self-interested inducement is offered to him for consulting them. It is essentially a doctrine of passive obedience; it inculcates submission to all authorities found established; who indeed are not to be actively obeyed when they command what religion forbids, but who are not to be resisted, far less rebelled against, for any amount of wrong to ourselves. And while, in the morality of the best Pagan nations, duty to the State holds even a disproportionate place, infringing on the just liberty of the individual; in purely Christian ethics, that grand department of duty is scarcely noticed or acknowledged. It is in the Koran, not the New Testament, that we read the maxim—"A ruler who appoints any man to an office, when there is in his dominions another man better qualified for it, sins against God and against the State." What little recognition the idea of obligation to the public obtains in modern morality is derived from Greek and Roman sources, not from Christian; as, even in the morality of private life, whatever exists of magnanimity, highmindedness, personal dignity, even the sense of honour, is derived from the purely human, not the religious part of our education, and never could have grown out of a standard of ethics in which the only worth, professedly recognised, is that of obedience.

I am as far as any one from pretending that these defects are necessarily inherent in the Christian ethics in every manner in which it can be conceived, or that the many requisites of a complete moral doctrine which it does not contain do not admit of being reconciled with it. Far less would I insinuate this of the doctrines and precepts of Christ himself. I believe that the sayings of Christ are all that I can see any evidence of their having been intended to be; that they are irreconcilable with nothing which a comprehensive morality requires; that everything which is excellent in ethics may be brought within them, with no greater violence to their language than has been done to it by all who have attempted to deduce from them any practical system of conduct whatever. But it is quite consistent with this to believe that they contain, and were meant to contain, only a part of the truth; that many essential elements of the highest morality are among the things which are not provided for, nor intended to be provided for, in the recorded deliverances of the Founder of Christianity, and which have been entirely thrown aside in the system of ethics erected on the basis of those deliverances by the Christian Church. And this being so, I think it a great error to persist in attempting to find in the Christian doctrine that complete rule for our guidance which its author intended it to sanction and enforce, but only partially to provide. I believe, too, that this narrow theory is becoming a grave practical evil, detracting greatly from the moral training and instruction which so many well meaning persons are now at length exerting themselves to promote. I much fear that by attempting to form the mind and feelings on an exclusively religious type, and discarding those secular standards (as for want of a better name they may be called) which heretofore coexisted with and supplemented the Christian ethics, receiving some of its spirit, and infusing into it some of theirs, there will result, and is even now resulting, a low, abject, servile type of character, which, submit itself as it may to what it deems the Supreme Will, is incapable of rising to or sympathising in the conception of Supreme Goodness. I believe that other ethics than any which can be evolved from exclusively Christian sources, must exist side by side with Christian ethics to produce the moral regeneration of mankind; and that the

Christian system is no exception to the rule, that in an imperfect state of the human mind the interests of truth require a diversity of opinions. It is not necessary that in ceasing to ignore the moral truths not contained in Christianity men should ignore any of those which it does contain. Such prejudice, or oversight, when it occurs, is altogether an evil; but it is one from which we cannot hope to be always exempt, and must be regarded as the price paid for an inestimable good. The exclusive pretension made by a part of the truth to be the whole, must and ought to be protested against; and if a reactionary impulse should make the protestors unjust in their turn, this one-sidedness, like the other, may be lamented, but must be tolerated. If Christians would teach infidels to be just to Christianity, they should themselves be just to infidelity. It can do truth no service to blink the fact, known to all who have the most ordinary acquaintance with literary history, that a large portion of the noblest and most valuable moral teaching has been the work, not only of men who did not know, but of men who knew and rejected, the Christian faith.

I do not pretend that the most unlimited use of the freedom of enunciating all possible opinions would put an end to the evils of religious or philosophical sectarianism. Every truth which men of narrow capacity are in earnest about, is sure to be asserted, inculcated, and in many ways even acted on, as if no other truth existed in the world, or at all events none that could limit or qualify the first. I acknowledge that the tendency of all opinions to become sectarian is not cured by the freest discussion, but is often heightened and exacerbated thereby; the truth which ought to have been, but was not, seen, being rejected all the more violently because proclaimed by persons regarded as opponents. But it is not on the impassioned partisan, it is on the calmer and more disinterested bystander, that this collision of opinions works its salutary effect. Not the violent conflict between parts of the truth, but the quiet suppression of half of it, is the formidable evil; there is always hope when people are forced to listen to both sides; it is when they attend only to one that errors harden into prejudices, and truth itself ceases to have the effect of truth, by being exaggerated into falsehood. And since there are few mental attributes more rare than that judicial faculty which can sit in intelligent judgment between two sides of a question, of which only one is represented by an advocate before it, truth has no chance but in proportion as every side of it, every opinion which embodies any fraction of the truth, not only finds advocates, but is so advocated as to be listened to.

We have now recognised the necessity to the mental well-being of mankind (on which all their other well-being depends) of freedom of opinion, and freedom of the expression of opinion, on four distinct grounds; which we will now briefly recapitulate.

First, if any opinion is compelled to silence, that opinion may, for aught we can certainly know, be true. To deny this is to assume our own infallibility.

Secondly, though the silenced opinion be an

error, it may, and very commonly does, contain a portion of truth; and since the general or prevailing opinion on any subject is rarely or never the whole truth, it is only by the collision of adverse opinions that the remainder of the truth has any chance of being supplied.

Thirdly, even if the received opinion be not only true, but the whole truth; unless it is suffered to be, and actually is, vigorously and earnestly contested, it will, by most of those who receive it, be held in the manner of a prejudice, with little comprehension or feeling of its rational grounds. And not only this, but, fourthly, the meaning of the doctrine itself will be in danger of being lost, or enfeebled, and deprived of its vital effect on the character and conduct: the dogma becoming a mere formal profession, inefficacious for good, but cumbering the ground, and preventing the growth of any real and heartfelt conviction, from reason or personal experience.

Before quitting the subject of freedom of opinion, it is fit to take some notice of those who say that the free expression of all opinions should be permitted, on condition that the manner be temperate, and do not pass the bounds of fair discussion. Much might be said on the impossibility of fixing where these supposed bounds are to be placed; for if the test be offence to those whose opinions are attacked, I think experience testifies that this offence is given whenever the attack is telling and powerful, and that every opponent who pushes them hard, and when they find it difficult to answer, appears to them, if he shows any strong feeling on the subject, an intemperate opponent.

But this, though an important consideration in a practical point of view, merges in a more fundamental objection. Undoubtedly the manner of asserting an opinion, even though it be a true one, may be very objectionable, and may justly incur severe censure. But the principal offences of the kind are such as it is mostly impossible, unless by accidental self-betrayal, to bring home to conviction. The gravest of them is, to argue sophistically, to suppress facts or arguments, to misstate the elements of the case, or misrepresent the opposite opinion. But all this, even to the most aggravated degree, is so continually done in perfect good faith, by persons who are not considered, and in many other respects may not deserve to be considered, ignorant or incompetent, that it is rarely possible, on adequate grounds conscientiously to stamp the misrepresentation as morally culpable; and still less could law presume to interfere with this kind of controversial misconduct. With regard to what is commonly meant by intemperate discussion, namely invective, sarcasm, personality, and the like, the denunciation of these weapons would deserve more sympathy if it were ever proposed to interdict them equally to both sides; but it is only desired to restrain the employment of them against the prevailing opinion: against the unprevailing they may not only be used without general disapproval, but will be likely to obtain for him who uses them the praise of honest zeal and righteous indignation. Yet whatever mischief arises from their use is greatest when they are employed against the comparatively defenceless; and whatever unfair advantage can be derived by any opinion from this mode of asserting it, accrues almost exclusively to received opinions. The worst offence of this kind which can be committed by a polemic is to stigmatise those who hold the contrary opinion as bad and immoral men. To calumny of this sort, those who hold any unpopular opinion are peculiarly exposed, because they are in general few and uninfluential, and nobody, but themselves feels much interested in seeing justice done them; but this weapon is, from the nature of the case, denied to those who attack a prevailing opinion: they can neither use it with safety to themselves, nor, if they could, would it do anything but recoil on their own cause. In general, opinions contrary to those commonly received can only obtain a hearing by studied moderation of language, and the most cautious avoidance of unnecessary offence, from which they hardly ever deviate even in a slight degree without losing ground: while unmeasured vituperation employed on the side of the prevailing opinion really does deter people from professing contrary opinions, and from listening to those who profess them. For the interest, therefore, of truth and justice, it is far more important to restrain this employment of vituperative language than the other; and, for example, if it were necessary to choose, there would be much more need to discourage offensive attacks on infidelity than on religion. It is, however, obvious that law and authority have no business with restraining either, while opinion ought, in every instance, to determine its verdict by the circumstances of the individual case; condemning every one, on whichever side of the argument he places himself, on whose mode of advocacy either want of candour, or malignity, bigotry, or intolerance of feeling manifest themselves; but not inferring these vices from the side which a person takes, though it be the contrary side of the question to our own; and giving merited honour to every one, whatever opinion he may hold, who has calmness to see and honesty to state what his opponents and their opinions really are, exaggerating nothing to their discredit, keeping nothing back which tells, or can be supposed to tell, in their favour. This is the real morality of public discussion: and if often violated, I am happy to think that there are many controversialists who to a great extent observe it, and a still greater number who conscientiously strive towards it.

# CHAPTER III

## OF INDIVIDUALITY, AS ONE OF THE
## ELEMENTS OF WELL-BEING

SUCH BEING THE REASONS WHICH MAKE IT imperative that human beings should be free to form opinions, and to express their opinions without reserve; and such the baneful consequences to the intellectual, and through that to the moral nature of man, unless this liberty is either conceded, or asserted in spite of prohibition; let us next examine whether the same reasons do not require that men should be free to act upon their opinions—to carry these out in their lives, without hindrance, either physical or moral, from their fellow-men, so long as it is at their own risk and peril. This last proviso is of course indispensable. No one pretends that actions should be as free as opinions. On the contrary, even opinions lose their immunity when the circumstances in which they are expressed are such as to constitute their expression a positive instigation to some mischievous act. An opinion that corndealers are starvers of the poor, or that private property is robbery, ought to be unmolested when simply circulated through the press, but may justly incur punishment when delivered orally to an excited mob assembled before the house of a corndealer, or when handed about among the same mob in the form of a placard. Acts, of whatever kind, which, without justifiable cause do harm to others, may be, and in the more important cases absolutely require to be, controlled by the unfavourable sentiments, and, when needful, by active interference of mankind. The liberty of the individual must be thus far limited; he must not make himself a nuisance to other people. But if he refrains from molesting others in what concerns them, and merely acts according to his own inclinations and judgment in things which concern himself, the same reasons which show that opinion should be free, prove also that he should be allowed, without molestation, to carry his opinions into practice at his own cost. That mankind are not infallible; that their truths, for the most part, are only half-truths; that unity of opinion, unless resulting from the fullest and freest comparison of opposite opinions, is not desirable, and diversity not an evil, but a good, until mankind are much more capable than at present of recognising all sides of the truth, are principles applicable to men's modes of action, not less than to their opinions. As it is useful that while mankind are imperfect there should be different opinions, so it is that there should be different experiments of living; that free scope should be given to varieties of character, short of injury to others; and that the worth of different modes of life should be proved practically, when any one thinks fit to try them. It is desirable, in short, that in things which do not primarily concern others, individuality should assert itself. Where, not the person's own character, but the traditions or customs of other people are the rule of conduct, there is wanting one of the principal ingredients of human happiness, and quite the chief ingredient of individual and social progress.

In maintaining this principle, the greatest difficulty to be encountered does not lie in the appreciation of means towards an acknowledged end, but in the indifference of persons in general to the end itself. If it were felt that the free development of individuality is one of the leading essentials of well-being; that it is not only a co-ordinate element with all that is designated by the terms civilisation, instruction, education, culture, but is itself a necessary part and condition of all those things; there would be no danger that liberty should be undervalued, and the adjustment of the boundaries between it and social control would present no extraordinary difficulty. But the evil is, that individual spontaneity is hardly recognised by the common modes of thinking as having any intrinsic worth, or deserving any regard on its own account. The majority, being satisfied with the ways of mankind as they now are (for it is they who make them what they are), cannot comprehend why those ways should not be good enough for everybody; and what is more, spontaneity forms no part of the ideal of the majority of moral and social reformers, but is rather looked on with jealousy, as a troublesome and perhaps rebellious obstruction to the general acceptance of what these reformers, in their own judgment, think would be best for mankind. Few persons, out of Germany, even comprehend the meaning of the doctrine which Wilhelm von Humboldt, so eminent both as a *savant* and as a politician, made the text of a treatise— that "the end of man, or that which is prescribed by the eternal or immutable dictates of reason, and not suggested by vague and transient desires, is the highest and most harmonious development of his powers to a complete and consistent whole"; that, therefore, the object "towards which every human being must ceaselessly direct his efforts, and on which especially those who design to influence their fellow-men must ever keep their eyes, is the individuality of power and development"; that for this there are two requisites, "freedom, and variety of situations"; and that from the union of these arise "individual vigour and manifold diversity," which combine themselves in "originality." [1]

Little, however, as people are customed to a doctrine like that of von Humboldt, and surprising as it may be to them to find so high a value attached to individuality, the question, one must nevertheless think, can only be one of degree. No one's idea of excellence in conduct is that people should do absolutely nothing but copy one another. No one would assert that people ought not to put into their mode of life, and into the conduct of their concerns, any impress whatever of their own judgment, or of their own individual character. On the other hand, it would be absurd to pretend that people ought to live as if nothing whatever had

1. *The Sphere and Duties of Government,* from the German of Baron Wilhelm von Humboldt, pp. 11-13.

been known in the world before they came into it; as if experience had as yet done nothing towards showing that one mode of existence, or of conduct, is preferable to another. Nobody denies that people should be so taught and trained in youth as to know and benefit by the ascertained results of human experience. But it is the privilege and proper condition of a human being, arrived at the maturity of his faculties, to use and interpret experience in his own way. It is for him to find out what part of recorded experience is properly applicable to his own circumstances and character. The traditions and customs of other people are to a certain extent, evidence of what their experience has taught *them;* presumptive evidence, and as such, have a claim to his deference: but, in the first place their experience may be too narrow; or they may not have interpreted it rightly. Secondly, their interpretation of experience may be correct, but unsuitable to him. Customs are made for customary circumstances and customary characters; and his circumstances or his character may be uncustomary. Thirdly, though the customs be both good as customs, and suitable to him, yet to conform to custom, merely as custom, does not educate or develop in him any of the qualities which are the distinctive endowment of a human being. The human faculties of perception, judgment, discriminative feeling, mental activity, and even moral preference, are exercised only in making a choice. He who does anything because it is the custom makes no choice. He gains no practice either in discerning or in desiring what is best. The mental and moral, like the muscular powers, are improved only by being used. The faculties are called into no exercise by doing a thing merely because others do it, no more than by believing a thing only because others believe it. If the grounds of an opinion are not conclusive to the person's own reason, his reason cannot be strengthened, but is likely to be weakened, by his adopting it: and if the inducements to an act are not such as are consentaneous to his own feelings and character (where affection, or the rights of others, are not concerned) it is so much done toward rendering his feelings and character inert and torpid, instead of active and energetic.

He who lets the world, or his own portion of it, choose his plan of life for him, has no need of any other faculty than the ape-like one of imitation. He who chooses his plan for himself, employs all his faculties. He must use observation to see, reasoning and judgment to foresee, activity to gather materials for decision, discrimination to decide, and when he has decided, firmness and self-control to hold to his deliberate decision. And these qualities he requires and exercises exactly in proportion as the part of his conduct which he determines according to his own judgment and feelings is a large one. It is possible that he might be guided in some good path, and kept out of harm's way, without any of these things. But what will be his comparative worth as a human being? It really is of importance, not only what men do, but also what manner of men they are that do it. Among the works of man, which human life is rightly employed in perfecting and beautifying, the first in importance surely is man himself. Supposing it

were possible to get houses built, corn grown, battles fought, causes tried, and even churches erected
and prayers said, by machinery—by automatons
in human form—it would be a considerable loss to
exchange for these automatons even the men and
women who at present inhabit the more civilised
parts of the world, and who assuredly are but
starved specimens of what nature can and will
produce. Human nature is not a machine to be
built after a model, and set to do exactly the work
prescribed for it, but a tree, which requires to grow
and develop itself on all sides, according to the
tendency of the inward forces which make it a living thing.

It will probably be conceded that it is desirable
people should exercise their understandings, and
that an intelligent following of custom, or even
occasionally an intelligent deviation from custom,
is better than a blind and simply mechanical adhesion to it. To a certain extent it is admitted that
our understanding should be our own: but there
is not the same willingness to admit that our desires
and impulses should be our own likewise; or that
to possess impulses of our own, and of any strength,
is anything but a peril and a snare. Yet desires and
impulses are as much a part of a perfect human
being as beliefs and restraints: and strong impulses are only perilous when not properly balanced; when one set of aims and inclinations is
developed into strength, while others, which ought
to co-exist with them, remain weak and inactive.
It is not because men's desires are strong that they
act ill; it is because their consciences are weak.

There is no natural connection between strong impulses and a weak conscience. The natural connection is the other way. To say that one person's desires and feelings are stronger and more various than those of another, is merely to say that he has more of the raw material of human nature, and is therefore capable, perhaps of more evil, but certainly of more good. Strong impulses are but another name for energy. Energy may be turned to bad uses; but more good may always be made of an energetic nature, than of an indolent and impassive one. Those who have most natural feeling are always those whose cultivated feelings may be made the strongest. The same strong susceptibilities which make the personal impulses vivid and powerful, are also the source from whence are generated the most passionate love of virtue, and the sternest self-control. It is through the cultivation of these that society both does its duty and protects its interests: not by rejecting the stuff of which heroes are made, because it knows not how to make them. A person whose desires and impulses are his own—are the expression of his own nature, as it has been developed and modified by his own culture—is said to have a character. One whose desires and impulses are not his own, has no character, no more than a steam-engine has a character. If, in addition to being his own, his impulses are strong, and are under the government of a strong will, he has an energetic character. Whoever thinks that individuality of desires and impulses should not be encouraged to unfold itself, must maintain that society has no need of strong natures—is not the better for containing many persons who have much character—and that a high general average of energy is not desirable.

In some early states of society, these forces might be, and were, too much ahead of the power which society then possessed of disciplining and controlling them. There has been a time when the element of spontaneity and individuality was in excess, and the social principle had a hard struggle with it. The difficulty then was to induce men of strong bodies or minds to pay obedience to any rules which required them to control their impulses. To overcome this difficulty, law and discipline, like the Popes struggling against the Emperors, asserted a power over the whole man, claiming to control all his life in order to control his character —which society had not found any other sufficient means of binding. But society has now fairly got the better of individuality; and the danger which threatens human nature is not the excess, but the deficiency, of personal impulses and preferences. Things are vastly changed since the passions of those who were strong by station or by personal endowment were in a state of habitual rebellion against laws and ordinances, and required to be rigorously chained up to enable the persons within their reach to enjoy any particle of security. In our times, from the highest class of society down to the lowest, every one lives as under the eye of a hostile and dreaded censorship. Not only in what concerns others, but in what concerns only them- selves, the individual or the family do not ask themselves—what do I prefer? or, what would suit my character and disposition? or, what would allow the best and highest in me to have fair play, and enable it to grow and thrive? They ask themselves, what is suitable to my position? what is usually done by persons of my station and pecuniary circumstances? or (worse still) what is usually done by persons of a station and circumstances superior to mine? I do not mean that they choose what is customary in preference to what suits their own inclination. It does not occur to them to have any inclinations, except for what is customary. Thus the mind itself is bowed to the yoke: even in what people do for pleasure, conformity is the first thing thought of; they like to be in crowds; they exercise choice only among things commonly done: peculiarity of taste, eccentricity of conduct, are shunned equally with crimes: until by dint of not following their own nature they have no nature to follow: their human capacities are withered and starved: they become incapable of any strong wishes or native pleasures, and are generally without either opinions or feelings of home growth, or properly their own. Now is this, or is it not, the desirable condition of human nature?

It is so, on the Calvinistic theory. According to that, the one great offence of man is self-will. All the good of which humanity is capable is comprised in obedience. You have no choice; thus you must do, and no otherwise: "Whatever is not a duty, is a sin." Human nature being radically corrupt, there is no redemption for any one until human nature is killed within him. To one holding this theory of life, crushing out any of the human faculties, capacities, and susceptibilities, is no evil: man needs no capacity, but that of surrendering himself to the will of God: and if he uses any of his faculties for any other purpose but to do that supposed will more effectually, he is better without them. This is the theory of Calvinism; and it is held, in a mitigated form, by many who do not consider themselves Calvinists; the mitigation consisting in giving a less ascetic interpretation to the alleged will of God; asserting it to be his will that mankind should gratify some of their inclinations; of course not in the manner they themselves prefer, but in the way of obedience, that is, in a way prescribed to them by authority; and, therefore, by the necessary condition of the case, the same for all.

In some such insidious form there is at present a strong tendency to this narrow theory of life, and to the pinched and hidebound type of human character which it patronises. Many persons, no doubt, sincerely think that human beings thus cramped and dwarfed are as their Maker designed them to be; just as many have thought that trees are a much finer thing when clipped into pollards, or cut out into figures of animals, than as nature made them. But if it be any part of religion to believe that man was made by a good Being, it is more consistent with that faith to believe that this Being gave all human faculties that they might be cultivated and unfolded, not rooted out and consumed, and that he takes delight in every nearer approach made by his creatures to the ideal conception embodied in them, every increase in any of their capabilities of comprehension, of action, or of enjoyment. There is a different type of human excellence from the Calvinistic: a conception of humanity as having its nature bestowed on it for other purposes than merely to be abnegated. "Pagan self-assertion" is one of the elements of human worth, as well as "Christian self-denial." [2] There is a Greek ideal of self-development, which the Platonic and Christian ideal of self-government blends with, but does not supersede. It may be better to be John Knox than an Alcibiades, but it is better to be a Pericles than either; nor would a Pericles, if we had one in these days, be without anything good which belonged to John Knox.

It is not by wearing down to uniformity all that is individual in themselves, but by cultivating it, and calling it forth, within the limits imposed by the rights and interests of others, that human beings become a noble and beautiful object of contemplation; and as the works partake the character of those who do them, by the same process human life also becomes rich, diversified, and animating, furnishing more abundant aliment to high thoughts and elevating feelings, and strengthening the tie which binds every individual to the race, by making the race infinitely better worth belonging to. In proportion to the development to his individuality, each person becomes more valuable to himself, and is therefore capable of being more valuable to others. There is a greater fullness of life about his own existence, and when there is more life in the units there is more in the mass which is composed of them. As much compression as is necessary to prevent the stronger specimens of human nature from encroaching on the rights of others cannot be dispensed with; but for this there is ample compensation even in the point of

2. Sterling's Essays.

view of human development. The means of development which the individual loses by being prevented from gratifying his inclinations to the injury of others, are chiefly obtained at the expense of the development of other people. And even to himself there is a full equivalent in the better development of the social part of his nature, rendered possible by the restraint put upon the selfish part. To be held to rigid rules of justice for the sake of others, develops the feelings and capacities which have the good of others for their object. But to be restrained in things not affecting their good, by their mere displeasure, develops nothing valuable, except such force of character as may unfold itself in resisting the restraint. If acquiesced in, it dulls and blunts the whole nature. To give any fair play to the nature of each, it is essential that different persons should be allowed to lead different lives. In proportion as this latitude has been exercised in any age, has that age been noteworthy to posterity. Even despotism does not produce its worst effects, so long as individuality exists under it; and whatever crushes individuality is despotism, by whatever name it may be called, and whether it professes to be enforcing the will of God or the injunction of men.

Having said that the individuality is the same thing with development, and that it is only the cultivation of individuality which produces, or can produce, well-developed human beings, I might here close the argument: for what more or better can be said of any condition of human affairs than that it brings human beings themselves nearer to the best thing they can be? or what worse can be said of any obstruction to good than that it prevents this? Doubtless, however, these considerations will not suffice to convince those who must need convincing; and it is necessary further to show, that these developed human beings are of some use to the undeveloped—to point out to those who do not desire liberty, and would not avail themselves of it, that they may be in some intelligible manner rewarded for allowing other people to make use of it without hindrance.

In the first place, then, I would suggest that they might possibly learn something from them. It will not be denied by anybody, that originality is a valuable element in human affairs. There is always need of persons not only to discover new truths, and point out when what were once truths are true no longer, but also to commence new practices, and set the example of more enlightened conduct, and better taste and sense in human life. This cannot well be gainsaid by anybody who does not believe that the world has already attained perfection in all its ways and practices. It is true that this benefit is not capable of being rendered by everybody alike: there are but few persons, in comparison with the whole of mankind, whose experiments, if adopted by others, would be likely to be any improvement on established practice. But these few are the salt of the earth, without them, human life would become a stagnant pool. Not only is it they who introduce good things which did not before exist; it is they who keep the life in those which already exist. If there were nothing new to be done, would human intellect cease to be necessary? Would it be reason why those who do the old things should forget why they are done, and do them like cattle, not like human beings? There is only too great a tendency in the best beliefs and practices to degenerate into the mechanical; and unless there were a succession of persons whose ever-recurring originality prevents the grounds of those beliefs and practices from becoming merely traditional, such dead matter would not resist the smallest shock from anything really alive, and there would be no reason why civilization should not die out, as in the Byzantine Empire. Persons of genius, it is true, are, and are always likely to be, a small minority, but in order to have them, it is necessary to preserve the soil in which they grow. Genius can only breathe freely in an *atmosphere* of freedom. Persons of genius are, *ex vi termini,* more individual than any other people—less capable, consequently, of fitting themselves, without hurtful compression, into any of the small number of moulds which society provides in order to save its members the trouble of forming their own character. If from timidity they consent to be forced into one of these moulds, and to let all that part of themselves which cannot expand under the pressure remain unexpanded, society will be little the better for their genius. If they are of a strong character, and break their fetters, they become a mark for the society which has not succeeded in reducing them to commonplace, to point out with solemn warning as "wild," "erratic," and the like; much as if one should complain of the Niagara river for not flowing smoothly between its banks like a Dutch canal.

I insist thus emphatically on the importance of

genius, and the necessity of allowing it to unfold itself freely both in thought and in practice, being well aware that no one will deny the position in theory, but knowing also that almost every one, in reality, is totally indifferent to it. People think genius a fine thing if it enables a man to write an exciting poem, or paint a picture. But in its true sense, that of originality in thought and action, though no one says that it is not a thing to be admired, nearly all, at heart, think that they can do very well without it. Unhappily this is too natural to be wondered at. Originality is the one thing which unoriginal minds cannot feel the use of. They cannot see what it is to do for them: how should they? If they could see what it would do for them, it would not be originality. The first service which originality has to render them, is that of opening their eyes: which being once fully done, they would have a chance of being themselves original. Meanwhile, recollecting that nothing was ever yet done which some one was not the first to do, and that all good things which exist are the fruits of originality, let them be modest enough to believe that there is something still left for it to accomplish, and assure themselves that they are more in need of originality, the less they are conscious of the want.

In sober truth, whatever homage may be professed, or even paid, to real or supposed mental superiority, the general tendency of things throughout the world is to render mediocrity the ascendant power among mankind. In ancient history, in the Middle Ages, and in a diminishing degree through the long transition from feudality to the present

time, the individual was a power in himself; and
if he had either great talents or a high social position, he was a considerable power. At present individuals are lost in the crowd. In politics it is
almost a triviality to say that public opinion now
rules the world. The only power deserving the name
is that of masses and of governments while they
make themselves the organ of the tendencies and
instincts of masses. This is as true in the moral and
social relations of private life as in public transactions. Those whose opinions go by the name of
public opinion are not always the same sort of
public: in America they are the whole white population; in England, chiefly the middle class. But
they are always in a mass, that is to say collective
mediocrity. And what is a still greater novelty, the
mass do not now take their opinions from dignitar-
ies in Church or State, from ostensible leaders, or
from books. Their thinking is done for them by
men much like themselves, addressing them or
speaking in their name, on the spur of the moment,
through the newspapers. I am not complaining of
all this. I do not assert that anything better is compatible, as a general rule, with the present low state
of the human mind. But that does not hinder the
government of mediocrity from being mediocre
government. No government by a democracy or a
numerous aristocracy, either in its political acts
or in the opinions, qualities, and tone of mind
which it fosters, ever did or could rise above mediocrity, except in so far as the sovereign. Many have
let themselves be guided (which in their best times
they always have done) by the counsels and influence of a more highly gifted and instructed One

or Few. The initiation of all wise or noble things comes and must come from individuals; generally at first from some one individual. The honour and glory of the average man is that he is capable of following that initiative; that he can respond internally to wise and noble things, and be led to them with his eyes open. I am not countenancing the sort of "hero-worship" which applauds the strong man of genius for forcibly seizing on the government of the world and making it do his bidding in spite of itself. All he can claim is, freedom to point out the way. The power of compelling others into it is not only inconsistent with the freedom and development of all the rest, but corrupting to the strong man himself. It does seem, however, that when the opinions of masses of merely average men are everywhere become or becoming the dominant power, the counterpoise and corrective to that tendency would be the more and more pronounced individuality of those who stand on the higher eminences of thought. It is in these circumstances most especially, that exceptional individuals, instead of being deterred, should be encouraged in acting differently from the mass. In other times there was no advantage in their doing so, unless they acted not only differently but better. In this age, the mere example of non-conformity, the mere refusal to bend the knee to custom, is itself a service. Precisely because the tyranny of opinion is such as to make eccentricity a reproach, it is desirable, in order to break through that tyranny, that people should be eccentric. Eccentricity has always abounded when and where strength of character has abounded; and the amount of eccentricity in a society has generally been proportioned to the amount of genius, mental vigour, and moral courage it contained. That so few now dare to be eccentric marks the chief danger of the time.

I have said that it is important to give the freest scope possible to uncustomary things, in order that it may in time appear which of these are fit to be converted into customs. But independence of action, and disregard of custom, are not solely deserving of encouragement for the chance they afford that better modes of action, and customs more worthy of general adoption, may be struck out; nor is it only persons of decided mental superiority who have a just claim to carry on their lives in their own way. There is no reason that all human existence should be constructed on some one or some small number of patterns. If a person possesses any tolerable amount of common sense and experience, his own mode of laying out his existence is the best, not because it is the best in itself, but because it is his own mode. Human beings are not like sheep; and even sheep are not undistinguishably alike. A man cannot get a coat or a pair of boots to fit him unless they are either made to his measure, or he has a whole warehouseful to choose from: and is it easier to fit him with a life than with a coat, or are human beings more like one another in their whole physical and spiritual conformation than in the shape of their feet? If it were only that people have diversities of taste, that is reason enough for not attempting to shape them all after one model. But different persons also require different conditions for their spiritual development; and can no more exist healthily in the same moral, than all the variety of plants can in the same physical, atmosphere and climate. The same things which are helps to one person towards the cultivation of his higher nature are hindrances to another. The same mode of life is a healthy excitement to one, keeping all his faculties of action and enjoyment in their best order, while to another it is a distracting burthen, which suspends or crushes all internal life. Such are the differences among human beings in their sources of pleasure, their susceptibilities of pain, and the operation on them of different physical and moral agencies, that unless there is a corresponding diversity in their modes of life, they neither obtain their fair share of happiness, nor grow up to the mental, moral and aesthetic stature of which their nature is capable. Why then should tolerance, as far as the public sentiment is concerned, extend only to tastes and modes of life which extort acquiescence by the multitude of their adherents? Nowhere (except in some monastic institutions) is diversity of taste entirely unrecognised; a person may, without blame, either like or dislike rowing, or smoking, or music, or athletic exercises, or chess, or cards, or study, because both those who like each of these things, and those who dislike them, are too numerous to be put down. But the man, and still more the woman, who can be accused either of doing "what nobody does," or of not doing "what everybody does," is the subject of as much depreciatory remark as if he or she had committed some grave moral delinquency. Persons require to possess a title, or some other badge of rank, or of the consideration of people of rank, to be able to indulge somewhat in the luxury of doing as they like without detriment to their estimation. To indulge somewhat, I repeat: for whoever allow themselves much of that indulgence, incur the risk of something worse than disparaging speeches—they are in peril of a commission *de lunatico,* and of having their property taken from them and given to their relations.[3]

There is one characteristic of the present direction of public opinion peculiarly calculated to make it intolerant of any marked demonstration of individuality. The general average of mankind are not only moderate in intellect, but also moderate in inclinations: they have no tastes or wishes

3. There is something both contemptible and frightful in the sort of evidence on which, of late years, any person can be judicially declared unfit for the management of his affairs; and after his death, his disposal of his property can be set aside, if there is enough of it to pay the expenses of litigation—which are charged on the property itself. All the minute details of his daily life are pried into, and whatever is found which, seen through the medium of the perceiving and describing faculties of the lowest of the low, bears an appearance unlike absolute commonplace, is laid before the jury as evidence of insanity, and often with success; the jurors being little, if at all, less vulgar and ignorant than the witnesses; while the judges, with that extraordinary want of knowledge of human nature and life which continually astonishes us in English lawyers, often help to mislead them. These trials speak volumes as to the state of feeling and opinion among the vulgar with regard to human liberty. So far from setting any value on individuality—so far from respecting the right of each individual to act, in things indifferent, as seems good to his own judgment and inclinations, judges and juries cannot even conceive that a person in a state of sanity can desire such freedom. In former days, when it was proposed to burn atheists, charitable people used to suggest putting them in a madhouse instead; it would be nothing surprising now-a-days were we to see this done, and the doers applauding themselves, because, instead of persecuting for religion, they had adopted so humane and Christian a mode of treating these unfortunates, not without a silent satisfaction at their having thereby obtained their deserts.

strong enough to incline them to do anything unusual, and they consequently do not understand
those who have, and class all such with the wild
and intemperate whom they are accustomed to
look down upon. Now, in addition to this fact
which is general, we have only to suppose that a
strong movement has set in towards the improvement of morals, and it is evident what we have to
expect. In these days such a movement has set in;
much has actually been effected in the way of increased regularity of conduct and discouragement
of excesses; and there is a philanthropic spirit
abroad, for the exercise of which there is no more
inviting field than the moral and prudential improvement of our fellow-creatures. These tendencies of the times cause the public to be more
disposed than at most former periods to prescribe
general rules of conduct, and endeavour to make
every one conform to the approved standard. And
that standard, express or tacit, is to desire nothing
strongly. Its ideal of character is to be without any
marked character; to maim by compression, like
a Chinese lady's foot, every part of human nature
which stands out prominently, and tends to make
the person markedly dissimilar in outline to commonplace humanity.

As is usually the case with ideals which exclude
one-half of what is desirable, the present standard
of approbation produces only an inferior imitation
of the other half. Instead of great energies guided
by vigorous reason, and strong feelings strongly
controlled by a conscientious will, its result is weak
feelings and weak energies, which therefore can
be kept in outward conformity to rule without any

strength either of will or of reason. Already energetic characters on any large scale are becoming merely traditional. There is now scarcely any outlet for energy in this country except business. The energy expended in this may still be regarded as considerable. What little is left from that employment is expended on some hobby; which may be a useful, even a philanthropic hobby; but is always some one thing, and generally a thing of small dimensions. The greatness of England is now all collective; individually small, we only appear capable of anything great by our habit of combining; and with this our moral and religious philanthropists are perfectly contented. But it was men of another stamp than this that made England what it has been; and men of another stamp will be needed to prevent its decline.

The despotism of custom is everywhere the standing hindrance to human advancement, being unceasing antagonism to that disposition to aim at something better than customary, which is called, according to circumstances, the spirit of liberty, or that of progress or improvement. The spirit of improvement is not always a spirit of liberty, for it may aim at forcing improvements on an unwilling people; and the spirit of liberty, in so far as it resists such attempts, may ally itself locally and temporarily with the opponents of improvement; but the only unfailing and permanent source of improvement is liberty, since by it there are as many possible independent centres of improvement as there are individuals. The progressive principle, however, in either shape, whether as the love of liberty or of improvement, is antagonistic to the sway of Custom, involving at least emancipation from that yoke; and the contest between the two constitutes the chief interest of the history of mankind. The greater part of the world has, properly speaking, no history, because the despotism of Custom is complete. This is the case over the whole East. Custom is there, in all things, the final appeal; justice and right mean conformity to custom; the argument of custom no one, unless some tyrant intoxicated with power, thinks of resisting. And we see the result. Those nations must once have had originality; they did not start out of the ground populous, lettered, and versed in many of the arts of life; they made themselves all this, and were then the greatest and most powerful nations of the world. What are they now? The subjects or dependents of tribes whose forefathers wandered in the forests when theirs had magnificent palaces and gorgeous temples, but over whom custom exercised only a divided rule with liberty and progress. A people, it appears, may be progressive for a certain length of time, and then stop: when does it stop? When it ceases to possess individuality. If a similar change should befall the nations of Europe, it will not be in exactly the same shape: the despotism of custom with which these nations are threatened is not precisely stationariness. It proscribes singularity, but it does not preclude change, provided all change together. We have discarded the fixed costumes of our forefathers; every one must still dress like other people, but the fashion may change once or twice a year. We thus take care that when there is a change, it shall be for change's sake, and not from any idea of beauty or convenience; for the same idea of beauty or convenience would not strike all the world at the same moment, and be simultaneously thrown aside by all at another moment. But we are progressive as well as changeable: we continually make new inventions in mechanical things, and keep them until they are again superseded by better; we are eager for improvement in politics, in education, even in morals, though in this last our idea of improvement chiefly consists in persuading or forcing other people to be as good as ourselves. It is not progress that we object to; on the contrary, we flatter ourselves that we are the most progressive people who ever lived. It is individuality that we war against: we should think we had done wonders if we had made ourselves all alike; forgetting that the unlikeness of one person to another is generally the first thing which draws the attention of either to the imperfection of his own type, and the superiority of another, or the possibility, by combining the advantages of both, of producing something better than either. We have a warning example in China—a nation of much talent, and in some respects, even wisdom, owing to the rare good fortune of having been provided at an early period with a particularly good set of customs, the work, in some measure, of men to whom even the most enlightened European must accord, under certain limitations, the title of sages and philosophers. They are remarkable, too, in the excellence of their apparatus for impressing, as far as possible, the best wisdom they possess upon every mind in the community, and securing that those who have appropriated most of it shall occupy the posts of honour and power. Surely the people who did this have discovered the secret of human progressiveness, and must have kept themselves steadily at the head of the movement of the world. On the contrary, they have become stationary—have remained so for thousands of years; and if they are ever to be farther improved, it must be by foreigners. They have succeeded beyond all hope in what English philanthropists are so industriously working at—in making a people all ᵥᵣ̲ᵥ̲ᵥ̲, all governing their thoughts and conduct by the same maxims and rules; and these are the fruits. The modern *régime* of public opinion is, in an unorganised form, what the Chinese educational and political systems are in an organised; and unless individuality shall be able successfully to assert itself against this yoke, Europe, notwithstanding its noble antecedents and its professed Christianity, will tend to become another China.

What is it that has hitherto preserved Europe from this lot? What has made the European family of nations an improving, instead of a stationary portion of mankind? Not any superior excellence in them, which, when it exists, exists as the effect not as the cause; but their remarkable diversity of character and culture. Individuals, classes, nations, have been extremely unlike one another: they have struck out a great variety of paths, each leading to something valuable; and although at every period those who travelled in different paths have been intolerant of one another, and each would have thought it an excellent thing if all the rest could have been compelled to travel his road, their attempts to thwart each other's development have rarely had any permanent success, and each has in time endured to receive the good which the others have offered. Europe is, in my judgment, wholly indebted to this plurality of paths for its progressive and many-sided development. But it already begins to possess this benefit in a considerably less degree. It is decidedly advancing towards the Chinese ideal of making all people alike. M. de Tocqueville, in his last important work, remarks how much more the Frenchmen of the present day resemble one another than did those even of the last generation. The same remark might be made of Englishmen in a far greater degree. In a passage already quoted from Wilhelm von Humboldt, he points out two things as necessary conditions of human development, because necessary to render people unlike one another; namely, freedom, and variety of situations. The second of these two conditions is in this country every day diminishing. The circumstances which surround different classes and individuals, and shape their characters, are daily becoming more assimilated. Formerly, different ranks, different neighbourhoods, different trades and professions, lived in what might be called different worlds; at present to a great degree in the same. Comparatively speaking, they now read the same things, listen to the same things, see the same things, go to the same places, have their hopes and fears directed to the same objects, have the same rights and liberties, and the same means of asserting them. Great as are the differences of position which remain, they are nothing to those which have ceased. And the assimilation is still proceeding. All the political changes of the age promote it, since they all tend to raise the low and to lower the high. Every extension of education promotes it, because education brings people under common influences, and gives them access to the general stock of facts and sentiments. Improvement in the means of communication promotes it, by bringing the inhabitants of distant places into personal contact, and keeping up a rapid flow of changes of residence between one place and another. The increase of commerce and manufactures promotes it, by diffusing more widely the advantages of easy circumstances, and opening all objects of ambition, even the highest, to general competition, whereby the desire of rising becomes no longer the character of a particular class, but of all classes. A more powerful agency than even all these, in bringing about a general similarity among mankind, is the complete establishment, in this and other free countries, of the ascendancy of public opinion in the State. As the various social eminences which enabled persons entrenched on them to disregard the opinion of the multitude gradually become levelled; as the very idea of resisting the will of the public, when it is positively known that they have a will, disappears more and more from the minds of practical politicians; there ceases to be any social support for nonconformity —any substantive power in society which, itself opposed to the ascendency of numbers, is interested in taking under its protection opinions and tendencies at variance with those of the public.

The combination of all these causes forms so great a mass of influences hostile to Individuality, that it is not easy to see how it can stand its ground. It will do so with increasing difficulty, unless the intelligent part of the public can be made to feel its value—to see that it is good there should be differences, even though not for the better, even though, as it may appear to them, some should be for the worse. If the claims of Individuality are ever to be asserted, the time is now, while much is still wanting to complete the enforced assimilation. It is only in the earlier stages that any stand can be successfully made against the encroachment. The demand that all other people shall resemble ourselves grows by what it feeds on. If resistance waits till life is reduced *nearly* to one uniform type, all deviations from that type will come to be considered impious, immoral, even monstrous and contrary to nature. Mankind speedily become unable to conceive diversity, when they have been for some time unaccustomed to see it.

# CHAPTER IV

## OF THE LIMITS TO THE AUTHORITY
## OF SOCIETY OVER THE INDIVIDUAL

WHAT, THEN, IS THE RIGHTFUL LIMIT TO THE sovereignty of the individual over himself? Where does the authority of society begin? How much of human life should be assigned to individuality, and how much to society?

Each will receive its proper share, if each has that which more particularly concerns it. To individuality should belong the part of life in which it is chiefly the individual that is interested; to society, the part which chiefly interests society.

Though society is not founded on a contract, and though no good purpose is answered by inventing a contract in order to deduce social obligations from it, every one who receives the protection of society owes a return for the benefit, and the fact of living in society renders it indispensable that each should be bound to observe a certain line of conduct towards the rest. This conduct consists, first, in not injuring the interests of one another; or rather certain interests, which, either by express legal provision or by tacit understanding, ought to be considered as rights; and secondly, in each person's bearing his share (to be fixed on some equitable principle) of the labours and sacrifices incurred for defending the society or its members from injury and molestation. These conditions society is justified in enforcing, at all costs to those who endeavor to withhold fulfillment. Nor is this all that society may do. The acts of an individual may be hurtful to others, or wanting in due consideration for their welfare, without going to the length of violating any of their constituted rights. The offender may then be justly punished by opinion, though not by law. As soon as any part of a person's conduct affects prejudicially the interests of others, society has jurisdiction over it, and the question whether the general welfare will or will not be promoted by interfering with it, becomes open to discussion. But there is no room for entertaining any such question when a person's conduct affects the interests of no persons besides himself, or needs not affect them unless they like (all the persons concerned being of full age, and the ordinary amount of understanding). In all such cases, there should be perfect freedom, legal and social, to do the action and stand the consequences.

It would be a great misunderstanding of this doctrine to suppose that it is one of selfish indifference, which pretends that human beings have no business with each other's conduct in life, and that they should not concern themselves about the well-doing or well-being of one another, unless their own interest is involved. Instead of any diminution, there is need of a great increase of disinterested exertion to promote the good of others. But disinterested benevolence can find other instruments to persuade people to their good than whips and scourges, either of the literal or the metaphorical sort. I am the last person to undervalue the self-regarding virtues; they are only second in importance, if even second, to the social. It is equally the business of education to cultivate both. But even education works by conviction and persuasion as well as by compulsion, and it is by the former only that, when the period of education is passed, the self-regarding virtues should be inculcated. Human beings owe to each other help to distinguish the better from the worse, and encouragement to choose the former and avoid the latter. They should be for ever stimulating each other to increased exercise of their higher faculties, and increased direction of their feelings and aims towards wise instead of foolish, elevating instead of degrading, objects and contemplations. But neither one person, nor any number of persons, is warranted in saying to another human creature of ripe years, that he shall not do with his life for his own benefit what he chooses to do with it. He is the person most interested in his own well-being: the interest which any other person, except in cases of strong personal attachment, can have in it, is trifling, compared with that which he himself has; the interest which society has in him individually (except as to his conduct to others) is fractional, and altogether indirect; while with respect to his own feelings and circumstances, the most ordinary man or woman has means of knowledge immeasurably surpassing those that can be possessed by any one else. The interference of society to overrule his judgment and purposes in what only regards himself must be grounded on general presumptions; which may be altogether wrong, and even if right, are as likely as not to be misapplied to individual cases, by persons no better acquainted with the circumstances of such cases than those are who look at them merely from without. In this department, therefore, of human affairs, Individuality has its proper field of action. In the conduct of human beings towards one another it is necessary that general rules should for the most part be observed, in order that people may know what they have to expect: but in each person's own concerns his individual spontaneity is entitled to free exercise. Considerations to aid his judgment, exhortations to strengthen his will, may be offered to him, even obtruded on him, by others: but he himself is the final judge. All errors which he is likely to commit against advice and warning are far outweighed by the evil of allowing others to constrain him to what they deem his good.

I do not mean that the feelings with which a person is regarded by others ought not be in any way affected by his self-regarding qualities or deficiencies. This is neither possible nor desirable. If he is eminent in any of the qualities which conduce to his own good, he is, so far, a proper object of admiration. He is so much nearer to the ideal perfection of human nature. If he is grossly deficient in those qualities, a sentiment the opposite of admiration will follow. There is a degree of folly, and a degree of what may be called (though the phrase is not unobjectionable) lowness or depravation of taste, which, though it cannot justify doing harm to the person who manifests it, renders him necessarily and properly a subject of distaste, or, in extreme cases, even of contempt: a person could not have the opposite qualities in due strength without entering these feelings. Though doing no wrong to any one, a person may so act as to compel us to judge him, and feel to him, as a fool, or as a being of an inferior order: and since this judgment and feeling are a fact which he would prefer to avoid, it is doing him a service to warn him of it beforehand, as of any other disagreeable consequence to which he exposes himself. It would be well, indeed, if this good office were much more freely rendered than the common notions of politeness at present permit, and if one person could honestly point out to another that he thinks him in fault, without being considered unmannerly or presuming. We have a right, also, in various ways, to act upon our unfavourable opinion of any one, not to the oppression of his individuality, but in the exercise of ours. We are not bound, for example, to seek his society; we have a right to avoid it (though not to parade the avoidance), for we have a right to choose the society most acceptable to us. We have a right, and it may be our duty, to caution others against him, if we think his example or conversation likely to have a pernicious effect on those with whom he associates. We may give others a preference over him in optional good offices, except those which tend to his improvement. In these various modes a person may suffer very severe penalties at the hands of others for faults which directly concern only himself; but he suffers these penalties only in so far as they are the natural and, as it were, the spontaneous consequences of the faults themselves, not because they are purposely inflicted on him for the sake of punishment. A person who shows rashness, obstinacy, self-conceit—who cannot live within moderate means—who cannot restrain himself from hurtful indulgences—who pursues animal pleasures at the expense of those of feeling and intellect—must expect to be lowered in the opinion of others, and to have a less share of their favourable sentiments; but of this he has no right to complain, unless he has merited their favour by special excellence in his social relations, and has thus established a title to their good offices, which is not affected by his demerits toward himself.

What I contend for is, that the inconveniences which are strictly inseparable from the unfavourable judgment of others, are the only ones to which a person should ever be subjected for that portion of his conduct and character which concerns his own good, but which does not affect the interest of others in their relations with him. Acts injurious to others require a totally different treatment. Encroachment on their rights; infliction on them of any loss or damage not justified by his own rights; falsehood or duplicity in dealing with them; unfair or ungenerous use of advantage over them; even selfish abstinence from defending them against injury—these are fit objects of moral reprobation, and, in grave cases, of moral retribution and punishment. And not only these acts, but the dispositions which lead to them, are properly immoral, and fit subjects of disapprobation which may rise to abhorrence. Cruelty of disposition; malice and ill-nature; that most anti-social and odious of all passions, envy; dissimulation and insincerity, irascibility on insufficient cause, and resentment disproportioned to the provocation; the love of domineering over others; the desire to engross more than one's share of advantages: (the πλεονεξία of the Greeks); the pride which derives gratification from the abasement of others; the egotism which thinks self and its concerns more important than everything else, and decides all doubtful questions in its own favour;—these are moral vices, and constitute a bad and odious moral character: unlike the self-regarding faults previously mentioned, which are not properly immoralities, and to whatever pitch they may be carried, do not constitute wickedness. They may be proofs of any amount of folly, or want of personal dignity and self-respect: but they are only a subject of moral reprobation when they involve a breach of duty to others, for whose sake the individual is bound to have care for himself. What are called duties to ourselves are not socially obligatory, unless circumstances render them at the same time duties to others. The term duty to oneself, when it means anything more than prudence, means self-respect or self-development, and for none of these is any one accountable to his fellow creatures, because for none of them is it for the good of mankind that he be held accountable to them.

The distinction between the loss of consideration which a person may rightly incur by defect of prudence or of personal dignity, and the reprobation which is due to him for an offence against the rights of others, is not a merely nominal distinction. It makes a vast difference both in our feelings and in our conduct towards him whether he displeases us in things in which we think we have a right to control him, or in things in which we know that we have not. If he displeases us, we may express our distaste, and we may stand aloof from a person as well as from a thing that displeases us; but we shall not therefore feel called on to make his life uncomfortable. We shall reflect that he already bears, or will bear, the whole penalty of his error; if he spoils his life by mismanagement, we shall not, for that reason, desire to spoil it still further: instead of wishing to punish him, we shall rather endeavour to alleviate his punishment, by showing him how he may avoid or cure the evils his conduct tends to bring upon him. He may be to us an object of pity, perhaps of dislike, but not of anger or resentment; we shall not treat him like an enemy of society: the worse we shall think ourselves justified in doing is leaving him to himself, if we do not interfere benevolently by showing interest or concern for him. It is far otherwise if he has infringed the rules necessary for the protection of his fellow-creatures, individually or collectively. The evil consequences of his acts do not then fall on himself, but on others; and society, as the protector of all its members, must retaliate on him; must inflict pain on him for the express purpose of punishment, and must take care that it be sufficiently severe. In the one case, he is an offender at our bar, and we are called not only to sit in judgment on him, but, in one shape or another, to execute our own sentence: in the other case, it is not our part to inflict any suffering on him, except

SOCIETY AND THE INDIVIDUAL

what may incidentally follow from our using the same liberty in the regulation of our own affairs, which we allow to him in his.

The distinction here pointed out between the part of a person's life which concerns only himself, and that which concerns others, many persons will refuse to admit. How (it may be asked) can any part of the conduct of a member of society be a matter of indifference to the other members? No person is an entirely isolated being; it is impossible for a person to do anything seriously or permanently hurtful to himself, without mischief reaching at least to his near connections, and often far beyond them. If he injures his property, he does harm to those who directly or indirectly derived support from it, and usually diminishes, by a greater or less amount, the general resources of the community. If he deteriorates his bodily or mental faculties, he not only brings evil upon all who depended on him for any portion of their happiness, but disqualifies himself for rendering the services which he owes to his fellow-creatures generally; perhaps becomes a burthen on their affection or benevolence; and if such conduct were very frequent, hardly any offence that is committed would detract more from the general sum of good. Finally, if by his vices or follies a person does no direct harm to others, he is nevertheless (it may be said) injurious by his example; and ought to be compelled to control himself, for the sake of those whom the sight or knowledge of his conduct might corrupt or mislead.

And even (it will be added) if the consequences of misconduct could be confined to the vicious or

thoughtless individual, ought society to abandon
to their own guidance those who are manifestly
unfit for it? If protection against themselves is
confessedly due to children and persons under age,
is not society equally bound to afford it to persons
of mature years who are equally incapable of self-
government? If gambling, or drunkenness, or in-
continence, or idleness, or uncleanliness, are as
injurious to happiness, and as great a hindrance
to improvement, as many or most of the acts prohibited by law, why (it may be asked) should not
law, so far as is consistent with practicability and
social convenience, endeavour to repress these
also? And as a supplement to the unavoidable im-
perfections of law, ought not opinion at least to
organise a powerful police against these vices, and
visit rigidly with social penalties those who are
known to practise them? There is no question here
(it may be said) about restricting individuality, or
impeding the trial of new and original experiments in living. The only things it is sought to prevent are things which have been tried and condemned from the beginning of the world until now;
things which experience has shown not to be useful or suitable to any person's individuality. There
must be some length of time and amount of experience after which a moral or prudential truth may
be regarded as established: and it is merely desired to prevent generation after generation from
falling over the same precipice which has been fatal
to their predecessors.

I fully admit that the mischief which a person
does to himself may seriously affect, both through
their sympathies and their interests, those nearly

connected with him and, in a minor degree, society at large. When, by conduct of this sort, a person is led to violate a distinct and assignable obligation to any other person or persons, the case is taken out of the self-regarding class, and becomes amenable to moral disapprobation in the proper sense of the term. If, for example, a man, through intemperance or extravagance, becomes unable to pay his debts, or, having undertaken the moral responsibility of a family, becomes from the same cause incapable of supporting or educating them, he is deservedly reprobated, and might be justly punished; but it is for the breach of duty to his family or creditors, not for the extravagance. If the resources which ought to have been devoted to them, had been diverted from them for the most prudent investment, the moral culpability would have been the same. George Barnwell murdered his uncle to get money for his mistress, but if he had done it to set himself up in business, he would equally have been hanged. Again, in the frequent case of a man who causes grief to his family by addiction to bad habits, he deserves reproach for his unkindness or ingratitude; but so he may for cultivating habits not in themselves vicious, if they are painful to those with whom he passes his life, or who from personal ties are dependent on him for their comfort. Whoever fails in the consideration generally due to the interests and feeling of others, not being compelled by some more imperative duty, or justified by allowable self-preference, is a subject of moral disapprobation for the failure, but not for the cause of it, nor for the errors, merely personal to himself, which may have remotely led to it. In like manner, when a person disables himself, by conduct purely self-regarding, from the perform-ance of some definite duty incumbent on him to the public, he is guilty of a social offence. No per-son ought to be punished simply for being drunk; but a soldier or a policeman should be punished for being drunk on duty. Whenever, in short, there is a definite damage, or a definite risk of damage, either to an individual or to the public, the case is taken out of the province of liberty, and placed in that of morality or law.

But with regard to the merely contingent, or, as it may be called, constructive injury which a per-son causes to society, by conduct which neither violates any specific duty to the public, nor oc-casions perceptible hurt to any assignable individ-ual except himself; the inconvenience is one which society can afford to bear, for the sake of the greater good of human freedom. If grown persons are to be punished for not taking proper care of themselves, I would rather it were for their own sake, than under pretence of preventing them from impairing their capacity or rendering to society benefits which society does not pretend it has a right to exact. But I cannot consent to argue the point as if society had no means of bringing its weaker members up to its ordinary standard of rational conduct, except waiting till they do some-thing irrational, and then punishing them, legally or morally, for it. Society has had absolute power over them during all the early portion of their ex-istence: it has had the whole period of childhood and nonage in which to try whether it could make them capable of rational conduct in life. The exist-

SOCIETY AND THE INDIVIDUAL

ing generation is master both of the training and the entire circumstances of the generation to come; it cannot indeed make them perfectly wise and good, because it is itself so lamentably deficient in goodness and wisdom; and its best efforts are not always, in individual cases, its most successful ones; but it is perfectly well able to make the rising generation, as a whole, as good as, and a little better than, itself. If society lets any considerable numbers grow up mere children, incapable of being acted on by rational consideration of distant motives, society has itself to blame for the consequences. Armed not only with all the powers of education, but with the ascendency which the authority of a received opinion always exercises over the minds who are least fitted to judge for themselves; and aided by the *natural* penalties which cannot be prevented from falling on those who incur the distaste or the contempt of those who know them; let not society pretend that it needs, besides all this, the power to issue commands and enforce obedience in the personal concerns of individuals, in which, on all principles of justice and policy, the decision ought to rest with those who are to abide the consequences. Nor is there anything which tends more to discredit and frustrate the better means of influencing conduct than a resort to the worse. If there be among those whom it is attempted to coerce into prudence or temperance any of the material of which vigorous and independent characters are made, they will infallibly rebel against the yoke. No such person will ever feel that others have a right to control him in his concerns, such as they have to prevent him from injuring them in theirs; and it easily comes to be considered a mark of spirit and courage to fly in the face of such usurped authority, and do with ostentation the exact opposite of what it enjoins; as in the fashion of grossness which succeeded, in the time of Charles II, to the fanatical moral intolerance of the Puritans. With respect to what is said of the necessity of protecting society from the bad example set to others by the vicious or the self-indulgent; it is true that bad example may have a pernicious effect, especially the example of doing wrong to others with impunity to the wrong-doer. But we are now speaking of conduct which, while it does no wrong to others, is supposed to do great harm to the agent himself; and I do not see how those who believe this can think otherwise than that the example, on the whole, must be more salutary than hurtful, since, if it displays the misconduct, it displays also the painful or degrading consequences which, if the conduct is justly censured, must be supposed to be in all or most cases attendant on it.

But the strongest of all the arguments against the interference of the public with purely personal conduct is that, when it does interfere, the odds are that it interferes wrongly, and in the wrong place. On questions of social morality, of duty to others, the opinion of the public, that is, of an overruling majority, though often wrong, is likely to be still oftener right; because on such questions they are only required to judge of their own interests; of the manner in which some mode of conduct, if allowed to be practised, would affect themselves. But the opinion of a similar majority, imposed as a law on the minority, on questions of self-regarding conduct, is quite as likely to be wrong as right; for in these cases public opinion means, at the best, some people's opinion of what is good or bad for other people; while very often it does not even mean that; the public, with the most perfect indifference, passing over the pleasure or convenience of those whose conduct they censure, and considering only their own preference. There are many who consider as an injury to themselves any conduct which they have a distaste for, and resent it as an outrage to their feelings; as a religious bigot, when charged with disregarding the religious feelings of others, has been known to retort that they disregard his feelings, by persisting in their abominable worship or creed. But there is no parity between the feeling of a person for his own opinion, and the feeling of another who is offended at his holding it; no more than between the desire of a thief to take a purse, and the desire of the right owner to keep it. And a person's taste is as much his own peculiar concern as his opinion or his purse. It is easy for any one to imagine an ideal public which leaves the freedom and choice of individuals in all uncertain matters undisturbed, and only requires them to abstain from modes of conduct which universal experience has condemned. But where has there been seen a public which set any such limit to its censorship? or when does the public trouble itself about universal experience? In its interferences with personal conduct it is seldom thinking of anything but the enormity of acting or feeling differently from itself; and this standard of judgment, thinly disguised, is held up to mankind as the dictate of religion and philosophy, by nine-tenths of all moralists and speculative writers. These teach that things are right because they are right: because we feel them to be so. They tell us to search in our own mind and heart for laws of conduct binding on ourselves and on all others. What can the poor public do but apply these instructions, and make their own personal feelings of good and evil, if they are tolerably unanimous in them, obligatory on all the world?

The evil here pointed out is not one which exists only in theory; and it may perhaps be expected that I should specify the instances in which the public of this age and country improperly invests its own preferences with the character of moral laws. I am not writing an essay on the aberrations of existing moral feeling. That is too weighty a subject to be discussed parenthetically, and by way of illustrations. Yet examples are necessary to show that the principle I maintain is of serious and practical moment, and that I am not endeavouring to erect a barrier against imaginary evils. And it is not difficult to show, by abundant instances, that to extend the bounds of what may be called moral police, until it encroaches on the most unquestionably legitimate liberty of the individual, is one of the most universal of all human propensities.

As a first instance, consider the antipathies which men cherish on no better grounds than that persons whose religious opinions are different from theirs do not practise their religious observances, especially their religious abstinences. To cite a rather trivial example, nothing in the creed or practice of Christians does more to envenom the hatred of Mahomedans against them than the fact of their eating pork. There are few acts which Christians and Europeans regard with more unaffected disgust than Mussulmans regard this particular mode of satisfying hunger. It is, in the first place, an offence against their religion; but this circumstance by no means explains either the degree or the kind of their repugnance; for wine also is forbidden by their religion, and to partake of it is by all Mussulmans accounted wrong, but not disgusting. Their aversion to the flesh of the "unclean beast" is, on the contrary, of that peculiar character, resembling an instinctive antipathy, which the idea of uncleanness, when once it thoroughly sinks into the feelings, seems always to excite even in those whose personal habits are anything but scrupulously cleanly, and of which the sentiment of religious impurity so intense in the Hindoos, is a remarkable example. Suppose now that in a people of whom the majority were Mussulmans, that majority should insist upon not permitting pork to be eaten within the limits of the country. This would be nothing new in Mahomedan countries.[1] Would this be a legitimate exercise of the moral authority of

1. The case of the Bombay Parsees is a curious instance in point. When this industrious and enterprising tribe, the descendants of the Persian fire-worshippers, flying from their native country before the Caliphs, arrived in Western India, they were admitted to toleration by the Hindoo sovereigns, on condition of not eating beef. When these regions afterwards fell under the dominion of Mahomedan conquerors, the Parsees obtained from them a continuance of indulgence, on condition of refraining from pork. What was at first obedience to authority became a second nature, and the Parsees to this day abstain both from beef and pork. Though not required by their religion, the double abstinence had had time to grow into a custom of their tribe; and custom, in the East, is a religion.

public opinion? and if not, why not? The practise is really revolting to such a public. They also sincerely think that it is forbidden and abhorred by the Deity. Neither could the prohibition be censured as religious persecution. It might be religious in its origin, but it would not be persecution for religion, since nobody's religion makes it a duty to eat pork. The only tenable ground of condemnation would be that with the personal tastes and self-regarding concerns of individuals the public has no business to interfere.

To come somewhat nearer home: the majority of Spaniards consider it a gross impiety, offensive in the highest degree to the Supreme Being, to worship him in any other manner than the Roman Catholic; and no other public worship is lawful on Spanish soil. The people of all Southern Europe look upon a married clergy as not only irreligious, but unchaste, indecent, gross, disgusting. What do Protestants think of these perfectly sincere feelings, and of the attempt to enforce them against non-Catholics? Yet, if mankind are justified in interfering with each other's liberty in things which do not concern the interests of others, on what principle is it possible consistently to exclude these cases? or who can blame people for desiring to suppress what they regard as a scandal in the sight of God and man? No stronger case can be shown for prohibiting anything which is regarded as a personal immorality, than is made out for suppressing these practices in the eyes of those who regard them as impieties; and unless we are willing to adopt the logic of persecutors, and to say that we may persecute others because we are right, and that they must not persecute us because they are wrong, we must beware of admitting a principle of which we should resent as a gross injustice the application to ourselves.

The preceding instances may be objected to, although unreasonably, as drawn from contingencies impossible among us: opinion, in this country, not being likely to enforce abstinence from meats, or to interfere with people for worshipping, and for either marrying or not marrying, according to their creed or inclination. The next example, however, shall be taken from an interference with liberty which we have by no means passed all danger of. Wherever the Puritans have been sufficiently powerful, as in New England, and in Great Britain at the time of the Commonwealth, they have endeavoured, with considerable success, to put down all public, and nearly all private, amusements: especially music, dancing, public games, or other assemblages for purposes of diversion, and the theatre. There are still in this country large bodies of persons by whose notions of morality and religion these recreations are condemned; and those persons belonging chiefly to the middle class, who are the ascendant power in the present social and political condition of the kingdom, it is by no means impossible that persons of these sentiments may at some time or other command a majority in Parliament. How will the remaining portion of the community like to have the amusements that shall be permitted to them regulated by the religious and moral sentiments of the stricter Calvinists and Methodists? Would they not, with considerable peremptoriness, desire these intrusively pious mem-

bers of society to mind their own business? This is
precisely what should be said to every government
and every public, who have the pretension that no
person shall enjoy any pleasure which they think
wrong. But if the principle of the pretension be
admitted, no one can reasonably object to its being
acted on in the sense of the majority, or other pre-
ponderating power in the country; and all persons
must be ready to conform to the idea of a Christian
commonwealth, as understood by the early settlers
in New England, if a religious profession similar to
theirs should ever succeed in regaining its lost
ground, as religions supposed to be declining have
so often been known to do.

To imagine another contingency, perhaps more
likely to be realised than the one last mentioned.
There is confessedly a strong tendency in the modern world towards a democratic constitution of
society, accompanied or not by popular political
institutions. It is affirmed that in the country where
this tendency is most completely realised—where
both society and the government are most democratic—the United States—the feeling of the majority, to whom any appearance of a more showy
or costly style of living than they can hope to rival
is disagreeable, operates as a tolerably effectual
sumptuary law, and that in many parts of the
Union it is really difficult for a person possessing a
very large income to find any mode of spending it
which will not incur popular disapprobation.
Though such statements as these are doubtless
much exaggerated as a representation of existing
facts, the state of things they describe is not only a
conceivable and possible, but a probable result of

democratic feeling, combined with the notion that the public has a right to a veto on the manner in which individuals shall spend their incomes. We have only further to suppose a considerable diffusion of Socialist opinions, and it may become infamous in the eyes of the majority to possess more property than some very small amount, or any income not earned by manual labour. Opinions similar in principle to these already prevail widely among the artisan class, and weigh oppressively on those who are amenable to the opinion chiefly of that class, namely, its own members. It is known that the bad workmen who form the majority of the operatives in many branches of industry, are decidedly of opinion that bad workmen ought to receive the same wages as good, and that no one ought to be allowed, through piecework or otherwise, to earn by superior skill or industry more than others can without it. And they employ a moral police, which occasionally becomes a physical one, to deter skillful workmen from receiving, and employers from giving, a larger remuneration for a more useful service. If the public have any jurisdiction over private concerns, I cannot see that these people are in fault, or that any individual's particular public can be blamed for asserting the same authority over his individual conduct which the general public asserts over people in general.

But, without dwelling upon suppositious cases, there are, in our own day, gross usurpations upon the liberty of private life actually practised, and still greater ones threatened with some expectation of success, and opinions propounded which assert an unlimited right in the public not only to prohibit by law everything which it thinks wrong, but, in order to get at what it thinks wrong, to prohibit a number of things which it admits to be innocent.

Under the name of preventing intemperance, the people of one English colony, and of nearly half the United States, have been interdicted by law from making any use whatever of fermented drinks, except for medical purposes: for prohibition of their sale is in fact, as it is intended to be, prohibition of their use. And though the impracticability of executing the law has caused its repeal in several of the States which had adopted it, including the one from which it derives its name, an attempt has notwithstanding been commenced, and is prosecuted with considerable zeal by many of the professed philanthropists, to agitate for a similar law in this country. The association, or "Alliance" as it terms itself, which has been formed for this purpose, has acquired some notoriety through the publicity given to a correspondence between its secretary and one of the very few English public men who hold that a politician's opinions ought to be founded on principles. Lord Stanley's share in this correspondence is calculated to strengthen the hopes already built on him, by those who know how rare such qualities as are manifested in some of his public appearances unhappily are among those who figure in political life. The organ of the Alliance, who would "deeply deplore the recognition of any principle which could be wrested to justify bigotry and persecution," undertakes to point out the "broad and impassable barrier" which divides such principles from those of the association. "All matters relating to thought, opinion, conscience, appear to me," he says, "to be without the sphere of legislation; all pertaining to social act, habit, relation, subject only to a discretionary power vested in the State itself, and not in the individual, to be within it." No mention is made of a third class, different from either of these, viz., acts and habits which are not social, but individual; although it is to this class, surely, that the act of drinking fermented liquors belongs. Selling fermented liquors, however, is trading, and trading is a social act. But the infringement complained of is not on the liberty of the seller, but on that of the buyer and consumer; since the State might just as well forbid him to drink wine as purposely make it impossible for him to obtain it. The secretary, however, says, "I claim, as a citizen, a right to legislate whenever my social rights are invaded by the social act of another." And now for the definition of these "social rights." "If anything invades my social right, certainly the traffic in strong drink does. It destroys my primary right of security, by constantly creating and stimulating social disorder. It invades my right of equality, by deriving a profit from the creation of a misery I am taxed to support. It impedes my right to free moral and intellectual development, by surrounding my path with dangers, and by weakening and demoralising society, from which I have a right to claim mutual aid and intercourse." A theory of "social rights" the like of which probably never before found its way into distinct language: being nothing short of this—that it is the absolute social right of every individual, that every other individual shall act in every respect exactly as he ought; that whosoever fails thereof in the smallest particular violates my social right, and entitles me to demand from the legislature the removal of the grievance. So monstrous a principle is far more dangerous than any single interference with liberty; there is no violation of liberty which it would not justify; it acknowledges no right to any freedom whatever, except perhaps to that of holding opinions in secret, without ever disclosing them: for, the moment an opinion which I consider noxious passes any one's lips, it invades all the "social rights" attributed to me by the Alliance. The doctrine ascribes to all mankind a vested interest in each other's moral, intellectual, and even physical perfection, to be defined by each claimant according to his own standard.

Another important example of illegitimate interference with the rightful liberty of the individual, not simply threatened, but long since carried into triumphant effect, is Sabbatarian legislation. Without doubt, abstinence on one day in the week, so far as the exigencies of life permit, from the usual daily occupation, though in no respect religiously binding on any except Jews, is a highly beneficial custom. And inasmuch as this custom cannot be observed without a general consent to that effect among the industrious classes, therefore, in so far as some persons by working may impose the same necessity on others, it may be allowable and right that the law should guarantee to each the observance by others of the custom, by suspending the greater operations of industry on a particular day.

But this justification, grounded on the direct interest which others have in each individual's observance of the practise, does not apply to the self-chosen occupations in which a person may think fit to employ his leisure; nor does it hold good, in the smallest degree, for legal restrictions, on amusements. It is true that the amusement of some is the day's work of others; but the pleasure, not to say the useful recreation, of many, is worth the labour of a few, provided the occupation is freely chosen, and can be freely resigned. The operatives are perfectly right in thinking that if all worked on Sunday, seven days' work would have to be given for six days' wages; but so long as the great mass of employments are suspended, the small number who for the enjoyment of others must still work, obtain a proportional increase of earnings; and they are not obliged to follow those occupations if they prefer leisure to emolument. If a further remedy is sought, it might be found in the establishment by custom of a holiday on some other day of the week for those particular classes of persons. The only ground, therefore, on which restrictions on Sunday amusements can be defended, must be that they are religiously wrong; a motive of legislation which can never be too earnestly protested against. "Deorum injuriæ Diis curæ." It remains to be proved that society or any of its officers holds a commission from on high to avenge any supposed offence to Omnipotence, which is not also a wrong to our fellow-creatures. The notion that it is one man's duty that another should be religious, was the foundation of all the religious persecutions ever perpetrated, and, if admitted, would fully justify them. Though the feeling which breaks out in the repeated attempts to stop railway travelling on Sunday, in the resistance to the opening of Museums, and the like, has not the cruelty of the old persecutors, the state of mind indicated by it is fundamentally the same. It is a determination not to tolerate others in doing what is permitted by their religion, because it is not permitted by the persecutor's religion. It is a belief that God not only abominates the act of the misbeliever, but will not hold us guiltless if we leave him unmolested.

I cannot refrain from adding to these examples of the little account commonly made of human liberty, the language of downright persecution which breaks out from the press of this country whenever it feels called on to notice the remarkable phenomenon of Mormonism. Much might be said on the unexpected and instructive fact that an alleged new revelation, and a religion founded on it, the product of palpable imposture, not even supported by the *prestige* of extraordinary qualities in its founder, is believed by hundreds of thousands, and has been made the foundation of a society, in the age of newspapers, railways, and electric telegraph. What here concerns us is, that this religion, like other and better religions, has its martyrs: that its prophet and founder was, for his teaching, put to death by a mob; that others of its adherents lost their lives by the same lawless violence; that they were forcibly expelled, in a body, from the country in which they first grew up; while, now that they have been chased into a solitary recess in the midst of a desert, many in this country openly declare that it would be right (only that it is not convenient) to send an expedition against them, and compel them by force to conform to the opinions of other people. The article of the Mormonite doctrine which is the chief provocative to the antipathy which thus breaks through the ordinary restraints of religious tolerance, is its sanction of polygamy; which, though permitted to Mahomedans, and Hindoos, and Chinese, seems to excite unquenchable animosity when practised by persons who speak English and profess to be a kind of Christians. No one has a deeper disapprobation than I have of the Mormon institution; both for other reasons, and because, far from being in any way countenanced by the principle of liberty, it is a direct infraction of that principle, being a mere riveting of the chains of one half of the community, and an emancipation of the other from reciprocity of obligation towards them. Still, it must be remembered that this relation is as much voluntary on the part of the women concerned in it, and who may be deemed the sufferers by it, as is the case with any other form of the marriage institution; and however surprising this fact may appear, it has its explanation in the common ideas and customs of the world, which teaching women to think marriage the one thing needful, make it intelligible that many a woman should prefer being one of several wives, to not being a wife at all. Other countries are not asked to recognise such unions, or release any portion of their inhabitants from their own laws on the score of Mormonite opinion. But when the dissentients have conceded to the hostile sentiments of others far more than could justly be demanded; when they have left the countries to which their doctrines were unacceptable, and established themselves in a remote corner of the earth, which they have been the first to render habitable to human beings, it is difficult to see on what principles but those of tyranny they can be prevented from living there under what laws they please, provided they commit no aggression on other nations, and allow perfect freedom of departure to those who are dissatisfied with their ways. A recent writer, in some respects of considerable merit, proposes (to use his own words) not a crusade, but a *civilisade*, against this polygamous community, to put an end to what seems to him a retrograde step in civilisation. It also appears so to me, but I am not aware that any community has a right to force another to be civilised. So long as the sufferers by the bad law do not invoke assistance from other communities, I cannot admit that persons entirely unconnected with them ought to step in and require that a condition of things with which all who are directly interested appear to be satisfied, should put an end to because it is a scandal to persons some thousands of miles distant, who have no part or concern in it. Let them send missionaries, if they please, to preach against it; and let them, by any fair means (of which silencing the teachers is not one), oppose the progress of similar doctrines among their own people. If civilisation has got the better of barbarism when barbarism had the world to itself, it is too much to profess to be afraid lest barbarism, after having been fairly got under, should revive and conquer civilisation. A civilisation that can thus succumb to its vanquished enemy; must first have become so degenerate, that neither its appointed priests and teachers, nor anybody else, has the capacity, or will take the trouble, to stand up for it. If this be so, the sooner such a civilisation receives notice to quit the better. It can only go on from bad to worse, until destroyed and regenerated (like the Western Empire) by energetic barbarians.

# CHAPTER V

## APPLICATIONS

THE PRINCIPLES ASSERTED IN THESE PAGES MUST be more generally admitted as the basis for discussion of details, before a consistent application of them to all the various departments of government and morals can be attempted with any prospect of advantage. The few observations I propose to make on questions of detail are designed to illustrate the principles, rather than to follow them out to their consequences. I offer, not so much applications, as specimens of application; which may serve to bring into greater clearness the meaning and limits of the two maxims which together form the entire doctrine of this Essay, and to assist the judgment in holding the balance between them, in the case where it appears doubtful which of them is applicable to the case.

The maxims are, first, that the individual is not accountable to society for his actions, in so far as these concern the interests of no person but himself. Advice, instruction, persuasion, and avoidance by other people if thought necessary by them for their own good, are the only measures by which society can justifiably express its dislike or disapprobation of his conduct. Secondly, that for such actions as are prejudicial to the interests of others, the individual is accountable, and may be subjected either to social or to legal punishment, if society is of opinion that the one or the other is requisite for its protection.

In the first place, it must by no means be supposed, because damage, or probability of damage, to the interests of others, can alone justify the interference of society, that therefore it always does justify such interference. In many cases, an individual, in pursuing a legitimate object, necessarily and therefore legitimately causes pain or loss to others, or intercepts a good which they had a reasonable hope of obtaining. Such oppositions of interest between individuals often rise from bad social institutions, but are unavoidable while those institutions last; and some would be unavoidable under any institutions. Whoever succeeds in an overcrowded profession, or in a competitive examination; whoever is preferred to another in any contest for an object which both desire, reaps benefit from the loss of others, from their wasted exertion and their disappointment. But it is, by common admission, better for the general interest of mankind, that persons should pursue their objects undeterred by this sort of consequences. In other words, society admits no right, either legal or moral, in the disappointed competitors to immunity from this kind of suffering; and feels called on to interfere, only when means of success have been employed which it is contrary to the general interest to permit—namely, fraud or treachery, and force.

Again, trade is a social act. Whoever undertakes to sell any description of goods to the public, does what effects the interest of other persons, and of society in general; and thus his conduct, in principle, comes within the jurisdiction of society: accordingly, it was once held to be the duty of governments, in all cases which were considered of importance, to fix prices, and regulate the processes of manufacture. But it is now recognised, though not till after a long struggle, that both the cheapness and the good quality of commodities are most effectually provided for by leaving the producers and sellers perfectly free, under the sole check of equal freedom to the buyers for supplying themselves elsewhere. This is the so-called doctrine of Free Trade, which rests on grounds different from, though equally solid with, the principle of individual liberty asserted in this Essay. Restrictions on trade, or on production for purposes of trade, are indeed restraints; and all restraint, *qua* restraint, is an evil: but the restraints in question affect only that part of conduct which society is competent to restrain, and are wrong solely because they do not really produce the results which it is desired to produce by them. As the principle of individual liberty is not involved in the doctrine of Free Trade, so neither is it in most of the questions which arise respecting the limits of that doctrine; as, for example, what amount of public control is admissible for the prevention of fraud by adulteration; how far sanitary precautions, or arrangements to protect workpeople employed in dangerous oc-

cupations, should be enforced on employers. Such
questions involve considerations of liberty, only in
so far as leaving people to themselves is always better, *cœteris paribus*, than controlling them: but
that they may be legitimately controlled for these
ends is in principle undeniable. On the other hand,
there are questions relating to interference with
trade which are essentially questions of liberty;
such as the Maine Law, already touched upon;
the prohibition of the importation of opium into
China; the restriction of the sale of poisons; all
cases, in short, where the object of the interference
is to make it impossible or difficult to obtain a difficult commodity. These interferences are objectionable, not as infringements on the liberty of the
producer or seller, but on that of the buyer.

One of these examples, that of the sale of poisons, opens a new question; the proper limits of
what may be called the functions of police; how
far liberty may legitimately be invaded for the
prevention of crime, or of accident. It is one of the
undisputed functions of government to take precautions against crime before it has been committed, as well as to detect and punish it afterwards. The preventive function of government,
however, is far more liable to be abused, to the
prejudice of liberty, than the punitory function;
for there is hardly any part of the legitimate freedom of action of a human being which would not
admit of being represented, and fairly too, as increasing the facilities for some form or other of
delinquency. Nevertheless, if a public authority,
or even a private person, sees any one evidently
preparing to commit a crime, they are not bound

141

to look on inactive until the crime is committed, but may interfere to prevent it. If poisons were never bought or used for any purpose except the commission of murder, it would be right to prohibit their manufacture and sale. They may, however, be wanted not only for innocent but for useful purposes, and restrictions cannot be imposed in the one case without operating in the other. Again, it is a proper office of public authority to guard against accidents. If either a public officer or any one else saw a person attempting to cross a bridge which had been ascertained to be unsafe, and there were no time to warn him of his danger, they might seize him and turn him back, without any real infringement of his liberty; for liberty consists in doing what one desires, and he does not desire to fall into the river. Nevertheless, when there is not a certainty, but only a danger of mischief, no one but the person himself can judge of the sufficiency of the motive which may prompt him to incur the risk: in this case, therefore (unless he is a child, or delirious, or in some state of excitement or absorption incompatible with the full use of the reflecting faculty), he ought, I conceive, to be only warned of the danger, not forcibly prevented from exposing himself to it. Similar consideration, applied to such a question as the sale of poisons, may enable us to decide which among the possible modes of regulation are or are not contrary to principle. Such a precaution, for example, as that of labeling the drug with some word expressive of its dangerous character, may be enforced without violation of liberty: the buyer cannot wish not to know that the thing he possesses has poisonous qualities. But to require in all cases the certificate of a medical practitioner would make it sometimes impossible, always expensive, to obtain the article for legitimate uses. The only mode apparent to me, in which difficulties may be thrown in the way of crime committed through this means, without any infringement worth taking into account upon the liberty of those who desire the poisonous substance for other purposes, consists in providing what, in the apt language of Bentham, is called "preappointed evidence." This provision is familiar to every one in the case of contracts. It is usual and right that the law, when a contract is entered into, should require as the condition of its enforcing performance, that certain formalities should be observed, such as signatures, attestation of witnesses, and the like, in order that in case of subsequent dispute there may be evidence to prove that the contract was really entered into, and that there was nothing in the circumstances to render it legally invalid: the effect being to throw great obstacles in the way of fictitious contracts, or contracts made in circumstances which, if known, would destroy their validity. Precautions of a similar nature might be enforced in the sale of articles adapted to be instruments of crime. The seller, for example, might be required to enter in a register the exact time of the transaction, the name and address of the buyer, the precise quality and quantity sold; to ask the purpose for which it was wanted, and record the answer he received. When there was no medical prescription, the presence of some third person might be required, to bring home the fact to the purchaser, in case there should afterwards be reason to believe that the article had been applied to criminal purposes. Such regulations would in general be no material impediment to obtaining the article, but a very considerable one to making an improper use of it without detection.

The right inherent in society, to ward off crimes against itself by antecedent precautions, suggests the obvious limitations to the maxim, that purely self-regarding misconduct cannot properly be meddled with in the way of prevention or punishment. Drunkenness, for example, in ordinary cases, is not a fit subject for legislative interference; but I should deem it perfectly legitimate that a person, who had once been convicted of any act of violence to others under the influence of drink, should be placed under a special legal restriction, personal to himself; that if he were afterwards found drunk, he should be liable to a penalty, and that if when in that state he committed another offence, the punishment to which he would be liable for that other offence should be increased in severity. The making himself drunk, in a person whom drunkenness excites to do harm to others, is a crime against others. So, again, idleness, except in a person receiving support from the public, or except when it constitutes a breach of contract, cannot without tyranny be made a subject of legal punishment; but if, either from idleness or from any other avoidable cause, a man fails to perform his legal duties to others, as for instance to support his children, it is no tyranny to force him to fulfill that obligation, by compulsory labour, if no other means are available.

Again, there are many acts which, being directly

injurious only to the agents themselves, ought not to be legally interdicted, but which, if done publicly, are a violation of good manners, and coming thus within the category of offences against others, may rightly be prohibited. Of this kind are offences against decency; on which it is unnecessary to dwell, the rather as they are only connected indirectly with our subject, the objection to publicity being equally strong in the case of many actions not in themselves condemnable, nor supposed to be so.

There is another question to which an answer must be found, consistent with the principles which have been laid down. In cases of personal conduct supposed to be blamable, but which respect for liberty precludes society from preventing or punishing, because the evil directly resulting falls wholly on the agent; what the agent is free to do, ought other persons to be equally free to counsel or instigate? This question is not free from difficulty. The case of a person who solicits another to do an act is not strictly a case of self-regarding conduct. To give advice or offer inducements to any one is a social act, and may, therefore, like actions in general which affect others, be supposed amenable to social control. But a little reflection corrects the first impression, by showing that if the case is not strictly within the definition of individual liberty, yet the reasons on which the principle of individual liberty is grounded are applicable to it. If people must be allowed, in whatever concerns only themselves, to act as seems best to themselves, at their own peril, they must equally be free to consult with one another about what is fit to be so done; to

exchange opinions, and give and receive suggestions. Whatever it is permitted to do, it must be
permitted to advise to do. The question is doubtful
only when the instigator derives a personal benefit
from his advice; when he makes it his occupation,
for subsistence or pecuniary gain, to promote what
society and the State consider to be an evil. Then,
indeed, a new element of complication is introduced; namely, the existence of classes of persons
with an interest opposed to what is considered as
the public weal, and whose mode of living is
grounded on the counteraction of it. Ought this to
be interfered with, or not? Fornication, for example, must be tolerated, and so must gambling;
but should a person be free to be a pimp, or to keep
a gambling-house? The case is one of those which
lie on the exact boundary line between two principles, and it is not at once apparent to which of
the two it properly belongs. There are arguments
on both sides. On the side of toleration it may be
said that the fact of following anything as an occupation, and living or profiting by the practice of it,
cannot make that criminal which would otherwise
be admissible; that the act should either be consistently permitted or consistently prohibited; that
if the principles which we have hitherto defended
are true, society has no business, *as* society, to decide anything to be wrong which concerns only the
individual; that it cannot go beyond dissuasion,
and that one person should be as free to persuade
as another to dissuade. In opposition to this it may
be contended, that although the public, or the
State, are not warranted in authoritatively decid-
ing, for purposes of repression or punishment, that

such or such conduct affecting only the interests of the individual is good or bad, they are fully justified in assuming, if they regard it as bad, that its being so or not is at least a disputable question: that, this being supposed, they cannot be acting wrongly in endeavouring to exclude the influence of solicitations which are not disinterested, of instigators who cannot possibly be impartial—who have a direct personal interest on one side, and that side the one which the State believes to be wrong, and who confessedly promote it for personal objects only. There can surely, it may be urged, be nothing lost, no sacrifice of good, by so ordering matters that persons shall make their election, either wisely or foolishly, on their own prompting, as free as possible from the arts of persons who stimulate their inclinations for interested purposes of their own. Thus (it may be said) though the statutes respecting unlawful games are utterly indefensible—though all persons should be free to gamble in their own or each other's houses, or in any place of meeting established by their own subscriptions, and open only to the members and their visitors—yet public gambling-houses should not be permitted. It is true that the prohibition is never effectual, and that, whatever amount of tyrannical power may be given to the police, gambling-houses can always be maintained under other pretences; but they may be compelled to conduct their operations with a certain degree of secrecy and mystery, so that nobody knows anything about them but those who seek them; and more than this society ought not to aim at. There is considerable force in these arguments. I will not venture to decide whether they are sufficient to justify the moral anomaly of punishing the accessary, when the principal is (and must be) allowed to go free; of fining or imprisoning the procurer, but not the fornicator—the gambling-house keeper, but not the gambler. Still less ought the common operations of buying and selling to be interfered with on analogous grounds. Almost every article which is bought and sold may be used in excess, and the sellers have a pecuniary interest in encouraging that excess; but no argument can be founded on this, in favour, for instance, of the Maine Law; because the class of dealers in strong drinks, though interested in their abuse, are indispensably required for the sake of their legitimate use. The interest, however, of these dealers in promoting intemperance is a real evil, and justifies the State in imposing restrictions and requiring guarantees which, but for that justification, would be infringements of legitimate liberty.

A further question is, whether the State, while it permits, should nevertheless indirectly discourage conduct which it deems contrary to the best interests of the agent; whether, for example, it should take measures to render the means of drunkenness more costly, or add to the difficulty of procuring them by limiting the number of the places of sale. On this as on most other practical questions, many distinctions require to be made. To tax stimulants for the sole purpose of making them more difficult to be obtained, is a measure differing only in degree from their entire prohibition; and would be justifiable only if that were justifiable. Every increase of cost is a prohibition, to those whose means do not come up to the augmented price; and to those who do, it is a penalty laid on them for gratifying a particular taste. Their choice of pleasures, and their mode of expending their income, after satisfying their legal and moral obligations to the State and to individuals, are their own concern, and must rest with their own judgment. These considerations may seem at first sight to condemn the selection of stimulants as special subjects of taxation for purposes of revenue. But it must be remembered that taxation for fiscal purposes is absolutely inevitable; that in most countries it is necessary that a considerable part of that taxation should be indirect; that the State, therefore, cannot help imposing penalties, which to some persons may be prohibitory, on the use of some articles of consumption. It is hence the duty of the State to consider, in the imposition of taxes, what commodities the consumers can best spare; and *a fortiori,* to select in preference those of which it deems the use, beyond a very moderate quantity, to be positively injurious. Taxation, therefore, of stimulants, up to the point which produces the largest amount of revenue (supposing that the State needs all the revenue which it yields) is not only admissible, but to be approved of.

The question of making the sale of these commodities a more or less exclusive privilege, must be answered differently, according to the purposes to which the restriction is intended to be subservient. All places of public resort require the restraint of a police, and places of this kind peculiarly, because offences against society are especially apt to originate there. It is, therefore, fit to confine the power of selling these commodities (at least for consumption on the spot) to persons of known or vouched-for respectability of conduct; to make such regulations respecting hours of opening and closing as may be requisite for public surveillance, and to withdraw the licence if breaches of the peace repeatedly take place through the connivance or incapacity of the keeper of the house, or if it becomes a rendezvous for concocting and preparing offences against the law. Any further restriction I do not conceive to be, in principle, justifiable. The limitation in number, for instance, of beer and spirit houses, for the express purpose of rendering them more difficult of access, and diminishing the occasions of temptation, not only exposes all to an inconvenience because there are some by whom the facility would be abused, but is suited only to a state of society in which the labouring classes are avowedly treated as children or savages, and placed under an education of restraint, to fit them for future admission to the privileges of freedom. This is not the principle on which the labouring classes are professedly governed in any free country; and no person who sets due value on freedom will give his adhesion to their being so governed, unless after all efforts have been exhausted to educate them for freedom and govern them as freemen, and it has been definitively proved that they can only be governed as children. The bare statement of the alternative shows the absurdity of supposing that such efforts have been made in any case which needs to be considered here. It is only because the institutions of this country are a mass of inconsistencies, that things find admittance into our practice which belong to the system of despotic, or what is called paternal government, while the general freedom of our institutions precludes the exercise of the amount of control necessary to render the restraint of any real efficacy as a moral education.

It was pointed out in an early part of this Essay, that the liberty of the individual, in things wherein the individual is alone concerned, implies a corresponding liberty in any number of individuals to regulate by mutual agreement such things as regard them jointly, and regard no persons but themselves. This question presents no difficulty, so long as the will of all persons implicated remains unaltered; but since that will may change, it is often necessary, even in things in which they alone are concerned, that they should enter into engagements with one another, and when they do, it is fit, as a general rule, that those engagements should be kept. Yet, in the laws, probably, of every country, this general rule has some exceptions. Not only persons are not held to engagements which violate the rights of third parties, but it is sometimes considered a sufficient reason for releasing them from an engagement, that it is injurious to themselves. In this and most other civilised countries, for example, an engagement by which a person should sell himself, or allow himself to be sold, as a slave, would be null and void; neither enforced by law nor by opinion. The ground for thus limiting his power of voluntarily disposing of his own lot in life, is apparent, and is very clearly seen in this extreme case. The reason for not interfering, unless for the sake of others, with a person's voluntary acts, is consideration for his liberty. His voluntary choice is evidence that what he so chooses is desirable, or at least endurable, to him, and his good is on the whole best provided for by allowing him to take his own means of pursuing it. But by selling himself for a slave, he abdicates his liberty; he foregoes any future use of it beyond that single act. He therefore defeats, in his own case, the very purpose which is the justification of allowing him to dispose of himself. He is no longer free; but is thenceforth in a position which has no longer the presumption in its favour, that would be afforded by his voluntarily remaining in it. The principle of freedom cannot require that he should be free not to be free. It is not freedom to be allowed to alienate his freedom. These reasons, the force of which is so conspicuous in this peculiar case, are evidently of far wider application; yet a limit is everywhere set to them by the necessities of life, which continually require, not indeed that we should resign our freedom, but that we should consent to this and the other limitation of it. The principle, however, which demands uncontrolled freedom of action in all that concerns only the agents themselves, requires that those who have become bound to one another, in things which concern no third party should be able to release one another from the engagement: and even without such voluntary release there are perhaps no contracts or engagements, except those that relate to money or money's worth, of which one can venture to say that there ought to be no liberty whatever of retractation. Baron Wilhelm von Humboldt, in the excellent essay from which I have already quoted, states it as his conviction, that engagements which involve personal relations or services should never be legally binding beyond a limited duration of time; and that the most important of these engagements, marriage, having the peculiarity that its objects are frustrated unless the feelings of both the parties are in harmony with it, should require nothing more than the declared will of either party to dissolve it. This subject is too important, and too complicated, to be discussed in a parenthesis, and I touch on it only so far as is necessary for purposes of illustration. If the conciseness and generality of Baron Humboldt's dissertation had not obliged him in this instance to content himself with enunciating his conclusion without discussing the premises, he would doubtless have recognised that the question cannot be decided on grounds so simple as those to which he confines himself. When a person, either by express promise or by conduct, has encouraged another to rely upon his continuing to act in a certain way—to build expectations and calculations, and stake any part of his plan of life upon that supposition—a new series of moral obligations arises on his part towards that person, which may possibly be overruled, but cannot be ignored. And again, if the relation between two contracting parties has been followed by consequences to others; if it has placed third parties in any peculiar position, or, as in the case of marriage, has even called third parties into existence, obligations arise on the part of both the contracting parties in any peculiar position, or, as in the case of which, or at all events the mode of fulfilment, must be greatly affected by the continuance or disruption of the relation between the original parties to the contract. It does not follow, nor can I admit, that these obligations extend to requiring the fulfilment of the contract at all costs to the happiness of the reluctant party; but they are a necessary element in the question; and even if, as von Humboldt maintains, they ought to make no difference in the *legal* freedom of the parties to release themselves from the engagement (and I also hold that they ought not to make *much* difference), they necessarily make a great difference in the *moral* freedom. A person is bound to take all these circumstances into account before resolving on a step which may affect such important interests of others; and if he does not allow proper weight to those interests, he is morally responsible for the wrong. I have made these obvious remarks for the better illustration of the general principle of liberty, and not because they are at all needed on the particular question, which, on the contrary, is usually discussed as if the interest of children was everything, and that of grown persons nothing.

I have already observed that, owing to the absence of any recognised general principles, liberty is often granted where it should be withheld, as well as withheld where it should be granted; and one of the cases in which, in the modern European world, the sentiment of liberty is the strongest, is a case where, in my view, it is altogether misplaced. A person should be free to do as he likes in his own concerns; but he ought not to be free to do as he likes in acting for another, under the pretext that the affairs of the other are his own affairs. The State, while it respects the liberty of each in what specially regards himself, is bound to maintain a vigilant control over his exercise of any power which it allows him to possess over others. This obligation is almost entirely disregarded in the case of the family relations, a case, in its direct influence on human happiness, more important than all others taken together. The almost despotic power of husbands over wives needs not be enlarged upon here, because nothing more is needed for the complete removal of the evil than that wives should have the same rights, and should receive the protection of law in the same manner, as all other persons; and because, on this subject, the defenders of established injustice do not avail themselves of the plea of liberty, but stand forth openly as the champions of power. It is in the case of children that misapplied notions of liberty are a real obstacle to the fulfilment by the State of its duties. One would almost think that a man's children were supposed to be literally, and not metaphorically, a part of himself, so jealous is opinion of the smallest interference of law with his absolute and exclusive control over them; more jealous than of almost any interference with his own freedom of action: so much less do the generality of mankind value liberty than power. Consider, for example, the case of education. Is it not almost a self-evident axiom, that the State should require and compel the education, up to a certain standard, of every human being who is born its citizen? Yet who is there that is not afraid to recognise and assert this truth? Hardly any one indeed will deny that it is one of the most sacred duties of the parents (or, as law and usage now stand, the father), after summoning a human being into the world, to give to that being an education fitting him to perform his part well in life towards others and towards himself. But while this is unanimously declared to be the father's duty, scarcely anybody, in this country, will bear to hear of obliging him to perform it. Instead of his being required to make any exertion or sacrifice for securing education to his child, it is left to his choice to accept it or not when it is provided gratis! It still remains unrecognised, that to bring a child into existence without a fair prospect of being able, not only to provide food for its body, but instruction and training for its mind, is a moral crime, both against the unfortunate offspring and against society; and that if the parent does not fulfil this obligation, the State ought to see it fulfilled, at the charge, as far as possible, of the parent.

Were the duty of enforcing universal education once admitted there would be an end to the difficulties about what the State should teach, and how it should teach, which now convert the subject into a mere battlefield for sects and parties, causing the time and labour which should have been spent in educating to be wasted in quarrelling about education. If the government would make up its mind to require for every child a good education, it might save itself the trouble of providing one. It might leave to parents to obtain the education where and how they pleased, and content itself with helping to pay the school fees of the poorer classes of children, and defraying the entire school expenses of those who have no one else to pay for them. The objections which are urged with reason against

State education do not apply to the enforcement of education by the State, but to the State's taking upon itself to direct that education; which is a totally different thing. That the whole or any large part of the education of the people should be in State hands, I go as far as any one in deprecating. All that has been said of the importance of individuality of character, and diversity in opinions and modes of conduct, involves, as of the same unspeakable importance, diversity of education. A general State education is a mere contrivance for moulding people to be exactly like one another: and as the mould in which it casts them is that which pleases the predominant power in the government, whether this be a monarch, a priesthood, an aristocracy, or the majority of the existing generation; in proportion as it is efficient and successful, it establishes a despotism over the mind, leading by natural tendency to one over the body. An education established and controlled by the State should only exist, if it exist at all, as one among many competing experiments, carried on for the purpose of example and stimulus, to keep the others up to a certain standard of excellence. Unless, indeed, when society in general is in so backward a state that it could not or would not provide for itself any proper institutions of education unless the government undertook the task: then, indeed, the government may, as the less of two great evils, take upon itself the business of schools and universities, as it may that of joint stock companies, when private enterprise, in a shape fitted for undertaking great works of industry, does not exist in the country. But in general, if the country contains a sufficient number of persons qualified to provide education under government auspices, the same persons would be able and willing to give an equally good education on the voluntary principle, under the assurance of remuneration afforded by a law rendering education compulsory, combined with State aid to those unable to defray the expense.

The instrument for enforcing the law could be no other than public examinations, extending to all children, and beginning at an early age. An age might be fixed at which every child must be examined, to ascertain if he (or she) is able to read. If a child proves unable, the father, unless he has some sufficient ground of excuse, might be subjected to a moderate fine, to be worked out, if necessary, by his labour, and the child might be put to school at his expense. Once in every year the examination should be renewed, with a gradually extending range of subjects, so as to make the universal acquisition, and what is more, retention, of a certain minimum of general knowledge virtually compulsory. Beyond that minimum there should be voluntary examinations on all subjects, at which all who come up to a certain standard of proficiency might claim a certificate. To prevent the State from exercising, through these arrangements, an improper influence over opinion, the knowledge required for passing an examination (beyond the merely instrumental parts of knowledge, such as languages and their use) should, even in the higher classes of examinations, be confined to facts and positive science exclusively. The examinations on religion, politics, or other disputed topics, should not turn on the truth or falsehood of opinion, but on the matter of fact that such and such an opinion is held, on such grounds, by such authors, or schools, or churches. Under this system, the rising generation would be no worse off in regard to all disputed truths than they are at present; they would be brought up either churchmen or dissenters as they now are, the State merely taking care that they should be instructed churchmen, or instructed dissenters. There would be nothing to hinder them from being taught religion, if their parents chose, at the same schools where they were taught other things. All attempts by the State to bias the conclusions of its citizens on disputed subjects are evil; but it may very properly offer to ascertain and certify that a person possesses the knowledge requisite to make his conclusions, on any given subject, worth attending to. A student of philosophy would be the better for being able to stand an examination both in Locke and in Kant, whichever of the two he takes up with, or even if with neither: and there is no reasonable objection to examining an atheist in the evidences of Christianity, provided he is not required to profess a belief in them. The examinations, however, in the higher branches of knowledge should, I conceive, be entirely voluntary. It would be giving too dangerous a power to governments were they allowed to exclude any one from professions, even from the profession of teacher, for alleged deficiency of qualifications: and I think with Wilhelm von Humboldt, that degrees, or other public certificates of scientific or professional acquirements, should be given to all who present themselves for examination, and stand the test; but that such certificates should confer no advantage over competitors other than the weight which may be attached to their testimony by public opinion.

It is not in the matter of education only that misplaced notions of liberty prevent moral obligations on the part of parents from being recognised, and legal obligations from being imposed, where there are the strongest grounds for the former always, and in many cases for the latter also. The fact itself, of causing the existence of a human being, is one of the most responsible actions in the range of human life. To undertake this responsibility—to bestow a life which may be either a curse or a blessing—unless the being on whom it is to be bestowed will have at least the ordinary chances of a desirable existence, is a crime against that being. And in a country either over-peopled, or threatened with being so, to produce children, beyond a very small number, with the effect of reducing the reward of labour by their competition, is a serious offence against all who live by the remuneration of their labour. The laws which, in many countries on the Continent, forbid marriage unless the parties can show that they have the means of supporting a family, do not exceed the legitimate powers of the State: and whether such laws be expedient or not (a question mainly dependent on local circumstances and feelings), they are not objectionable as violations of liberty. Such laws are interferences of the State to prohibit a mischievous act—an act injurious to others, which ought to be a subject of reprobation, and social stigma, even when it is not deemed expedient to superadd legal punishment. Yet the current ideas of liberty, which bend so easily to real infringements of the freedom of the individual in things which concern only himself, would repel the attempt to put any restraint upon his inclinations when the consequence of their indulgence is a life or lives of wretchedness and depravity to the offspring, with manifold evils to those sufficiently within reach to be in any way affected by their actions. When we compare the strange respect of mankind for liberty, with their strange want of respect for it, we might imagine that a man had an indispensable right to do harm to others, and no right at all to please himself without giving pain to any one.

I have reserved for the last place a large class of questions respecting the limits of government interference, which, though closely connected with the subject of this Essay, do not, in strictness, belong to it. These are cases in which the reasons against interference do not turn upon the principle of liberty: the question is not about restraining the actions of individuals, but about helping them; it is asked whether the government should do, or cause to be done, something for their benefit, instead of leaving it to be done by themselves, individually or in voluntary combination.

The obligations to government interference, when it is not such as to involve infringement of liberty, may be of three kinds.

The first is, when the thing to be done is likely to be better done by individuals than by the government. Speaking generally, there is no one so fit to conduct any business, or to determine how or by whom it shall be conducted, as those who are personally interested in it. This principle condemns the interferences, once so common, of the legislature, or the officers of government, with the ordinary processes of industry. But this part of the subject has been sufficiently enlarged upon by political economists, and is not particularly related to the principles of the Essay.

The second objection is more nearly allied to our subject. In many cases, though individuals may not do the particular thing so well, on the average, as the officers of government, it is nevertheless desirable that it should be done by them, rather than by the government, as a means to their own mental education—a mode of strengthening their active faculties, exercising their judgment, and giving them a familiar knowledge of the subjects with which they are thus left to deal. This is a principal, though not the sole, recommendation of jury trial (in cases not political); of free and popular local and municipal institutions; of the conduct of industrial and philanthropic enterprises by voluntary associations. These are not questions of liberty, and are connected with that subject only by remote tendencies; but they are questions of development. It belongs to a different occasion from the present to dwell on these things as parts of national education; as being, in truth, the peculiar training of a citizen, the practical part of the political education of a free people, taking them out of the narrow circle of personal and family selfishness, and accustoming them to the comprehension of joint interests, the management of joint concerns—habituating them to act from public or semi-public motives, and guide their conduct by aims which unite instead of isolating them from one another. Without these habits and powers, a free constitution can neither be worked nor preserved; as is exemplified, by the too-often transitory nature of political freedom in countries where it does not rest upon a sufficient basis of local liberties. The management of purely local business by the localities, and of the great enterprises of industry by the union of those who voluntarily supply the pecuniary means, is further recommended by all the advantages which have been set forth in this Essay as belonging to individuality of development, and diversity of modes of action. Government operations tend to be everywhere alike. With individuals and voluntary associations, on the contrary, there are varied experiments, and endless diversity of experience. What the State can usefully do is to make itself a central depository, and active circulator and diffuser, of the experience resulting from many trials. Its business is to enable each experimentalist to benefit by the experiments of others; instead of tolerating no experiments but its own.

The third and most cogent reason for restricting the interference of government is the great evil of adding unnecessarily to its power. Every function superadded to those already exercised by the government causes its influence over hopes and fears to be more widely diffused, and converts, more and more, the active and ambitious part of the public into hangers-on of the government, or of some party which aims at becoming the government. If the roads, the railways, the banks, the insurance offices, the great joint-stock companies, the universities, and the public charities, were all of them branches of the government; if, in addition, the municipal corporations and local boards, with all that now devolves on them, became departments of the central administration; if the employees of all these different enterprises were appointed and paid by the government, and looked to the government for every rise in life; not all the freedom of the press and popular constitution of the legislature would make this or any other country free otherwise than in name. And the evil would be greater, the more efficiently and scientifically the administrative machinery was constructed—the more skillful the arrangements for obtaining the best qualified hands and heads with which to work it. In England it has of late been proposed that all the members of the civil service of government should be selected by competitive examination, to obtain for these employments the most intelligent and instructed persons procurable; and much has been said and written for and against this proposal. One of the arguments most insisted on by its opponents is that the occupation of a permanent official servant of the State does not hold out sufficient prospects of emolument and importance to attract the highest talents, which will always be able to find a more inviting career in the professions, or in the service of companies and other public bodies. One would not have been surprised if this argument had been used by the friends of the proposition, as an answer to its principal difficulty. Coming from the opponents it is strange enough. What is urged as an objection is the safety-valve of the proposed system. If indeed all the high talent of the country *could* be drawn into the service of the government, a proposal tending to bring about that result might well inspire uneasiness. If every part of the business of society which required organised concert, or large and comprehensive views, were in the hands of the government, and if government offices were universally filled by the ablest men, all the enlarged culture and practised intelligence in the country, except the purely speculative, would be concentrated in a numerous bureaucracy, to whom alone the rest of the community would look for all things: the multitude for direction and dictation in all they had to do; the able and aspiring for personal advancement. To be admitted into the ranks of this bureaucracy, and when admitted, to rise therein, would be the sole objects of ambition. Under this *régime,* not only is the outside public ill-qualified, for want of practical experience, to criticise or check the mode of operation of the bureaucracy, but even if the accidents of despotic or the natural working of popular institutions occasionally raise to the summit a ruler or rulers of reforming inclinations, no reform can be effected which is contrary to the interest of the bureaucracy. Such is the melancholy condition of the Russian empire, as shown in the accounts of those who have had sufficient opportunity of observation. The Czar himself is powerless against the bureaucratic body; he can send any one of them to Siberia, but he cannot govern without them, or against their will. On every decree of his they have a tacit veto, by merely refraining from carrying it into effect. In countries of more advanced civilisation and of a more insurrection-

ary spirit, the public, accustomed to expect everything to be done for them by the State, or at least
to do nothing for themselves without asking from
the State not only leave to do it, but even how it is
to be done, naturally hold the State responsible for
all evil which befalls them, and when the evil
exceeds their amount of patience, they rise against
the government, and make what is called a revolution; where-upon somebody else, with or without
legitimate authority from the nation, vaults into
the seat, issues his orders to the bureaucracy, and
everything goes on much as it did before; the bureaucracy being unchanged, and nobody else being
capable of taking their place.

A very different spectacle is exhibited among a
people accustomed to transact their own business.
In France, a large part of the people, having been
engaged in military service, many of whom have
held at least the rank of non-commissioned officers,
there are in every popular insurrection several
persons competent to take the lead, and improvise some tolerable plan of action. What the
French are in military affairs, the Americans are
in every kind of civil business; let them be left
without a government, every body of Americans is
able to improvise one, and to carry on that or any
other public business with a sufficient amount of
intelligence, order, and decision. This is what every
free people ought to be: and a people capable of
this is certain to be free; it will never let itself be
enslaved by any man or body of men because these
are able to seize and pull the reins of the central
administration. No bureaucracy can hope to make
such a people as this do or undergo any thing that

they do not like. But where everything is done through the bureaucracy, nothing to which the bureaucracy is really adverse can be done at all. The constitution of such countries is an organisation of the experience and practical ability of the nation into a disciplined body for the purpose of governing the rest; and the more perfect that organisation is in itself, the more successful in drawing to itself and educating for itself the persons of greatest capacity from all ranks of the community, the more complete is the bondage of all, the members of the bureaucracy included. For the governors are as much the slaves of their organisation and discipline as the governed are of the governors. A Chinese mandarin is as much the tool and creature of a despotism as the humblest cultivator. An individual Jesuit is to the utmost degree of abasement the slave of his order, though the order itself exists for the collective power and importance of its members.

It is not, also, to be forgotten, that the absorption of all the principal ability of the country into the governing body is fatal, sooner or later, to the mental activity and progressiveness of the body itself. Banded together as they are—working a system which, like all systems, necessarily proceeds in a great measure by fixed rules—the official body are under the constant temptation of sinking into indolent routine, or, if they now and then desert that mill-horse round, of rushing into some half-examined crudity which has struck the fancy of some leading member of the corps; and the sole check to these closely allied, though seemingly opposite, tendencies, the only stimulus which can keep the ability of the body itself up to a high standard, is liability to the watchful criticism of equal ability outside the body. It is indispensable, therefore, that the means should exist, independently of the government, of forming such ability, and furnishing it with the opportunities and experience necessary for a correct judgment of great practical affairs. If we would possess permanently a skillful and efficient body of functionaries—above all, a body able to originate and willing to adopt improvements; if we would not have our bureaucracy degenerate into a pedantocracy, this body must not engross all the occupations which form and cultivate the faculties required for the government of mankind.

To determine the point at which evils, so formidable to human freedom and advancement, begin or rather at which they begin to predominate over the benefits attending the collective application of the force of society, under its recognised chiefs, for the removal of the obstacles which stand in the way of its well-being; to secure as much of the advantages of centralised power and intelligence as can be had without turning into governmental channels too great a proportion of the general activity—is one of the most difficult and complicated questions in the art of government. It is, in a great measure, a question of detail, in which many and various considerations must be kept in view, and no absolute rule can be laid down. But I believe that the practical principle in which safety resides, the ideal to be kept in view, the standard by which to test all arrangements intended for overcoming the difficulty, may be conveyed in these words:

the greatest dissemination of power consistent with efficiency; but the greatest possible centralisation of information, and diffusion of it from the centre. Thus, in municipal administration, there would be, as in the New England States, a very minute division among separate officers, chosen by the localities, of all business which is not better left to the persons directly interested; but besides this, there would be, in each department of local affairs, a central superintendence, forming a branch of the general government. The organ of this superintendence would concentrate, as in a focus, the variety of information and experience derived from the conduct of that branch of public business in all the localities, from everything analogous which is done in foreign countries, and from the general principles of political science. This central organ should have a right to know all that is done, and its special duty should be that of making the knowledge acquired in one place available for others. Emancipated from the petty prejudices and narrow views of a locality by its elevated position and comprehensive sphere of observation, its advice would naturally carry much authority; but its actual power, as a permanent institution, should, I conceive, be limited to compelling the local officers to obey the laws laid down for their guidance. In all things not provided for by general rules, those officers should be left to their own judgment, under responsibility to their constituents. For the violation of rules, they should be responsible to law, and the rules themselves should be laid down by the legislature; the central administrative authority only watching over their execution, and if they were not properly carried into effect, appealing, according to the nature of the case, to the tribunals to enforce the law, or to the constituencies to dismiss the functionaries who had not executed it according to its spirit. Such, in its general conception, is the central superintendence which the Poor Law Board is intended to exercise over the administrators of the Poor Rate throughout the country. Whatever powers the Board exercises beyond this limit were right and necessary in that peculiar case, for the cure of rooted habits of maladministration in matters deeply affecting not the localities merely, but the whole community; since no locality has a moral right to make itself by mismanagement a nest of pauperism, necessarily overflowing into other localities, and impairing the moral and physical condition of the whole labouring community. The powers of administrative coercion and subordinate legislation possessed by the Poor Law Board (but which, owing to the state of opinion on the subject, are very scantily exercised by them), though perfectly justifiable in a case of first-rate national interest, would be wholly out of place in the superintendence of interests purely local. But a central organ of information and instruction for all the localities would be equally valuable in all departments of administration. A government cannot have too much of the kind of activity which does not impede, but aids and stimulates, individual exertion and development. The mischief begins when, instead of calling forth the activity and powers of individuals and bodies, it substitutes its own activity for theirs; when, instead of informing, advising, and, upon occasion, denouncing, it makes them work in fetters, or bids them stand aside and does their work instead of them. The worth of a State, in the long run, is the worth of the individuals composing it; and a State which postpones the interests of *their* mental expansion and elevation to a little more of administrative skill, or of that semblance of it which practice gives, in the details of business; a State which dwarfs its men, in order that they may be more docile instruments in its hands even for beneficial purposes—will find that with small men no great thing can really be accomplished; and that the perfection of machinery to which it has sacrificed everything will in the end avail it nothing, for want of the vital power which, in order that the machine might work more smoothly, it has preferred to banish.

# Gateway Titles

**Jane Austen** was born in Hampshire in 1775. The daughter of a country rector, without advantages of education or travel, she wrote novels which established her as one of the great writers of any age. These include *Sense and Sensibility*, *Pride and Prejudice*, *Emma* and *Northanger Abbey*. Jane Austen did not marry and died in 1817.

In 1869, from the Vicarage at Bray, her nephew wrote in his memoir of Jane Austen, 'There was in her nothing eccentric or angular; no ruggedness of temper; no singularity of manner; none of the morbid sensibility of exaggeration of feeling, which not unfrequently accompanies great talents . . . Hers was a mind well balanced on a basis of good sense, sweetened by an affectionate heart, and regulated by fixed principles; so that she was to be distinguished from many other amiable and sensible women only by that particular genius which shines out in her works.'